Cyrus Jay

Recollections of William Jay, of Bath

SALZWASSER
VERLAG

Cyrus Jay

Recollections of William Jay, of Bath

Reprint of the original, first published in 1859.

1st Edition 2023 | ISBN: 978-3-37514-201-8

Verlag (Publisher): Salzwasser Verlag GmbH, Zeilweg 44, 60439 Frankfurt, Deutschland
Vertretungsberechtigt (Authorized to represent): E. Roepke, Zeilweg 44, 60439 Frankfurt, Deutschland
Druck (Print): Books on Demand GmbH, In de Tarpen 42, 22848 Norderstedt, Deutschland

RECOLLECTIONS OF WILLIAM JAY.

RECOLLECTIONS

OF

WILLIAM JAY,

OF BATH:

WITH

OCCASIONAL GLANCES AT SOME OF HIS CONTEMPORARIES AND FRIENDS.

BY HIS SON

CYRUS JAY.

LONDON:
HAMILTON, ADAMS, AND CO., PATERNOSTER ROW.
MDCCCLIX.

WILLIAM JAY.

Æt: 19.

Copied from a Print published as the Act directs, October 24th 1789, by J. Goldar.

TO

THE READERS

OF

WILLIAM JAY'S MORNING AND EVENING EXERCISES

THIS VOLUME

IS RESPECTFULLY DEDICATED

BY HIS SON

CYRUS JAY.

PREFACE.

This volume is partly intended as a supplement to the Autobiography of my late father, the Rev. William Jay, of Bath, a work published some months after his decease by his literary executors. At the time he commenced writing it, he was well advanced in years. To this cause, and to the fact that he kept neither diary nor memoranda, must be attributed the omission of many interesting events of his useful and lengthened career. It should also be recollected, that a man in narrating his own life labours under many disadvantages. He can neither praise nor censure himself; nor can he criticise his actions, or give any account of his domestic habits and pursuits, without the imputation of egotism.

Shortly after the publication of the Autobiogaphy, many communications were addressed to my late father's executor, wherein the writers (several of whom described themselves as "the Readers of Jay's Morning and Evening Exercises") expressed a desire that some account should be sent forth to the world of the personal and domestic habits of a man who had been so long before the public both as a preacher and an author.

I had occasionally been in the habit of relating to

several friends and admirers of my late father (amongst others, to Mr. John Simpson of Skinner Street, a gentleman of whom mention is made in one of the chapters of these Recollections) several of the anecdotes contained in this volume; and on informing them of the communications to which I have just referred, they suggested that I should attempt to satisfy the wishes of the writers. I at first hesitated; but on the task being pressed upon me, I yielded to the request. This must be received as my apology for presuming to publish this work.

I once heard my late father remark, that the author of a single essay or sermon generally launches it into the world by stating that it is published "*by request*," without naming (which would perhaps be impossible) the persons by whom the "request" was made. Such is not exactly my case, as the foregoing statement proves.

I have written these Recollections under many disadvantages, having been compelled to trust entirely to memory, being without any documents to which I could refer, and not having visited Bath for more than one day since my father's death, in December 1853.

15 Sergeant's Inn, Fleet Street,
February 1859.

CONTENTS.

CHAPTER I.

CHAPTER II.

CHAPTER III.

CHAPTER IV.

CHAPTER V.

CHAPTER VI.

CHAPTER VII.

CHAPTER VIII.

CHAPTER IX.

CHAPTER X.

CHAPTER XI.

CHAPTER XII.

CHAPTER XIII.

CHAPTER XIV.

CHAPTER XV.

CHAPTER XXIII.

CHAPTER XXIV.

CHAPTER XXV.

CHAPTER XXVI.

CHAPTER XXVII.

CHAPTER XXVIII.

CHAPTER XXIX.

CHAPTER XXX.

CHAPTER XXXI.

CHAPTER XXXII.

CHAPTER XXXIII.

CHAPTER XXXIV.

CHAPTER XXXV.

CHAPTER XXXVI.

CHAPTER XXXVII.

CHAPTER XXXVIII.

CHAPTER XXXIX.

CHAPTER XL.

CHAPTER XLI.

CHAPTER XLII.

CHAPTER XLIII.

CHAPTER XLIV.

William Jay

In his 85th Year and the 62nd of his Pastorate at Argyll Chapel.

J Netherclift lith. 143, S^t. Martin's Lane

RECOLLECTIONS OF WILLIAM JAY.

CHAPTER I.

Birth and parentage of William Jay—His progress at the village-school—Employed under his father at Fonthill Abbey—Attracts the attention of Mr. Turner—Introduced to Cornelius Winter—Educated by him at Marlborough College—Preaches his first sermon at the age of sixteen—Anecdotes of early preaching—Marquis of Lansdowne and Priestley—A well-timed rebuke—The disadvantages of the want of popularity to a Dissenting minister.

THE late William Jay of Bath was born at Tisbury in Wiltshire, on the 6th of May 1769. He was the only male child of an industrious mason. His parents, who were religious, really and practically, were able by frugality and diligence to support themselves, and bring up a family in the decencies and comforts of a village life.

He was sent at a very early age to the village-school, where there was nothing to be gained beyond the common elements of reading, writing, and the first rules of arithmetic. At first he did not show any thing like precociousness of talent. Indeed, he acquired reading with so much labour, that his eldest sister, when questioned concerning his first years, said: "We thought he never would have learned." In allusion to this period of his life, Mr. Jay, in his Autobiography, says, "I always felt a strange love of withdrawing myself from my playmates, and roving alone; and while pausing among the scenes of nature of surrendering myself to musings which carried me away, and often left me lost, in doing or enjoying something indistinctly different from what I had ever witnessed."

At the age of fourteen he commenced working as a mason under his father on the works of Fonthill Abbey, situated about two miles from Tisbury. About this time Mr. Thomas Turner, the memoir of whose wife has been published by Dr. Bogue, having been successful in business at Trowbridge, returned to his native village of Tisbury, where he took a house, and licensed and opened it for preaching. The punctual attendance of young Jay at this place of worship attracted the attention of Mrs. Turner. One of the first supplies was Cornelius Winter, who was much struck with the comely appearance of the lad and his pious demeanour. About a year afterwards Mr. Winter came again to preach at Tisbury on a week evening; and he beheld, seated in the chapel, the youth with his flannel jacket and his white leather apron, just as he had left his work at Fonthill, listening with deep attention to his discourse. After the conclusion of the sermon, young Jay was, at Winter's especial request, introduced to him by Mrs. Turner. Winter began to talk to him in a manner which disarmed him of his fears, and made inquiries of him as to his religious views and feelings. At the close of this interview the preacher desired the youth to call on him on the following day, which he joyfully did. After inquiring of him whether he should not like, and did not long, to communicate to others what he felt himself, Mr. Winter observed that he had an academy of young men for the ministry, and would gladly receive him as a pupil, free of any expense, if upon reflection his parents should be disposed to give their consent. It was not long before this invitation was accepted.

As Cornelius Winter rated learning very high, his young pupil was obliged to fag hard. At first the difficulties were not only trying, but seemed insuperable; but in a little time he felt encouraged, and soon found pleasure in the languages. The literary acquisitions of the students were not a little impeded by what the tutor deemed justifiable interruptions. The state of the country was then very different from what it now is as to an Evangelical ministry. The real labourers were few, the spiritual condition of many of the villages was deplorable, and the people were perishing for lack of knowledge. So it was with the vicinages all round Marlborough; and their spiritual wants, if not their wishes, cried aloud, "Come and help us." Mr. Winter therefore obtained and licensed various private houses to preach in, and not only went as often as he was able himself, but also sent his young students to instruct these poor creatures, and show unto them the way of life. The first sermon which young Jay preached was at Ablington, a village near Stonehenge. He was then a little more than sixteen years of age; and between that period and his first appearance at Surrey Chapel, at the age of nineteen, he had preached, in various of the small towns and villages in Wiltshire, nearly a thousand sermons.

In many of these places, where the chapels and towns did not afford sufficient accommodation for the hearers, Winter's pupils addressed them in the open air. In allusion to this system, Mr. Jay, in his Autobiography, says: "In the milder seasons, which would allow of it, we often addressed large numbers out of doors; and many a clear and calm evening I have preached down the day on a corner of a common, or upon the green turf before a cottage-door."

One of these open-air preachings was at a small town in Wiltshire called Calne, where the Marquis of Lansdowne has a magnificent seat and large estate. On one fine summer's evening young Jay had to preach in this town in a small room; but the crowd being very great, it became necessary to adjourn to the open air; and the spot selected was the side of a high wall bounding the marquis's estate, on which he mounted, as being the most eligible spot from whence to address his rural auditors. Whilst in the middle of the sermon, he happened to look round, and to his astonishment espied on the other side of the wall, quite out of sight from the congregation, the late Marquis of Lansdowne, and Priestley the philosopher. At first their appearance somewhat startled the youthful preacher; but observing that they were attentive listeners and took great interest in his discourse, their presence assisted and encouraged him rather than otherwise. The late marquis allowed a handsome pension to the philosopher, then the Unitarian minister at Birmingham. Priestley had a brother, also a minister, who held orthodox opinions. Mr. Jay had heard that the philosopher had, on one occasion only, allowed his brother to preach in his pulpit; and that whilst in the vestry, just previous to entering the chapel, the astute philosopher said to him: "Enter into no controversy, I beseech you." His brother, without making any reply, ascended the pulpit, and gave out the following text: "And without controversy great is the mystery of godliness."

The following anecdote, in relation to Mr. Jay's early preaching, I had from his own lips:

"Mr. Winter being unable, through ill health, to comply with an engagement to preach a few miles in the country on the following day (Sunday), requested me to officiate for him. I told my tutor, that although he had given me but little time for preparation (it then being late in the evening), yet I would do the best I could to acquit myself of the duty. On reaching the village where the service was to be performed quite fatigued, having travelled on foot, I inquired for the residence of Winter's friend, a wealthy farmer, who was the head of the religious interest of the place and the surrounding neighbourhood. On arriving there, I gave a timorous rap at the door, and on its being opened, informed the female servant that I wished to see the gentleman of the house. The domestic asked me what I wanted with her master at so late an hour. My reply was, that Mr. Winter had sent me in his place to supply the chapel on the Sunday, and had desired me personally to see her master on the subject. The servant, after bidding me go into the kitchen, said she would deliver my message; which she did, with a smile on her countenance, telling her master that Mr. Winter had sent a farmer's boy, with hobnail shoes and worsted stockings, to preach in his stead. Upon the gentleman farmer making his appearance in the kitchen, he, after eyeing me from head to foot, said: 'So, my young friend, Mr. Winter has sent you to preach here; is it so?' 'Yes, sir,' was my reply. The gentleman, without entering into further conversation with me, said in a low tone of voice to the servant, which I overheard: 'Who will Winter send here next?' and then, after bidding the servant to give me some supper, and get a bed ready for me in the top room of the house, abruptly took his departure.

"The next morning, whilst I was on the road on foot to the chapel to perform my duties there, a carriage passed by me containing the rich farmer and his lady, who although they saw, yet would not recognise me. This slight did not much disconcert me; for my mind was intent upon the preparation of my discourse, from a text which had occurred to me whilst in bed, as being appropriate to the circumstances of my reception, my appearance as to dress, and my youth. The text was from the sixth chapter of John, ninth verse: 'There is a lad here which hath five barley loaves and two small fishes.' In the course of my extemporaneous discourse, which soon riveted the deep attention of the rural audience, I exclaimed: 'Did God despise a lad who supplied the Son of man with food for the great multitude, in number about five thousand? No. Was it not a lad—a ruddy-faced lad—who slew Goliath the giant, and afterwards cut off his head with the great sword of that Philistine, thereby giving deliverance to Israel? Yes. And was it not a lad by whose lips God reproved the aged and hoary-headed Eli? Yes. Why, then, despise a lad?'

"When I retired to the vestry, the wealthy farmer, who was there waiting for me, shook me heartily by the hand, thanked me in the most flattering terms for what he was pleased to style my excellent discourse, and made me his guest until my departure on the following day. I need hardly mention, that instead of returning from the chapel to the gentleman's residence on foot, I was invited into the carriage, and treated with the greatest hospitality."

I have heard old farmers in Wiltshire, who knew Mr. Jay at this period, state that his youthful appearance even for his age was most remarkable, and that in some few instances the deacons refused on that account to allow him to preach. His youth was sometimes made a matter of reproach to him, as appears by the following fact, related by him in his work: "Shortly after I had begun my early career, I went to supply for a Sabbath at Melksham. At this time was residing there an old gentleman from London, a very wise man, at least in his own conceit. I called upon him on the Monday morning. He received me rather uncourteously. He did not indeed censure my preaching; but rudely said he had no notion of *beardless* boys being employed as preachers. 'Pray, sir,' said I, 'does not Paul say to Timothy, Let no man despise thy youth? And, sir, you remind me of what I have read of a French monarch who had received a young ambassador, and complaining, said: 'Your master should not have sent me a beardless stripling.'

'Sir,' said the youthful ambassador, 'had my master supposed you wanted a beard, he would have sent you a goat.'"

Before introducing young Jay to a London congregation, it does not seem out of place to record an opinion which I have frequently heard him express as to the treatment of Dissenting ministers by their people. "In the Established Church," said he, "let a clergyman's appearance or poverty be what it may, he is always treated as a gentleman, and is entitled by right of his sacred office to be admitted, and is received, into the first society upon a footing of equality. So it is with the Catholic Church. But far different is it with the Dissenting public. Amongst them there is a barometer of popularity to regulate their conduct. If a minister of theirs attain the highest, the attentions he receives are too overpowering and suffocating; but if, on the other hand, this barometer points near, at, or below the zero of popularity, then the less fortunate of the Dissenting ministers, who comprise the main body, and are the most useful and zealous of that class, are treated out of the pulpit with a degree of coldness, of which ice gives you some idea."

CHAPTER II.

Mr. Jay joins Rowland Hill as a supply at Surrey Chapel at the age of nineteen — His success and popularity—Retires to Christian Malford—Leaves it to officiate at Hope Chapel, Clifton—Lady Maxwell—Samuel Wesley—Ordained pastor of Argyle Chapel by Cornelius Winter—His marriage—His estimate of his wife's good qualities.

THE Rev. Rowland Hill, who had become acquainted with the young preacher whilst he was yet a student at Marlborough, engaged him to go to supply Surrey Chapel for eight weeks. This he did with the consent of his tutor. Here it was that his great popularity commenced, at the early age of nineteen, and which continued unabated until his death, a period of sixty-five years. He was then styled "young Jay, the boy-preacher." The portrait fronting the title-page is, as I have been informed, an admirable likeness of him at that age, and is a copy of a print published at the time, thousands of which were sold. I had also two other likenesses of him of the same date, but have mislaid or lost them. I have often heard him relate that hundreds of persons anxious to hear him could not gain admission; and that when the service was over, crowds remained round the parsonage-house, and would not depart until he addressed them from the windows. The great success of the youthful preacher was the commencement of a very close friendship between himself and Rowland Hill, which continued unabated until the decease of that well-known and popular preacher. When it is stated that Mr. Jay preached annually for his friend at the Surrey Chapel for upwards of sixty years, he must, as a matter of course, have become acquainted with all his peculiarities and eccentricities; a few of which I shall in a further part of this volume bring under the reader's notice, and shall also allude to the funeral sermon which he preached at that place of worship on the occasion of his friend's death, after his interment there.

I do not know whether it was upon this or the succeeding visit to London that young Jay, whom I shall henceforward designate as Mr. Jay, preached before a numerous congregation at Tottenham Court Tabernacle, built by Whitfield the great pulpit orator. I have heard him say, that the fact of Whitfield having held forth in that chapel, at first created some timidity on his part; but that he soon overcame it. I may mention, that here it was that Bacon, the royal academician and sculptor, worshiped, and that to his memory there is a marble tablet erected in the Tabernacle, where he was buried.

Mr. Jay, after having fulfilled his engagement with Rowland Hill, returned back to the country with the full conviction that if he wished to retain the popularity acquired so early in life, he must increase his stock of knowledge. He accordingly retired for nearly two years to Christian Malford, and resided in a tradesman's house. Here he devoted his time to his studies; and was, notwithstanding he had made so great a sensation in London, always more content to preach to the villagers of the place, than to the large congregations of Bath and the neighbouring towns, which he was so frequently solicited to do.

Mr. Jay left Christian Malford, at the request of Lady Maxwell, to officiate as minister at Hope Chapel, Hot Wells, Clifton, belonging to her ladyship. It had not been long opened at the time when he undertook the service. A congregation had, in fact, to be formed; and though young, not being quite twenty years of age, he succeeded by his labours in drawing large audiences. Shortly after commencing his ministry here, he had the pleasure of dining at her ladyship's house, and meeting there the venerable and celebrated divine, Mr. Wesley, who kindly noticed him, and inquired after his tutor Cornelius Winter, adding that he was an excellent man. He several times afterwards met Mr. Wesley at Clifton, and one evening accompanied that venerable preacher to Bristol in his carriage, and heard him preach from the text, "Ye were sometimes darkness, but now are ye light in the Lord: walk as children of light." It was the only opportunity which he ever had of hearing this truly apostolical man. The whole scene was very picturesque and striking; several preachers stood in the large pulpit around him; the sermon was short; the language terse and good, but utterly devoid of expansion and imagery; while the delivery was low and unanimated. This surprised Mr. Jay, who thought it must have been the effect of age; for if it had been originally the same, how did it happen, argued he, that Wesley became so popular among the multitudes which always attended him, and so hung upon his lips?

Mr. Jay officiated at Hope Chapel more than

twelve months; and no doubt might have remained there, having been much pressed both by her ladyship and the people to become the permanent minister, had it not been for a difference which took place between him and a religious landlady at Clifton, to whom her ladyship delegated the secular concerns of the place. This female wished to dictate to the preacher on doctrinal points; an interference to which he would not submit.

At the very time of this difference there came an invitation from the Independent Chapel at Bath, then vacant by the death of the Rev. Thomas Tupper, which he immediately accepted, and remained in that far-famed city as the pastor of Argyle Chapel to within thirteen months of his death.

Mr. Jay was not unknown to the Rev. Thomas Tupper's congregation when this invitation was made to him. When that pastor was laid aside by sickness, the deacons applied to him, both whilst he was at Christian Malford and at Clifton, to supply for a season their lack of service, with which he complied. Mr. Tupper after a short period revived, but soon relapsed again, and his illness was severe and long; yet some hope was entertained of his recovery, and this occasioned delay in the opening of Argyle Chapel, which, encouraged by the help of Lady Glenorchy, and excited by his growing success, he had been induced to build; for he naturally wished, and his hearers also, that he who had been the instrument of rearing it should open it himself. At length, however, it being deemed inexpedient to wait any longer for the dedication, Mr. Jay was applied to for this purpose; and so great was his popularity that he preached both parts of the day. The text of the sermon (which at the especial request of the congregation was published) was: "The hour cometh, and now is, when the true worshipers shall worship the Father in spirit and in truth; for the Father seeketh such to worship him. God is a Spirit; and they that worship him must worship him in spirit and in truth." This service took place on the 4th of October 1789. When Mr. Tupper's recovery was quite despaired of, the deacons of the church repaired to his dying chamber, and expressed a wish to hear his advice and recommendation with regard to his successor, observing that although his opinion might not absolutely determine the choice of the people, it would tend much to influence, unite, and guide them. He only and instantly mentioned Mr. Jay's name; and as this fell in with the conviction and wish of the members and attendants, he was, without further deliberation, invited to take, and accepted, the pastorate of Argyle Chapel, as I have before stated. In due time he was ordained over the congregation. At this solemnity his venerated tutor Cornelius Winter prayed, and gave him the charge.

On Mr. Jay's first journey to London as a supply to Surrey Chapel, of which I have already given a slight account, Cornelius Winter gave him a letter of introduction to the Rev. Edward Davies, first rector of Bengeworth, Worcestershire, and afterwards of Coychurch. Mr. Jay called and delivered it. During the eight weeks he was in London, he was often invited to the house; and finding in the reverend gentleman's daughter Ann a powerful attraction, he contrived to call without an invitation. It was just prior to Mr. Jay's settling in Bath that Mr. Davies obtained a dispensation for non-residence at his living, and accepted the curacy of Batheaston, a pleasant village two miles from the city. Nothing could be more gratifying to the feelings, and more friendly to the intercourse, of the young parties than this unexpected approximation of residences. The lady's father having given his consent to the union, Mr. Jay journeyed to London, where the elect was on a visit to her most intimate friend, Mrs. Rowland Hill. The marriage took place at St. Peter's Church, Cornhill, on the 6th day of January 1791, Rowland Hill performing the service. On returning to Bath, the young couple paid their first visit to Mr. and Mrs. Winter. This was shortly before Mr. Jay's ordination to the pastorate of Argyle Chapel. Mr. Jay, speaking of his courtship, says: "My intended must have deemed me rather an awkward and not a very satisfactory correspondent; for I always disliked letter-writing, and I had little leisure for courting by post,—a part of what some of her sex would have deemed wanting in me was, I can truly say, the effect of design and principle. I always felt for women who are flattered to adoration before marriage, and obliged to put up with, at least comparative, neglect and indifference afterwards; and I resolved to raise no expectations which I could not hope to realise, and not to suffer the husband to belie and disgrace the suitor."

Mr. Jay truly describes my mother as the best of women, and says: "I was always desirous and anxious to be a good husband; nothing in my estimation and remarkings ever being able to atone for the want of consistency and excellency here, especially in a minister. But I must have been one of the basest of men had I not always endeavoured to act worthily towards the wife of my youth, to whom I am under so many obligations. It was she who contributed to give me that exalted idea of the female character which I have always entertained and expressed. She excluded perfectly the entrance of every notion and feeling of submission or authority, so that we had no rights to adjust, or duties to regulate. She possessed every requisite that could render her a helpmate. Her special qualities were admirably suited to my defects. Her domestic virtues rendered my house a complete home, —the abode of neatness, order, punctuality, peace, cheerfulness, comfort, and attraction. She calmed my brow when ruffled by disappointment and vexation; she encouraged me when depressed; she kept off a thousand cares, and left me to attend to the voice of my calling; she reminded me of my engagements when I was forgetful, and stimulated me when I was remiss, and always gently enforced the *present* obligation, as 'the duty of every day required.'"

CHAPTER III.

Mrs. Hannah More—Anecdotes respecting her—William Jay's estimate of her as an authoress—Lady Huntingdon—Brighton—The Prince of Wales and Fox—Whitfield—Rev. R. Bolton—Rev. Mr. Sortain of Brighton—A sermon at Colerne—Good Friday—Rural walks with his children on that day—Christmas Day—A deputation—Reply to it—Dr. Parry, M.D.

A SKETCH of Mrs. Hannah More, whose name among our female authors of genius and piety will always occupy a high place, having appeared in the Autobiography of Mr. Jay, I shall merely mention a few circumstances relating to that lady, which may perhaps be interesting. She attended Mr. Jay's preaching at Argyle Chapel a considerable time; and I have often heard him declare under what obligations he was to her, in the early part of his ministry at Bath, for the valuable hints she gave him as to delivery and composition.

Mr. Jay was a constant visitor at this lady's house, where he met a great many of the aristocracy, to whom he was introduced. He was the first person to whom she read her manuscripts of *The Shepherd of Salisbury Plain, The Two Shoemakers,* and other religious tracts; and so pleased was he with them, that she, on his recommendation, determined to have them printed. Mr. Jay met at dinner a day or two after he had seen the manuscripts the late Earl Bathurst, who admired them so much, that he also recommended their publication. It is needless to add how many editions of these tracts have been sent forth to the world.

Although Mrs. Hannah More was so tolerant in her religious principles as to attend repeatedly at Argyle Chapel, she was nevertheless very bigoted in many respects. She was an enthusiastic admirer of that celebrated statesman William Pitt; and on one occasion took a journey from Bath to Cambridge expressly to see the fine statue of him in the Senate House, and also the rooms which he inhabited whilst a graduate at Pembroke Hall. When Mr. Jay was at Cambridge many years ago, he was informed by one of the heads of houses, that Mrs. Hannah More, on entering these rooms, which were of miserable appearance, immediately knelt down and kissed the floor; a circumstance which Mr. Jay would not have credited, had he not received it from so good a source. But there can be no doubt of the fact; for I have heard the late Dr. Lamb, the master of Corpus Christi and Dean of Bristol, relate the same circumstance. This lady was also at one time a great admirer of the late Sir Robert Peel, and had an admirable likeness of him hanging up in one of her rooms. Mr. Jay called on her one day after Sir Robert had changed his opinion on the Catholic question, and on being informed thereof, she immediately went up to the likeness, and turning its face to the wall, said: "I have now done with my old friend, and cannot with pleasure any longer look at his portrait." Mr. Jay, who could not suppress a smile, in vain tried to persuade her that such an act of toleration was quite compatible with principle and the doctrines of Christianity.

Little or nothing has been mentioned about Mr. Jay in the life of Hannah More, written by Mr. Robert; but that she had the greatest regard for him is evidenced by her leaving him in her will a very handsome legacy, which was paid to him by the executors free of duty. She also noticed all the family of Mr. Jay in their youthful days, and constantly made them presents. Mr. Jay had an application from Messrs. Cadell's, the great booksellers of the Strand, who published her works, to write the memoirs of her life, knowing his great intimacy with her; but her papers being in other hands, he at once declined the offer. Mr. Jay's estimate of Mrs. Hannah More as an authoress was, that she possessed a most vigorous mind and masculine understanding, and that her writings abound in the richest illustrations and appeals. He greatly admired her *Essay on St. Paul*, her *Strictures on Female Education*, and her *Practical Piety*, and considered that her *Cœlebs* contained some very beautiful writing.

Mrs. Hannah More was a daily reader of Mr. Jay's Morning Exercises.

Mr. and Mrs. Jay were acquainted very early in life with the late well-known Countess of Huntingdon. My mother had the pleasure of accompanying her ladyship and Miss Hannah More to Westminster Hall to hear the trial of Warren Hastings. They were seated in a gallery appropriated exclusively to ladies. The dress worn on that occasion by my mother being presented to her by the countess, was afterwards treasured up with pride. The countess being a peeress in her own right, exercised a privilege, not then disputed, of taking a house in each of the principal fashionable cities and towns of the kingdom, building a chapel adjoining it, and appointing a clergyman to preach there without consecration,—a privilege which, I believe, a legal decision has since abolished. The countess had erected such a chapel at Brighton. About sixty-three years ago, Mr. Jay, being on a visit to that town, preached in it to a very large congregation. At that time, this fashionable watering-place, now consisting of miles of palaces, was just emerging from being a fishing village. On the Monday (after preaching on the Sunday), Mr. Jay, as was his wont, took a solitary walk along the sea-shore. After rambling about a mile, he observed two gentlemen in close conversation; and on passing them, he at once recognised one of them as Charles James Fox, and the other as the Prince of Wales, afterwards George IV. Fox, who had his hands in his breeches-pockets, was talking with much animation to the prince, his generous and noble countenance showing itself off to much advantage. The prince, who Mr. Jay thought was the finest man he had ever seen, although picking up the pebbles, and endeavouring to perform the schoolboy trick of duck-and-drake upon the water, appeared to be listening with much attention to the great statesman's conversation. Mr. Jay, by no means an inquisitive man, said, in relating this occurrence, that he was very anxious at the time to know what the conversation was about; but he presumed that it had some connection with politics, which then ran very high.

The chapel alluded to was opened by the celebrated Whitfield; and in the vestry there is an engraving from an original portrait of him, of great value and fidelity, formerly in the possession of Mr. Jay's son-in-law, the late Rev. Robert Bolton, whose father, a large and opulent merchant in Savannah, treated Whitfield, when in that city, with great hospitality. Mr. Jay's tutor Cornelius Winter, who accompanied Whitfield to America, enjoyed the same kindness. Some years after Mr. Jay had been settled at Bath, Cornelius Winter introduced Mr. Bolton's son to him, and a marriage with Mr. Jay's daughter was the result. The Rev. Mr. Sortain is now the pastor of the same chapel, and has been so for many years: he was by Mr. Jay considered to be one of the most popular preachers in this country. The celebrated Charles Phillips, no mean authority, informed me that he was of the same opinion, and that he always attended Mr. Sortain's chapel in his autumnal visits to that watering-place. Indeed, very few persons of any note ever visit Brighton without hearing him.

Mr. Jay was greatly attached, from his earliest public efforts and associations, to preaching in villages, particularly in the neighbourhood of Bath. One of these was Colerne in Wiltshire, a village situated on a high hill about six miles from Bath, where its church and a high-built brewery in the vicinity are prominent objects as you enter the western city from London, and witness them on your right on emerging from "Box" railway tunnel. In early life he preached there in a large barn, or out-house, belonging to Mr. Sumsion the respected brewer, one of the principal inhabitants of the place. After a long lapse of years, Mr. Jay came again to the village (which had been occasionally aided by the services of "supplies" of lay-preachers connected with the Home Missionary Society), for the purpose of laying the foundation-stone of the present Independent chapel there. He was then the guest of the son of his old (then deceased) friend Mr. Sumsion, who, at Mr. Jay's request, accompanied him to view the spots of early associations. He stood under the large village-tree in the centre of the place, and remembered that the inclemency of the weather precluded his preaching there on a former visit; and he thence interestingly sought out the old out-house where long since he had addressed the villagers. This was shown, and gratified him. I was amongst the auditory at his service of laying the foundation-stone. He preached in the open air. I sat on a side-wall with others from Bath. There was a temporary awning for the ladies, which was densely filled. The clergyman of the parish at that time was a man of High-Church principles and doubtful character. The hungry village "sheep" weekly looked up to him, and were not fed. The villagers, therefore, attended where they could hear the "Gospel" preached in its simplicity. On this occasion, I recollect Mr. Jay giving unintentional offence to the *baker* of the village, by remarking that if the parish bread was not genuine and wholesome, the villagers must seek a supply of this "article of life" from other sources. Mr. Jay meant no reflection; but simply spoke in a spiritual sense. However, the remark hit; for it was said that the literal bread was not what it ought to have been, and therefore it was not to be wondered at that the baker should feel highly offended at the preacher's apt illustration.

Mr. Jay, contrary to the usual practice of Dissenting ministers, always preached upon the days appointed for religious festivals, though he did not otherwise keep them very strictly. On every Good-Friday evening he had a service at Argyle Chapel, and among his hearers on such occasions were many church people. My mother frequently attended divine service at the parish church of Bath on the morning of that day, she being a member of the Church of England. I recollect her playfully upbraiding Mr. Jay one Good-Friday morning, on her meeting him coming into the house from the garden, where he had been digging, in these words: "Dear Mr. Jay, what will the neighbours, who have been eyeing you working in the garden on such a day as this for the last two hours, think of you as a minister?" Turning to her, with a kind look, he replied: "Do you think there is any harm in it? I do not."

Good Friday was a glorious morning for all of us in our childhood. He would, if the weather permitted, take us a very long walk up one of the valleys near Bath, and was delighted to see us gather primroses, violets, and other wild flowers; whilst he, with all the freshness of a boy, was prowling about for birds' nests, which he was sure to discover, if there were any near the spot,—for he knew every thing about English birds, their habits, and their haunts; but he never would permit us to take away the eggs. Sometimes he would bend over a brook to gather watercresses, with which he loaded us. He always appeared in the highest spirits on these rambles; and I have heard him say, when alluding to these happy days, that he had prepared his sermon for the evening of Good Friday days before, in order to have his mind disengaged from his duties.

He always preached on the morning of Christmas

Day; and on this festival his chapel was very much thronged with strangers. Some of the good people of Argyle Chapel, not satisfied with this act of liberality in an Independent minister, wished him to preach also on the evening of that day; and for this purpose they once upon a time elected a deputation from amongst themselves to wait upon him full a month before Christmas Day. They went on their mission, confident of success; and on their arrival at Percy Place were shown into the library, where they were received most cordially by Mr. Jay. After stating to their pastor the object of their call, and adducing several arguments in support of their application, to which he lent an attentive ear, he suddenly exclaimed: "Gentlemen, you need not trouble yourselves with any further arguments on the subject, my mind being made up; for I never will preach on Christmas evenings to roast beef and plum-pudding."

That eminent physician, the late Dr. Parry of Bath, for the last twenty years of his life, often visited Mr. Jay; and it was generally thought that during this period he had the largest practice of any man in England. Bath was then in its palmy days. One morning the doctor, in the course of conversation, stated to Mr. Jay that he had seen on the preceding day upwards of eighty noblemen, besides numerous distinguished characters, on the Orange Grove and Parade of the city. No doubt his great reputation brought many of them to Bath for the purpose of consulting him. Irrespective of his professional knowledge, he was a man of great science and literary attainments, was the author of many celebrated works, and the introducer of Spanish sheep into this country. The doctor, whenever he called upon Mr. Jay, went into the library. I was once present when he came in there. On that occasion he said: "Mr. Jay, I cannot remain with you for more than two or three minutes; for I have this long list of agriculturists and farmers to visit during the day; and I find cases from these useful classes of society are greatly on the increase: formerly I had very seldom any such cases to attend to." "How do you account for that, doctor?" inquired Mr. Jay. "Why, in this way,—that the agriculturists and farmers have of late years given themselves up to ease by riding on horseback over their estates and farms; whereas formerly they were content to walk over them, and live in a less luxurious manner than they now do."

The doctor was a very fine-looking man, had an extremely handsome countenance, was upwards of six feet in height, and his figure was that of perfect symmetry. Admiral Sir Edward Parry, R.N., the celebrated explorer of the northern regions, was his son.

He invariably refused to accept any fee from Mr. Jay,—I presume, as much out of regard to him, as from the circumstance of his own father being a Dissenting minister at Cirencester.

CHAPTER IV.

Dr. Haweis—Anecdotes respecting him—A walk on Marshfield Road near Bath—A sermon preached by Mr. Jay in aid of the Propagation of Christian Knowledge in the Highlands of Scotland—Duke of Athol—Sermon on the death of the Princess Amelia—Commentaries—Benefits resulting to Christianity from the opposite views taken by commentators of the different parts of Scripture.

The late Dr. Haweis, rector of Aldwinkle,—a living which he held until the day of his death, the duties of which were performed by his curate,—preached for several years at the Countess of Huntingdon's chapel at Bath; but it having been deserted by the greater part of the congregation on account of his very long sermons, he left it, and afterwards attended Argyle Chapel, being a great admirer of Mr. Jay's discourses. The doctor reached to a very old age, and lived in good style. He was remarkable for his loud voice, even in conversation; and had a very peculiar way, during divine service, of shouting out most energetically "Amen," when any point in Mr. Jay's discourse pleased him, much to the annoyance of the congregation, as well as to that of the preacher.

Mr. Jay, at this period of his life, devoted many hours of his time in attending to the sick; and many were the notes, letters, and livery-servants constantly coming to Percy Place, pressing for his attendance on them. He usually left his house on these visits of mercy a little after three o'clock in the afternoon, and on reaching Bath would devote a few minutes in looking at the London newspapers at the public library in Milson Street. I shall never forget, when once going into the hall of the library with him, observing him peeping through the glass-door in all directions, and his suddenly taking hold of my arm, exclaiming, "I shall not go in; for I see that Dr. Haweis sitting there. You have no idea how he annoyed me yesterday when I went into the library, the room being filled with ladies, gentlemen, admirals, generals, and members of Parliament. No sooner had I got hold of the *Times* than the doctor espied me, and with his stentorian voice exclaimed, 'Brother Jay, that was a blessed, blessed meeting that we attended last night.' The company thought the doctor mad, and their attention was also directed to me; and as I am determined not to be annoyed in a similar way for the future, I shall never enter the library again whilst the doctor's there, having such an aversion to any thing approaching to *cant*, but especially before persons who know nothing about religious matters."

Mr. Jay was not a very attentive hearer when he considered a subject badly handled. On one occasion I attended with him at the Countess of Huntingdon's chapel when the doctor was preaching one of his long discourses. I innocently thought, after the lapse of an hour, that he was about to close his sermon; but Mr. Jay turning round to me, said with a smile, "Do not suppose that he is about to finish yet; he is just what fighting-men term getting second wind, and he is good for another half-hour;" and so it proved. How Mr. Jay got hold of the expression I cannot say; for I am certain that he never witnessed a fight, and I should have thought had never read an account of one; but he was a very general reader, and possessed a most retentive memory. This reminds me of a striking remark of his, in reference to the passage, "They laid down their clothes at a young man's feet whose name was Saul." "The young persecutor," exclaimed Mr. Jay, "fiercely said to the murderers, 'Strip! and go at it. I'll hold your clothes!'" There is another anecdote of the doctor which Mr. Jay used to relate. "The doctor, when a young man, was very fond of hunting, a diversion which at that period was by no means uncommon amongst the clergy. At that time, the doctor, who always professed evangelical principles, whilst pursuing the hare, shouted out with great delight, with the voice of a hunter, 'Nothing will save her!' when one of the red-coats said, 'Why, doctor, won't faith save her?' The doctor never hunted again."

One summer's Sunday morning I accompanied Mr. Jay on one of his early walks in the direction of Marshfield, a small town six or seven miles from Bath on the Gloucester road. On our return, we espied a gentleman walking very fast towards us. Mr. Jay informed me that he was the Unitarian minister of Marshfield, that he resided at Bath, and that he walked to that place and back every Sunday, regardless of the weather, after preaching there morning and afternoon. On remarking to Mr. Jay what a cold and bleak-looking place Marshfield appeared, he said, "You would think so, if you were to see the congregation the doctor preaches to. A farmer from that place told me the other day that it never consists of more than three or four people, although the chapel, which was formerly a Presbyterian one, is a very neat building, and had some small endowment." When Mr. Jay came up to the doctor, he put out his hand to him, and after a hearty shake, asked him his opinion of the weather. He replied, "I think you are the best judge of that, as you are such an early riser." Mr. Jay then said, "Well, doctor, what do your prayers now consist of?" He immediately replied, "*Adoration, sir;*" and proceeded on his journey. Mr. Jay smiled at the answer. Before the doctor's death I drove Mr. Jay, on a beautiful day, over to Marshfield, he having to open a large commodious chapel just erected there. The town was all commotion; there were vehicles of all sorts along the main street, and every stable was occupied. It appeared to me that all the inhabitants had opened their houses for the reception of their friends. I drove him back directly after the service, he refusing to dine with the ministers and managers of the chapel at the inn. I should mention, that difference of opinion on points of religion never influenced Mr. Jay in his personal friendships; and I have a perfect recollection of his being very intimate with Mr. Jardine, the Unitarian minister of Trim-Street Chapel, Bath, the father of the present recorder of that city, who is also the worthy police-magistrate at Bow Street.

In the year 1803 Mr. Jay preached a sermon before the Correspondent Board in London of a society, incorporated by royal charter, for the Propagation of Christian Knowledge in the Highlands and Islands of Scotland; and the Duke of Athol and other distinguished individuals formed part of his congregation on that occasion. At a meeting of the board, the noble duke being in the chair, it was unanimously resolved that their thanks should be given to Mr. Jay for the sermon, and that he should be requested to permit the same to be printed for the use of the society. Such permission was given. The text was, "Skin for skin; yea, all that a man hath will he give for his *life*." When the proof-sheets of the sermon were sent to Mr. Jay for correction, he found that the printer had printed the text thus, "Skin for skin; yea, all that a man hath will he give for his WIFE." Instead of correcting the error in the usual way, he wrote in the margin, underlining the word "wife," "*That* depends on circumstances."

I cannot help quoting the following paragraph, forming one of the divisions of this sermon, on account of the strong common sense of the language, and the great impression which I am told it made on Mr. Jay's hearers. It is in these words: "If human life be so precious, you should not expose it to injury and hazard. I know that there is no cure for mortality; but a physician of no common reputation has told us that not one in a thousand dies a natural death; and a higher authority has declared that the wicked shall not live out half their days. In many ways persons may be chargeable with suicide, beside swallowing poison, acting the madman in a duel, or playing the fool in a balloon. Life may be taken away slowly as well as suddenly, by negligence as well as by violence. What think you of the man who indulges himself in all the excesses of intemperance, which breed and nourish all manner of diseases? What think you of the man who harbours evil passions, and suffers anger to consume him, envy to gnaw him, anxiety to corrode him? What think you of the man who, by pursuing too much business, oppresses nature, injures his faculties, deprives himself of rest and relaxation and ease? He forgets 'that the life is more than meat, and the body than raiment.' What think you of those who, to amass money, will deny themselves the conveniences and necessaries of life? What think you of those martyrs of vanity, who, to appear in the fashion, will avail themselves of modes of apparel, I will not say incompatible with decency, but hazardous to health? What think you of those who carelessly or presumptuously disregard the beginnings of disorder, and suffer that which might be easily checked at first to become inveterate and fatal? 'A little cold,' says an original writer, 'is a little death; a little more chills us to clay, and fits us for the damps of the grave.' What think you of those who lie long and late in bed,—relaxing the fibres, unstringing the nerves, evaporating the animal spirits, till they start at their own shadow? We would not have you finical and delicate; but a proper regard to health is a duty enforced by the most awful considerations."

On the death of the Princess Amelia, the youngest daughter of George III., Mr. Jay selected his text from the second of Kings, ninth chapter, thirty-fourth verse: "Bury her; for she is a king's daughter." Whilst the preacher was in the midst of his discourse, a curious incident occurred. One of the fashionable visitors at Bath, attracted no doubt by his popularity and general repute, having overcome her scruples of entering a Dissenting place of worship, was of course accommodated with a seat in a conspicuous place of the chapel. Mr. Jay began by portraying the diabolical character of Jezebel, to whom the text immediately referred. This was merely his dark background upon which he designed to bring out in strong relief a modern specimen of female excellence, also "a king's daughter." The lady, however, would not wait for the cheering contrast of character; but got up, left the pew, slamming the door, and indignantly walked out of the chapel, the eyes of the congregation and preacher, who was nothing disconcerted, being fixed on her as an object to be pitied. She had come to hear of Amelia, she had only heard of Jezebel. Had she retained her seat but for a short period longer, she would have been delighted by one of the most beautiful, affecting, and deserved eulogiums ever pronounced. But she left before the preacher had turned the angle of his discourse: "If Jezebel, being 'a king's daughter,' was deserving of burial, rather than that her ignominious remains should be mangled and desecrated by the very dogs in the street; how infinitely more meritoriously entitled to sepulchral respect, veneration, and a nation's mourning, was a princess, whose greatest lustre was her piety, her filial and domestic affection, and the unobtrusive and varied benevolence characteristic of her brief and sorrowing career." Mr. Jay often related this circumstance, smiling at the folly of the lady, whose name was duly reported to him, and thanked Providence that as he grew older a more tolerant spirit existed between the various sects of the Christian family.

Such was the liberality of Mr. Scott, the great commentator, whose Commentaries have gone through so many editions, that although a Churchman, he applied to Mr. Jay, who was just then of age, to bestow his patronage on the work in the form of a letter, who with equal liberality complied with the request. This letter, which highly recommended the work to the attention of the public, was printed on the blue cover of the first published number. Mr. Jay's opinion was, that, taking the book altogether, it was one of the best commentaries in circulation. I never knew him to read them at family worship, or any other commentary, except Job Orton's (the successor of Dr. Doddridge), and that was very seldom.

Mr. Jay also wrote a recommendation of a commentary by Mr. Williams, entitled *The Cottage Bible*, a work which he very much admired, and which deservedly had a very extensive circulation. I have heard him mention a commentary, written by that celebrated Wesleyan minister Dr. Cook, formerly a fellow at a college at Oxford, which he said was, in the main, not much more than a transcript of Dr. Dodd's,—a work then very scarce, and not very likely to be reprinted, that divine, as is well known, having been found guilty of forgery, and executed. Dr. Cook published it on his own account at a very great expense; and it not selling at all, he thought he had hit upon a very good plan of disposing of it, by the aid of canvassers in different parts of the country. After a little time, he complained that the canvassers cost him a great deal of money; and he consulted a very clever man in Cornwall whether he should proceed with this plan, who, after examining the accounts of the printing, publishing, and canvassing, at once said: "Doctor, it will be cheaper to have only one canvasser; but that not for the purpose of selling, but of giving the work away."

Mr. Jay had in his extensive library the works of all the commentators, excepting those of Dr. Clarke; but I know that he had, from time to time, read the doctor's commentaries whilst on his annual visit to Surrey Chapel; for I have gone with him, repeatedly, to borrow the numbers of a young gentleman of the name of Simpson (who was in a large establishment in Fleet Street), to whom he was very partial, and who, I am happy to say, has been very successful in business.

Henry's Commentaries was a very favourite book with Mr. Jay: he considered it the best work of its class for devotional purposes and perusal in the closet. It is remarkable that the preface to the last beautiful edition of this work was written by the late Mr. Bickersteth, a Churchman, though the learned and eminent commentator was a Dissenter.

Mr. Jay was of opinion that the different views taken by commentators and religious parties on some portions of the Scriptures had been of the greatest possible benefit to the cause of religion; for, says he, "It is better for Christians to love one another, than to pry through the same keyhole of opinion. Hence religion has been more regarded in all its extent. One class urging more the doctrinal, another the practical, and the third the disciplinarian and ritual parts, no portion has been left unexplored or unenforced. One thing must be conceded with regard to all religious parties,—they have proved salutary checks upon each other, so as to render interpolations and expunctions of the Scriptures impossible. Had a Trinitarian been so disposed, he could not have inserted a verse or sentence in favour of his creed; the Arians would have detected and exposed him. Or had the Socinian attempted to erase a passage that bore on the divinity of the Son of God, some of the orthodox would have exploded the treachery. The same may be said of the advocates or opponents of all other principles: however widely they have erred, they have been, by their mutual hatred and jealousy, vouchers for the originals and versions of the Scriptures."

CHAPTER V.

Mr. Jay and his friend the Milkman at an auction-room at Bath—A bank cheque—Mr. Jay's good fortune—Gains a prize in the lottery—Anecdotes of two acts of rascality connected with the lottery system—The Rev. Mr. Howells.

Mr. Jay said that the only reason why he should have liked to have been the possessor of a large fortune was, that it would have afforded him the delight and satisfaction of assisting with small sums of money farmers' labourers, and industrious young men just starting into life. Yet, without a fortune, he would often assist the deserving. The following anecdote, which I well remember, is illustrative of his kindness of heart in this respect, as well as his simplicity of character, and freedom from bigotry. It should be mentioned that Mr. Jay was a very early riser. In his morning rambles he became acquainted with a very industrious and well-conducted milkman of the name of Poole, who, besides being a good husband, was a fine, tall, and handsome man. His knowledge of this individual, like that of many other industrious persons whom he thus met, generally commenced by an inquiry about the weather, and what sort of a day it was likely to turn out. One morning Poole solicited Mr. Jay to lend him 10*l.*, in order to enable him to purchase a cow, which was during the day to be sold by auction along with the household furniture, plate, and other effects of a deceased wealthy old gentleman. Mr. Jay, without the least hesitation, granted the favour; Poole having on several previous occasions punctually repaid him former loans. Mr. Jay made his appearance in the room of the mansion where the sale took place some time after it had commenced, and found the whole company convulsed with laughter. It appeared that an old state-carriage had been put up by the auctioneer, and no advance having been made on the sum of 9*l.* odd, the milkman made a bidding of 10*l.*, when it was immediately knocked down to him at that sum; so that instead of purchasing a cow, he purchased a state-carriage, which he was soon informed by some kind friends in the room was only fit to be broken up for firewood. Mr. Jay joined in the general laugh against the milkman; but his glee was of brief duration; for shortly after the milkman's act of folly, four silver massive candlesticks were put up by the auctioneer at 6*s.* per ounce. Mr. Jay thought that the price put upon these candlesticks was 6*s.* only, instead of 6*s.* per ounce, and he accordingly bid 6*s.* 6*d.* for them; and the auctioneer thinking that Mr. Jay was desirous of becoming their purchaser, knocked the lot down to him, who, on tendering the sum of 6*s.* 6*d.* to the auctioneer, was informed, amidst roars of laughter, to the evident delight of the milkman, that the amount to be paid for the candlesticks was 78*l.*, they having been knocked down to him at 6*s.* 6*d.* per ounce. After paying the 78*l.*, Mr. Jay soon beat his retreat from the sale-room, accompanied by his humble friend the milkman, one moralising with the other, and confessing that each of them was unfit to enter an auction-room; Mr. Jay archly telling his unfortunate companion that he might possibly make money by the carriage if he were to exhibit it as the first state-carriage that had ever been made, it having all the signs of great antiquity about it. But the divine had the best of the milkman; for a liberal silversmith of Bath, hearing of Mr. Jay's simplicity, took the candlesticks off his hands at the auction price, whereas the milkman parted with the carriage at the loss of 5*l.* To show how little bigotry there was in Mr. Jay's character, it should be mentioned that although this milkman had never on any occasion attended, or could be induced to enter, Argyle Chapel, yet Mr. Jay, during a long illness, visited him at his bedside every afternoon, and cheered his dying moments.

Mr. Jay very seldom troubled himself about financial matters; and never kept any banker. A gentleman having left him a legacy of 100*l.* free of duty, the executor gave him a cheque for that amount on one of the Bath banks. One morning he called at the —— Bank with the cheque, which had been in his possession nearly a month, and presented it to the cashier, to whom he was known. Having been asked how he would have it paid, he replied, *Bank*, much to the surprise of the cashier, who gave him Bank-of-England notes. An hour afterwards the bank stopped payment.

A gentleman who met Mr. Jay in the evening, said: "I have heard from the cashier of the —— Bank how fortunate you were in getting your cheque changed; and really, sir, every one says that you seem to know as much about commercial as you do about religious matters." "What do you mean?" said Mr. Jay. "Why, sir, if you had answered the cashier's inquiry by the word *Notes* instead of *Bank*, he would have given you their useless paper. It was the word *Bank* that brought you Bank-of-England notes." "Well," said Mr. Jay, "it was certainly a piece of good fortune, for I neither knew that the bank was insolvent, nor that the word *Bank* meant Bank-of-England notes. I said *Bank*, as the most natural answer to a simple inquiry. It was the first cheque I ever presented in my life, and I think it will be the last, as it seems to have made quite a sensation."

There was a second piece of good luck which befell Mr. Jay. A Welsh gentleman of the name of Butler made him a present of a sixteenth of a lottery-ticket, which turned up a prize of upwards of 100*l*. His first printer, Mr. Gye, of Bath, who was agent for a lottery-office in London, and sold more tickets than perhaps any man in the West of England, had the good fortune to obtain a prize of 20,000*l*. One would have supposed that these two fortunate events would have induced Mr. Jay to be a purchaser of tickets; but he was proof against the temptation.

I have heard Mr. Jay relate, in company, two cases of rascality connected with the lottery system.

The first swindle case was this. A keeper of a lottery-office one morning sold to a lady's-maid—a respectable character—four sixteenths of a ticket, which she booked by paying a small sum. They produced 5000*l*. The morning after the drawing of the lottery she called at the office to ascertain her fate, when the keeper said that he was very sorry to inform her that her tickets had turned up blanks. He then, under some excuse or another, made an appointment to see her in the evening, which he punctually kept; and he so ingratiated himself into her good opinion, that in the course of one week he made her an offer of marriage, which was accepted and solemnised. It turned out a most unhappy union. The deluded wife, upon her learning shortly after her marriage the imposition which had been practised upon her,—that her husband had only feigned love to her to obtain the money, that his salary was small, and that his debts exceeded the amount of the prize,—was so disgusted with him that she left him; nor could any thing ever induce her to live with him again.

The other swindle was one of a very different character, the particulars of which Mr. Jay had obtained from Sir Richard Phillips, a bookseller, and the author of many useful works, and who had served the office of Sheriff of London. A small tradesman in the country, who united a lottery-office with his other business, circulated a report that he had obtained a prize of 20,000*l.*; and, to confirm it, gave a large dinner to his friends, and illuminated his house at night. The prizes not being payable for some time after the day of drawing, he borrowed money of every one he knew, who freely lent him what he required. But this was not all. He got the paragraph in the country papers setting forth his success copied in the London journals, left the country, purchased an extensive business in London without parting with any money, and obtained a large amount of credit, it being his intention to dispose of the business and stock with all promptitude, so as to be out of the way in due time. But the full extent of his views was frustrated; for one morning a very curious friend examined the books at Somerset House, and found that the whole tale was an entire fabrication. This real bad news circulated quicker than the false good news; and, as may be imagined, the rogue was not slow in loading himself with all the ready cash and valuables he could lay his hands on, and leaving the country. He was made a bankrupt and outlaw; but what afterwards became of him was never ascertained.

The Rev. Mr. Howells, a clergyman of the Church of England, preached for many years at the Long-Acre Chapel, and became very popular with a certain class of his hearers, many of the aristocracy forming part of his congregation. It was a melancholy place of worship inside; and over the entrance was painted, in black letters on a white board, "Long-Acre Episcopal Chapel." On one of Mr. Jay's visits to London he spent a long day with the late William Wilberforce, and in the evening they went to hear Mr. Howells preach. When the service was over, one of Mr. Howells' great admirers, a friend of Mr. Wilberforce's, followed him out of the chapel, and speaking about the sermon, regretted that it was not one of the preacher's first-rate discourses. Mr. Wilberforce smiled at the apology; and as he went away with Mr. Jay, said, "I have heard him three times, and the same excuse has always been made for him." Mr. Jay thought nothing of the sermon, and was satisfied with one hearing. Perhaps there never was a preacher so little calculated to interest Mr. Wilberforce or Mr. Jay. Mr. Howells was a very high Calvinist. He had a very remarkable countenance, and a most peculiar Welsh voice, so that many of his hearers could not understand him.

The gentleman who read prayers for him—a Mr. Knight—had for many years been the reader at Surrey Chapel, and was quite worn out before he went to Long-Acre Chapel. The curate was well known for burying in such places as St. Clement Danes, and similar public strips of churchyards in the metropolis, at very low charges. One Sunday evening Mr. Howells (such was his eccentricity) thus addressed poor Mr. Knight, who had been a very long time in travelling through the service: "Mr. Knight, I now tell you in public what I have repeatedly told you in private, that you drawl over the prayers so much that you leave me no time for the sermon." This admonition was certainly in bad taste.

I was once with Mr. Jay when Mr. Howells came into a book-shop where we were: he followed us out, and entered into a long conversation about Catholic emancipation; he being much opposed to that question, whilst Mr. Jay was in favour of it. Mr. Jay seemed quite delighted when he took his leave, saying to me, "My friend has been boring me about a matter in which he has not advanced a single new idea." Mr. Howells, notwithstanding his eccentricity, was considered a kind and good-hearted man. He had been for a long time acting as curate to Mr. Jay's father-in-law, the Rev. Mr. Davies, rector of Coychurch, so that no man knew better than Mr. Jay what sort of popularity Mr. Howells possessed. He died before he was an old man, and was never married. His medical attendant, a friend of mine, told me that he injured himself very much by constantly taking opening medicine.

CHAPTER VI.

Mr. Jay's punctuality in the performance of his duties at Argyle Chapel—Anecdotes—A sermon suddenly brought to a conclusion by way of reproof—The burying-ground—An exception to Mr. Jay's punctuality—An interview in the vestry between him and a Dutch gentleman—An ordination sermon—The ex-minister.

Mr. Jay was a model of punctuality. When in the vestry of his own chapel he would say, "I wait for nobody. When the hour of worship arrives I begin." Exactly as the clock of Argyle Chapel was striking the hour of eleven in the morning, and six in the evening, the congregation would be sure to see him, with his large Bible under his arm, either ascending the stairs of the pulpit, or just entering it. Having walked from his house to the chapel alone, he would enter an inner vestry, and remain there in retirement for two or three minutes before the commencement of the service; and on coming into the outer vestry would ask for the clerk and organist, telling the former what hymns to give out, and frequently requesting the latter to play a particular tune. When preaching from home he was all anxiety to see the clerk before service; for he used to say, "I never trust clerks with a hymn-book, for they appear to have no judgment, and frequently give out a hymn of ten or twelve verses, never taking into account the heat and crowded state of the chapel;" for he was always sure to attract a large congregation. He often astonished a clerk by giving him the number of a very long hymn, and telling him only to give out one particular verse, which he would name; he very often saying, "I will close the service without singing."

How frequently have I heard him request the gentleman who was going to precede him by prayer to be sure not to be very long. Mr. Jay, at his own chapel, always preferred going through the whole of the service himself; and on one occasion he quaintly said to a minister who had offered to pray before the sermon, "No, sir. I am much obliged to you for your kind offer; but I like to whet my own scythe." The congregation generally thought he could whet it better than any one else; and he always considered that the prayers, which seldom occupied more than a quarter of an hour, including the Lord's Prayer, which he invariably repeated, prepared his mind for the sermon. It is a remarkable fact, that on entering the pulpit he would open the Bible at that part where the Lord's Prayer appears, having on several occasions forgotten part of it, which so much annoyed him that he adopted this mode of preventing any future vexation on this point.

Visitors have often remarked that there was a greater stillness on the part of Mr. Jay's congregation than in any other place of worship they had ever entered, which was no doubt to be attributed to his highly impressive manner both of praying and preaching. This stillness would bring its annoyances, as it enabled him to hear the least sound. On one occasion, after the conclusion of the service, he desired the pew-opener to inform a gentleman with whom he was well acquainted that he wished to see him in the vestry; and on his making his appearance, Mr. Jay, after shaking hands with him, said with a smile on his countenance, "Really it is not affectation on my part, but the noise you make with your teeth and tongue so disturbs me, that I am sure you will endeavour to prevent it in future." On another occasion, a gentleman, the moment after Mr. Jay had given out the text, pulled out from his pocket a watch with a large bunch of seals attached to it, in order to time the discourse. The seals made such a rattling noise, that Mr. Jay turned his eyes towards the gentleman, and would not commence the sermon until he saw the watch safely deposited in its owner's pocket. Nothing could equal his aversion to any person entering the chapel after the commencement of the sermon; and on one occasion, after he had been preaching for the space of forty minutes, he, on observing a gentleman entering the chapel and leisurely walking down one of the aisles, stopped short his discourse, and eyeing the intruder, said to him, "Sir, you have come in to hear the amen.—*Amen.*" He immediately sat down; and the singing commenced. It should in justice be mentioned, that the gentleman came into the vestry immediately after the conclusion of the service, and apologised to Mr. Jay, stating that he did not know when it commenced.

There was a burying-ground belonging to Argyle Chapel, which imposed the same heavy duties on Mr. Jay as if he had been rector of some populous parish. Formerly Bath was a much more frequented place for invalids than it is at present; and many who came there to recruit their health never left that city alive.

This burying-ground was situated at the side of Bacon Cliff, one of the very high hills which surround Bath. Mr. Jay could, by opening the door of his house in Percy Place, discern the funeral procession winding up the hill to its destination; and being, as already observed, punctuality itself, could ascertain to a nicety how long it would take him to run up the hill to reach it,—for he always avoided, if possible, riding in the mourning-coaches with the procession. One of his servants, who was on these occasions his time-keeper, always informed him of the hour of the funeral. How often have I seen him open the door, and return either into his garden or study, saying, "I have a good ten minutes yet." When he once started from his residence to perform the duty imposed upon him, he would, even in the latter years of his life, run up the hill with all the agility of a young man, reaching the burial-ground before the procession.

It is much to be regretted that some of his orations over the dead have not been secured to the public. They were elegant in style, and abounded in deep pathos. He scarcely alluded to the deceased, but addressed the mourners and spectators in words of sympathy, and consolation, and admonition. I have on many of these occasions accompanied him on the road to the burial-ground, and was astonished to hear him converse upon trivial matters, even politics; but generally he would make some allusion from nature, and draw my attention to the wild flowers in the hedgerows, and to the neatness of the cottagers' gardens, as he passed along. But when arrived at the ground, he would turn round, and say: "It is not this melancholy procession, or that mournful countenance of the undertaker, which affects me; but it is the sight of the children there, leaping over the tombstones, and playing at their infantile games, full of health and spirits, and with faces lightened up with laughter, regardless of death." Often have I seen him eye their artless movements rather than watch the funeral procession enter the burial-ground. In reference to one of these burials, Mr. Jay says: "I remember some years ago to have buried a corpse. In the extremity of the audience that surrounded me I discovered a female wrinkled with age and bending with weakness; one hand held a motherless grandchild, the other wiped away her tears with a woollen apron. I pressed towards her when the service was closed. 'Have you too lost a friend?' She heaved a melancholy sigh; 'The Lord bless her memory!' I soon found that the deceased had allowed her for several years sixpence a-week. O, my God! is it possible that the appropriation of a sum so inconsiderable should cause a widow's heart to sing for joy, and save the child of the needy?"

The only exception (and it will be seen that it turned out a most providential one) to Mr. Jay's want of punctuality in attending to his ministerial duties, as far as I ever heard, occurred under the following circumstances:

Mr. Jay had entered into an engagement to preach one evening at Painswick in Gloucestershire. A two-horse coach passed every day by his house to that town, and most usually there were very few passengers either in the inside or out; so that he thought it unnecessary to book his place, which he was generally accustomed to do, travelling so much as he did. On the day in question he had a most painful toothache; and it so happened that when the coach drew up to the door, he found there was no room either inside or out. He was therefore obliged to return to his study; and being in excruciating pain, said that he should not go to Painswick by any private vehicle, as there was every excuse for not attending to preach there as advertised. He soon retired to rest. About twelve o'clock at night he was awakened by the cry of fire. The workmen and neighbours had entered the house, and soon ascertained that a room, in which his third son, a fine young lad of seven or eight years of age, was sleeping, was full of flames and smoke. The watchman refusing, from want of nerve, to enter the room to rescue the youth from almost instant death, Mr. Jay, with the greatest presence of mind, and regardless of danger, rushed into it with only his night-shirt on, and snatching up his son from the midst of the flames, took him to a place of safety. This was the work of a moment; and again rushing into the burning apartment threw open the window, and catching hold of the bedding and curtains, which were in flames, he bundled them all out of it, and succeeded in putting a stop to the fire in the other parts of the room, but not without some difficulty, his hands and legs being very much burnt.

A gentleman of fortune, of Dutch extraction, and who had, I believe, been early in life a consul in Holland, was a constant attendant at Argyle Chapel. On one occasion Mr. Jay preached on the salvability of infants in virtue of the infinite meritoriousness of the death of Christ. In the course of the sermon he said: "There are some wretches who believe there are in hell infants a span long." After the service, the gentleman intruded himself into the vestry, and thus addressed Mr. Jay: "I am, sir, one of those wretches you have described." "I am sorry for it," replied Mr. Jay, and turned upon his heel.

At the ordination of Independents, it is customary for the ordaining minister, after the confession of faith, and a prayer for the divine blessing and influence to attend the union that has been publicly recognised between the pastor and the church, to address to each of the parties a charge, containing suitable instructions, cautions, admonitions, and encouragements with regard to their respective duties. No person was more calculated than Mr. Jay to perform strictly, and without favour or affection, this part of his vocation. He had observed a growing evil amongst his brethren, with the cause of which he was well acquainted, and he therefore determined to rebuke and denounce it. When in the midst of an ordination sermon he thus addressed some candidates for admission into the church of Christ as Independent ministers: "My young brethren, it is deeply to be regretted that many young men, after having been educated for the church, who has thus a claim on their services, no sooner enter the ministry than they begin to look about them for a wife, taking care, however, that she be possessed of a fortune: if successful in their search, after a time they begin to grow weary in well-doing. They take cold; it results in a cough, or a spitting of blood; they are so weak that they cannot attend to the duties of their office. They resign, and live upon their wife's fortune. I know *five cases of this kind;* may it never be your lot!"

During the delivery of this keen rebuke, there was a young minister, or rather an ex-minister, who did not seem very comfortable. After the service was closed, the merits of the discourse were canvassed; and the general opinion was, that it was such a one as could be delivered only by Mr. Jay. "How did you like Mr. Jay?" said one of the hearers to the ex-pastor: "it was fine; quite a treat, wasn't it?" "Well, I liked him very well," replied the ex-pastor; "but I think he was rather personal." "Personal, eh! how so?" "Why you must have noticed his reference to ministers out of health resigning." "Yes, yes, he was a little close there, I must admit." "I shall speak to him about it," said the delicate, fastidious ex-minister, who, true to his word, sought the vestry, and found Mr. Jay there. He congratulated him on his health and discourse, but hinted that he was personal in his remarks, and would like to know if he referred to him. "Personal," said Mr. Jay, "personal, eh! in what part of the discourse?" "When you were speaking about ministers resigning," replied the ex-pastor. "O," said Mr. Jay, "I see you have resigned." "Yes, sir." "Did you marry a rich wife?" "Yes, sir." "Did you have a cough, and become disabled for service?" "Yes, sir." "Ah, my friend," said Mr. Jay, "yours is the *sixth case*, then." This young man, having reaped the reward of his folly, retired confused and abashed.

CHAPTER VII.

Reminiscences of Cobbett—Anecdote of an American Quaker—Cowper—The poet's favourite walks—The parish church.

I WAS acquainted for many years with the late celebrated political writer, William Cobbett, who frequently was a guest at my house in Sergeant's Inn. I remember that on one occasion when he dined there, in company with the late Sydney Taylor (the then sub-editor of the *Morning Herald*) and the late Mr. Francis Bacon (the then sub-editor of the *Times*), his saying to me, "Jay, I have the pleasure of knowing your father. I personally became acquainted with him when he was on a visit to his brother-in-law, the Rev. Mr. Gauntlett, then about quitting Botley, where he had been a curate for some years, for the vicarage at Olney. I purchased all Gauntlett's furniture at a valuation, and, like all parsons, I need not tell you he had the best of me. I once heard your father preach, and I greatly admired his style of language and delivery." It should be mentioned that Botley was the place where Cobbett resided for many years, and where, during the period of such residence, he dated his *Register* from. Mr. Bensley of Bolt Court, Mr. Jay's printer, was also Cobbett's printer. I was on a visit at Bath when Mr. Bensley forwarded to Mr. Jay some proof-sheets of one of his works, and enclosed in the same parcel a number of Cobbett's *Register* of the 7th Dec. 1825. He read it through, and was particularly struck with the following passages, which I will quote:

"Reader, did you ever pass a winter near the sand-hills of Surrey; did you, after a long and dreary season, the ground half the time covered with snow, and the other half drenched with wet,—did you ever at the end of such a winter's last frost, followed by a gentle thaw, find yourself, just after sunrise, upon a hillock, scores of linnets singing in an oak-tree, or a ploughboy's whistle keeping time to the jingle of the traces to the right, the hounds at unequal intervals giving tongue in the thicket in the vale below, and then all at once bursting out in full cry, come rattling up to the spot where you stood: did you ever feel *this joy?*—Did you ever, after being months and weeks longer at sea than you expected to be, sit moping in the cabin, hating the look of victuals, looking at your half-washed hands, thinking of your dirty face, execrating the ship, the sea, the crew, the captain, and thinking life hardly worth preserving for another day? did you ever, thus being and thus feeling, hear from the deck (no matter if in the devil's voice) the cry of land? did you ever feel *this joy?*—Did you ever, after having married a beautiful young woman, the very touch of whose garments once made the blood dance through your veins from the sole of your foot to the crown of your head, see her in a fair way of producing her or your like? did you ever, with unceasing anxiety, watch her every look for six or seven months, your hope and fear both going on and increasing all the while; and at last, after fear alone had got possession of your heart, and was on the point of producing distraction, did you ever at that moment creep softly, and with your shoes off, to the bedside, and there, the clothes being slowly drawn down, see the little creature, and see the mother's smile upon it, and feel its almost boneless hand: did you ever feel *this joy?*—Were you ever snatched in dead of night from your wife and children, hoisted away and crammed into a dungeon, in consequence of the bills brought in by Sidmouth and Castlereagh? did you ever hear or read the speeches made on that occasion; and did you, O, did you ever hear of that same Castlereagh cutting his own throat at North Cray, Kent? did you ever feel *this joy?* Have you felt *these joys?* If you have not felt all of them,—not one, two, or three of them, but the *whole four*,—you can have but a faint idea of the joy which I at this moment feel at the alarm, the dreadful forebodings, the tormenting embarrassments, and all the other evils, present and expected, real, imaginery, contingent, and even possible, that now assail, or stare in the face, the merchants and bankers of London, together with all their relations, friends, dependants, abettors, and well-wishers in every part and corner of the kingdom. God is *just;* and as man is said to be made in the image of God, man should be just too; and to forget, or not to punish as far as we are able and legally can punish, moral offences, is a neglect of a sacred duty."

Mr. Jay could hardly conceive that such a concentration of beautiful sentences could end in such a denunciation and burst of joy at the ruin which had fallen on the merchants and bankers of the metropolis.

This was the first time he had ever had a number

of Cobbett's *Register* forwarded to him, and so pleased was he at the writer's style, that he ordered a stamped copy of the *Register* to be sent to him by post every week. He well knew the day on which it would arrive at Percy Place; and I have seen him, after the postman's knock, come from his study with a paper-knife in his hand, seize the *Register*, and return back with it into his study. We were sure after dinner to have the most striking parts read to us. But to return back to the quotation I have made, I should mention that after the perusal of the *Register* in which it was contained, he put it into his pocket, and having to call on Mr. Wilberforce, he thought he would read him the passage; but to his astonishment Mr. Wilberforce said, "I have taken in Cobbett's *Register* for many years: being a public man, I am desirous of hearing what is going on in the political world; besides which I admire his style of writing."

On one of my visits to Mr. Jay, when speaking of Cobbett, and his strong prejudice against many persons, especially Quakers,—for whom Mr. Jay entertained great respect, so much so that he sent me to a Quaker's school, where I was the only scholar not of that persuasion,—I related to him the following anecdote, which I had from Cobbett's own lips, as illustrative of his prejudice against Quakers, whom he unjustly regarded as liars: "I was," said he, "while residing in Long Island in America, acquainted with a well-disposed young gentleman of large fortune, whose only fault was the habit of swearing,—such a habit that he often declared that he would give half his fortune to get rid of it. This desire came to the ears of a Quaker, who thereupon had an interview with the young gentleman, and said, 'I can cure thee of that bad habit;' whereupon the youth caught hold of the Quaker's hand and gave it a hearty shake, saying, 'How can you perform that miracle?' The reply was, 'I can tell thee. I have heard that thou art going this day to travel for a period of six weeks; thou art just my size; nobody will know thee; thou shalt come to my house, put on the cocked-hat, the coat without buttons, the knee-breeches, and the shoe-buckles; and thou wilt find that the strangeness of the dress will have such an effect on thee when thou art going to talk, that it will restrain thee from swearing,—as thou perhaps knowest, my friend, that we Quakers never swear.' The young man cheerfully assented to the proposal, and accompanied the Quaker to his house, where after changing his clothes he took his departure in the garb of a Quaker, and went his way rejoicing. The period of the young gentleman's tour having elapsed, the Quaker all anxiety started on the road to meet him. Having met him, he said, 'Well, friend, how hast thou got on?' The reply was, 'Very well.' 'Hast thou sworn so much with that dress on thee?' inquired the Quaker. The young man, rubbing the sleeves of his coat, replied, 'Certainly not; but I feel a d—d inclination to lie.'"

I was one day at Cobbett's office in Bolt Court, when it was announced to him that a deputation from the popular vestry of Marylebone wished to wait upon him for the purpose of soliciting him to take the chair at a large dinner to be given in Lord's Cricket-ground. I was about retiring, but he requested me to remain. The deputation having been shown in and introduced to him, their speaker stated to him that the parishioners would feel greatly indebted to him if he would take the chair. Cobbett made no reply; but smiled. The speaker then said, by way of inducement, that it would be the largest dinner ever given; that there would be present Daniel Whittle Harvey, and many first-rate speakers. Cobbett again smiled, and said, "*I* can speak. Have you got any good *listeners?*" The deputation, finding that Cobbett would not comply with their wishes, withdrew, laughing heartily at his remarks.

The late Lord Denman, when he was Attorney-General, prosecuted Cobbett by a criminal information for a political libel. Previous to the trial, which came on before Lord Tenterden at the Guildhall of the City of London, Cobbett wrote a letter to me, which I have in my possession, requesting me to furnish him with the list of the jury, who, as it fortunately happened, were impanneled in the ward of Farringdon Street Without, near Sergeant's Inn. I knew the politics of most of the jury, so that I was enabled to strike out the names of those most opposed to him in politics. I sat next to him in court on the trial, which took place on a very cold morning. When he entered the court he was evidently somewhat nervous; but on seeing one of the jury, an admirer of his politics, with whom he had spent the evening of the night before the trial, and who would have died rather than have given a verdict of guilty, enter the jury-box, he took courage, and called out to the door-keeper: "Shut the door, or it will cut my head off, as the Attorney-General wishes to do." The chief defence of Cobbett in his speech to the jury (for he appeared without counsel) was an unjust attack upon the Whigs; and I was astonished to observe that Lord Tenterden seemed to enjoy it. He was found "Not guilty."

Cobbett published a volume of Sermons, a copy of which he forwarded to Mr. Jay, who remarked to me that he considered them very ably written, and much to the point, and that the texts were extremely well selected. He added, that he liked them better than most of the sermons he had seen printed; and that if Cobbett had been a clergyman instead of a political writer, he would have been one of the most popular preachers of the day.

Mr. Jay was a great admirer of Cowper, and more frequently quoted from him than from any other poet, with the single exception of Watts, whom he aptly designated the poet of the Scriptures, the poet of the sanctuary. "Cowper's poems," said Mr. Jay, "are so natural, so chaste, so eloquent; they abound in such fine expressions, and in such great principles; they are so purely English, and so truly Christian,—that I have never found any other poet take so strong hold of my thoughts and affections; and as to his hymns, what can be more chaste, more tender, more exquisite? The muse of Cowper is the muse of England."

Mr. Jay, on one of his visits to Cambridge, made it a point to spend a long day at the neighbouring town of Huntingdon, where the poet so long resided, merely to view his residence. He frequently visited Olney; and from the poet's friend, the Rev. Mr. Newton, the former vicar of that place, and from his brother-in-law, the Rev. Mr. Gauntlett, the then vicar, he knew the favourite walks and haunts of the poet, which he would frequently pace in contemplative mood. He particularly delighted to ramble on the banks of the Ouse, which the poet has immortalised in verse. It was in one of these rambles by the river's side that Mr. Jay said that he composed that passage in reference to a stream in one of his Morning Exercises. It is so natural that I cannot help transcribing it. Here it is: "Nothing can be more pleasing or interesting to those who relish the simple beauties of nature than to walk by the side of living streams, to see the fish playing and disappearing, the green weeds waving their long streamers in the water, the reeds bending and recovering themselves again, the rippling of the shallows, and the glassy reflections of the deep, while the bushes and trees form a quivering shade on the banks. Here is enough to fix the tasteful mind, and to induce the poet to take out his pen, and the painter his pencil."

Whilst on his visits to his brother-in-law at Olney, Mr. Jay often made the parish church his place of study; and on letting himself into the sacred edifice with the vicar's key, he would immediately betake himself to the pew where Cowper had so many years sat and worshiped. Often was the dinner-time announced to him whilst seated and meditating in the pew; and he would come out, saying that he enjoyed his new study more than any other, with the single exception of his own at Percy Place. Here he composed, on his last visit to his relative, the sermon which he preached at the dissenting chapel at Olney.

Mr. Jay, in one of his discourses, thus alludes to the affection of Cowper for the memory of his mother, so beautifully and feelingly described by the poet on viewing her portrait: "Where should we think of looking for affection, if not among those who are attached by ties of nature, by habits of early intercourse, by mutual participations of every youthful enjoyment, by the reciprocal performance of a thousand tender and endearing offices! But conceive of whatever is attractive and binding in the fond image of a *mother*, one who, after nameless pains and perils, gave thee birth, nursed thee on her knees, fed thee at her breast, and, through sleepless nights and anxious days, watched over thy tender progress; bring before your mind a man all genius and sensibility, viewing the picture of a mother,

'Faithful remembrancer of one so dear,'

recalling maternal smiles, and the dress in which, with blessings, she dismissed him to school; forgetting a thousand other things, but remembering her 'nightly visits,' her 'morning bounties,' her 'constant flow of love that knew no fall.'"

Mr. Jay had in his possession several of Cowper's autograph letters, which he highly prized. He much admired the epistolary style of the poet, than which he considered nothing could be finer, being, as he termed, full of heart, and free from affectation. I have often seen him, just before sitting down to breakfast, take from his library a volume of the poet's letters, and get one of my sisters to read some of them to him during the repast. He had for years an engraving of the well-known portrait of the poet, which the Rev. Mr. Newton said was a most striking likeness, hanging up in his study.

CHAPTER VIII.

Robert Hall and anecdotes — The title of D.D. conferred upon Mr. Jay — A dinner-party — Percy Place.

Mr. Jay's intimacy with Robert Hall commenced early in life, and continued uninterrupted until the death of that eminent man. Nothing afforded Mr. Jay greater delight than to be in the company of his friend. He preached a funeral sermon at Argyle Chapel on the occasion of his death, which I regret was never printed.

It is well known in the religious world that Robert Hall was an inveterate smoker, and it appeared to be the only thing which afforded any relief to the malady, or rather complication of maladies, to which he was for so many years a victim, making his body, in the language of his physician, "an entire machine of physical suffering." Mr. Jay's horror of smoking was so great that he never would endure it in any company except that of Robert Hall, and John Newton the rector of St. Mary Woolnoth, in whose favour he relaxed the rule, well knowing that in Hall's case the habit relieved the pain, and animated his conversation, which was not less his congenial element than contemplation. Whilst smoking, he kept on apologising to Mr. Jay for the annoyance to which he was sure he was subjecting him, saying, that he had first taken to a pipe in self-defence, having been so much in the company of Dr. Parr, the celebrated Grecian, who was a very great smoker.

Robert Hall, in his love of smoking, followed the example of his great episcopal namesake, the amiable and admirable Bishop Hall. A friend once said to the prelate when indulging in this enjoyment, "Well, venerable bishop, I see you are worshiping your idol again." "Yes," was the instant reply, "I am burning him."

I cannot refrain from relating the following anecdotes, which I have heard Mr. Jay tell in company, connected with his friend:

Mr. Hall told Mr. Jay that three sermons were advertised to be preached on a week-day at a large village on the borders of Cambridgeshire, and that he was selected to preach the first of them. The vicinity of this village was noted for its coursing; and the prize given in those days to the young farmers was "a laced hat," which is to this day a sign of some of the public-houses in that district. The morning was a very fine one, and many were the carriages, other vehicles, and horses, which came in quick succession to the village, bearing most of the rank and population of the surrounding villages, all eager to hear the eloquent preacher. Mr. Hall had, a short time prior to the commencement of the service, rambled down a narrow lane, with a pipe in his mouth, for retirement and reflection. He was much amused in hearing a dialogne between two farmer's labourers, who were occupied in fixing some hurdles. One said to the other: "John, I say, what is the meaning of such a lot of carriages, gigs, carts, and horses coming into the village; it is surely not the great coursing meeting for the 'laced hat,' is it?" "No," answered the other; "but they say that there is going to be a batch of preaching the whole day for a laced hat, to be given as a prize to the best preacher." This colloquy much amused the listener; and it came across his mind two or three times during the course of the sermon.

On another occasion, having to preach at some village, Robert Hall got out of his gig at a small public-house not far from the chapel. He was seen entering it by one of the deacons, a very religious man, who, thinking such an act the height of sin, followed him into the house to rebuke him for his conduct. He found the preacher sitting on a chair with a pipe in his mouth; who, surmising that the good man, for whom he had much respect, was about to lecture him, prevented him from doing so, by instantly saying to him: "My dear friend, we cannot be sufficiently thankful to God for these small public-houses." He then resumed his smoking, much to the discomfiture of the deacon, who made a speedy exit.

Robert Hall had a great aversion to a high pulpit. On one occasion of his preaching at Argyle Chapel, after having entered the pulpit, he unceremoniously took up the cushion from the desk, and having pushed it aside as a useless incumbrance, placed the Bible on the plain board of the desk. He then commenced a most simple and sublime prayer, a part of the service in which he always excelled. The sermon which he preached on that occasion was equal to his highest efforts. Next day Mr. Jay directed his son Edward to call on Robert Hall, who was staying at Mr. Smith's, the banker, at Bath, to inquire how he was after the labour of the preceding day. After the usual compliments, Hall said to Mr. Jay's son: "Sir, I am very much obliged to your father for his kind inquiries. Tell him I am pretty well, although fatigued. But allow me to say, sir, that your father's is a very high pulpit. I never like to preach in a high pulpit, sir, and am much surprised that he has not reduced it in height, and brought himself nearer to his auditory. No preacher, sir, should hold forth in a high pulpit. To reduce my altitude, I kicked the stool away, and cast the cushion aside."

The late Dr. Porteous, Bishop of London, who was a great admirer of Robert Hall, invited him to spend a day with him at his palace at Fulham. The invitation was given in so kind a manner, that he could not refuse to accept it, although he never sought for high society. Hall spent a most interesting day with the prelate. After dinner, Mrs. Porteous, a lady whose education was not of the highest order, suddenly addressed Robert Hall, asking him, "What are Baptists?" The bishop naively winked his eye at his guest, as much as to say, you must not consider the question an insult. Hall took the cue, and very simply answered the lady's question, doing it in so clear a manner, that the bishop in the course of the evening alluded to his admirable definition of Baptists, saying, "Hall, do you know you have half made my wife a convert?"

"I was very much astonished," said Mr. Jay, "when dining once in company with Robert Hall, to observe how regardless he was in respect of his diet; not that he was a great eater. Seeing him take many slices of cucumber, after he had just been helped twice to a dish of trifle, and knowing how much his health depended on his digestion, I said to him, 'Will that agree with your stomach?' 'It must,' he said quickly, 'or it's no stomach to me.' We all laughed heartily, and I never afterwards interfered with his eating propensities." No person was more competent to give advice on a subject of this kind than Mr. Jay, who was very simple in his diet, rarely partaking of more than one of the dishes on the table.

One morning one of Robert Hall's friends called on him, and found him on the parlour floor, stretched on the carpet, after a night of disturbed and intermitted repose, suffering most acutely. His friend remarked to him that he appeared to be in great agony. "Agony, sir!" replied Hall; "go to hell for a word; you will not find one upon earth to express what I am now enduring, and have been throughout the night." This intensity of language was evidently as concentrated as his sufferings were.

A professional gentleman at Bath, who had been all his life a dissipated man, suddenly became religious, and connected himself with the Baptist chapel of that city. The convert after a little time became extremely troublesome, and soon caused a division in the church. Mr. Hall was very much annoyed at the circumstance; and in telling Mr. Jay of it, spoke in terms of great acrimony of the conduct of this individual, when Mr. Jay suddenly replied, "I liked him much better before his conversion;" an observation which so tickled Hall's fancy, that he forgot the grievance in a loud laugh.

No preacher assumed less of the Reverend than Mr. Jay. In the title-page of all his works he simply styled himself *William Jay*, a designation by which he was so well known. In the year 1810 the degree of Doctor of Divinity was conferred upon him by the College of New Jersey in North America, a country where his works were then, and have since been, in such extensive circulation; and although he duly acknowledged the honour, he never adopted the "Doctor" as a prefix to his name, or the "D.D." after it, except upon one occasion, in travelling, when, in order to insure attention to a case of manuscripts, which he was obliged to leave at a large inn, he knowingly described himself on the direction as the "Rev. Dr. Jay." When the diploma reached his hands, his family described him as Dr. Jay; but he immediately put a stop to the use of the title. In the year 1817 a like degree was conferred by the Faculty of Marischal College, Aberdeen, upon Robert Hall, in testimony of his high talents and character; but although he felt much gratified by this mark of their good opinion of him, he never would adopt the title.

I have heard Mr. Jay state that he was one day dining in company with that celebrated minister at the house of a friend, where there were present several D.D.'s, who constantly kept challenging one another thus: "Doctor, shall I take wine with you?" Robert Hall, on leaving the room with Mr. Jay, said: "What do you think of the Doctors to-day? We ought both to rejoice that we have not availed ourselves of the dignity." To which Mr. Jay replied: "If there was no other reason for my not assuming the title, this dining-room scene would have prevented me. It has almost made me sick."

For several years there was no name on the door

of Mr. Jay's residence; and so frequent were the complaints made by numerous persons who had occasion to call on him of the difficulty of finding it out, that Mrs. Jay, in his absence from home, and without his knowledge, ordered a brass plate to be fixed on the door, with these words engraved thereon, "Rev. William Jay." On his return home, he saw, to his astonishment and mortification, the plate. After the usual salutations between himself and wife, he said: "My dear, I cannot permit that piece of brass to remain on the door, for I am no *Reverend.* I shall go into the city at once, and order it to be immediately removed; but I have no objection, by way of compromise, to have a plate with the word 'Jay' engraved on it." Such plate was substituted for the other obnoxious one, and it remains fixed on the door to this day.

CHAPTER IX.

Rowland Hill in early life — His admission into deacon's orders — Builds Surrey Chapel, and also a chapel at Wotton-under-Edge —Mr. Jay visits him at his country retreat — Meets there Lord Hill — A strange introduction — The peace-offering and its results—Pulpit anecdotes of Rowland Hill—The effects of flattery —Mr. Jay preaches the funeral sermon of his departed friend at Surrey Chapel — Lord Hill chief mourner—The sermon printed, and dedicated to his lordship.

I HAVE already stated the long friendship which existed between Mr. Jay and the Rev. Rowland Hill, and how it commenced. I shall now present the reader with a few recollections and anecdotes of the last well-known preacher, as related by Mr. Jay in his private circle, but to which he has not alluded in his reminiscences of him.

When a young man, Rowland Hill was described, and very truly so, as possessing a very gentlemanly deportment; and this, together with his condition of life, sprightliness of imagination, and earnestness of address, produced an amazing attention and effect on the part of his auditors. He was educated first at Eton, and afterwards graduated at Cambridge. On quitting that University he was admitted into deacon's orders, but could not obtain from the bishop any further ordination, unless with a promise of regularity, he having preached in the open air, a condition with which he peremptorily refused to comply.

Being thus driven out of the pale of the church, he built Surrey Chapel, and also a chapel at Wotton-under-Edge, and attached to each of them dwelling-houses.

Rowland Hill always made the dwelling-house at Wotton-under-Edge the centre of his retreat and excursions when in the country. Mr. Jay was on a visit to his friend whilst the late Lord Hill was a guest there. This was at the time when, during the Peninsular war, his lordship was obliged to leave Spain for a few months on account of his health. Mr. Jay was much pleased with his lordship, and greatly admired the feeling he manifested on reading in the daily journals an account of one of the sanguinary sieges in that theatre of war, tears rolling down his cheeks in the perusal of the loss sustained by so many of his brave companions in arms. The feelings of grief manifested by his lordship were soon interrupted by a scene of a totally different nature. Rowland Hill was called out of the room by his servant. It appears that one of the managers of his chapel, by trade a dyer, a little man, called on him in his working dress, besmeared with blue, about the chapel arrangements. This business settled, Mr. Hill said, "I should like, my good friend, to introduce you to my nephew, the great general." Upon which the little dyer replied, "Look, respected sir, at my hands and clothes; I should be ashamed to face him." No sooner was the sentence finished than Rowland Hill, without more ado, caught hold of the dyer's hands, slapped him on the back, and brought him into the room, then letting him down, said to his nephew, "There is my deacon; and I can assure you that he is one of the best of men living." Lord Hill, like a true gentleman, took particular notice of the dyer, and made various inquiries of him about his trade.

Rowland Hill entertained a personal dislike of the late Mr. Huntingdon, between whom and himself a pulpit war had been carried on; Mr. Huntingdon being a high Antinomian, against the tenets of which Mr. Hill was known to entertain a great aversion. Mr. Huntingdon, by way of a peace-offering, took a copy of his book on Faith to Surrey Chapel to present it to his opponent. He knocked at the door, and on the servant opening it, said, "Tell your master that William Huntingdon has brought his book on Faith as a present to him, and that he wishes to present it personally." This message the servant duly delivered to his master, who thereupon seized the fire-tongs, and putting them behind him, walked to the street-door. Mr. Huntingdon, little dreaming what was to follow, then offered his book, which Mr. Hill seized with the tongs (until then concealed), and running into the room, where there was a glorious fire, pursued by Huntingdon frantic with rage, threw it on the fire in the presence and to the astonishment of its Antinomian donor, who soon beat a retreat.

After this affair, several Antinomians who were attendants at Surrey Chapel left it, and congregated at a small meeting-house near the Elephant and Castle, selecting for a minister a man of no very great reputation either for learning or morality. There was at that time no name to the street in which this chapel was situated. A meeting of its members took place to give the chapel a name or description; which coming to the ears of Rowland Hill, he said to a friend,

"Go and present my compliments to the reverend gentleman officiating there, and tell him he had better call it *Scum Chapel;* for I have got rid of all the disagreeables belonging to my place of worship."

It was for many years a frequent custom with Rowland Hill, before the evening commencement of the service at Surrey Chapel, to take a stroll as far as the foot of Blackfriars' Bridge. On one of these strolls he overheard a dissipated rakish-sort-of-looking young man say to a companion of like appearance, "Let's go to old Rowland Hill's chapel, and have a lark." "So we will," replied the companion. Rowland Hill watched them go into the chapel, and observed the pew in which they were placed. During the sermon, discovering that these young men were laughing and making all sort of grimaces, he intensely cast his eyes towards them, and pointing at them with his finger, exclaimed in a very loud voice, "There is no peace to the wicked, saith my God. There's a lark!" Report says that this exclamation was the cause of their reformation.

On another occasion Rowland Hill, at the close of a sermon at the Surrey Chapel on a Sunday night, called out of his pulpit at the very top of his voice, "There is a great cry, that there's a want of employment: steal some more umbrellas and hats, and you shall have, I warrant you, lots of work. caused three of such persons to be tried yesterday at the Surrey sessions, and they have got twelve months' employment at the treadmill."

So frequent was the picking of pockets at Surrey Chapel on Sunday nights, that it became such a source of annoyance to Rowland Hill, that at the conclusion of one of his sermons he said, in reference thereto, "I understand that many of the congregation lost their purses last Sunday night; and if any of the thieves should be present, I would tell them that they are in the house of God, and that God sees them, which I should have thought would have been sufficient to have prevented such crimes; but if this will not be sufficient to prevent it, I am happy to inform them that there are twelve police-officers stationed in different parts of my chapel."

A poor's-rate having been assessed on Surrey Chapel, Rowland Hill determined to appeal against the payment thereof at his own expense. The appeal came on for hearing at the Surrey sessions, Rowland Hill appearing by counsel under his written instructions, and Mr. Spankie, afterwards a Sergeant-at-Law, appearing as counsel for the respondents. Rowland Hill, like all advocates in person, imported into his case that which had really nothing to do with it, but which was nevertheless true to the very letter,—that he had collected more moneys at his chapel for religious and charitable purposes than any other preacher in the metropolis. Mr. Spankie was equally irregular; for, not content with arguing the case on the behalf of the parish on legal grounds, he travelled out of the way to attack and abuse the reverend appellant. The appeal succeeded.

On the following Sunday, Rowland Hill, in the course of his sermon, which he preached in aid of some charity, said: "My friends, I have been called a good divine, but I now begin to think I must be a good lawyer; for I beat Counsellor Spankie and all his crew the other day upon every one of their points.

They wanted to dip their hands deeply into the funds which we collect for charitable purposes, but I wouldn't let them. If this Spankie is in the congregation, I wish he would make his appearance in the vestry after the collection of this morning, and dare to abuse me there as he did at the Court-house of the Surrey Sessions: I think he would find his match."

Rowland Hill was very susceptible to flattery. A tradesman residing near his chapel, observing this foible in his minister, ingratiated himself, in process of time, into his good opinion and friendship by obsequious attentions and fulsome adulation. The office of tax-collector having been offered to the tradesman, provided he could obtain a surety for 2000*l.*, he hastened without delay to inform Rowland Hill thereof, who, on hearing the condition upon which the appointment could be obtained, voluntarily offered to become the surety, and was quite restless until he signed the bond. After the lapse of a year or two the tradesman failed, and ran away with the government money. It was late on a Saturday evening that Rowland Hill received a letter from the solicitor of the Treasury, stating that if the sum of 2000*l.* for which he had become bound was not paid forthwith, legal proceedings would be immediately taken against him to recover the amount thereof. This notification greatly annoyed and mortified him; but he kept the matter to himself, not even divulging it to his wife, for a few hours at least, as you shall hear. The following day happened to be Sacrament Sunday. No sooner had he made his appearance in the chapel than his congregation observed that something more than ordinary was on his mind, but what it was they could not conjecture. At length, during the administration of the sacrament, the cause of his depression of spirits was revealed. He could no longer keep the secret. Scarcely had the curate read the passage, "He that giveth to the poor lendeth unto the Lord," than he immediately exclaimed to the communicants: "I hope you will not forget the plates as you pass by; I am going to give all the money I have about me, rather than the devil should have it." And then, pulling his nose, he added: "A scoundrel for whom I became a surety for 2000*l*. has taken me in, and I shall have to pay for it to-morrow. What makes it more certain that the devil has had a hand in the fraud is, that I have been preaching all my life against one person becoming surety for another."

Mr. Jay, in his Autobiography, in alluding to the difficulty which Rowland Hill must have experienced in repressing his humour in the pulpit, says: "This was indeed overruled for good; and the expectation of hearing something droll and witty drew many to hear him, who though they came to laugh, returned to pray. A man should never dive who cannot swim. Mr. Hill could come up again; and we have often seen the smile which he excited soon followed by the tear. Yet these outbreaks of wit and humour sometimes gave offence, and caused his good to be evil spoken of; and, it must be owned, that his ideas, like rich clusters of grapes, sometimes, for want of proper support, fell down, and were soiled upon the ground."

Upon the death of Rowland Hill, Mr. Jay was selected to preach the funeral sermon. I accompanied him to Surrey Chapel-house, and almost immediately on his arrival there he retired into one of the bed-rooms, so that he might not be seen by any of the numerous clergymen and ministers who were expected on that occasion. He desired me to ask the late Dr. Collyer, of Peckham, who was appointed to read the prayers, to come up to him. On seeing the Doctor, he requested him to leave out part of the prayers and one of the lessons, saying, in his innocent way, "How can I preach before persons who have been in the crowded chapel since nine o'clock in the morning?" On Lord Hill's arriving in his carriage, decorated in his blue riband, as chief-mourner, he immediately inquired for Mr. Jay. I told his lordship that he had retired to one of the bed-rooms, he not wishing to see any one before the service; but as I knew that his lordship, independently of his being chief mourner, was acquainted with him, I took him to the place of retirement. His lordship, after shaking hands with Mr. Jay, held a short conversation with him respecting his lordship's last interview with his deceased uncle. Many were the inquiries after Mr. Jay by many very distinguished characters, who made it a point of conscience and respect to be present on the occasion of the funeral sermon; but he stuck to the bed-room until the hymn before the sermon was partly sung. I have often thought that Mr. Jay's retirement previous to preaching, either in a room or his garden, was one of the grand causes of his popularity. The text was, "Howl, fir-tree; for the cedar is fallen." Lord Hill was much affected during the discourse, and particularly so when Mr. Jay came to that part of his sermon, "When such a man finishes his course, we surround his death, not indeed without weeping, as we shall presently see, but with songs of deliverance. Each one is ready to exclaim, 'Well done, thou hast gained the day; thy warfare is accomplished; thou hast nobly fought, and conquered.' We rejoice, as the Scripture says, that no man took his crown; he left it uninjured, unsullied; and we lay the moral coronet on his coffin, and shout the plaudit he has heard in another world, 'Servant of God, well done.' 'Well done, thou good and faithful servant, enter thou into the joy of thy Lord.'"

Mr. Jay, at Lord Hill's request, printed the sermon, under the title of *Sensibility at the Fall of Eminence*, and it was dedicated to his lordship, then Commander-in-Chief of her Majesty's Forces, in the following words: "My Lord, the sermon which your lordship's candour approved in the delivery, and whose chief merit consists in the well-meant endeavour to appreciate the worth and to improve the death of your eminently pious, and useful, and honoured relation, is, with all respect due to the high renown you have so justly acquired, and still more to the excellences of your personal character, inscribed by your lordship's most humble and obedient servant, William Jay."

CHAPTER X.

Mr. Jay writes the preface to the Memoirs of Mrs. Sarah Savage—Extracts therefrom—Preaches for the Home Missionary Society at Salter's Hall in 1820—Extract from the sermon—Collections for charitable purposes—An anecdote—Collection for the repairs of Argyle Chapel—The contribution of a millionnaire—The excuse of a rich tradesman—Welsh ministers—Boatswain Smith.

MR. JAY, when preaching at Shrewsbury in 1818, was the guest of Sir John Bickerton Williams, who was then writing the life and character of Mrs. Sarah Savage, eldest daughter of the Rev. Philip Henry, M.A., and sister of Matthew Henry the commentator. At the request of his host Mr. Jay wrote a preface to the work, and felt much gratification, whilst on his task, in having the opportunity afforded him of perusing all the manuscripts of the pious lady, which chiefly consisted of a diary. Mr. Jay, in allusion to the benefit of having such a daily remembrancer, says in his preface, "The species of writing in which this gracious woman so largely indulged was far more common in her days than it is in ours. It has been abused and rendered ridiculous by its minuteness, and too frequently publication; yet, properly conducted, it would prove eminently conducive to usefulness." And further on in the preface he adds, "Some diaries were written, either for the express purpose of meeting the public eye, or in the apprehended probability of it. When this is known to be the case, we cannot peruse them with the same degree of pleasure and confidence as when they were written for their own sake, and betray no wish to produce effect. Nothing was further from the mind of Mrs. Savage than the public exhibition of what she wrote. It was solely inscribed for her own use and edification. Her views in it she has thus recorded: 'It is in my thoughts to do something in the nature of a diary, being encouraged by the advantage others have gained thereby, and the hope that I may be furthered by it in a godly life, and be more watchful over the frame of my heart, when it shall be kept on record. I would approve myself to God, who alone knows my sincerity. To him I have made known my request herein; and I heartily beg that what I shall at any time put down may be the workings of my heart, and that in nothing I may bear witness against myself.' In this temper of mind the whole seems to have been penned; and nothing can be more pleasing and edifying than the perusal of such unstudied, undisguised representations of her conscience and character."

Mr. Jay, in another part of his preface, says: "The experience of Mrs. Savage shows us that religion is not always begun abruptly, or in a manner bordering on prodigy. It is often derived, under divine agency, from pious education, family worship, parental instruction, holy example. It is certain that many of the most eminent and useful ministers among the Puritans and Nonconformists were not converted from a course of profligacy, but were trained up in the nurture and admonition of the Lord; from children they knew the Holy Scriptures; and the change in them was as gradual in its progress, as it was proved to be real and divine in its effects. . . . . I never knew a professor of religion who fell by certain temptations, but had been, previously to his connection with the Christian world, the victim of vice. Moral and virtuous habits produce delicacy, and impose restraint. Former scenes of guilt will often revive in the imagination, and though they are not entertained there, yet by passing through the mind they defile it and distress it. . . . . Though morality is not religion, yet it is a social benefit; but the man called from the dregs of profaneness has to look back upon the injury he has done to others, and to mourn over effects which he cannot repair."

In the year 1820, Thomas Tompson, of Pounsford Park, Somersetshire, applied to Mr. Jay to preach the first sermon for the Home Missionary Society at Salter's Hall, London, that gentleman being one of its first movers and most zealous and liberal supporters. Mr. Jay, feeling much interest in the success of the society, cheerfully undertook the task. The attendance at the chapel was very numerous, and the sum collected great, although at this time there was much distress in the country, to which he alluded in the following touching and pertinent sentences: "Many are not aware of the sufferings of the poor, unless in general rumour, which obtains slight credit, and produces little impression. How destitute of comfort, of attendance, of accommodation, of conveniences, of needful supplies, are many of the aged and sick! How many infantile cries for relief pierce and agonise a father's or mother's ear in vain! How many are there who never touch a morsel of meat of their own from one month to another; yea, whose homely board is frequently spread with the most common vegetables, unaccompanied, not only with meat, but even bread and salt! How many are there wretchedly apparelled, as well as starvingly fed, and who, by a sense of decency stronger than their feeling of piety, are ashamed to appear at public worship! How many are there who, when He sendeth abroad His ice like morsels, and you exclaim, 'Who can stand before His cold?' encounter the adversity in tattered garments, through paneless windows, and with scanty, casually-collected, pilfered fuel! How many are heard begging,—for what?—labour, toil, drudgery! My God! what a state of society is that, in which, what was originally pronounced as a curse, —'In the sweat of thy face shalt thou eat bread, till thou return unto the ground,'—is prized, and implored as a boon, and implored too in vain! O my countrymen, if your complaints reach not the ears of the great, they shall, by our prayers for you, enter the ears of the Lord God of Sabaoth!"

Mr. Jay, in the course of his discourse, after stating that every preacher produced by the efforts of the society would become an official advocate, and be empowered to render it, by his sermons, as well as his life, important service, thus alludes to himself: "And is even this an impossible or an improbable result? It is not delicate for a speaker to refer to himself, otherwise it might be observed that your preacher of this morning was the fruit of village-preaching, and preaching of a very humble kind too. Three others also," continues he, "by the same means, were called to labour in the word and doctrine out of the same obscure vicinity." These individuals were not mentioned by Mr. Jay, but I have heard him allude to those eminent preachers, Mr. Toplady and Dr. Williams, as having been awakened by village-preaching, with both of whom he was well acquainted.

Perhaps Mr. Jay preached more sermons for collections for different charities than any other minister of his time. When his great popularity is taken into account, this is not to be wondered at; for wherever he preached the chapels were sure to be crowded more than upon any other occasion. Sometimes he would select a text appropriate to the subject of the charity, but oftener would preach a sermon on a popular text, without reference to the collection, in which case he would conclude his discourse with a few sentences containing deep pathos. But if the sermon was entirely devoted to the subject of the charity, he would frequently conclude it with something facetious. I recollect on one occasion his narrating to a large audience at the close of his discourse the following anecdote: "My friends, a few weeks ago, at a collection at my chapel at Bath, whilst I was talking, after the conclusion of the service, with some gentlemen in the vestry, who were engaged in counting out the money, a sturdy and determined-looking man, in a humble station of life, suddenly made his appearance before us, and approaching the table threw down a sixpence, exclaiming in a loud voice, 'There it is!' 'What is?' I inquired. 'Why, the other sixpence.' 'What other sixpence?' I asked him. 'Why, sir, your last sentence had such an effect upon me, that I determined to drop a shilling in the plate; but I followed a very well-dressed gentleman, and I observed that he only put in sixpence, and I thought I would do the same. So I gave up my good resolution, and followed his example: but after I had left the chapel my conscience was pricked, and my good resolution returned,—and that is the other sixpence which I intended to put in the plate.'" After quaintly telling this anecdote, Mr. Jay said: "I shall feel much obliged to gentlemen who are very well dressed, and who are going to put into the plate a sixpence, to have the kindness to remain the last in the chapel, so that their bad example may not lead to bad effects."

Argyle Chapel having been enlarged at a very heavy expense, Mr. Jay, during one of his annual visits to London for a month, determined to use his personal exertions to collect a sufficient sum of money to pay off the necessary incumbrance on the building. I accompanied him several times in this embassy of his, and was much amused in observing how very reluctantly he performed the self-imposed task, although he met with more success than any other applicant. It appeared to me that his character, reputation, and fine joyous countenance, had a great deal to do with the unloosing of the purse-strings. Where he expected the most, he oftentimes obtained the least. One morning he called at my house, and requested me to accompany him to the residence of a millionnaire in one of the Squares, who was, he said, a constant hearer of his whenever and wherever he preached in London. I am certain, from what Mr. Jay stated on the road, that he expected that these two facts would cause a very handsome subscription towards the chapel. We arrived at the gentleman's house; and when the servant announced our names we were ushered into the breakfast-room. He appeared delighted to see Mr. Jay; but it struck me, by his countenance, that he guessed the object of the call. Mr. Jay, after the usual conversation, told his tale, and presented the subscription-book to the rich man, who, with evident pain, gave a sovereign. I looked at Mr. Jay's countenance, and he appeared to be in a perfect state of amazement, and immediately left the room. When we reached the bottom of the stairs we had to make our way through rows of old china jars and basins standing on each side of the hall on marble slabs. Just before reaching the street-door Mr. Jay turned round to me, saying: "I am quite sick." I said: "You have just passed a china basin in the hall, which perhaps is kept for people in your condition to use." When we emerged into the street I saw that he was annoyed at the small amount of the contribution, although I had for the moment tickled his fancy by my observation. "I am not sorry, Cyrus, that the gentleman has given me so little; my regret is that he is so very rich."

The next day Mr. Jay related this story, in my presence, to a reverend gentleman, who was accustomed to these things. He said: "I think there ought to be white basins in very many of the houses where we call." He then related the various excuses which religious professors make for not giving, although they wish to pass in the eyes of the world as very liberal. One excuse which the reverend gentleman related was this: A poor Dissenting minister from a rural district came into the counting-house of one of these gentry, a rich tradesman, with his book in his hand, and made his application. The gentleman immediately seized the book, and said: "Let me see it; for I have a rule which regulates my giving. Let me see how much you have done in your own district." He observed to the applicant that a small sum only had been there collected. "True, sir; but we are so very poor." The tradesman then returned the book to the Dissenting minister without a donation, and bowed him out of the counting-house. By this plan the religious professor never had to part with his money, inasmuch as applications of this nature only came from districts where the poverty of the inhabitants compelled then to seek for aid elsewhere. Mr. Jay, it should be mentioned, collected several hundred pounds during his brief visit in London; and was highly gratified with the general and generous reception he met with on most occasions.

Mr. Jay frequently gave a great deal of money away to poor Dissenting ministers, particularly those from Wales, who called upon him at Bath. I have observed, that after looking at the case written in the book of a Welsh minister, he would ask him one or two questions, and then would say: "How did you come from Wales to Bath?" The poor divine would innocently say: "I have walked the whole way, to save expense." This was enough for the inquirer, who would slip his hand into his pocket, draw out thence a sovereign, present it to his less fortunate friend, and sign his name in the book, an act proving of more advantage to the poor Welshman in his future collections than the money.

I happened to be at Bath one day, when Mr. Jay was much amused by Boatswain Smith, accompanied by his little children, who were dressed in naval and military uniforms, calling upon him at Percy Place. The children having sung a verse of a hymn, he gave the Boatswain a sovereign, and wished him and the children good afternoon. After taking their departure I was surprised to hear him say, that the Boatswain was a very good preacher.

CHAPTER XI.

A sermon at sea—The conduct of one of the passengers—Rev. Mr. Venn—Scarcity of clergy—Mr. Jay preaches at Paddington Chapel on the appointment of the Rev. Mr. Stretton as its pastor—Extracts from the sermon—A few notices of the Rev. Mr. Foster the celebrated essay-writer.

ALTHOUGH Mr. Jay had in his younger days, and upon particular occasions afterwards, preached in the open air, yet he nevertheless considered that there was this objection to the practice, viz. that in open-air preaching there were many surrounding objects, as well as temporary incidents, tending to draw off the attention of the auditors. This observation of his brings to my recollection an anecdote respecting a sermon preached by him at sea on his return homewards by a steam-vessel from Glasgow (where he had been preaching for Dr. Chalmers at the Tron Church) to Liverpool. Hardly had he set his foot on board the steamer before he was recognised. The sea being very smooth, the captain, crew, and passengers, with the exception of an elderly and supercilious-looking gentleman, surrounded him, and requested him to preach. At first he declined to accede to their wishes; but at length, overcome by their importunity, he consented. At the given time he took up his position on the deck, encircled by the captain, crew, and passengers minus the venerable dissentient, who just as the service was about to commence, stepped up to Mr. Jay, and with a view, no doubt, of putting a stop to what he considered an act of desecration, said to him in a stern and sarcastic manner, "Sir, I should like to know whether or not the stokers are present, as the machinery must not be deserted;" after the uttering of which he made his exit from the deck into the cabin. The query, to which Mr. Jay did not deign to give any reply, somewhat disconcerted him for the moment; but quickly recovering his self-possession, he, as a prelude to his discourse, gave out the following verse from one of Dr. Watts's hymns, informing his auditors to what tune it was to be sung:

"Let them refuse to sing
Who never knew the Lord;
But children of the heavenly King
Will shout his name abroad."

At the conclusion of the hymn, in which all present joined, he delivered a short but most interesting and appropriate address, which was no sooner finished than the elderly gentleman abandoned his retreat in the cabin, and made his re-appearance on deck. It was really laughable to observe with what contempt he looked upon Mr. Jay as he passed by him on the deck of the steamer; but the cause of such uncourteous conduct was soon explained by one of the passengers, who, after describing the elderly gentleman as being a doctor of divinity, the possessor of a large income, a man of little charity, and a very high and bigoted Churchman, said that he was such a contemner of all Dissenting ministers, that he invariably avoided being seen in their company. The doctor condescended to ask one of the passengers who that *man* (meaning Mr. Jay) was, that had turned religion into ridicule; and on being informed that he was William Jay of Bath, the popular Independent preacher, and that he was possessed of too much piety to deserve the censure cast upon him, the doctor said, "Well, he is the best of the *set*, and better perhaps than some of our low Churchmen; but as for popularity in a preacher, I despise it." This sentiment the doctor could well afford to entertain; for if report did not belie itself, he would have laboured in vain to have acquired that which he professed to hold in abhorrence.

Mr. Jay was intimate with the Rev. Mr. Venn, one of the most influential episcopal clergymen of the evangelical party of his day, and the author of a religious work entitled *Venn's Duty of Man*, which Mr. Jay highly admired and commended for its sterling and peculiar excellence, and as being a most able and impressive hortatory volume of divinity. Whenever this reverend gentleman went to the sea-side, or to any locality where he was known, he never was invited by the resident clergy to officiate for them solely on account of his evangelical principles, which were then but little in the ascendant. On one occasion Mr. Jay, on meeting him, said, "Why, my good sir, I have to my great surprise heard of your preaching at several churches in the West of England. How have you accomplished this miracle, after the strong prejudice which most of the clergy have against your doctrines?" "Very easily," answered his friend. "I always go to the post-office myself and inquire whether there are any letters for the *Rev. Mr. Venn.*

It soon gets abroad that there is a clergyman in the place, and I have invariably found that the rector or incumbent, after my being pointed out to them, and observing that I carry about with me a jolly and red face, have invited me to preach for them, a request which I never refuse; but I need not tell you that I am never asked a second time." Mr. Jay laughed heartily at the answer to his question and the allusion which the Rev. Mr. Venn made to his own red and burly face, which gave him the appearance of being fond of port wine and brandy, whereas the contrary was the fact; for he was one of the most abstemious men that Mr. Jay had ever met with.

It should be observed that at this period there were very few clergymen in comparison to those of the present day, so that it became extremely difficult for any clergyman to obtain a supply.

On the 18th of November 1818 Mr. Jay called at my then chambers in Gray's Inn Square early in the morning, and whilst at breakfast he informed me, to my surprise, that he had to preach that morning at the ordination of the Rev. James Stretton over the church and congregation of Paddington Chapel, and inquired of me if I knew in what part of that place the chapel was situated. I answered that I knew where Paddington was, which was all the information I could afford him; for I should remark that that suburb of London was then a different place to what it is now. He appeared to be alarmed at my being unable to give him the required information, saying, "How can we find it out?" "O, easily enough," said I. "We will get into the New Road, or any of the places leading to Paddington, and we shall be sure to see many persons that follow you whenever you preach." He took the course I had pointed out to him, and we soon discovered a gray-headed and venerable-looking Christian ploughing along in the direction of Paddington. Him we followed, having overtaken many other individuals going in the same direction and apparently with the same object, and at length reached the chapel, which was crowded to excess. I then separated from Mr. Jay, who went immediately into the vestry. He preached an excellent sermon from these words of Scripture, "Now know I that the Lord will do me good, seeing that I have a Levite to my priest;" and in the course of it made the following graphic and pertinent observations in reference to subjects which have more recently affected the religious public mind, viz. apostolical succession and baptismal regeneration: "Micah thought nothing of the character of his priest, if he had Levitical blood in him. He might be as wicked as Satan, if he could prove legitimate descent; and therefore, although he knew him to be an idle, time-serving, hungry hireling, prostituting himself to the service of idols to get a piece of bread, he was satisfied, and sung out his superstitious confidence, 'Now know I that the Lord will do me good, seeing that I have a Levite to my priest.' What ignorance and delusion to expect that the divine blessing would assuredly flow through such fingers, merely because of the tribe to which he belonged! And yet are there not persons in a much more enlightened period who approximate the same folly? Some, whatever may be his gifts or grace, would not for the world hear a man that is not episcopally sanctioned, yet will hear any thing upon earth that is. Yea, we have been told in this country, all who worship out of the Established Church are left to the uncovenanted mercies of God; that all their ministers are destitute of a legitimate authorisation, and therefore all their ministrations are invalid. Yet it is not many years since the venerable Secker filled our metropolitan chair; yet he was baptised by the hands of Dissenters, without either godfathers or godmothers to be answerable for him; yet he ordained numbers to the sacred office, and what is more lamentable still, he baptised his present majesty [George III.], the head of the church; all of which, according to this principle, was null and void, as being performed by an officiator who either had no baptism himself, or a useless one. Nor was this a solitary instance. It is well known that Bishop Reynolds in England, and Hopkins in Ireland, and Cooper and Leighton in Scotland, were in the same dilemma; so that all they did personally, and all that was done by those on whom they laid hands, was illegal and ineffectual; and now, alas, it is to be feared that it is too late to stop consequences, or even to ascertain the multiplied directions in which the unhallowed streams have run. And are there persons pretending to serious religion, who know the importance of doctrine and of holiness in a minister, and yet can recommend people to attend on a man merely because he is a Levite, however wretched in living and teaching too, while God has placed near them a man of acknowledged godliness, and who preaches 'all the words of this life?'"

Mr. Jay, in the same sermon, alluding to persons who in a preacher regard only genius and splendid abilities, says, "Dr. Owen, in the early part of his ministry, went to hear Dr. Calamy, one of the most famous preachers of the day. After waiting in the place for some time, he saw ascending the pulpit a plain countryman, and he felt disposed to withdraw; but reverence forbad. He was soon struck with his prayer, and still more with his sermon. His text was, 'O ye of little faith, wherefore do you doubt?' and he entered so experimentally into the doubts of God's people, and so satisfactorily solved them, that the mind of this prince of divines, as Cecil calls him, was so effectually released from a burden of distress, that from that hour he went on his way rejoicing."

Mr. Jay has remarked to me, that Dr. Owen, on hearing the immortal John Bunyan preach, expressed his approbation in the highest terms of eulogy, and said that he was incompetent himself to produce any thing so affecting and powerful.

I will now make a third quotation from this sermon. Pointing to the Rev. James Stretton, he said: "It is, my dear brother, the sublime and momentous end of your function that reflects such honour upon it, and attaches so much importance to it. Things common or mean in themselves may acquire unspeakable excellence and grandeur by association and destiny. Your office is frequently held forth in the Scripture by images derived from employments abstractedly considered rather humble than glorious; but the weight it acquires from relation and design is never for a moment left out. You are a 'soldier,' but it is in 'the good fight of faith;' you are a 'fisher,' but 'a fisher of men;' you are a 'labourer,' but 'a labourer together with God;' you are a 'builder,' but it is in 'God's building;' you are a 'watchman,' but you 'watch for souls.' Thus a small insignificant piece of paper is converted into a bank-note, and by a sovereign impression becomes current for a thousand pounds. Thus Raphael took a roll of canvas, of which the weaver thought nothing, and the vendor nothing; but he threw down upon it his immortal tints, and bade it become the admiration of the world. And thus, sir, your office rises into ineffable greatness by taking the soul of man for its subject, and eternity for its aim."

Mr. Jay having in his Autobiography given an able sketch of the late Rev. John Foster, the celebrated essay-writer, with whom he was upon the most intimate terms of friendship, I shall merely mention a few circumstances relating to this great man, not alluded to in the sketch.

One morning Mr. Jay, addressing himself to me, then on a visit to him at Percy Place, said: "I shall require you to go out into the front garden, and remain there until you see Mr. Foster opposite the gate, for he is coming to breakfast with me. He is of so absent a mind, that he is sure to pass the house, and keep on walking, unless you stop him." I had scarcely entered the front garden, when I espied him passing the house, with his slippers on; whereupon I sallied out of the gate, overtook him, brought him back with me, and safely deposited him in Mr. Jay's library.

The conversation between Mr. Jay and his visitor at the breakfast-table was worth listening to. Among other topics, Mr. Foster alluded to Mr. Dickens' works, and spoke in very high commendation of them.

"They have," said he, "afforded me more amusement and recreation than I have met with through a long life. I have read them over and over again, and upon each perusal I discover fresh beauties; and you know how such works must exhilarate the spirits of one so naturally melancholy as I am. Have you read them?" "I had them read to me," replied Mr. Jay, "whilst visiting at the sea-side, and they highly amused me. I was much pleased with the moral and good feeling which pervade the whole of Dickens' works, attributes which seldom pertain to these works of fiction. I am certain that he must be a kind-hearted man." Mr. Foster was upon this occasion, as well as upon most other occasions when he visited Mr. Jay (which was somewhat frequent, they both residing in the same neighbourhood), very talkative. Although possessing a remarkable capacity for every kind of conversation, it was very difficult to draw his talent out in that line, he being usually taciturn and reserved in company, speaking but little, unless he had, to use his own expression, an individual or two, not to talk *upon*, but to talk *with*.

I was present on another occasion when Mr. Foster called upon Mr. Jay, who found his friend in a peculiar state of despondency. The subject introduced was that of metaphysics. Mr. Jay, just prior to Mr. Foster's taking leave of him, said to him: "Why, my good friend, your metaphysics appear to depress you. You had better be hanged at once than constantly live under the gallows." I may here add that, as far as I could form an opinion, Mr. Jay regarded metaphysical theology with some degree of indifference. I recollect a friend once asking him what was his opinion of metaphysics. His instant reply was: "Why, sir, I am a Jay, and not an owl, and therefore cannot see in the dark."

Mr. Foster always seemed to have an inherent abhorrence of pretension. His mind possessed in a high degree the element of simplicity, the characteristic of all great minds. He once remarked, that "all eloquence is in the idea, and not in the phraseology."

In his *Essay on Decision of Character*, he in his original edition forcibly said: "A resolute mind is omnipotent; difficulty is a stimulus and a triumph to a strong spirit; the joys of conquest are the joys of men." A feeble-minded but conscientious member of Mr. Foster's communion remonstrated with him on the seeming blasphemy of the sentiment in trespassing upon the attribute of omnipotence in God. Mr. Foster, feeling himself justly reproved by his friend, amended the passage thus: "A resolute mind is *almost* omnipotent." Mr. Jay, upon being informed of this hypercriticism, and of the consequent correction, remarked that Mr. Foster had done wrong in listening to his censor, for that the passage stood best as it was originally penned. "All great teachers," said Mr. Jay, "never qualify; they leave their hearers to do this. Our blessed Saviour said absolutely, 'Take no thought for the morrow,' &c.; meaning, of course, no unnecessary or anxious thought, and leaving his hearers to add the qualification."

Mr. Jay, in speaking of his friend, said, in allusion to his essays and writings: "Although I must ever consider Foster as one of the greatest and profoundest of writers, yet he is ponderous, and somewhat heavy;

and, as a sequence, it is no easy thing to read much of him at a time. His sarcasms are powerful; his illustrations original, and often most beautiful; and his appeals at once striking and impressive. I greatly admire his essays, and would particularly single out his *Popular Ignorance* and his *Missionary Sermon* as writings of the first order. Many of his reviews are uncommonly fine, and his introductory essay on Doddridge's *Rise and Progress* is magnificent."

Mr. Jay could never induce Foster, who was thrice settled near him, viz. at Downhead, at Frome, and at Stapleton, and who frequently passed a Sabbath at Bath, to preach for him. He declined commonly by saying with complacency and pleasantry, "You know that neither you nor your people would ever ask me again. I am never desired to preach a second time." He frequently said in company: "Mr. Jay is the prince of preachers."

CHAPTER XII.

Publication by Mr. Jay of the *Domestic Minister's Assistant, or Prayers for the Use of Families*—A quotation from the work—Family worship at Percy Place—William Etty the Royal Academician—Paints the portrait of Mr. Jay and his youthful daughter—Notice and anecdotes respecting him.

In the year 1820 Mr. Jay published the *Domestic Minister's Assistant, or Prayers for the Use of Families.* The work had an immense circulation, and went through many editions both in this country and America. He stated that he used the word "minister" in rather an unusual latitude, its adjective serving to explain and restrict it. The 'domestic minister' means not, as Mr. Jay stated, the pastor or preacher, nor the servant of the most high God who officially shows unto men the way of salvation; but he who adopts the resolution of Joshua, "as for me and my house we will serve the Lord." His rules for prayer, both at the family altar and in the pulpit, were, brevity; scriptural diction, there being a distinction between an address to God and that to man; the least artificial mode of uttering one's thoughts; the non-employment of any figure of speech, unless such figure was as familiar as the literal expression; and a kneeling posture. With regard to appropriateness, Mr. Jay said, we might as well expect to find a shoe to fit every foot, as a form of prayer to suit every purpose.

It is remarkable that, although a Dissenter, Mr. Jay has, in the publication alluded to, introduced forms of prayer for Christmas-Day, Good-Friday, and Whitsuntide, and also for other fasts and thanksgiving days; and there is even a prayer for the early rising of a servant entering a family. What can transcend in point of simple sublimity the following opening of the prayer for the first morning of the new year? "Of old Thou hast laid the foundation of the earth, and the heavens are the work of thy hands. They shall perish, but thou shalt endure; yea all of them shall wax old like a garment; as a vesture shalt Thou change them, and they shall be changed: but Thou art the same, and thy years shall have no end. Through all the successions of time, which with us constitute the past, the present, and the future, I AM is thy name, and this is thy memorial in all generations. We desire, O God, with the profoundest reverence to contemplate the eternity of thy nature. May our minds be filled with elevation and grandeur at the thought of a Being with whom one day is as a thousand years, and a thousand years as one day; a Being who, amidst all the revolutions of empire and the lapse of worlds, feels no variableness nor shadow of turning. How glorious, with eternity attached to them, are all thy attributes! and how secure are the hopes and happiness of all those who know thy name and put their trust in Thee!"

In the library of Percy Place Mr. Jay assembled his household morning and evening for family worship. His prayers here were brief, appropriate, simple, and touching; and he bestowed the same care in their delivery as if he had been in the pulpit. At each service he read out of his large Bible a certain portion of a chapter, leaving off, at his discretion, at a particular verse. In order to fix the attention of his servants, he invariably inquired of them at the next service at what verse he had stopped; a query to which a simultaneous and correct reply was sure to be given. In this Bible he had been in the habit of bracketing in ink every text upon which he had preached; so that after his decease it appeared to be put into complete mourning from the great number of these black and distinctive marks.

Dr. Bridges, a clergyman who preached at St. Mary Redcliffe, Bristol, spent much of his time at Bath, and frequently breakfasted with Mr. Jay at Percy Place, on all of which occasions he attended family worship. I remember when a boy being present with the doctor at such worship, and, on turning round, seeing him with a pencil in his hand taking down Mr. Jay's prayer as it was delivered.

One fine May morning, a clergyman of the Established Church from Dublin, of the name of Shaw, breakfasted at Percy Place with Mr. Jay, by whom he was requested to perform family worship. He readily consented; but so lengthy and prosy was he in his prayers, that it appeared as if he never would bring the service to an end. One of my sisters, then a young child, who had previously been playing most joyously in the garden, was present. Mr. Jay and myself observing that a faintness was coming over her, conducted her immediately into the adjoining room. She soon recovered; whereupon Mr. Jay archly remarked to me, "I wish the faintness had occurred earlier; for it would have saved us from the fatigue of listening for so long a time as we did to our friend's long and misapplied devotion."

Mr. Jay having informed me that at the height of the great commercial panic he prayed to God, in his chapel, that his congregation might be prevented from giving, accepting, or negotiating, accommodation-bills, I expressed my astonishment at his having introduced such a subject into the pulpit; when, in reply to my observation, he said, that he wished such a prayer had been offered up in every church and chapel in the kingdom.

The late William Etty, the Royal Academician, was for many years upon very intimate terms of friendship with Mr. Jay; and to this celebrated artist the religious public are indebted for the excellent likeness of the preacher, an engraving from which first appeared in the *European Magazine* for 1819, and now forms the frontispiece to his Autobiography. The portrait, which is in the possession of Mr. Jay's son-in-law, the Rev. Mr. Bolton, was painted by Etty whilst on a visit to Mr. Jay for a week; and I shall never forget the delightful conversations which took place between them during that time. Etty always considered this portrait as one of his best productions in that line, and placed this and another small portrait of one of Mr. Jay's daughters (then in her seventeenth year) in the Royal Academy at Somerset House as the only two productions for the year. The latter portrait is exquisitely beautiful, and the late Sir Thomas Lawrence much coveted to be its possessor. Very soon after the opening of that year's exhibition the artist was elected an Associate of the Royal Academy.

Some of the admirers of Mr. Jay have objected to the languid expression which Etty has thrown into the preacher's countenance, whose face was generally brightened up by cheerfulness; but at the time the portrait was taken, Mr. Jay was subject to such severe headaches, that on several occasions he was obliged, whilst preaching, to pause for a few minutes; and on more than one occasion has fallen down senseless in the pulpit in the midst of his discourse. He always spoke with great feeling of Mr. Wilberforce's providential kindness towards him in giving him a letter to the celebrated physician Dr. Baillie, through whose skill and attention he was restored to perfect health.

I should mention that Etty, upon this visit, soon discovered the position in which his friend the preacher most usually sat when unoccupied, viz. with his right hand in his pocket, and his left hand on the arm of an easy chair. This is the position of the portrait, in the painting of which Etty took, as he expressed himself to several friends, an unusual interest, not only on the score of friendship, but on account of what he was pleased to call the handsome head and fine countenance of Mr. Jay, regretting that he had not taken him whilst in the act of preaching. Talking of position, Etty said to Mr. Jay, "I consider position one of the most essential things to be studied in a portrait, inasmuch as it serves to indicate the character of the man." "I quite agree with you, Etty," said Mr. Jay, "and your opinion as to position puts me in mind of the following anecdote: An attorney, a sharp practitioner in the West of England, who had by plausibility, cunning, and various artifices, accumulated a large sum of money, must needs build himself a mansion; and as its founder, he resolved to have a full-length likeness of himself painted and hung up in the hall. He sent for a poor painter, a perfect stranger in the place, who represented him standing in a library, with one hand in his breeches-pocket, and the other holding a law-book. The likeness and attitude were considered extremely good; but that was not the opinion of a burly farmer who had been his client, and no doubt bled by him; for on being asked by the painter, who had then more than half finished the portrait, what he thought of it, innocently replied, that it could be improved and made more natural by altering the position. Upon which the painter, who was of the same opinion as myself, asked him, 'How?' to which the farmer replied, 'To make the picture natural, you must alter it. You have painted the lawyer with his hand in his own breeches-pocket, when you ought to have painted it in the pocket of one of his clients.'"

It was during this visit, which Etty always referred to with much satisfaction, that Mr. Jay was surprised to find that he had never read Crabbe's works. The poems being on one of the shelves of the library where Etty was then painting, Mr. Jay took down one of the volumes, and read him some extracts from the "Annals of the Poor" with such feeling and pathos, that tears trickled down the painter's face, and putting the brush aside, he exclaimed, "Mr. Jay, you must desist; it is too much for me." Mr. Etty, who was a man of very sensitive feelings, on his return home purchased an edition of the poet's works.

Etty was of a very weak constitution, and subject to a sort of asthma; a complaint no doubt increased by his having located for many years near the Thames, at the bottom of Arundel Street, Strand, from which place he removed to Hungerford Street, his last residence in the metropolis; for notwithstanding his complaint, he always preferred living by the side of the river.

He spent some considerable time in Florence, Rome, and Naples, studying the works of some of the great masters. Whilst at the latter place he wrote a very interesting and affecting letter to Mr. Jay, wherein he spoke despondingly of his health, and stated that the light air of that city was far worse for his complaint than the fog, mist, and smoke of the metropolis. I wish I could have found that letter amongst the papers of Mr. Jay, who usually was not a very great preserver of private correspondence.

The vacations of the last few years of Etty's life were spent by him in his native city of York, where he was constantly to be seen in the Minster, listening to the peals of the organ, and gazing with rapture at the beautiful painted windows. In that city he died. It is very much doubted whether he ever recovered from the shock which he sustained in beholding the greater number of his paintings collected, as an exhibition, under one roof. It was a noble triumph for genius, and the crowning act of his life. Well might so sensitive and simple-hearted a man be affected.

I met Etty in the Strand a few weeks before he died; and I, in a jocular manner, said to him, that I had just seen his last two paintings, but that I did not think he painted better then than he did when he painted the portraits of Mr. Jay and his daughter. To my astonishment he replied: "I am sure I do not."

Etty had frequently heard Mr. Jay preach, and was one of his greatest admirers, thinking that there was a freshness and an originality in his sermons. He was very much pleased with a sermon on "Neutrality in Religion exposed," the text being, "No man can serve two masters," &c. The following passages he often alluded to, and repeated from memory to many of his professional friends, amongst whom was the late Sir Thomas Lawrence, who was much struck with their beauty: "You say religion demands of us a succession of services from which you are exempted. But, O ye votaries of the world, let us examine your claims, and see wherein your preëminence appears. Have you, then, no services to render? Think of your privations, and sacrifices, and submissions; think of the numerous and arbitrary laws you have to obey, —the laws of opinion, the laws of custom, the laws of extravagance, the laws of folly. Yes; I sometimes think, if religion were to require of me such duties as the world imposes upon its enslaved followers; if it required me to turn day into night, and deprived me of seasonable repose; if it required me to embrace indecent and injurious fashions, and to expose at once my modesty and my health; if it required me to adopt expensive modes of life, which devoured my substance, and involved me in pecuniary disgrace; if it required me to spend my evenings from home, and to resign domestic enjoyments, to rove from one insipid amusement to another; if it required me to give up all that is easy and simple and natural for ceremonies, visits, and crowds, where all is artificial, studied, and forced; if it required me to convert my dwelling into the confusion and disorder of a rout, to stoop to the absurdity of a masquerade; to hazard my own life and the life of my fellow-creature, because I had received an offence perhaps unintentionally given, and allowed me not the choice of a refusal,—then I should conceive a disgust, then I would long to emancipate myself from such capricious despotism. I should sigh for liberty; for what liberty could I enjoy while compelled to submit to what is unreasonable and foolish, to what is dishonourable and shameful, to what is injurious and ruinous? But remember, ye followers of the vain world, *these* are the commands *you* obey, *these* are the services *you* render. Still you tell us that our Master requires us even to deny ourselves; that this is the grand law of His kingdom; and without obeying it we cannot be His disciples. But we contend that you are precisely in the same circumstances. We can prove that you also are required to exercise self-denial; and that this is the chief command you have to comply with in the service of the world. And mark the difference between us. Our Master requires us to deny only what is false and vain; yours what is solid and true. Ours requires us to deny what would only make us disorderly and miserable; yours what would render you peaceful and happy. Ours requires us only to deny the voice of passion and appetite; yours the voice of reason and of conscience. Ours requires us to deny the body for the sake of the soul; yours the soul for the sake of the body. Ours requires us to give up nothing but what He will more than repay; yours to surrender an interest, for the loss of which you cannot be indemnified in time or eternity. Since, then, it appears that you cannot serve two masters, and since it is equally certain that you will serve one, we plead for God, and call upon you to serve Him."

Etty, who had heard Rowland Hill preach at Surrey Chapel, where Mr. Jay, as already stated, at the very early age of nineteen years, first gained a notoriety in London as an eminent preacher, introduced and coloured with his own hand, in an interior view of that chapel painted in water-colours by an architect, various figures, which were remarkably clever; there were some groups singing out of a hymn-book, and in the pulpit he painted Rowland Hill; and though, of necessity, the figure of that well-known preacher was upon a very minute scale, yet Mr. Jay pronounced it to be the best likeness of him that he had seen.

Mr. Jay, who was very fond of paintings, and could very fairly estimate their merits, considered that Etty was, with all his great talent, no judge of beauty in the female countenance.

CHAPTER XIII.

Mr. Jay preaches at the Union Chapel, Islington—Anecdotes of his susceptibility—His aversion to anonymous letters—The big Welsh parson—A platform speech—His aversion to platform speaking—Preaches a funeral sermon on the death of Lord Byron—A preacher and his gloves.

MANY years ago, Mr. Jay preached for some charitable purpose at the Union Chapel, Islington, where a large and respectable congregation always attended, and where the Church-prayers were invariably read. He arrived in London from Bath on Saturday, and was the guest of a strict Nonconformist, a rich man, who lived near the chapel.

I mention two little circumstances which, although trifling in themselves, somewhat annoyed Mr. Jay. On the Sunday morning he said to his friend at the breakfast-table: "You know how plain I am about my dinner; therefore I hope you will not go out of your way on my account." When Mr. Jay seated himself down to dinner, he found that his host had not required any hint as to the entertainment, for there was nothing but cold mutton on the table. I caught Mr. Jay's eye, and saw that he felt chagrined, knowing that he required, on the Sunday, after the exertion of preaching, a hot joint, which he relished more on that than any other day, always being then in very joyous spirits. He had no sooner got over the disappointment of seeing the cold mutton on the table, than his host informed him that he had not been in the chapel in the morning, but had gone to his old place of worship in the city. If Mr. Jay, compelled by necessity, could have had any appetite for the cold mutton, this announcement took it quite away, particularly as it was at the especial request of this gentleman that he undertook a journey from Bath to preach the charity sermons. In the evening the chapel was crowded to excess, as it was also in the morning. The text was, "Such honour have all his saints." In the course of the sermon, Mr. Jay, in alluding to the many applications of the word "saints," said: "It is applied by way of reproach to a section in the House of Commons, of which Mr. Wilberforce is the worthy leader. I know many of that distinguished band well; and better men and better Christians than they are I have never met with." Amongst other allusions to saints, he said: "You will find a man who, having been suddenly detected in a crime, will endeavour to palliate it by saying, 'At any rate, I am no saint.' No," said the preacher, raising his voice, and exclaiming in an animated manner, "no, you are not; who said you were?" I thought it a most impressive sermon, and so did one of the sons of Mr. Wilberforce, who came into the vestry, and after shaking hands with the preacher, thanked him for speaking so highly of his father.

I will here mention another trifling circumstance, which I think annoyed Mr. Jay more than the cold mutton:

A gentleman of large fortune, who had been high-sheriff of the county in which he resided, made repeated applications to Mr. Jay to preach at the chapel near his mansion. Overcome at length by them, he consented to do so, although at much personal inconvenience to himself, thinking that he might be the instrument of doing some good in the neighbourhood. I was his companion on this occasion. On our arrival at the station, a distance of two or three miles from the mansion, he found, to his astonishment, that the gentleman had not sent his carriage, nor was there any fly or other vehicle to be hired that morning. I observed that he was much annoyed at the occurrence, the more so as he knew that the gentleman kept many horses. On our arrival at the mansion, the gentleman held out his hand to Mr. Jay; but he soon discovered, by the preacher's manner, that something had depressed his spirits; observing which, he said: "I hope, Mr. Jay, you are not ill." "No, sir; but I am much hurt that you did not pay me sufficient respect to send your carriage for me. I will do every thing in my power to serve any person, but I will not be slighted by any man." I need not add, that Mr. Jay returned back to the station in one of the gentleman's best carriages.

Mr. Jay would never take the least notice of the numberless anonymous and slanderous letters which were addressed to him, reflecting on the character of others. On discovering the nature of such communications, which he could instantly do by a mere glance of his eye, he would invariably tear or burn them. When dining with him one day at Worthing, he informed me that he had received three letters from a man respecting my having neglected his business, but that on perceiving that they were written in a very abusive style, he had destroyed them. "What is the man's name?" I inquired of Mr. Jay. On his giving it to me, I said: "O, it is a person who came backwards and forwards to my chambers for the space of two months, annoying me about the recovery of an estate; and he belongs to that class of men who wish to turn the right owner out of possession. As I wanted to get rid of his further annoying me, I told him that he need not trouble me any more on the subject; when, to my astonishment, he said, 'Then I will write to your father.'" "What answer did you make?" inquired Mr. Jay. "I said, 'You may write to any body you please, so that you do not write to me.'" Mr. Jay smiled, saying, "It was very kind of you to fasten him on me; but it is exactly the same answer which I should have given." I then informed him that I had lately given much umbrage to a big Welsh parson, and said that it would not at all surprise me if *he* had also written to him on the subject. "What is that about?" said Mr. Jay; "for I have had no letter from him."

I then related the following circumstance: "This personage had, during my absence from my chambers, called there two or three times; but not meeting with me, would not leave his name, or state the nature of his business. One morning I met him coming out of the street-door; and on his perceiving me, he sharply said, 'I have called here many times without seeing you;' at the same time thrusting his hand into a side-pocket, as if with the intention, as I thought, of serving me with a subpœna, or other legal proceeding. I stated that the cause of my absence was being engaged with my father, who had been spending a few days in London prior to his going to Worthing; when he, upon this explanation, instead of serving me with any legal proceeding, exclaimed in a loud voice, 'How is the worthy pilgrim?' and thereupon placing in my hands a dirty little book, requested my subscription to building some chapel in Wales. His breath smelt so strong of rum, that I immediately returned him the book, and bid him good morning." Mr. Jay said, "What a remarkable coincidence! I know the man. He called on me at Bath for a subscription, which, upon glancing at the case in his dirty book, I refused, because of his smelling so strongly of spirituous liquors. I would not trust such a man with money. Indeed, my aversion to that smell is so great, that I think I should have refused to subscribe even to the building of Noah's Ark, had the collector been a dram-drinker."

A meeting was held on behalf of the London Missionary Society, some thirty years ago, at the Vineyards Chapel, Bath, at which the Rev. Rowland Hill and Mr. Jay were present. The former divine presided, and his address on the occasion was excellent and much to the point. "All Christians of every denomination," he said, "should unite in the sacred and paramount obligation of gospel missions to the heathen. We cannot all get into the same boat for departure; I only wish we could; but let us all go either personally or by representation." The concluding speech was by Mr. Jay, who, it should be observed, had a great repugnance to platform speaking, and who very seldom made his appearance as a public speaker, often declaring, when requested to do so, that he was not born under the platform dispensation. After some pertinent remarks, he said: "The evening is advanced, and I much dislike detaining people out late from their families and domestic duties. Our platform speeches are, I think, much too long. More condensation and point are desirable. It was thus, my friends, that the attendant groom gently reproved his worthy master: 'Here, John,' said the gentleman to his servant on horseback in the rear, 'come forwards, and just take hold of my horse whilst I dismount; and, after I am dismounted, John, you dismount too. Then, John, ungirth the saddle of your horse, and put it down; and then you will please ungirth the saddle of my horse, and put it down. Then, John, take up the saddle of your horse, and put and girth it on my horse. Afterwards, John, take up the saddle of my horse, and put and girth it on your horse. Then, John, I will seat myself in your saddle, and you can seat yourself in mine, and we will resume our journey.' 'Bless me, master,' said the man, 'why couldn't you have simply said, Let's change saddles.'" I need hardly describe the ludicrous effect of this racy anecdote on the departing auditory, especially after the reading of a long report at the meeting, which contained much repetition.

Mr. Jay preached the Jubilee Sermon for the society at the Surrey Chapel. Whilst walking down the Strand with him on the following day, we passed Exeter Hall, at which there was then held a numerous meeting of the same society. I asked him if he had ever been in the interior of that building. He said he had not, but should much like to see it, if it were not that he might be recognised, and importuned to speak, which would be a source of great annoyance to him. At my persuasion, however, he went in. I conducted him up the back-stairs to the rear of the platform. Dr. Bunting was speaking at the time. Mr. Jay had no sooner seated himself, in a spot where he thought he should be out of observation, than he was immediately recognised all over the hall, and welcomed by a general clapping of hands; upon which he took hold of my arm and departed, only regretting, as he said, that he had not followed his own judgment.

At the first meeting of an association, called the Christian Alliance, at Exeter Hall, Mr. Jay so highly approved of its objects, that he left Worthing, where he was then staying, and came up to London expressly to attend the meeting, but positively refused to move any resolution, or make any speech. It was the most numerously-attended meeting ever assembled under the roof of that spacious building; and every one present will recollect the reception which he met with the moment he was seen on the platform, a reception more marked and enthusiastic than that bestowed on any other individual. The Rev. Mr. Bickersteth, and several other gentlemen, begged of him in the most earnest manner to address a few words to the audience, but it was of no avail. He said, that his sole object in attending there was to mark his high approval of the association by his presence.

Mr. Jay was deeply affected on hearing of the death of Lord Byron. I was present at Percy Place when he received the announcement with profound emotion, and immediately exclaimed: "All flesh is as grass, and all the glory of man as the flower of grass: the grass withereth, and the flower thereof falleth away: but the word of the Lord endureth for ever." On the following Sunday he took this as his text, and preached from it the poet's funeral sermon. The congregation appeared deeply affected. I recollect a mere sentence (for the sermon was never published): "Here is a genius which might have ranked with a Milton! No knell of departed greatness ever more solemnly sounded forth this sentiment, 'All flesh is as grass, and the glory of man as the flower of grass.'"

Little circumstances would sometimes arrest the attention of Mr. Jay, as the following anecdote will illustrate:

One Sunday, in the heat of summer, a reverend gentleman from London, then in the West of England on a tour, accepted an invitation from Mr. Jay to preach at Argyle Chapel. There was on this occasion a crowded congregation. Mr. Jay, according to his custom, was conducting the preacher to the pulpit-stairs, when all at once he suddenly stopped, and said to him, "Why, my good friend, I observe you have forgotten to take your gloves off." "O," replied the preacher, "I always preach with them on, and it is a very common practice with us in London." "The more to be pitied," rejoined Mr. Jay. The next morning the minister called at Percy Place, and was shown into the library. Mr. Jay, who at the time was in the garden cleaving wood,—a frequent occupation of his,—on being informed of the call, hastened up the garden, and entering the library a little out of breath, pulled off his garden-gloves, and laying them on the library-table, jocosely said to his friend, "I will make you a present of these gloves to preach in."

CHAPTER XIV.

A sermon at the opening of Hanover Chapel, Peckham — The late Duke of Sussex present—Rev. Edward Irving—The respective discourses delivered by that divine and Mr. Jay at Bedford on the same day contrasted — A ward in chancery — A dinner-party at Richmond — A funeral sermon on the death of the Rev. Mr. Thorp — The Bath coachman.

MR. JAY was invited by the late Dr. Collyer to preach at the opening of Hanover Chapel, Peckham. The attendance was very numerous, it being expected that two of the sons of George the Third would be present, Dr. Collyer being on most intimate terms with the Duke of Kent, the father of her present Majesty. His royal highness the Duke of Sussex attended, and kept the congregation waiting some time. Mr. Jay, who was always punctual in the commencing of divine service, was very much astonished at the managers of the chapel postponing it. He preached an excellent sermon; although several of his hearers were astonished at his boldness in alluding to noblemen and gentlemen assisting by their contributions in the erection of religious edifices into which, perhaps, they never entered; comparing them to the scaffolding, which, when the beautiful building is finished, is swept away. There was a sumptuous dinner given after the service, and a seat was reserved for Mr. Jay next the royal duke; but he, disliking public dinners, preferred dining quietly with two ladies at Denmark Hill. But Mr. Jay's son had his father's ticket, and sat next to his royal highness, who expressed great disappointment at Mr. Jay's absence; and who, after taking wine with him, alluded to the sermon in terms of great praise.

I should mention, that after the service was over, Mr. Jay was introduced to the duke, who requested him to send him a complete set of his works, a requisition with which he cheerfully complied. The next morning Mr. Jay sent to his bookseller's for the works, which he forwarded to the duke with the following letter: "Sire, when I had the honour of an interview with your royal highness, your royal highness was pleased to express the gracious willingness to possess that which I now present. It was an offering which I could not have had presumption enough to solicit, and it must be viewed as an instance of that condescension which, instead of detracting from greatness, adds grace to dignity. The sovereign providence of God, which allied your royal highness with majesty, caused the author to emerge from an obscure original, and denied him the facilities of early literature; but for the sentiments themselves the author makes no apology, being fully persuaded that he could preach them before kings, and not be ashamed." I took a copy of the letter before it was sent to Kensington Palace; but, having lost it, I quote from recollection. There were a few more sentences, which I have entirely forgotten. Mr. Jay received a most kind letter from his royal highness, requesting him to spend a day at Kensington Palace, and look over his valuable collection of Bibles.

Mr. Jay, during one of his annual visits to London, called upon that well-known preacher the late Rev. Edward Irving, when in the zenith of his popularity. His object in making this call was to warn his friend, as a Christian counsellor and brother minister of age and experience, not to be led astray by popularity, an ordeal which he (Mr. Jay) had in early life passed through unscathed. He always spoke of Mr. Irving (until that preacher adopted the aberration of the unknown tongues) in the highest terms of respect and affection, although his own views were on many points (especially those regarding prophetical and millenarian subjects) in antagonism with his Scotch friend.

Although Mr. Jay had been several times in company with Mr. Irving in Scotland, when that gentleman was assistant to the late Dr. Chalmers, yet he had only heard his friend preach once, and that was at Bedford, in the morning, Mr. Jay officiating in that town in the evening of the same day. Nothing could exhibit a greater contrast between these preachers than their respective discourses on that occasion. Mr. Irving, on the one hand, complained that there was no true religion in the world; and that Christianity was all profession, and merely a name without reality. Mr. Jay, on the other hand, took a most cheering view of Christianity, and preached a very joyous sermon, stating to the congregation that all the Bible, missionary, and tract societies, Sunday-schools, and the numerous increase of churches and chapels of every denomination, were demonstrative of the great effect of the spread of true religion in this country; that when he first commenced his ministry there were many houses and cottages in the West of England where there was no Bible, and that this was more particularly the deplorable case at that time of day in Wales. Mr. Jay states, that there was then such a scarcity of the sacred volume in the Welsh language, "that it was no uncommon thing for several householders to have one Bible between them as a joint property, and to keep it alternately, for reading, by the week. It was Mr. Charles, the pious clergyman of Bala, who announced the affecting truth; and one of the first efforts of the rising society in town was to meet the want. When the people of his parish learned that the first burden of the Lord was approaching, a number of them went forth to meet the vehicle, and removing the horses, drew it themselves into the market-place, where, in the course of a few hours, the whole supply of Bibles and Testaments was disposed of. What followed? Some kissed the book; some pressed it to their bosoms. The young seemed in ecstasy at the prize; while many a labourer took the treasure a-field, and refreshed his toil by reading it at his meals."

Mr. Jay had been appointed by the Lord Chancellor guardian to a ward in chancery; a lady of considerable property, who took it into her head one fine summer's morning to run away to Gretna Green with a gentleman, a friend of Mr. Irving's. When they were afterwards re-married in England, Mr. Irving, Mr. Jay, and other friends of the young couple, spent the day with them at the Star and Garter at Richmond. Both Mr. Irving and Mr. Jay were in excellent cue for talking. Mr. Jay, who was always partial to the Scotch accent, mentioned, after dinner, the following anecdote to Mr. Irving: "Lady Ross, and her son Colonel Ross, of the Grenadier Guards, who was afterwards killed in battle, had a large establishment at Queen Square, at Bath. They were both extremely partial to me, particularly the colonel. On going to dine there one day, I met Mr. Lowell, the Independent minister of Bristol, a pleasant companion and great mimic, who had just returned from Scotland, where he had heard the preacher whom Lady Ross and the colonel attended when in that country. Soon after dinner Mr. Lowell gave an imitation of the Scotch divine; and upon the door being suddenly opened, all the Scotch servants were discovered listening, much to the amusement of the colonel; and so correct was the imitation, that the listeners thought it was their Scotch pastor."

Mr. Irving had, as is well known, a peculiar physical obliquity of eye, so that when conversing with him you scarcely knew whether he was looking at yourself or at some other immediate object. Mr. Jay considered this defect to have been felicitously described by a witty writer of the day as "the cross-fire of the preacher's double vision;" and remarked, that a *squint* was a misfortune to a minister; for he recollected a worthy man having an infirmity of this character, who once injudiciously chose as a text (which of course he practically could not avoid violating throughout the whole of the sermon) the words, "Let thine eyes look *right on*, and thine eyelids *straight* before thee" (Proverbs iv. 25).

The texts of preachers here remind me of a pleasantry which provoked Mr. Jay's hearty laugh. A good man, whose anticipations of the marriage-state were by no means realised in the Xantippe of a wife to whom he unfortunately had united himself, was accustomed, *before* marriage, to preach from "The *Song* of Solomon." *Afterwards*, however, he more frequently (with intensity of disappointment, and amidst the sarcastic titters of those who knew his domestic griefs) selected his theme from "The *Lamentations* of Jeremiah."

The late Mr. Thorp, of Bristol, an eloquent Dissenting minister of that city, when dying, requested that Mr. Jay, whom he had known for years, should bury him. On the day appointed for the burial, Mr. Jay (instead of leaving Percy Place the night before, as was his usual custom when he had to perform service away from home), after partaking of an early breakfast, requested my brother to drive him through bye-lanes and over Lansdown Hill, a solitary ride which he very much enjoyed, liking to get out of the vehicle and walk up the hills. When Mr. Jay was entering Bristol, he observed a great many window-shutters up; and inquiring the cause, found, what he had little dreamed of, that it was out of respect to Mr. Thorp. As he proceeded further, he observed that the same mark of respect was almost universal. On arriving at the house of the deceased, he was informed that the pall was to be supported by twelve resident clergymen of the Established Church. Mr. Jay, instead of waiting to be introduced to them, ran up-stairs to one of the bedrooms to prepare himself for the service, having only about twenty minutes for that purpose. When the time arrived, he ascended the pulpit, and delivered, to a crowded congregation, an address which gave very great satisfaction,

I mention this little circumstance from a remark which Mr. Jay made to me, that it was the only instance, through a long life, in which he made so little preparation, thinking that his hearers would have been confined to the members of the chapel, whereas, in point of fact, it was almost a public funeral. Inpendently of the talents of the deceased, perhaps politics had to do with the great respect paid to his memory; for he was a very high Tory, and, like the generality of the Bristol people of that period, a violent opponent of the Catholic question.

Mr. Jay, on one occasion, had to travel from Bath to Bristol, to address some divinity students at the latter city; and it being a very fine summer's morning, he took his seat on the box just behind the coachman, who was not so communicative as persons of that class of society proverbially were. One of the outside passengers, a most loquacious gentleman, after talking first with one and then with another of his fellow-travellers, much to the inconvenience of Mr. Jay, who was doubtless studying his address, at length fastened himself on the coachman; and after asking him a multiplicity of trivial questions, said: "Coachman, whose villa is that?" "I do not know," was the answer. Proceeding further on the journey, the gentleman said: "Coachman, where does that new road lead to?" There was the same answer, "I do not know." At last, passing by a large mansion, he asked the coachman, "Who lives there?" "I do not know," was the reply. "Then," said the gentleman, quite out of patience at this answer, "do you know any thing?" To which the coachman replied, "I know how to drive."

Mr. Jay, my informant tells me, after naively relating this anecdote to the Bristol students, immediately closed his address to them with this sentence: "Recollect, my young friends, that the chief object of your studies has been to prepare you as preachers; and however comparatively ignorant you may be in any other pursuit, at all events be thoroughly conversant with your own peculiar one, and know, in the words of the Bath coachman, 'how to drive.'"

CHAPTER XV.

Dr. Chalmers—His work on Establishments—A dinner-party at Denmark Hill—The Rev. Mr. Melville—Rammohun Roy—Legality—An awkward question.

Mr. Jay was intimate with the late Dr. Chalmers; and many years ago, when that eminent and most justly popular divine resided at Glasgow, preached for him on a Sunday at the Tron Church in that city, he having the unusual privilege of access to most of the pulpits in the Scottish Church. Some years afterwards Mr. Jay was engaged to preach at Oxford, at the opening of a chapel there, but was obliged to leave that city without performing that duty, owing to the alarming and first illness of his wife. Dr. Chalmers, who happened to be at Oxford, kindly volunteered to officiate for him, very much, no doubt, to the gratification of many members of the University.

Mr. Jay was well acquainted with the doctor's works, and much admired them, though the style of writing was not exactly suited to his taste. The doctor was fond of using long and involved sentences, and tiring out an argument; and Mr. Jay, who, on the other hand, was partial to short sentences, on one occasion remarked: "Chalmers's arguments put me in mind of a door moving on its hinges—motion without progress." I was present when the doctor's work on Establishments was read to Mr. Jay; and when finished, he said, "That quotation from Cobbett's *Register*, speaking of the Church as a machine or apparatus, is better than all the arguments in the book." The quotation is in these words: "Go upon a hill in Hampshire and Wiltshire, and look to the church-steeples, one in about every four square miles. Imagine a man, of small learning at the least, to be living in a genteel and commodious house by the side of every one of these steeples, almost always with a wife and family; always with servants,—natives of the parish,—gardener, and other servants; a large farmyard, barns, stables, threshers, a carter or two, more or less of glebe and of farming. Imagine this gentleman having an interest—an immediate and pressing interest—in the productiveness of every field in the parish, being probably the largest corn-seller in the parish, and the largest ratepayer; more deeply interested than any other man can possibly be in the happiness, harmony, morals, industry, and sobriety of the people in his parish. Imagine his innumerable occasions for doing acts of kindness, his immense power in preventing the strong from oppressing the weak, his salutary influence coming between the hard farmer and the feeble or simple-minded labourer. Imagine all this to exist close alongside of these steeples; and you will at once say to yourself, Hurricanes and earthquakes must destroy the island before that Church can be overthrown. And when you add to all this, that this gentleman sets the example of good manners, of mildness, and of justice; that his life and conversation are constantly keeping themselves before the eye of his parishioners; when you add to all this, that one day in every week he has them assembled together, to sit in silence to receive his advice, his admonition, his interpretation of the will of God as applicable to their conduct and their affairs; that, too, in an edifice rendered sacred in their eyes, from their knowing that their forefathers assembled there in ages past, and from its being surrounded by the graves of their kindred; when this is added, and when it is recollected that the children pass through his hands at their baptism, that it is he alone who celebrates the marriage, and performs the last sad service over the graves of the dead;—when you think of all this, it is too much to believe that such a Church can fall. Yet fall it will."

Some years after Dr. Chalmers had preached at Oxford, I dined with him at the house of the Lord Mayor elect, at Denmark Hill, when he alluded with much pleasure to his preaching in that city, and inquired very kindly after Mrs. Jay's health, and very flatteringly stated before the company that Mr. Jay was the most popular preacher and religious writer of the day. My friend the late Mr. Sydney Taylor the barrister, a man of much intellect, who knew Mr. Jay, and had often heard him preach at Surrey Chapel, was also present, and he quite coincided with the doctor's opinion. A rich intellectual treat was anticipated; but to our great annoyance, Alderman Sir Claudius Stephen Hunter, who formed one of the company, engrossed the whole of the conversation, talking upon trifles which he made more trifling. I saw Sydney Taylor much annoyed at the incessant gabble of the alderman, he wishing to listen to the conversational talents of the doctor. Sydney Taylor, who was sitting next but one to me, slipped into my hand his card, with this pencil-writing on it, "Shall I pitch into the alderman?" I whispered, "Certainly;" but he had not pluck enough to quiet him; so that what was expected to have been a very great treat ended in disappointment. It was through Sydney Taylor that those beautiful lines, written by Wolfe, on the death of Sir John Moore, first came to light; Taylor and Wolfe being both first men of the year at Dublin University.

In the evening I went with Dr. Chalmers to hear the Rev. Mr. Melville preach at Camberwell Chapel. The doctor was much gratified with the discourse and manner of that great preacher, and asked me if Mr. Jay had ever heard him. I said, "I believed not; but my father had once dined with him, and thought most highly of his talents."

On leaving the chapel, the doctor said to me, "I want to find out a street near the Elephant and Castle; will you accompany me?" to which request I cheerfully assented. In walking along, the doctor said: "What a clatter the alderman set up! I wanted to hear Sydney Taylor talk, but no one could get a word in edgeways." I then told him the following anecdote: Sir Claudius Stephen Hunter and two other aldermen were present one morning at Surrey Chapel, and my father was arguing that worldly men could not understand spiritual things: "You may," said he, "as well attempt to read Greek to an alderman;" on hearing which the doctor laughed most heartily. I soon discovered for him what I call a *thin* street, where I learned that a poor brother of his resided. I waited outside of the house for him; and

I observed, when he entered it, that he had some bank-notes in his hand, which no doubt he presented to his relative. Be that as it may, when he came out of the house he appeared very happy, as if he had done a good act: but he said nothing to me on the subject. I could hardly refrain from laughing on seeing him tie a belcher handkerchief round his neck, which made him look more like a prize-fighter than a divine.

The next time I had the pleasure of seeing the doctor was at Cambridge, at the philosophical meeting held in that town; and although surrounded by noblemen and heads of houses, he came up to me, and after heartily shaking me by the hand, inquired very kindly after the health of Mr. and Mrs. Jay.

The late Rajah Rammohun Roy was introduced by the late rector of St. Saviour's, in the Borough, and Mr. Alderman Gibbs, to Mr. Jay, who in his Autobiography has made some mention of that well-known Indian prince. In the month of June 1832 Mr. Jay preached a sermon at Surrey Chapel, the text of which was, "I drew them with cords of a man, with bands of love; and I was unto them as they that take off the yoke on their jaws; and I laid meat unto them." The prince, who was present, and most attentive to the discourse, requested Mr. Jay to allow him to print it for distribution amongst his friends; to which, after a little hesitation, the preacher gave his consent. When the prince sent back the copy of the sermon, which had been taken down in short-hand for his perusal, Mr. Jay's attention was particularly drawn to two passages, around both of which the rajah had drawn a pencil-line. The first passage was in these words: "When Dr. Doddridge asked his little daughter, who died so early, why every body seemed to love her, she answered, 'I cannot tell, unless it is because *I* love every body.' This was not only a striking but a judicious reply. It accords with the sentiment of Seneca, who gives us a love-charm: and what do you suppose the secret is? 'Love,' says he, 'in order to be loved.'"

The other passage which the rajah had marked as interesting to him was upon "the yoke of Judaism," which he no doubt considered as applicable to the yoke of Sutteeism, from which he had freed himself, when, through conviction, he embraced the doctrines of Christianity. It was in these words: "I know not how it strikes others, but it has always appeared to me a convincing proof that Moses was no impostor, and was known to have received from God the system which he delivered, that such an untoward, unruly people as the Jews ever submitted, for a year or a month, to such bondage as it placed them under. Think of the painful nature of some of its rites, and the expense and troublesomeness of others. You complain of being so often called upon to give in the service of God; did you ever reflect upon the sums the devotion of a Jew required of him? You sometimes complain of difficulties attending the service of God, and mere trifles will often keep you from it; but a Jew, whatever was the road, or the weather, or the distance, was obliged to appear three times every year before the Lord in Jerusalem. You are affected by no distinction of meat but such as your health or your taste may impose; but how many things, and some of them very inviting, were forbidden him! If he touched a dead body or a grave, he was sent home and shut up for a week. How often had he to observe days, and months, and times, and years! He had precepts for building, travelling, ploughing, sowing, reaping. The very substance and make of his garment, and even the cutting of his hair, were subject to ordinances. In a word, a Jew could hardly stir without danger of violating something pertaining to his religion; and when we consider how numerous and trying were its rules, restraints, and impositions, we see with what propriety Peter called it a '*yoke* which neither we,' says he, 'nor our fathers could bear.'"

A day or two after the delivery of this discourse, Mr. Jay dined at the Mansion House with the rajah, Dr. Dale, the Rev. Mr. Melville, and Mr. Poynder; several other gentlemen, as well as myself, being of the party. A brisk conversation, on the subject of Christianity, took place after dinner, in which the rajah, and most of the gentlemen present, participated. When we were about joining the ladies, my father said slyly to me, "I really think the rajah had the best of the argument." A minute or two afterwards I told Mr. Melville what Mr. Jay had said; upon which he replied, "I think the prince a Jesuit." Mr. Jay said of the rajah, after his decease, that although he was persuaded that that remarkable individual, on his first embracing Christianity, was Unitarian in his views, yet that soon after he arrived in this country he became a sincere and earnest inquirer after evangelical truth, and would no doubt have professed his adoption of it, had he not been prematurely removed by death. I should add, that the rajah was not only an exceedingly handsome man, which was displayed to great advantage by his wearing the costume of his country, but was also possessed of a most intellectual mind, and spoke the English language like a native.

Mr. Jay not only considered that a minister of religion ought to be guided by the rules of morality, but that it was his duty to inculcate the observance of them from the pulpit. In a preface to one of his published sermons on this point, he says, "that he never has been afraid to preach on practical subjects;" that he "despises the charge of legality" brought against him on this very account; that he "considerably dislikes the exclusive application of evangelical to doctrinal preaching;" and that "he has been accustomed to seize events and circumstances as they arise, to engage attention, and diversify public instruction." It was in this union of works and faith that Mr. Jay, in combination with other qualities, excelled as a preacher and writer.

On the subject of practical preaching, Mr. Jay used to relate the following anecdote: "On the death of my daughter Statira, I went to Cheltenham, in order by a change of scene to divert my mind from that severe bereavement. I became the guest of a lady of that town who was a member of the Established Church. She informed me, with deep sorrow, that they had a minister at their church who, as they feared, did not preach the Gospel; and she desired me to go and hear him, in order to judge for myself. I went, and on leaving the church was asked, whether that was preaching the Gospel. 'Why, really, my dear madam, that is a very awkward question for me to answer; for it was my own sermon.'"

CHAPTER XVI.

A commemoration sermon—Mr. Jay's liberality in religion—His politics—Gore Langton—Mr. Roebuck—Lord Ashley—Lord Duncan—Municipal Reform Act—General Palmer—Sir John Moore.

It having been generally known at Bath that Mr. Jay was, on the 4th October 1835, to deliver a sermon in commemoration of that day, being the three-hundredth year of the publication of the first complete edition of the Bible in English, Argyle Chapel was crowded to excess, a great portion of the auditory consisting of members of the Established Church, amongst whom were several Episcopalian clergymen. It so happened, that this very day was also the forty-sixth anniversary of the opening of that chapel by Mr. Jay, the only minister employed in the service of its dedication, and who was soon after called upon to take the charge of the sanctuary, a duty in which he laboured with zeal and faithfulness during that long period. The sermon, the text of which was taken from the ninth chapter of the Hebrews, tenth verse, "The time of reformation," was published by Mr. Jay, in compliance with the request contained in two written addresses presented to him for that purpose, one of which was from a liberal Churchman, a gentleman of property, piety, philanthropy, and talent. Whilst Mr. Jay, in this discourse, condemned the doctrines, spiritual despotism, and superstitions of Popery, and set forth the great advantages which had resulted from the Reformation, yet he avowed himself a friend to the enjoyment by Catholics of civil and religious liberty; and amongst the cogent reasons why he, as a Protestant Dissenting minister should so declare himself, he thus expressed himself: "Your preacher remembers hearing the late excellent Wilberforce say, with great firmness, when rather reflected upon for his decided approbation of the Emancipation measure, 'I am a friend to the bill, because I am an enemy to Popery.' Nor need you, my friends, be surprised at this remark. If any fact be more clear than another from history, it is that sects and parties are most likely to relax and languish as they are left alone. They flourish most when they are persecuted. Restraint operates upon them like a dam thrown across the river, which makes the water rise higher and spread wider. Opposition unites them more closely, blends the pride of resistance with the steadiness of belief, and confirms the zeal and the firmness of martyrs, and calls out resources which the agents would not have known they possessed had they not been stimulated and called forth. And do we not see this in this day? Has it not caused a reaction, and raised a zeal in the Catholic Church such as was scarcely ever witnessed?"

Further on in his discourse, Mr. Jay declared "that he was sometimes dreadfully afraid of the Popery of Protestantism;" and, in alluding to ministers of this stamp in the Established Church, said: "What is High Churchism but Popery in the bud, or in the embryo? I know excellent Churchmen who are not bigots; they have their convictions and prejudices (and who would forbid them to any man?), but it is no part of *their* religion to condemn, or *even unchurch* others. But he who deems it sinful to enter any place of worship but his own; or treats it as a most lamentable offence that one of his own flock has, once in his life, communed at the table of a brother as much 'holding the head' as himself, and differing from him only in non-essentials; or who refuses or murmurs to bury a child baptised by a Dissenter, or not baptised at all; or considers all other churches but his own as unscriptural, and all administration of ordinances in them as invalid; let him rail as long and as loud as he chooses against Popery; be assured he is a Papist at heart and in principle. Liberty of conscience is his grievance. He would willingly recall it if it were in his power, and let loose the dogs of war, or employ the fetters of spiritual despotism. He secretly calls for fire from heaven; but the comfort is, that there is no one there to hear him. Elizabeth said to some of her bishops: 'When you argue against the Papists you are Puritans, and when you dispute against the Puritans you are Papists.'"

One would hardly have supposed that Mr. Jay's advocacy in this sermon, that Catholics should enjoy the same equal rights and privileges as other Christian sects, coupled as it was with his reasons for such a line of policy, would have given rise to much misrepresentation; but so it was. In alluding to such misrepresentation, Mr. Jay, in his Autobiography, says: "I am thankful that though a man's writings will always have a tinge of his own opinions, I have published nothing that can fairly or justly give offence to any religious parties amongst those who 'hold the head.' Let a man, if he please, state and defend his own peculiar views in a work of itself, and professing its own purpose; but I always disliked the smuggling of particular sentiments into a subject designed and adapted to general usefulness. I do not consider my sermon on the Reformation as excepted to this remark. The occasion was singular, and allowed and required me to speak freely. If any suppose that because I conceded to the Catholics their civil rights, I was too candid towards the doctrines and superstitions of Popery, they have but to peruse the sermon to see that they are mistaken. If any members of the Established Church were offended, it was only those who did not hear the sermon, but only heard of it in connection with a great misrepresentation, which ignorance reported and bigotry spread, and which was soon rectified by public denials. These denials, however, the author never called for, always having followed an advice given to him by a very wise and good man, namely, never to notice any thing said of him in newspapers and periodicals."

Mr. Jay, in politics, was a Whig of the old school; but in politics, as in religion, he generally took the liberal side, and never allowed difference of opinion on any subject to interfere with friendship. Years ago, it was well known that he intended to vote for Gore Langton, the candidate for the county of Somerset; and on the day he recorded his vote for that gentleman, Sir Thomas Lethbridge, Bart., resigned. Mr. Jay requested that neither the carriage which conveyed him to the hustings should be decked with, nor any of his numerous friends who accompanied him should wear, the colours of the candidate.

Bath being a close borough until the passing of the Reform Bill, Mr. Jay had not the opportunity of recording his vote as an elector for that city; but the first time he exercised his franchise he did it manfully, and was at the hustings by eight o'clock in the morning, voting for General Palmer and Mr. Roebuck. It was soon circulated over Bath that he had recorded his vote for these two candidates, who were elected by a large majority. This was the first time that Mr. Roebuck had entered Parliament; so that, in point of fact, he was an untried man. Mr. Jay, who was not altogether pleased with Mr. Roebuck as a member of Parliament, informed that learned gentleman, when he called upon him for a renewal of his vote, that he (Mr. Roebuck) was much too confident and positive on all subjects, and that he thought *himself* right, and *every one else* who differed from him in opinion wrong; a state of things, added Mr. Jay, which never existed. When Mr. Roebuck was taking his leave, Mr. Jay cunningly inquired of him whether he meant to support the government in all their measures. "Certainly not," replied Mr. Roebuck, who evidently thought the answer would please his inquirer. "Then," said Mr. Jay, without a moment's hesitation, "if that's your determination, I cannot vote for you; for I think the administration, taken as a whole, is as good as can be." Mr. Jay thought it somewhat strange that, on the Sunday following this interview, Mr. Roebuck should form one of the congregation at Argyle Chapel.

Mr. Roebuck's committee being most anxious to

obtain Mr. Jay's vote, and with it an amount of influence, used every argument to induce him to support their candidate, and offered to convey him by a special train from Worthing, where he was then staying, to Bath; but he was firm in his refusal. Mr. Roebuck lost his election, and with it his temper, attacking Mr. Jay most unwarrantably in his speech from the hustings. Many were the squibs and caricatures representing the divine kicking Mr. Roebuck out of Bath. The abuse and sarcasm of the rejected member was pointed out, for the first time, to Mr. Jay, in the newspapers, by a reverend doctor, master of one of the halls at Oxford; but he only smiled at it, and was soon afterwards seen talking to some of the fishermen on the beach. At this election, Lord Ashley, now the Earl of Shaftesbury, succeeded; and it was astonishing how many applications were made to Mr. Jay, personally and by letter, to vote for his lordship; one of such letters, which I was very much struck with, was from the late Mr. Bickersteth, brother of the late Lord Langdale, than whom no clergyman was more respected in the Church. The Tory party also tormented him for his interest; and two clergymen called upon him to solicit his vote for their candidate, and after using various arguments without effect, stated that a great many of his congregation were Tories; upon which he replied, "Gentlemen, I like Tories very much in the House of God, but not in the House of Commons."

A brother of mine, residing at Bath, called on Mr. Jay early one morning, on the eve of a general election, and found him busily employed digging in his garden. He informed his father that the object of his visit was to request him to give his first signature to a requisition calling on Lord Duncan to become a candidate for the representation of the city in Parliament. Although contrary to Mr. Jay's practice to do any thing without giving it some previous consideration, yet on this occasion he desired my brother, without one moment's hesitation, to go into the library and bring him out into the garden (for he would not leave off his digging) a pen and ink, on which being produced, he signed the requisition, saying after having done so, "I feel much pleasure in heading the requisition, as the Earl of Camperdown is a great friend to Bath, has a house in the city, and spends every winter here. I was acquainted with his father, the famous Lord Duncan, who gained the battle of Camperdown. Whenever the great admiral was at Portsmouth or Bath, he always attended the Independent chapels of both places; and his wife, the Dowager Lady Duncan, who lived to a very advanced age, was a constant attendant at my chapel. You and your brothers must surely recollect her ladyship's great kindness to you in her having always presented each of you, on your returning back to school after the vacations, with pocket-money. I sincerely hope his lordship will be at the head of the poll, as I like the man as well as his politics." Mr. Jay's wish was gratified.

On the Sunday after the election, Mr. Jay preached a sermon for the Bath Hospital, an institution which he very much admired. The Earl of Camperdown brought with him to the chapel Mr. Philips, the then member for Manchester, and several other friends, as well to hear Mr. Jay's discourse as to aid the institution by their contributions. The text was, "Let him that stole, steal no more; but rather let him labour, working with his hands the thing which is good, that he may have to give to him that needeth." The subject was ably handled. His lordship and friends, after the conclusion of the sermon, came into the vestry, and thanked Mr. Jay for his excellent discourse. A very handsome sum was collected for the hospital.

The Municipal Reform Act divided Bath, which had been previously a close corporation, into many wards, to which were apportioned an alderman and a certain number of common councilmen. At that time politics, both of a general and local nature, ran very high in the corporation, and many were the dissensions amongst them even upon trivial matters. For instance, the hot springs, for which that city has been from time immemorial celebrated, and which always belonged to the corporation, had its committee called the Hot-Water Committee, which Mr. Jay said was a most appropriate appellation for a body who were always squabbling together upon trivial points. There was also a building committee, the members of which could never agree; and so high were the disputes amongst them, that a paper war was carried on between one section of such committee and the other respecting it. Mr. Jay, who always read the local newspapers, preached on the Sunday morning, either by design or accident, on the subject of Noah's ark, many of the corporation being present. After making a suitable introduction, and treating the subject of his text with more than usual ability, he remarked that there were many other observations besides those which he had addressed to his hearers which might occur to an imaginative mind; but one thing was certain, said the preacher, that in the construction of the ark there was no building committee, or it never would have been built. The manner and tone of voice with which this unexpected reproof was uttered caused a titter amongst the whole of the congregation, the members of the corporation then present not excepted.

Mr. Jay was acquainted with Mr. Palmer, a member of the old corporation, who was the originator of the mail-coaches, for which he received a large annuity from the Government. This gentleman's son, General Palmer, who represented the city of Bath both before and after the Reform Bill, and for whom Mr. Jay recorded his vote, sold his interest in the mail-coaches for a large sum of money. Mr. Jay was informed by the general, who served under Sir John Moore in Spain, and was present at the battle of Corunna, of a fact not generally known to the public,—that that hero was one of the most showy dressers in the whole army. No wonder that this should especially attract the notice of General Palmer, he having been the best-dressed man in London, and the leader of fashion for years.

CHAPTER XVII.

Mr. Jay's library—An impromptu—His love of music—Lord Barham —Earl of Gainsborough—Conversion of the Jews—A conversation about prophecies—Lord A—— at Exeter Hall.

Mr. Jay possessed a very extensive collection of books, all of which were in first-rate condition. The library was a beautiful room; it looked upon an elegant garden, backed by bold and lovely hills. Many of the sets of books had been presented to him by men of rank and distinction out of respect to his character and admiration for his talents. Not only had he complete sets of the different reviews,—the *Monthly*, the *Edinburgh*, the *Quarterly*, the *Christian Observer*, and the *Eclectic*,—but he had a large collection of works on old divinity in fine preservation, and many of them very scarce. He had also a good collection of works on history, philosophy, science, and general literature. Early in the morning Mr. Jay might be seen leaving the library to go into his garden for exercise, which generally consisted in digging and wheeling the barrow. He had all through life a very strong idea that a slight glow of perspiration was conducive to health, and produced cheerfulness of mind. It was in his library, in which Mr. Jay took so much pleasure, that he had spent the greater part of his life. "How precious," would he frequently exclaim, "is this room to me! Here I have composed the most of my sermons; here I have prepared the best of my works for the press; here I have received my friends; and here I have spent the happiest hours of my life with my family. I never leave my study without regret."

Over the door of the library was suspended a painting by an American artist, representing the seat and grounds of General Washington at Mount Vernon. It was presented to Mr. Jay by his eldest son, the late William Jay, who died at the Mauritius, holding a government situation there. Mr. Jay, underneath the painting, wrote the following impromptu:

"There dwelt the *Man*, the flower of human kind,
Whose visage mild bespoke the noble mind;
There dwelt the *Soldier*, who his sword ne'er drew
But in a righteous cause, to freedom true;
There dwelt the *Hero*, who ne'er killed for fame,
Yet gained more glory than a Cæsar's name;
There dwelt the *Statesman*, who, devoid of art,
Gave soundest counsels from an upright heart.
And, O Columbia, by thy sons confessed!
There dwelt the *Father* of the realms he blest,
Who felt no wish to make his mighty praise,
Like other chiefs, the means himself to raise;
But there retiring, breathed in pure renown,
And felt a grandeur that disdain'd a crown."

Had not Mr. Jay made the above impromptu, as it were, public, I should not have inserted it in my recollections of him. He had written several poetical pieces, one of which, of considerable length, entitled "The Garden," he at one time intended to publish. But he afterwards altered his mind, falling back on his early resolution,—to make every thing subservient to preaching. It was his especial desire that none of his poetry should be sent forth to the publio after his death.

Mr. Jay, to use the words of my late sister, Mrs. Ashton, "was strongly excited by music, of the pleasure of which he was susceptible in the highest degree. He had an ear formed to enjoy the simplest melody, and, though little cultivated, he relished its highest charms." I remember having once accompanied him to hear the oratorio of the "Messiah," by Handel; and he was so deeply affected with various portions of it, that I thought I should have had to lead him out of the cathedral. On returning home, he said that he should attend no more musical festivals, as the grandeur and beauty of an oratorio was too much for his nerves. Although his ear could instantly detect any false note in music, yet he could never, during the whole course of his ministry, pitch any tune, or lead any singing with his voice,—a circumstance which he very much regretted; and knowing his own defect, it was his invariable recommendation to the tutors of the Dissenting colleges that the students should be instructed in psalmody.

Mr. Jay frequently preached at farmhouses, where it often happened that those present were either unable or too shy to lead the singing, or join in it. On one of these occasions he officiated at the house of a wealthy farmer, where a number of neighbours and rustics were assembled together to hear his discourse. Many attempts having been made to launch one of Dr. Watts's hymns in the right musical channel, both by Mr. Jay and his hearers, without success, Mr. Jay said: "My brethren, we had better give the thing over, for it is quite evident that our singing will never get us to heaven. I will therefore *read* the hymn." Perhaps no person ever read a hymn with a finer voice, or more pathos, than he did; and it was in reference to this quality that I heard Robert Hall once say, that he would rather hear Mr. Jay read one of Watts's hymns than he would hear many people preach. These gatherings were managed by Mr. Jay with the greatest dexterity; and in order to induce his rustic hearers to join in singing the hymn, he would, immediately on giving it out, endeavour to overcome their shyness and timidity by addressing one or more of the farmers thus: "What a very fine field of wheat is yours!" or, "How fine is the weather for the harvest!"

After the marriage of Mr. Jay's daughters, he was in the habit of entertaining some young ladies at his house as visitors; and I have thought that, in the selection of such guests, he had an eye to their musical qualifications. One of these ladies, a Miss Thompson, of Cirencester, was perhaps the best pianist and ballad-singer off the stage; and there was hardly one of Burns's songs which she did not sing. The late Earl Northesk, the third commander at the battle of Trafalgar, and whose remains lie next to Lord Nelson's at St. Paul's, was for many years a constant attendant at Mr. Jay's chapel, and a frequent visitor at his house. Many times have I seen his lordship go down the garden to Mr. Jay, and after a little conversation, would say to him, "Let us have one of those beautiful ballads of Burns;" upon which they would both retire into the house for that purpose. The lady always reluctantly acceded to these requests, though one would have thought that no entreaty would have been necessary to oblige a minister whom she so much admired, and a naval commander who had gained so much distinction. But how different was it with her on a Sunday night, when Mr. Jay came home from the chapel excited and wearied! for then she would anticipate his wishes, by going to the piano, and playing some of the beautiful music from Handel and other composers.

Mr. Jay was personally acquainted with Mr. Middleton, who was, at the time of the battle of Trafalgar, first lord of the Admiralty. In consequence of that glorious victory, the peerage was extended to his female issue, whereby his daughter, the Hon. Miss Noel, who was on intimate terms with Mr. Jay, and a constant attendant at Argyle Chapel during her different sojourns at Bath, became a peeress in her own right. This pious lady married Sir Gerald Noel, Bart., by whom she had a numerous family. At her death her eldest son became Lord Barham (afterwards created the Earl of Gainsborough), between whom and Mr. Jay a friendship of many years had existed. To Lord Barham he dedicated his *Morning Exercises for the Closet for every Day in the Year*, the excellence of which work has been fully demonstrated by its extensive circulation ever since its publication in 1828.

One morning I met Mr. Jay coming out of his study in a great hurry, having to leave Bath to proceed to Frome, to preach there that day; and he said, I have just received a letter from Lord Barham, in which, among other things, his lordship has asked my advice whether he ought, as a Christian, to sell his estate at Barham Court, in Kent, to Mr. Rothschild, he being a Jew, having some scruples as to its propriety. Mr. Jay's answer to such question was very laconic. It was, as near as I can remember, in the following words: "My dear Lord Barham, in answer to your letter, received this morning, as to the sale of Barham Court, my only fear is, that the Jew will get the best of the Christian in the bargain."

One morning, one of my sisters had been reading some notices in the library, which had been recently left there, respecting the conversion of the Jews. It caught the eye of Mr. Jay, who had just come into the library from the garden. "I am sorry," said he, "that all our young people trouble themselves so much about the Jews, when there is so much ignorance and poverty in the smaller towns of our western counties." The fact is, that Mr. Jay never took much interest in the Jews; and I have often observed, that when any question about their return to Jerusalem was started in company, he would dextrously turn the conversation, to avoid giving an opinion. Indeed, he thought such conversation was useless and trifling.

I was one day dining with Dr. Lee, the Hebrew Professor at Cambridge, in company with Mr. Jay, when the conversation turned upon the prophecies respecting the Jews. Mr. Jay appeared to be quite conversant with the professor's work on Prophecy, quoting largely therefrom, and debating several points with the learned host. The conversation at length flagging, Mr. Jay asked me to repeat to the professor the following story, which I had told him a few days before. I complied. It was as follows: Lord A— had much to do with Jews, in London and the country, in raising money which was never paid, in accepting bills which were never honoured, and in giving bonds which were not worth the paper on which they were written. It so happened, that a zealous youth in London had received from a brother of his in Jerusalem, who was almost mad on prophecy, a letter, wherein it was stated that he had just seen a missionary who had lately discovered another tribe of Jews in some part of Asia. Immediately on the receipt of such communication, the young enthusiast called a meeting at one of the small rooms of Exeter Hall, having previously advertised it in some of the religious publications, stating the fact, and that the discovery would lead to additional evidence in support of the authenticity of the Holy Scriptures; and got a nobleman to take the chair. To the surprise of the meeting, in came my Lord A—, which caused great mirth to the chairman, who, in accosting his lordship, expressed his great delight in seeing him at such a meeting; upon which his lordship said: "I have seen the interesting advertisement respecting this wealthy new tribe of Jews, and I am come to learn more particulars about them." The chairman jocosely remarked, that his lordship would not like to visit them. "But indeed I should," was the instant answer of Lord A—; "and that is what has brought me here. I have had the best of every Jew in *this* country, and I should like to have some *fresh* ones." The professor laughed heartily at this anecdote; and the conversation about prophecies ended.

I remember one of Mr. Jay's oldest hearers saying to him in conversation, "Sir, I have observed that you have been the instrument, under Providence, of converting two Jews who have attended your chapel for some time." Mr. Jay immediately replied: "I may have convinced, but I do not know about converting them." I have heard him apply the same observations to miracles, saying, that in general they merely convinced the Jews for a time, but failed in making converts of them.

CHAPTER XVIII.

Early walks—The Rev. Mr. Nelson—Lord Nelson—A Church-of-England dignitary—A delay on the road—A recognition—The poet Crabbe.

In the days of coaching, Mr. Jay was well known to all the coachmen on the Bath road, with whom he was an especial favourite, not only on account of the knowledge they had acquired of him from the numerous journeys he had undertaken by coach to preach at a greater or less distance from home, but also by their daily passing him on the road during his early morning walks.

Frequently have I accompanied Mr. Jay, as early as five o'clock in the morning of a spring day, on the Gloucester road as far as a wood, into which he would enter by a gate, and commence the operation of cutting down several long sticks for his peas; an act of labour which he almost daily repeated at this season of the year until he procured a number sufficient for the purpose for which he required them. On each of these occasions he would carry them on his shoulder. I have overheard the Bath coachman, when passing Mr. Jay thus loaded, inform the outside passengers that he was the well-known preacher at Bath. On arriving at Percy Place, it was quite laughable to see the care with which he laid the sticks together until they were required for use. He invariably, until the last few years of his life, stuck the peas himself; and his peas were observed to be finer and more prolific than those of his neighbours. I should mention that before Mr. Jay would attempt to commence his career as a pea-stick cutter, he asked permission of the proprietor of the wood to be allowed to do so, who instantly granted the request, saying, with a smile, "You may take the whole wood away if you like, Mr. Jay."

It was during the latter part of the last century that Mr. Jay, in his early morning walks on this road, met with a gentleman, as little of a sluggard as himself, who bore a great resemblance to the great John Wesley, not only in appearance and dress, but in the style of his hair, which fell in profusion on his shoulders. From these early morning meetings an acquaintanceship soon sprang up between Mr. Jay and the gentleman, who turned out to be no less a personage than the Rev. Mr. Nelson, the father of the celebrated admiral, Lord Nelson. Mr. Jay had frequently seen the naval hero, when not afloat, at Mr. Beckford's old house, and also at Bath.

I remember, when a lad, walking one day with Mr. Jay on the London road, when we met the mail-coach, covered with laurel, driving towards Bath at an unusual speed. Mr. Jay, on inquiring of the keeper of the toll-gate, whom he knew well, what was the occasion of the coach being so decorated, was informed by him, that he had learnt from the guard that Lord Nelson had gained a most glorious victory at Trafalgar, and had been killed during the action. "I expected to hear as much," said Mr. Jay; "for when I saw the laurel I thought of the cypress. His late father more than once prophesied to me that such would be the termination of his son's career."

On the 5th of December 1805, the day appointed for a general thanksgiving for the glorious victory, Mr. Jay preached a sermon at Argyle Chapel, the text of which was, "The victory that day was turned into mourning." He mentioned in his discourse, that upon the news of the victory the city of Edinburgh was illuminated, but not entirely. One street refused its lustre. In it lived the bereaved widow of the gallant Captain Duff, who fell in the action. It was a striking exception. Darkness best suited an anguished mind whose hope had fled. "It is remarkable," said Mr. Jay, "that the ship in which Lord Nelson fell was the *Victory;* and thus the words we have chosen were circumstantially accomplished,—the '*Victory* was that day turned into mourning.' The cabin-boy and the captain wept; the groan spread from the ship through the whole fleet; villages and cities shared the grief, till the tears of the sovereign mingled with the people. Nelson, farewell! thou hast more than repaid the confidence thy king and thy country reposed in thy patriotism and thy talents. Thy warfare is accomplished: but long shall thy fame live; long shall thy example stimulate; thy memory shall be embalmed in our grateful recollections; and history shall record that a whole nation, sensible of their obligations to thee, by their presence or their sympathy, attended thy funeral, and followed thy awful remains to their august and final abode."

The sermon concluded thus: "Men and brethren, it is scarcely necessary for me to mention the particular purpose for which your liberality is to be exercised this morning. You well know that a collection is to be made this day through the whole kingdom for the relief of the families of those who suffered in the late action. While all our fellow-citizens are coming forward, I am sure this congregation will readily coöperate with them. The claim upon you is a claim of gratitude, of justice. It addresses you as Christians, as Britons, as men. Suppose all these victims of bereavement were now assembled before you, dressed in mourning, and wiping their weeping eyes,—could you be insensible? Ah, ye brave countrymen, who fought to defend us, and who generously perished that we may continue in the possession of all our comforts; ye, descending wounded and gory into your watery graves,—ye said, 'We lament not our own destiny; we have fallen at our posts; but to you we commend our mothers, our wives, our children, our babes; deprived for ever of our support, let them find succour in you.' Valiant sailors! there is not a British heart but awaits and melts at your call. Ye have indeed done *your* duty, and we hasten to perform *ours*."

Mr. Jay did not appeal to his auditory in vain; the collection being the largest of any of the churches and chapels in Bath.

I remember, on one occasion, being Mr. Jay's companion in an early morning walk, when the Worcester coach overtook us. On passing, the coachman took off his hat to Mr. Jay, and gave a knowing nod. "You seem to be very good friends with the coachman," I observed. "Yes," said he; "and besides being a worthy man, he can keep a secret better than you can, although you are a lawyer." "What secret is that?" I inquired. "You shall hear. I was returning on Saturday from Worcester, having fulfilled an engagement there on the preceding day. On my stepping into the coach, I found there was only one inside passenger. It so happened, that although we were not previously known to each other, I recognised in the person of my fellow-companion a dignitary of the Church of England. On the coach passing through Lord Ducie's park, I pointed out some stables near the mansion built like a church, saying, 'That's a *sham church;*' upon which the dignitary, nudging me, said, '*Is it not all a sham?*' When the coach stopped to change horses, I alighted, and upon the coachman coming down from the box I requested him not to mention my name to my fellow-traveller. When I returned to the coach, the dignitary, after some trifling conversation, said: 'Do you know that, out of curiosity, I am going to Bath to hear that fellow Jay, who has made such a great noise, preach to-morrow; do you know him?' I said, 'I somewhat know him;' which was the fact; for what person is there that *really* knows himself? On reaching Percy Place, I alighted, leaving the dignitary alone in the coach. On the Sunday morning, as I was giving out the text, my eye alighted on my fellow-traveller, seated in a conspicuous part of the chapel; a circumstance which somewhat disconcerted me in the introductory part of my discourse, as I could well see that he had recognised me."

Although Mr. Jay had travelled for years in almost every part of England and Scotland by coach, he never was delayed on the road, except once, when the wheel came off. It being a very cold frosty morning, Mr. Jay, who was always very active, alighted from the coach, and walked up and down the road in order to keep himself warm. Not so one of the gentleman-passengers, a very irritable and impatient individual. He began swearing at the top of his voice, cursing the coachman, cursing the coach, cursing the wheel, cursing the horses, and cursing the frost. At length he accosted a boy who happened to be passing by, and asked him how far it was to the place where they could get a post-chaise; and on being informed that it was two miles off, solicited the lad to go and hire one for them. Finding from the reply that the lad could not do so, as he was going in a contrary direction, the gentleman turned round to Mr. Jay, who, as he observed, was the most active of the party, and asked him whether he would go and hire the post-chaise. "I would go directly, sir, but I cannot swear;" and without making any further observation, Mr. Jay kept walking up and down the road as before, until the wheel of the coach was replaced.

Mr. Jay's style of preaching, both as to the matter, mode, delivery, and quality of voice, aided by a fine eye and expressive face, left an impression on the hearer which was not speedily effaced. The following anecdote is illustrative of the power which he thus successfully exercised. On one occasion, being about six miles from Bath, he hailed the coachman journeying to that city, asking him if he had room for him upon the box. "We will make room there for you, sir, with pleasure," was the reply. He had no sooner taken his place on the box, than a gentleman, who was seated behind the coachman, thus accosted him: "Sir, if I do not mistake, you are Mr. Jay, of Bath." "I am, sir," was the reply. Upon which the gentleman said: "I have never heard you preach but once, since which time I have been in India for twenty years, and have just returned home. Your voice fascinated me; I recognise it again, and am happy to have met you. Do you still officiate at Argyle Chapel?" "I do," was the answer. "Then," said the gentleman, "although I intended to have left Bath on Saturday for London, I shall postpone my departure until Monday, in order to have the pleasure of hearing you preach on the Sunday."

Mr. Jay was on friendly terms with the Rev. George Crabbe, who died at Trowbridge in Wiltshire, of which parish he had been nineteen years the rector.

Mr. Jay was an ardent admirer of Crabbe's poetry, and highly extolled his accuracy, originality, power, and vivid painting; but said that he could not read much of it at a time. Mr. Jay one day meeting the poet at Bath, to which city he was a frequent visitor (Trowbridge being within the distance of ten miles), the subject of conversation turned upon poetry. Mr. Jay, having alluded to the early date of Crabbe's first tale, the poet said, "I should not have gone to the press again, had it not been for the purpose of obtaining money to assist me in sending my son to the University."

Upon another occasion, when Mr. Jay overtook Crabbe on the road, he, after repeating some of the poet's most exquisite and touching lines, asked him which he thought were the best lines he had ever written; when Crabbe instantly replied, "In that part of one of my poems beginning, *there are real mourners*," wherein is portrayed the sailor's death, and the surviving sweetheart, "a fair sad girl, mild, suffering, and serene." Often have I heard Mr. Jay, when, espying a young female in a burial-ground, repeat with much pathos the following and concluding lines of this very touching picture of innocent love, misfortune, and resignation, all of them taking a tinge of additional sweetness and tenderness from the humble condition of the parties:

> "Here will she come, and on the grave will sit,
> Folding her arms in long abstracted fit;
> But if observer pass will take her round,
> And careless seem, for she would not be found;
> Then come again, and thus her hour employ,
> While visions please her, and while woes destroy."

Mr. Jay read with much pleasure the *Life of Crabbe*, by his son; and said that it was a very touching and beautiful specimen of biography. The son, in one part of his work, alluding to the Parson-Adams-like simplicity of his father, says, that "he had the most complete exemption from fear or solicitude (while officiating as a minister). 'I must have some money, gentlemen,' he would say, in stepping from the pulpit. This was his notice of tithe-day. Once or twice, finding it grow dark, he abruptly shut up his sermon, saying, 'Upon my word, I cannot see; I must give you the rest when we meet again.' Or he would walk into a pew near a window, and stand on the seat and finish his sermon with the most admirable indifference to the remarks of his congregation." Mr. Jay seemed to have somewhat of the like fearlessness in his character.

CHAPTER XIX.

Anecdotes respecting undertakers—A cause of abstraction in the pulpit—A few words upon Mr. Jay's visit at the Mansion House in Dublin—The fortieth anniversary of his pastorate over Argyle Chapel, and its celebration.

It is well known amongst Mr. Jay's friends that he entertained a strong prejudice against undertakers, whose calling he considered had a tendency to make them callous to the best feelings of human nature. He had, during the long course of his pastorate at Argyle Chapel, visited many a house of mourning; so that he could not fail of having some knowledge of this class of tradesmen. I have accompanied him upon several of these visits, when we most usually found the passage lined with undertakers, all eagerly pressing towards him to obtain his influence for the *performance* of the funeral. But he invariably declined to interfere. They had, however, pretty good friends in the nurse and medical attendants, particularly in the palmy days of Bath, when death was rampant amongst the numerous wealthy and invalid visitors who then resorted to that city.

It was Mr. Jay's fate to be annoyed every three or four months by some one of these undertakers at his house in Percy Place, between whom and my mother there was a regular barter, she exchanging silk hatbands and long scarfs (which after use became her perquisites) for cloth or money. I have seen him at the moment of high change open the door of the sitting-room, and then, after closing it, retreat back again to his library. Of course the undertaker got the best of my mother. Although Mr. Jay received so many mourning rings, he would only wear them on the Sunday morning, having a great aversion to jewellery of any kind; and on his return home from Argyle Chapel would take them off and present them to my mother.

Mr. Jay often used to repeat in company the following story; but how or from whom he obtained it I know not:

A rich undertaker had in his employ a faithful servant, who had acted in the capacity of principal *weeper* at funerals for the long period of thirty years without receiving any increase of wages. One morning the undertaker being in an unusual flow of spirits on account of the many deaths which had recently taken place, and having in consequence to *perform* on the following day a great number of funerals, said to the weeper, "John, you have now been with us a long time, and I am determined to increase your wages." John thanked his master, and retired in first-rate spirits. The undertaker observing the next day to his utter astonishment that John was standing at the door of death with a countenance changed from *grief* to *mirth,* inquired of him the cause, and the reply was, "Sir, I have been in such high spirits since the increase of wages, that I am all joy instead of sadness;" whereupon the undertaker said, "John, if you cannot *act* the serious weeper upon the increased wages, I must reduce them."

Another story which Mr. Jay often repeated about

undertakers was the following: A gentleman of large estate from Yorkshire, and an enthusiastic fox-hunter, having the rheumatic gout, although otherwise of a strong constitution, took lodgings on the first-floor of a house at the North Parade, Bath. The first morning, after his breakfast, he was wheeled to the window of the front room, where he sat the greater part of the day to amuse himself. At a certain hour in the evening, he observed a man walk up and down for some time before the house, looking up at the windows, and secretly eyeing him. Observing this man for four or five days in succession make his appearance at the same time before the windows of the house, the gentleman inquired of his man-servant what all this prowling about the house meant. He replied, that the strange conduct of the man induced him to make a like inquiry of the landlady, who said, "Why, he is an undertaker, and is watching to see if your master is dead and the shutters are closed, to get the job of the funeral: he has learnt your master's name, knows of his great wealth, and that if he died at Bath he would be buried in Yorkshire." The fox-hunter said to his servant, "Samuel, we will quickly put a stop to this annoyance. Just before the time he usually makes his appearance, close the shutters, and then I will get upon the bed, and you must cover me over with sheets, and place a horsewhip by my side, and I will appear as if I were dead." This being done, a gentle rap at the door soon followed; and upon its being opened, the sneaking undertaker said to the gentleman's man-servant in a soft and mournful voice, "So your poor master is gone to his long home," at the same time slipping a five-pound note into the servant's hand, who then invited him up-stairs. The undertaker ascended the stairs, and at once proceeded to the bed with his measuring tape in hand. Placing the measure on the supposed corpse, and while passing it from the head to the foot to ascertain the length, the gentleman sprang up in bed, caught hold of him, and gave him a sound horse-whipping. The terrified undertaker ran away without the funeral and without the note.

I related to Mr. Jay the following anecdote respecting three undertakers, which much amused him: A gentleman of my acquaintance was appointed one of a committee of four to inquire into some parochial matter connected with a certain district, and the three other members associated with him were undertakers. At the first meeting, the *shortest* of them, much to the disgust of my friend, saluted him thus: "I am happy to see you here, sir, amongst us. You must know I have a great liking for this parish, for I have married out of it four wives." The second undertaker (a *tall man*) then rose from his seat, and approaching my friend, said: "Sir, will you stand up back to back with me, and see which of us is the tallest." No sooner had my friend excused himself from complying with this requisition, than the third undertaker (a *fat man*) said to him in a very familiar manner: "Come, my brother-committeeman, let me measure you round the waist, and see which of us is the stoutest." An idea having entered into the mind of my friend, who, although a tall, was yet a very nervous man, that they were measuring him for a coffin, he speedily made his exit from the room full of fear and trembling.

I also related to Mr. Jay at the same time the following story: A gentleman, the proprietor of a large and old-established coffee-house in London, having just died, his widow was sitting in the bar, weeping most bitterly, and waiting most anxiously for the arrival of the undertaker. No sooner did he appear, than he walked up to the mourner, and after shaking her by the hand and recommending her to keep up her spirits by taking some brandy-and-water, said: "I have picked out a *nice warm grave* for your husband:" whereupon she, after faintly thanking him, went off into a violent fit of hysterics.

A sharp and intelligent tradesman with whom Mr. Jay was one day conversing on the subject of the heavy amount of an undertaker's bill, and of the folly of paying it without due investigation, said: "O sir, a man of this calling has means to disarm investigation, particularly if the payment has to come from a lady. He contrives to introduce amongst his many charges several articles, such, for instance, as black kid-gloves, which are put down by him at a sum very considerably less than what he gave for them; and the smallness of the charge so strikes her, that she exclaims that she could not purchase them in any shop at double the price, and that she is confident the other portion of the bill is equally reasonable; and being thus deluded, she pays it without a murmur." "And I make no doubt," said Mr. Jay, "that many an executor has been deceived by a like manœuvre. But it gives me great pleasure to reflect that expensive funerals are daily getting out of fashion. Ridicule has done much to effect this desirable result."

Mr. Jay says, in one of his discourses, that "we

read that 'the rich man died and was buried,'—no doubt with great pomp and magnificence. But what does the Book say? 'In hell he lifted up his eyes, being in torment;' probably while they were returning from the funeral, and reading the will."

In the month of January 1831, having received an especial invitation from Mr. Jay to be his guest on the occasion of the completion of the fortieth year of his pastorate over Argyle Chapel, I took my departure to Bath a fortnight previously, and arrived at Percy Place on a Friday. During the course of dinner I remarked that the potatoes (in the growth of which he greatly prided himself) would be much improved by being served up with their jackets on. "I think so too," he replied; "for while I was in Ireland, on a visit to the Lord Mayor of Dublin, at the Mansion House, I well recollect that we had them put on table in the manner you suggest, and I thought then that that mode of treating them was superior to our own." On the Saturday morning, on coming out of the garden, Mr. Jay told his cook to serve-up the potatoes with their skins on; but, to his great disappointment, she forgot his direction, and sent them up peeled. On Sunday morning, just before starting for chapel, I heard him tell her to be sure and serve-up the potatoes as he had directed her on the preceding day, and not disappoint him a second time. On returning from the chapel to dinner, he appeared greatly to enjoy the potatoes so served; and at the close of the dinner, he turned round to me, and asked me if I knew where the text from which he had preached his discourse was from; an inquiry which he was very apt to make of any person in whose company he happened to be after the service. I said, "Really I forget; but it was a most capital sermon." To which he suddenly replied, "Why, you were thinking more about the potatoes with their skins on than my discourse." I said, "I certainly did think about the potatoes." Laughingly he said, "And so did I, and it annoyed me through a part of my sermon." And he added with a sort of lament, "What poor creatures we preachers are at the best, when even such a trifle can engage our thoughts, and distract them from weighty matters!"

Mr. Jay's visit at the Mansion House in Dublin was during the Rebellion, and at the time when Lord Fitzgerald was taken prisoner. Mr. Jay's name was written outside of the Mansion House, such being the case with every one residing in Dublin, martial-law having been proclaimed. This unfortunate state of things prevented him from preaching at most of the places in that city, as he would otherwise have done, his appearance in the pulpit being mostly before the Lord Mayor, officers and servants of the Mansion House. Whenever he preached in the sister-country he was very popular; for he was then very well known to many of the first families in Ireland, who had been his hearers at Bath, a city then much frequented by the Irish aristocracy.

I will now revert, in a few words, to the especial object of my visit to Percy Place.

The members of the church and congregation of Argyle Chapel being desirous to attest the deep interest which they felt on the occasion of the fortieth anniversary of Mr. Jay's pastorate, on the 30th of January 1831, unanimously resolved to present him with some lasting memorial of their affection and esteem towards him. Their gift was a handsome carriage, accompanied by a silver inkstand bearing a suitable inscription.

This anniversary was also celebrated by a sermon preached by Mr. Jay in the morning of the Lord's Day, January 30, 1831, to a crowded and deeply-affected audience, from a very appropriate text, the words of which I do not recollect. In this discourse (which, by the way, is not included in his collected works) he says, in reference to the gift bestowed upon him by his congregation, "Though I do not consider kindness shown to ministers as eleemosynary, yet I cannot but publicly express my thanks to those who have all along shown me so much of their esteem and regard. I never burdened any one in any instance or degree; and at the end of forty years I have no obligation in reference to them to acknowledge,—a boast which perhaps few ministers of my standing or acceptance in the kingdom can make."

CHAPTER XX.

Governesses—The commencement of three sermons—A day at Cheshunt—Copyright.

During the long course of Mr. Jay's ministry, he had occasion to visit, from time to time, many parts of the country, for the purpose of opening chapels or preaching for charities. He was domiciled chiefly on these occasions at some gentleman's house where governesses usually formed part of the establishment, and he invariably paid them the same attention as he did to the lady of the house. I have heard him say, in reference to this class of females: "I feel very much for governesses, and have subscribed to their institutions. They are generally ladies of good education, whose parents have died without having been able to make provision for their family, or who have failed in some pursuit of life. Their education makes them more sensible to neglect or tyranny. The wife may be jealous of them, or the husband may be one day kind to them; and on the following day, if any thing in the interval has gone wrong with him, or ruffled his temper, quite the reverse. Poor creatures! I have been informed that more of this class of females become inmates of lunatic asylums in proportion to their number than do those of any other class." At the same time I have heard him repeat the following quotation from Robert Hall: "The situation of females without fortune in this country is indeed deeply affecting. Excluded from all the active employments in which they might engage with the utmost propriety, by men who, to the injury of one sex, add the disgrace of making the other effeminate and ridiculous, an indigent female—the object probably of love and tenderness in her youth, at a more advanced age a withered flower—has nothing to do but to retire and die. Thus it comes to pass that the most amiable part of our species, by a detestable combination in those who ought to be their protectors, are pushed off the stage, as though they were no longer worthy to live when they ceased to be the objects of passion."

If many of Mr. Jay's texts were singular, equally so was the commencement of some of his sermons. He would thereby awaken the attention of his auditors to a pitch, which in a less practised preacher it would have been difficult to keep up. He commenced a discourse, taken from the tenth chapter of Hebrews and the twenty-eighth and twenty-ninth verses, by repeating the words of the text, and making a most startling deduction therefrom, thus: "'He that despised Moses' law died without mercy under two or three witnesses: of how much sorer punishment, suppose ye, shall he be thought worthy, who hath trodden under foot the Son of God, and hath counted the blood of the covenant, wherewith he was sanctified, an unholy thing, and hath done despite unto the spirit of grace?' What do we read,—a much sorer punishment than dying without mercy! This is fearfulness beyond the power of language to realise or convey."

On another occasion he thus singularly commenced a sermon on the parable of the "Great Supper," beginning at the sixteenth and ending at the twenty-fourth verse of the fourteenth chapter of St. Luke: "A certain man, says our Saviour in this parable, made a great supper, to which he had invited many. When all things were ready, he sent his servant to them that were bidden to announce that fact to them, and to request their attendance; but they all with one consent began to make excuse. The first said to him, 'I have bought a piece of ground, and I must needs go and see it: I pray thee have me excused.' A fool! Why did he not go and see it before he bought it? But this was *his* 'excuse.' Another said, 'I have bought five yoke of oxen, and I go to prove them: I pray thee have me excused.' Another fool! Why did he not go and prove them before he bought them? A grazier of the present day would have done so; but this was *his* 'excuse.' Another said, 'I have married a wife, and therefore I cannot come.' Fool again! Surely he need not have come alone. Could he not bring his wife with him? But this was *his* 'excuse.'"

I remember hearing Mr. Jay preach a sermon on the text of St. John, "God is love," which was thus beautifully and touchingly commenced: "Simonides, an ancient philosopher, was once asked by his sovereign, 'What is God?' The philosopher, in reply, requested a day to consider the question. He then asked for two days; then for four; until at length, being pressed by the monarch for an answer, he candidly confessed, 'The more I consider this question, the less am I able to answer it.'

"Now, my dear hearers, we will leave the philosopher, and go together to a shepherd-boy tending his fleecy charge on the plains of Bethlehem, and put the question to him. Here he is. 'David, what is God?' 'God! he is our refuge and strength, a very present help in trouble. He is my shepherd; I shall not want. He maketh me to lie down in green pastures; He leadeth me beside the still waters. He restoreth my soul; He leadeth me in the paths of righteousness, for His name's sake. Yea, though I walk through the valley of the shadow of death, I will fear no evil; for Thou art with me: Thy rod and staff shall comfort me.' Now let us away to some fishermen of Galilee, and ask them. Here is one of them. 'Peter, what is God?' 'God! He is the God of all grace, who hath called us unto His eternal glory by Christ Jesus.' Well, here is another fisherman; let us ask him too. Here is John. 'John, what is God?' 'God! what more can I say of Him, what less? God is love; and he that dwelleth in love dwelleth in God, and God in him.'"

On the 7th of July 1842, Mr. Jay delivered a long discourse at the Countess of Huntingdon's Chapel at Cheshunt, in commemoration of the fiftieth anniversary of the founding, by that noble lady, of a college in that place for the education of a number of Dissenting ministers. He was solicited to preach this sermon by its trustees; and at their desire he afterwards published and dedicated it to them, under the title of *Paul's Commission explained and applied.*

I formed one of the party who accompanied Mr. Jay to Cheshunt. It was a beautiful summer's day. A special-train left the Shoreditch station in time for the service. The chapel was so crowded, that the managers had one of its windows taken out, and a temporary pulpit was immediately erected in its stead, so that the numerous persons assembled outside could hear the sermon as well as those within.

Mr. Jay in this sermon says: "At the commencement of the present institution [the college], I had been a pastor more than a year, and a preacher for several years. Though I did not attend the opening, I remember it well, and my concern towards it; for I felt a kind of relationship, Whitfield having been her ladyship's chaplain, and he bringing forward in the ministry the excellent Cornelius Winter, who introduced into the work your present preacher. I knew personally the noble foundress, and I more than once conversed with her; and I am liable to no mistake when I say that the grand and only design in this work of faith and labour of love was founded entirely on the words of our Saviour to Paul, to send forth as speedily as possible a number of preachers whose hearts should teach their lips, and whose lives should be consecrated 'to open the eyes of sinners, and to turn them from darkness to light, from the power of Satan unto God, that they might receive the forgiveness of sins, and inheritance amongst them that were sanctified by faith in Christ.'"

Speaking of ministers of the Gospel (an appropriate topic for the occasion), the preacher says: "If they are instruments, that instrument is the best, not which has the finest handle, but that which does its work the best. He is the most enviable preacher who succeeds most in bringing souls to God, whatever comparative disadvantages he labours under. There are some persons who lay down one quality after another for a minister, and a great deal frequently goes to make up a complete reverend. They connect a minister with a certain dress, or with a college or academy, or with some peculiar studies and attainments; and when they hear of the one, they are led to think of the other. But we should distinguish between what is essential and what is preferable, or accessory or accidental. A minister is not a dandy, but a dandy may be a minister: a minister is not a gentleman, but a gentleman may be a minister: a minister is not a man of genius, but a man of genius may be a minister: a minister is not a classic, but a classic may be a minister. What is a minister, then? Go and ask Jesus Christ. He will send you to this commission. A minister is the text embodied—alive—in motion. 'I will send thee to open their eyes, and to turn them from darkness to light, and from the power of Satan unto God, that they may receive forgiveness of sins, and inheritance among them which are sanctified by faith that is in me.'"

In another part of this sermon Mr. Jay had a rap at some modern *reverends*, in the following words: "They show no little self-confidence by choosing difficult topics, and expressing themselves with dogmatism where others feel difficulty. By lengthiness they take for granted their peculiar acceptance; and instead of bespeaking the candour of their audiences by at least apparent modesty and diffidence, they challenge their judgment and demand their approbation by a fearless and daring kind of address. They sometimes show also, by a satisfied and careless demeanour, that they are above the usual auxiliaries needful to some of their brethren and fathers. I one day heard of a young minister of this calibre (I know not if he is in this crowd, but if he be, it will not signify), who, being about to preach, was asked whether he did not wish to *retire* before he went into the pulpit. 'No,' said he; 'I am charged and primed.' He was *primed*, indeed, but not *chargèd*. When he went off, it was only a flash in the pan."

Mr. Jay, in concluding his sermon, thus forcibly addressed his hearers on the duty which was imposed on them as Christians to contribute to the funds of the college: "And must I stand here this morning to *beg* of those who are *able* to give? I will not beg. I have been a beggar for considerably more than half a century, and I will beg no more, at least where the Saviour's cause is concerned. I will do nothing but plead in His name, and enforce His claims,—*His* claims who died for you and rose again. And is there one here but cries, 'Lord, what wilt thou have me to do?'"

After the service, Mr. Jay dined by invitation at the house of Mr. Taylor, which was pleasantly situated by the New River, which ran at the bottom of the lawn. The party at the dinner-table consisted mostly of ladies. After dinner, Mr. Jay withdrew from the table, and apologised to the ladies for so doing, stating that he was so fatigued that he must betake himself to the sofa; but hoped that that would not interrupt the conversation. In about half an hour he beckoned to me, saying, "I should like to see the artificial river." When walking on its banks, he said he had heard the conversation respecting the sermon, and that Mrs. Taylor, in alluding to the meadows and wagon of a Christian, had hit that part which pleased him the most, and that he was surprised at the tenacity of that lady's memory in repeating such portion almost word for word as he had uttered it. I here quote it: "Christian, call to remembrance the commencement of your religious course. Ah, how peculiar and sacred the people of God then appeared! Ah, you said, *you* are safe, *you* are happy, *you* are the seed which the Lord hath blessed. They seemed the only things worthy of your regard. If the wagon of a Christian passed you on the road, the very *name* on the vehicle seemed to endear it. If you leaned upon the gate, and looked down upon his meadow, it seemed as the smell of a field which the Lord had blessed. You surveyed their goings, and their worship, and wept, and said with Cowper:

'Clothed in sanctity and grace,
How sweet it is to see
Those that love Thee as they pass,
And as they wait on Thee!'

And when you looked down from the gallery, and saw the household of faith, and the King sitting at his table, was not this your most feeling wish,—'O that I were counted worthy, and could make one with you!'"

Mr. Jay felt considerable annoyance whenever any of his sermons were taken down in short-hand, and sent into the world without his permission.

In reference to a discourse preached by him in aid of some society, which had been published, he thus expresses himself: "In this way I have been frequently treated: no remonstrance has been available to prevent the gross impropriety of sending a man out before the public against his inclination, or the obvious injustice, when he himself publishes, of forestalling him and injuring the sale. Surely the law ought to protect every species of substance; and a man's sermons, even when preached, while unprinted, do not cease to be his property, as he may be required to preach them again in other places, and on similar occasions; or be disposed to print them on his own account separately or collectively. In both these respects I have been robbed by this unjust practice, which many are unprincipled or inconsiderate enough to encourage by taking the pilfered produce in. The receiver of stolen goods is ranked with the thief." On another and subsequent occasion, Mr. Jay publicly alludes in one of his sermons to the same practice, thus: "I have been obliged to omit and abridge what I intended to deliver; but this can be rectified in the published discourse. I say published, for it does not depend upon the preacher whether it shall be published; he must do it in his own defence, as indecency and injustice will have stolen a *defective publication* for sale in a few hours:—the sale, indeed, was advertised before the sermon itself was prepared or delivered."

In what indignant terms of reprobation would Mr. Jay have expressed himself, had he been alive, at the barefaced manner in which a volume of what are termed his sermons was ushered into the world by a short-hand writer under a catching title! Whether this reporter had talent enough to take down *all* that the preacher said, or omitted any thing he *did* say, or added any thing out of his own brains or that of others, I do not know. All I can say on the subject is, that I have seen the sermons, and that they do not bear the impress of being in the language in which they were uttered from the pulpit. Ignorance is generally allied to cunning, which was exemplified in this person having had the indecency to send the first copy of the sermons to a member of Mr. Jay's family, who had the good sense, without the least deliberation, to return it immediately. It is somewhat doubtful whether the law can lay hold of this description of theft. I laid a statement connected with this publication before an eminent Queen's Counsel, who, after some consideration, said, that inasmuch as the law was uncertain (though I was of a different opinion), he advised me not to move in the matter, as it could easily be discovered whether the sermons were genuine or not.

Common sense points out that there are many words, expressions, and sentences delivered in extemporaneous discourses which a preacher would rather not see in print; and Mr. Jay, in allusion to this subject, said,—what was carrying the principle much higher,—that he never read any of his own printed works, for he well knew that he might have improved or altered them; a reflection which would have caused regret for what could not be remedied.

CHAPTER XXI.

Week-day evening services at Argyle Chapel—Barristers—Young the tragedian—Captain Wall—Sir Robert Inglis—Voltaire and Hallyburton contrasted.

There was a service held at Argyle Chapel every Thursday evening, which commenced punctually at seven, and concluded at eight o'clock to a minute; the singing and a short prayer being omitted if necessary, rather than it should exceed the hour. In consequence of this restriction of time, Mr. Jay had on these evenings a very large congregation, amongst whom were to be seen many noblemen, clergy, and others, visitors at Bath. He prepared as much for this service as he was accustomed to do for that of the Sunday; and always had the tea half an hour earlier on the table on this than any other day, so that he might have a greater time for retirement. The last time I and my brother-in-law, Mr. Ashton, attended this weekly service, we saw, on its conclusion, leaving the chapel Lord Godolphin, who for many years, prior to his accession to the peerage, was member of parliament for the county of Cambridge, and in the House of Commons was the most strenuous advocate for the repeal of the Test and Corporation Acts. His lordship, who was in the company of two or three gentlemen from Cambridge, beckoned to Mr. Ashton, and after shaking hands with him, said, "I have been living at Bath for the last two or three months, attending Lady Godolphin, in consequence of a cold caught in my yacht in the summer. She is using the baths. But, do you know, Mr. Ashton, I consider Bath is now so very dull a city, that if it had not been for Mr. Jay's preaching, I could not have remained so long in it. I do not think I have missed an opportunity of hearing him." When we arrived at Percy Place, Mr. Ashton mentioned this conversation to Mr. Jay, and described his lordship to him as being a very tall man. "Why," said Mr. Jay, "I have seen him in my chapel for the last three months, and could not tell who he was; but I observed that he listened very attentively to my discourses."

Mr. Jay was popular as a preacher amongst barristers, many of whom, including the late well-known Mr. Sergeant Pell, being in the habit, during the assizes, of attending at Argyle Chapel. This popularity was not confined to Bath, for many of the long robe formed part of the congregation at Surrey Chapel when he officiated there during his annual visits to London; and nearly the last time I had any conversation with the late Lord Truro, then the Attorney-General, he particularly inquired after Mr. Jay, and said that he had heard him frequently at that chapel with much delight.

The late Mr. Phillpotts, member of parliament for Gloucester, and brother to the Bishop of Exeter, told me that he and a number of gentlemen of the Oxford circuit formed part of Mr. Jay's congregation on the last Sunday he preached at Gloucester.

Speaking of Mr. Phillpotts, brings to my recollection the following anecdote, which he related to Mr. Jay: "I was one day walking with Dr. Ryder, then Bishop of Gloucester, through one of the streets of that city, when his lordship, observing Mr. Bishop the Independent minister, facetiously said, 'That gentleman is *Bishop* of Gloucester. He is a most respectable man, and has officiated in his chapel very many years.'" Mr. Jay ever afterwards addressed him in the inside of the letters he wrote to him as *Bishop of Gloucester*.

Mr. Jay being personally acquainted with a great many barristers, seemed to take an interest in their profession, and would occasionally, whenever any trials were going on, attend the law-courts; but he soon got tired of listening to the speeches of counsel and the examination of witnesses. During a long life he never was subpœnaed as a witness, or engaged in a law-suit. His wife was not quite so fortunate; for one day, prior to the assizes for Taunton, she was served with a subpœna to attend in court as a witness in a cause which was to be tried there within two days. Mr. Jay, seeing her much agitated by the service, said to her, "There is really nothing to be annoyed at. All that you have to do in the witness-box is to answer each question the counsel asks you with a simple *yes* or *no*, and never attempt to explain, or enter into any anecdote." No barrister could have given better advice than this; but Mrs. Jay, to her great delight, was not put to the ordeal of following it, the cause having been settled out of court.

One Sunday morning a gentleman of an intelligent and intellectual appearance was shown, before the commencement of the service, into a pew in Argyle Chapel, in which was seated the Rev. Thomas Wallis, a friend of Mr. Jay's. Mr. Wallis offered the stranger his hymn-book, and they both sang out of it together. The preacher's discourse, which was from the beautiful and touching request of the Psalmist, "Say unto my soul, Thou art my salvation," was listened to with the deepest attention and interest by the gentleman, who, at its close, observed to Mr. Wallis: "We have had an admirable sermon this morning. Mr. Jay wears well. I have heard him occasionally for more than thirty years." On the following morning Mr. Wallis called on Mr. Jay, who, in the course of conversation, said to him: "Do you know with whom you were worshiping on Sunday morning last, and who was singing out of your hymn-book?" "I was not aware that you observed us," was the reply. "O," said Mr. Jay, "I had my eyes upon the gentleman, who was no less a person than Charles Young the great tragedian. He often comes to hear me, and he is a very gentlemanly and intelligent man. He has been visiting the Bishop of Bath and Wells, and was, I suppose, stopping in the city."

Mr. Jay had never, during the whole course of a long life, been in a theatre; but there was to be found in his library the works of several of the great dramatists, with which he was well acquainted, particularly with those of Shakespeare; and he had heard of the great excellence of Charles Young in that actor's personifications of King Lear, Othello, Hamlet, Macbeth, and other characters.

I cannot speak of Charles Young without introducing the following instance of that celebrated tragedian's sympathy for misfortune and Christian benevolence, as related by a writer in *Bentley's Miscellany*, and which Mr. Jay brought under my notice: "Returning from the theatre one night, the tragedian was accosted by a female. There was something in the tone and manner of the woman that arrested his attention. After a few inquiries, he desired her to call on him next morning. She did so, and told her tale. It was one of heartless seduction, of estrangement of friends, and three nights upon the streets of London. The truth of this statement was ascertained, and she was placed by Mr. Young in a respectable home, with an annuity of 26*l.*, which was duly paid her for three-and-thirty years. She is dead now, but out of her little stipend of 10*s.* per week she had saved 18*l.* for sickness and her funeral expenses, and she died blessing her benefactor."

It is well known in the theatrical world that Bath was formerly the chief nursery of the stage, and that all the great actors of the day occasionally performed there. Indeed, there was scarcely an actor of celebrity visiting that city, either professionally or for pleasure, who was not to be seen at Argyle Chapel, listening with great attention to Mr. Jay's discourses. Mr. Cooper, the very eminent actor, who has been before the theatrical public for nearly forty years, and whom I frequently have the pleasure of meeting at a friend's house, informed me that whenever he visited Bath, which was for many weeks in every year, he attended Argyle Chapel. I mention this circumstance the more particularly from the fact of this gentleman having had greater experience in teaching elocution to the clergy of the Established Church than perhaps any other person, and from his having stated to me that he held up Mr. Jay in many respects as one of his models as a preacher.

General Wall, more commonly known to the public as Governor Wall, and as having been most unjustly executed through political motives upon a conviction for murder during the mutiny at the Nore, left a son, a most humorous and kind-hearted man, who was captain of one of the Highland regiments. The captain was often at Bath, and was acquainted with Mr. Jay, to whom he was so partial, that he always made it a point, whenever he was staying in that city, to attend every Sunday morning at Argyle Chapel. I remember the captain, on his return from one of his usual annual continental trips, making a call at Percy Place, while I was on a visit there, and keeping Mr. Jay in a continual state of laughter by his humorous anecdotes. Amongst other things, that which amused Mr. Jay the most was the captain's stating that when he travelled abroad he invariably took with him an *Army List*. "And I did so," said he, "because I fell in company at the different *tables-d'hôte* with persons who styled themselves colonels and captains. My plan with any one of these titled gentlemen whom I suspected to be an impostor was to inquire of him, before the assembled company, to what regiment he belonged. Upon receiving his answer, I would immediately pull out of my pocket an *Army List*, and casting my eye over it at the proper place, would reply, 'Why, my good sir, I do not see your name there.' It may easily be imagined that the self-dubbed officer was silenced, and that he took the first opportunity of making his exit from the hotel, for the purpose of becoming a guest at another where he could be less easily detected."

When the humorous captain had wound up this anecdote, I said to Mr. Jay: "I can testify to the truth of my friend's statement; for when I was at Rome, Florence, and other places on the Continent, I was often in his company, and heard him detect many persons in the manner he has described. Indeed, he thinned many hotels." Mr. Jay, turning round to me, archly said: "And what do you pass for amongst these grand officers?" "Certainly not," replied I, "as a colonel or captain, nor as a lawyer; but on several occasions, when the conversation was running close, and many of the company were boasting largely of their rank and pedigree, I said: 'Gentlemen, I am the son of a Dissenting minister at Bath, of the name of William Jay.' I found that this plan succeeded better for me than it did for the self-dubbed colonels and captains; for there were generally some of the company who knew you well, and I was, in consequence of your being my father, frequently invited to their private apartments. It was from being recognised as such at Florence by Sir Harry Inglis, M.P. for Oxford, that he inquired very kindly after you, and said that he had met you at the late Mr. Wilberforce's and the late Mr. Thornton's, and that he was a great admirer of your writings. This politeness on Sir Harry's part was not all. The next day he invited me to accompany him to a fête, or fair, held on one of the hills near that beautiful city on some religious festival, where I spent several pleasant hours in his society, and was delighted with his observations."

The worthy baronet having remarked to me during the course of conversation, "Why, this fête seems to be held more for the purpose of drinking and dancing than for a religious commemoration," I, in reply to his observation, stated that Mr. Jay had declared, in relation to our chief religious festivals, as follows: "It is lamentable to think how Christmas (I do not like the word, it is a popish word;—it means Christ's mass; and what have we to do with masses? Nothing, but to abhor them),—I say that it is lamentable to think how Christmas is kept; so that if a stranger were to come amongst us, he would think we were celebrating the birth of Bacchus. And how many are there who revive the works of the devil, which Christ was manifested to destroy! It is nothing better with regard to Whitsuntide. One might imagine we were celebrating the descent of intemperance, licentiousness, and disorder, rather than the descent of the Spirit of holiness and truth."

I remember being present at a conversation between Mr Jay and a religious friend, when the name of Voltaire came uppermost as the great antagonist of revealed truth. "Yes," said Mr. Jay; "but after all, he did not die game,—conscience made him a coward at the last. 'Men may live fools; but fools they cannot die.' The delusions of time perish at the approach of eternity. Little children always believe. Would that men were like them! Many, alas, doubt, deny their God and Saviour, and die in impenitence and apostasy. The infidel practically makes 'God a liar,' as the Apostle's phrase is."

At the time of this conversation, Mr. Jay was composing his *Morning Exercises*. In the evening he read one of them to us, wherein he quoted, from the works of Voltaire and the excellent and pious Hallyburton, passages as illustrative of the different views of human existence in the eyes of an infidel and Christian. These passages I will here quote:

"Who," says Voltaire, "can, without horror, consider the whole world as the empire of destruction? It abounds with wonders; it also abounds with victims. It is a vast field of carnage and contagion. Every species is without pity pursued and torn to pieces through the earth and air and water. In man there is more wretchedness than in all the other animals put together. He loves life, and yet he knows that he must die. If he enjoys a transient good, he suffers various evils, and is at last devoured by worms. This knowledge is his fatal prerogative: other animals have it not. He spends the transient moments of his existence in diffusing the miseries which he suffers,—in cutting the throats of his fellow-creatures for pay, in cheating and being cheated, in robbing and being robbed, in serving that he might command, and in repenting of all he does. The bulk of mankind are nothing more than a crowd of wretches equally criminal and unfortunate; and the globe contains rather carcasses than men. I tremble at the review of this dreadful picture to find that it contains a complaint against Providence itself; and *I wish I had never been born.*"

"I," says Hallyburton, "shall shortly get a very different sight of God from what I have ever had, and shall be made meet to praise Him for ever and ever. O, the thoughts of an incarnate Deity are sweet and ravishing! O, how I wonder at myself that I do not love Him more, and that I do not admire Him more! What a wonder that I enjoy such composure under all my bodily pains, and in the view of death itself! What a mercy that, having the use of my reason, I can declare his goodness to my soul! I long for his salvation; I bless his name. I have found Him, and die rejoicing in Him. O, blessed be God that *I was born!* O that *I* was where *He* is! I have a father, and mother, and ten brothers and sisters in heaven, and I shall be the eleventh. O, there is a telling in this Providence, and I shall be telling it for ever! If there be such a *glory* in his conduct towards me *now,* what will it be to *see the Lamb* in the midst of the throne! Blessed be God that ever *I was born!*"

CHAPTER XXII.

Mr. Jay at Sidmouth—The Isle of Wight and Lynmouth—Description of Lynmouth—His annual visits to Worthing—His avocations and mode of life at that watering-place—Mr. Hume, M.P.—Extract from one of Mr. Jay's discourses—Anecdotes.

MR. JAY'S labours as an author were, except within a very few years of his death, principally pursued at watering-places during a relaxation of a few weeks in summer. He gives the following interesting account of these labours in the last edition of the *Exercises.*

"At Sidmouth he began the *Domestic Minister's Assistant,* and wrote many of the family prayers. In the Isle of Wight he composed *A Charge to a Minister's Wife,* and the *Wife's Advocate.* At Lynmouth he finished his *Christian Contemplated,* and wrote the preface with *Hints on Preaching.*

"But the latter place must be a little more noticed. There, for several years successively, he passed a month, the most perfectly agreeable and happy he ever experienced in a life of lovingkindness and tender mercy.

"Linton and Lynmouth are nearly connected, the one being at the top and the other at the bottom of a declivity, covered with trees and verdure, interspersed with several houses. Linton has been remarked for its sublimity, and Lynmouth for its beauty, and their united aspects have been called Switzerland in miniature.

"Lynmouth was to the author the most interesting spot. Here two narrow and craggy valleys, obviously once ruptured by a convulsion of nature, terminate; and down these, tumbling from rock to rock, two streams—one running from the east, and the other from the south—unite, and then in a small distance empty themselves into the sea.

"At the time of his first going there, it was hardly known, or considered a watering-place. It had not as yet fallen into the corruptions of such receptacles; nor had its inhabitants been taught to make visitors a prey. The villagers were very respectful, and strangers felt a sense of safety.

"Here the author fixed his residence. He took a whole cottage: it was far from elegant, but it was neat and agreeable: it wanted some accommodation and comfort; but he had what he more prized, rural and enchanting scenery and solitude. Yet not without some to hear the exclamation, 'How sweet this solitude is!' for he had society too: his company was small, consisting of his wife and a female friend.

"The cottage we occupied has since been spoilt by improvements, and is now a kind of tawdry little mansion; and the whole village of Lynmouth itself, which taste might have altered and yet left it a village still, is aping a paltry town.

"Here our party found themselves at liberty to meet or separate, to read or to write, to converse or to walk, as inclination prompted. As to himself, the author opened his parlour, and spoke on the Sabbath-Day evening to any of the neighbours who would attend. But having been struck with the design, and having been urged to undertake something of the kind, he now began his *Morning Exercises*. Of these he often wrote two, and sometimes three a day, and always read one of them in the morning and another in the evening devotion, and not often without the approbation of his companions, which most excited and encouraged him to proceed.

"Here he composed the greater part of these *Morning Exercises*, and here also, in after visits, he wrote the greater part of the *Evening*."

Mr. Jay, for the last twenty years of his life, was in the habit, during the months of July and August, of spending six weeks at Worthing; a locality which he chose partly from its being a very retired watering-place, and partly from its being a convenient spot where he could meet his son, who resided in London, and his daughter and son-in-law (Mr. and Mrs. Ashton), who resided at Cambridge. At these visits Mr. Jay gave himself up entirely to relaxation. He was always to be seen rambling by the sea-side as early as five o'clock in the morning, watching the fishing-boats as they came in, and entering into conversation with the fishermen. At seven o'clock precisely he was at the breakfast-table, and after breakfast there was family worship. The morning was spent in reading, or by a walk. At one o'clock dinner was on table. At the conclusion of this meal he invariably took a short nap, after which one of the party would read to him some interesting new publication. He partook of tea at five o'clock, and when it was finished would stroll either on the downs or through the woods and lanes. There was family worship at nine o'clock, at the conclusion of which he, after a short conversation, retired to rest, leaving his family and guests to themselves. In fact, his habits of life at this sea-side retreat were pretty much the same as they were at Percy Place.

It is incredible the number of volumes read by or to Mr. Jay during these annual visits to Worthing, including every variety of subject. If a work did not interest him, he was not a good listener, as the following incident will show. The late Captain Maryatt, who wrote several nautical tales, and who was a client of mine, gave me his last work before he went to America, which I took down with me to Worthing. One morning, on my return from a walk before dinner, I found that Mr. Ashton was reading it aloud to the whole party, they evidently all seeming to enjoy it but Mr. Jay. After a little while I said that I should take another walk, upon which Mr. Jay rose from his seat, and said, "So will I, for I cannot stand it any longer." When he got into the open air, he expressed himself greatly pleased at what he termed my having come to his rescue.

Mr. Jay, on his first visit to Worthing, found the little chapel there but thinly attended. Its minister, who had been a student at Dr. Bogue's academy at Gosport, was not by any means popular, although possessed of good talents. Out of a small income the minister had to support himself, a sick wife, and a large family. It was interesting to see how Mr. Jay endeavoured to assist him; and he consented to preach at the chapel the first Sunday after his first visit at that place, on condition that a collection should be made for the minister's support. This was agreed to, and the chapel was crowded to excess by visitors staying at that watering-place. Some persons, friends of

Mr. Jay's, held the plates, and to the surprise and gratification of the minister more than 20*l.* was collected, whereas the usual collections hardly amounted to so many shillings. This act of kindness Mr. Jay repeated twice during every visit to Worthing, so long as this minister resided there. After he left, two other ministers in succession settled over the congregation, each of whom subsequently entered into holy orders in the Established Church, one being ordained by the Bishop of Chichester, and the other by the Bishop of Exeter. On one of these occasions I sat in the same pew with the late Joseph Hume, M.P., and, at the conclusion of the sermon, I heard him express to the lady who accompanied him the great gratification he had experienced in listening to Mr. Jay's discourse. I followed this celebrated economist out of the chapel, and, to my great astonishment, I found that upon this occasion at least he did not study economy, for he slipped into the plate a sovereign with much evident satisfaction.

Whenever it was known at Worthing that Mr. Jay was to preach, the chapel was sure to be crowded to excess, not only by the inhabitants of the place, but by its fashionable visitors. The sermon which Mr. Hume heard was from this text: "And he went and beheaded John in prison," upon which text he wrote one of his Evening Exercises. In this sermon, after alluding to the character of John, and giving the history of his life, and of his early and violent death through the revenge of Herodias, in having, with unflinching fidelity, reproved Herod for having had a criminal intrigue with her who was his brother's wife, and fearlessly telling him that kings were no more above the law than their subjects, thus strikingly spoke of the woman and her daughter, in language which much arrested the attention of Mr. Hume: "Nothing can equal the revenge, the restlessness, and the cunning of an imperious whorish woman. With her, when there is a will, a way will soon follow. Herodias seizes an opportunity for her foul purpose on the king's birthday: she introduces her daughter to dance,—the dance, it is presumed, is what they now call waltzing. It excited and charmed Herod, whereupon he promised with an oath to give her whatsoever she should ask. And she, being instructed of her mother, said, 'Give me here John Baptist's head in a charger.' And the king was sorry; nevertheless, for his oath's sake and them which sat with him at meat, he commanded it to be given to her. Not a person present, male or female, interposed one word in his behalf. The barbarous deed was done without even the form of a trial,—done privately, and in prison. Perhaps John was praying, perhaps sleeping, when the executioner arrived. But he was ready for the event, and the axe would only release him into the glorious liberty of the sons of God. Yet the head, the veins bleeding, the hair clotted with gore, the eyes all wan and half opened, was brought in a charger, and given to the damsel, and she brought it to her mother, who, according to Josephus, stuck the tongue full of needles, (what tenderness and delicacy!)—and yet these females often affected to tremble at the shaking of a leaf. But there is no ground for general reflections here. A virtuous woman need not feel herself dishonoured by wretches who have disowned her sex and renounced their very nature. Two things the disciples did: they took up the body and buried it. Whether the head was returned for interment with the body, or whether the ladies kept it for further insult, we know not; but doubtless the disciples obtained it if they could."

For the first few years of Mr. Jay's annual visits to Worthing, the rector of Broadwater and prebendary of Chichester, the Rev. Peter Wood, whose lady prior to her marriage Mr. Jay had met at Mrs. Hannah More's, always called and left his card upon each arrival, and Mr. Jay acknowledged this mark of attention by returning the call. For the last few years the rector neglected to perform this act of courtesy, but for what reason Mr. Jay could never ascertain.

Walking one day with Mr. Jay, he, pointing to a neat tenement, said, "Do you see that house? You must know that its owner married one of Mr. Wood's servants, in whose family she had resided as lady's-maid for many years, and was highly respected by him and his lady. This female, who was brought up at Bath, of which city she was a native, was much attached to my preaching. The rector, after performing the marriage-service, inquired of her where she was going to pass the honeymoon. 'At Bath, sir,' was the reply. 'Well,' said the rector, 'I have one request to make to you, which is, that you do not go to Argyle Chapel next Sunday to hear Mr. Jay preach.' She smiled, but made no answer. On the Sunday morning she attended my chapel, and, to her astonishment, she saw sitting before her her master the rector. I do not think he cared in the least about her attending to hear me preach; but knowing that he should be in Bath that Sunday, and that it was his intention to be present at my chapel, he without doubt did not wish that his late servant should know that he had formed part of a Dissenting minister's congregation, he being a very strict Churchman."

During Mr. Jay's final visit to Worthing, I remember his reading with much interest the *Life of Southey,* a work which raised the poet higher than ever in his estimation. He had met Mr. Southey some years before at Worthing, and was intimately acquainted with that poet's friend, Mr. Cottle, a bookseller and poet of Bristol, who, by the way, was the early patron of Coleridge, whose life he wrote. Mr. Jay was on terms of friendship with Mr. Cottle, and usually slept at that gentleman's house whenever he had occasion to go to Worthing. I also remember his reading here, at this or some prior visit, the *Duke of Wellington's Despatches,* edited by Colonel Gurwood, which he very much admired. I mention this circumstance in order to introduce the following anecdote: I one day accompanied Mr. Jay to make a return-visit to Mr. Secondary James, then residing at this watering-place. The conversation turning upon the subject of these despatches, the Secondary remarked, that if the name of God had been oftener used in them, he should have liked them much better; whereupon Mr. Jay instantly rejoined: "By no means do I agree with you. The less that the name of God is mentioned in relation to battles the better."

Mr. Jay listened with great attention to the *History of England,* by Macaulay, in two volumes, which the late Mr. Ashton (a most excellent reader) read aloud to him and the whole family-party, finishing the task in three days. I remember Mr. Jay calling

Mr. Ashton one morning down-stairs as early as five o'clock, saying, "I must have some more of that history directly." Mr. Ashton soon made his appearance, and cheerfully continued the reading until breakfast-time, and again resumed it after that repast. Mr. Jay said that Macaulay's history, taken as a whole, had interested him more than any work of that class ever had. He was a great admirer of the articles written by him in the *Edinburgh Review*, and more particularly his review on Milton. Both Mr. Macaulay (now Lord Macaulay) and his father had been hearers of Mr. Jay.

CHAPTER XXIII.

Mr. Jay preaches for the Wesleyans an annual missionary sermon in London — Also preaches for them at Bath — His observations on them and on psalmody — Rev. Richard Watson — Dr. Bunting — An account of the commemoration of the fiftieth year of Mr. Jay's pastorate over Argyle Chapel — The poets James and Robert Montgomery.

Mr. Jay was on friendly terms with the gentlemen of the Methodist connection who went the Bath circuit; and from having been personally acquainted with Mr. Wesley and the earlier preachers, he was much sought after by them. He was the first minister, I believe, in England, not belonging to their connection, who was selected to preach their annual Missionary Society sermon at their large chapel in Great Queen Street, Lincoln's-Inn Fields. I accompanied him there, and left him in the vestry. There was a very crowded audience, an excellent sermon, and a large collection. At the conclusion of the service, I called for him, by his desire, at the vestry. He appeared anxious to take leave of the ministers as speedily as he could. I accompanied him to the lady's house where he was staying, and on the road he expressed his surprise at their tallness and fine healthy appearance, saying that they put him in mind of Life-guardsmen dressed in black. He made the same observation at the dinner-table of his hostess, saying that the celebrated preacher, Mr. Newton, a fine tall man, would give her some idea of their height. The conversation turning upon Richard Watson, their celebrated minister, Mr. Jay said that he considered him in the pulpit not only vigorous, but profound; and that his *Sermons, Biography, Conversations for the Young,* and *Expositions* showed him also to have been a great man. "He was," added Mr. Jay, "a most indefatigable secretary to the Wesleyan Missionary Society, into which he threw the whole of his energies. By his death the Wesleyans lost their most distinguished member."

I should mention that, on a subsequent occasion, Mr. Jay was requested by the president of the conference of the Wesleyans at Bath to preach the opening service in that city on the Sunday morning, he (the president) reading the prayers.

When Mr. Jay began to appear in public, a number of the original converts of Wesley were yet living, some of whom he knew intimately, and who made an impression on him not to be forgotten. "They were," said he, "certainly better acquainted with and more endeared to each other than the larger proportion of professors now are. . . . . . I was also much struck with their general freedom from the fear of death. They never seemed unwilling to be reminded of its approach. They spoke of it with pleasure; and in conversing with their dying friends, they appeared concerned to reconcile them to the thought of *recovery* (should this be the event) rather than to their dissolution."

Mr. Jay, in a preface to a volume of hymns which he had collected as an appendix to Dr. Watts (many of which were his own composition, although he does not affix his name to them), speaking of the Wesleyans as the true founders of pure psalmody, said: "They were a band of heralds, whose hearts the Lord had touched; and they flew like angels, having the everlasting Gospel to preach unto them that dwell upon the earth. They roused a slumbering nation, called the attention to the truth as it is in Jesus, and commenced a revival of evangelical religion, from which Churchmen and Dissenters have derived advantages for which they should not be ashamed to be thankful. The leaders in this work also understood human nature; and, like Calvin and Luther in the Reformation abroad, they did almost as much by their psalmody as by their preaching. They rescued singing from the usual drawling of the clerk in the desk, or the insulated conceit of the choir in the gallery. They electrified and engaged the *people,*—*all* the people. Their singing was popular; their tunes and their hymns were popular. Some of the tunes, and many of the hymns by which they did such execution, have come down to us. The generation is now gone which witnessed their first efforts. Yet the words took hold of their successors, and there are many who now feel from them very early and powerful recollections."

With the late well-known Dr. Bunting, who was often at Bath, having married a lady from Bradford, Mr. Jay was on terms of intimacy. The doctor, when not preaching at the Methodist chapel in that city, was a frequenter of Argyle Chapel. I was a visitor at Percy Place a year or two before Mr. Jay's death, and one evening I accompanied him to hear the doctor preach. The text selected was from the fourth chapter of the first Epistle of Peter, and the sixteenth verse, being the same text as that of a published sermon of Mr. Jay's under the title of *The Christian*. He listened most attentively to the discourse, which he greatly admired both as to style and delivery, but considered that it was wanting in simplicity;—in fact, Mr. Jay was so accustomed to what was plain and chaste, that he disliked, in language, that which was over-painted or elaborated.

Mr. Jay's sermon of *The Christian*, to which I have incidentally alluded, was published at the request of his second wife, and he therein refers to the death of her only brother through an accident, whom he describes as a young man of good talents, and who had feared the Lord from his youth. "He was never," said Mr. Jay, "more in his element than when he was doing good. On the morning of his death he had gone over to a neighbouring village to endeavour to reconcile two individuals who had been at variance. He had succeeded according to his wishes, and was returning; but as he mounted his horse, the animal started; he was thrown to the ground, and after a few hours of unconsciousness, expired. Is it true that the path of duty is the path of safety? That in keeping His commandments there is great reward? That blessed are the peacemakers, for they shall be called the sons of God? It *is* true."

It was on the 30th day of January 1841 that Mr. Jay completed the fiftieth year of his pastorate over Argyle Chapel.

The members of his church and congregation, as well as a wide circle of friends, being desirous of celebrating an event to which they looked forward with much interest, in an appropriate manner, lost no time in setting on foot a subscription, in order to present him with a purse of money as a tribute of Christian esteem, affection, and gratitude for his long and zealous service as their minister. The sum of 650*l.* was soon collected.

Mr. Jay, in the bosom of his own family, expressed his averseness to accept a pecuniary offering, alleging that its appropriation to a charity would be the more fitting way of applying it. It was urged by his family that the subscribers intended it for his own personal benefit; that divines of the Church of England frequently received such tokens of affection from their congregations; that the length of his pastorate demanded a pecuniary recompense; and that he had zealously devoted his whole energies in the service of a church which had not its prizes like those of the Established Church. These arguments at length overcame his scruples, with one sole reservation, in which his family acquiesced. "There is," said he, "one who is dear to all of us, and who has had the hand of suffering upon her for many years. It is my dear wife,—your mother. My wants are few; but that is no reason why hers should be restricted. The money shall be hers, for her service and comfort. I wish her not to know of my resolve until I can present it to her with my own hand."

After this digression, I will now return back to the celebration of the jubilee.

The first meeting—one for devotion—was held on Sunday January 31, 1841, at Argyle Chapel, at seven o'clock, when thanksgiving and prayers were offered. At eleven o'clock public service was held in the chapel, and Mr. Jay preached from the text, "What is our hope, or joy, or crown of rejoicing? Are not even ye in the presence of our Lord Jesus Christ at his coming?" The sermon contained highly interesting instruction addressed to the disciples of the Gospel under the different classes of those who *encourage*, those who *solace*, and those who *dignify* ministers. After the general discussion of the text, the preacher entered into a detail of the circumstances which led to his settlement at Bath, and a review of his lengthened ministry.

On the evening of the same day, the Rev. Mr. East, then of Birmingham, delivered a very appropriate discourse from the text, "They that turn many to righteousness shall shine as the stars for ever and ever." Thus terminated the proceedings of the day.

On Tuesday morning following, a public breakfast took place at the Assembly Rooms. The number of persons present was 820, the ministers attending both from the city and neighbourhood. Henry Godwin, Esq. was called to the chair.

This gentleman, after making very sensible and appropriate observations on the occasion, read before the meeting a touching and feeling address, from the members of the church and congregation, to Mr. Jay, and at its conclusion offered to him on their behalf an elegant silver salver, and purse containing 650*l.*, as a token of their united affection and gratitude.

After the presentation, Mr. Jay, who was surrounded by his wife and all the members of his family then in England, addressed the assembly in a suitable speech, in the course of which he expressed himself thus: "I should be sorry if any had been led to imagine, because I had been generally successful in life, that I had now well feathered a nest for myself, or for one dearer to me than myself. But I can glory in saying that such is not the case. While, therefore, with regard to the pecuniary part of this oblation, I am not at a loss to employ it, especially relatively and prospectively, yet it is not with this that I am principally impressed. 'How long have I to live, that I should go up to the king to Jerusalem?' I hope providence and grace have taught me, in whatever state I have been, therewith to be content. Nor can I expect to derive any immediate comfort from this present; but as a testimony of respect and approbation I exceedingly prize it; and there are few things which could have afforded me more pleasure, considering the principle from which the gift has sprung, and the various expressions of esteem and regard with which it has been accompanied. I feel also the unsectarian nature of the boon, as it has come from Churchmen and Dissenters, and from the various religious parties for whom I have often preached, and for whom I always prayed, saying, 'Grace be with all them that love our Lord Jesus Christ in sincerity;' for 'whosoever shall do the will of my Father which is in heaven, the same is my mother, and sister, and brother.' From the rank and office of some of the contributors in church and state, perhaps it may be expected that there should be a more distinct acknowledgment. I am very willing to render to them the praise which is their due; but you will allow me to say, I have been most affected with the poor of my flock; and nothing will so long remain written on the fleshly table of my heart as the generosity of one individual who presented sixpence to one of my deacons, adding, 'I only wish it were a hundred pounds.' I have only one thing more to add. I take this purse, and present it to you, madam," (addressing Mrs. Jay, in whose hands he placed it, amidst the warm applause of the company); "I present it to you, madam, who have always kept my purse, and therefore it has been so well kept. Consider it as entirely sacred to your pleasure, your use, your service, your comfort. I know this has been perfectly unexpected by you, but it is also perfectly deserved by you." And then turning to the assembly, he finished his address by pronouncing a well-merited eulogium on his wife.

The younger members of the congregation having determined to take part in the celebration, presented their pastor with a handsome gold medal and a silver salver. On the one side of the medal was a likeness of Mr. Jay, with the following inscription: "The Rev. William Jay completed a pastorate of fifty years January 30, 1841." On the reverse of the medal was the front elevation of Argyle Chapel, with the inscription, "Argyle Chapel, Bath, erected 1789,—first enlargement 1804,—second enlargement 1821." The salver bears the following inscription: "The juvenile members of the church and congregation of Argyle Chapel present this salver, bearing a gold medal commemorative of the event, as a tribute of affection to their highly esteemed pastor the Rev. William Jay, on the completion of the jubilee of his ministerial labours, with the sincere hope that he may long be spared to them as their shepherd. Bath, 30th January 1841."

James Montgomery (the Sheffield poet), whose long friendship Mr. Jay cherished in a high degree, and who had often been his hearer and admirer, composed two hymns in commemoration of the jubilee, which were sung at the conclusion of the presentation-meeting. The committee having sent the poet, by way of acknowledgment, a jubilee medallion, he, in a letter to their chairman, Mr. Godwin, after expressing his thanks for the gift, says in relation thereto: "The workmanship seems admirable, the likeness of your pastor excellent, and the simple register of dates on either side the most appropriate of inscriptions in such a case." I make this quotation solely because the poet was well acquainted with Mr. Jay's countenance, and understood the merit of a medallion, having resided in Sheffield the greater part of his life; and I can also certify that, notwithstanding the many paintings, prints, and busts of Mr. Jay, the medallion, although executed in metal, is the best likeness of him. Speaking of James Montgomery as a poet, I have heard Mr. Jay say, "How I value his poetry, particularly his hymns and lyrical pieces, with the excellency of which few can compete! He will be admired as long as the English language shall endure, or Christianity be loved." This good man, in early life, suffered imprisonment for a political libel; and he solaced his captivity, as he informed Mr. Jay, by the composition of poetry and a novel, the latter of which he subsequently burnt,—a circumstance much to be regretted, as no doubt it would have ranked in reputation with *Cœlebs in Search of a Wife*, by Mrs. Hannah More; "for it was impossible," said Mr. Jay, "that such a work from the poet's hands could have any other than a moral tendency."

I will now say a few words about the other poet

of the same name (Robert), with whom Mr. Jay was well acquainted. He was born at Bath, where he resided many years. During his residence in that city he attended Mr. Jay's ministry; and I have often seen him, after the conclusion of the Thursday night's service, return homewards with the preacher, they residing in the same direction. It may not be generally known to the public that the name of the poet's father was Gomery, who was for many years the box-office keeper at the Bath Theatre, and who, as report says, had at one time been a celebrated theatrical clown, and in his boyhood a companion of Grimaldi. Whether the name was an assumed one, as is usual on the stage, whilst his real name was Montgomery, or whether the son elongated the true name into Montgomery, were questions which Mr. Jay was unable to solve, although the poet himself declared that his father was the son, or grandson, of the General Montgomery who figured in the American war. Yet there is a great doubt on the subject: he may have been a legal or natural descendant. Be that as it may, I have ascertained that the poet was christened in 1807, under the name of Montgomery, at the pretty little village of Weston, now almost forming part of Bath, clearly proving that the story of *his* having *assumed* the name by which he has become known to public has no foundation in fact. Mr. Jay was of opinion that Robert Montgomery, both as preacher and poet, had gained sufficient fame, without the aid of ancestral honours; and although no very great admirer of his friend's poetry, he thought that however able Mr. Macaulay's review of it was, yet it was too severe.

But to return again for a few moments to the clown: did he always go under the name of *Gomery?* I ask this question the more particularly because, in my researches to clear up that point, my eye lighted upon a number of the *Globe* newspaper of the 26th of December 1806, wherein it was announced, that a *Mr. Montgomery* would make his *first* appearance on the boards of Drury Lane Theatre as Urchin the Clown in a new comic opera, entitled *The Enchantress, or Harlequin Sultain.* Who of the present day could believe that in this self-same journal there should appear such a paragraph as the following in justification of assassination: "There are many full-length *portraits* of Bonaparte. The artist who should make a *bust* of him would deserve well of mankind."

CHAPTER XXIV.

The death of Mr. Jay's Sister, and a brief account of her family—The Tisbury curate—The deaths of Mr. Jay's daughter Statira, Grandson, eldest Son, Granddaughter, and Wife.

The first domestic affliction which befell Mr. Jay after his marriage was the death of his favourite sister, Mrs. Coombes, whom he described as having been possessed of considerable wit and cleverness. She was, moreover, a handsome woman; but what is far better than that, a kind one, as I can vouch, having been frequently in her company in my youthful days. She died, after a long and happy union with her husband, a man of property, not at a very advanced age. I was at Bath when the news of her decease arrived, which greatly affected Mr. Jay, who, on the following Sunday, alluded to the event in his sermon.

I will now say a few words about Mr. Coombes and his family, and of Mr. Jay's visits to that gentleman's house at Tisbury.

Mr. Coombes was a fine, tall, and intelligent man, and understood the science of draining and water-courses better perhaps than any other person in the county of Wilts, and was always consulted in such matters by Mr. Beckford of Fonthill Abbey, and Mr. Bennet, M.P. He was possessed of property, and was the proprietor of a large flour-mill and an adjoining residence, beautifully situated by a clear stream abounding with fish of various kinds. Mr. Jay enjoyed his visits at Mr. Coombes's residence more than he did at any other place. I and my late brother William (then both of us young) were often his companions there. During such visits he would frequently, on a spring or summer's morning, go out angling,—his favourite amusement,—and on his return would spend some time in studying or writing. He was quite delighted to observe, after tea was concluded, the fine young sons of his sister pursuing their algebraical and mathematical studies; and he never visited Tisbury without presenting them with books upon those subjects. It was with a peculiar pleasure that he preached in his native village; and whenever he did so, the chapel was sure to be crowded with men wearing smock-frocks, and women wearing red cloaks. Mr. Coombes and all his family regularly attended the Dissenting chapel at Tisbury. One evening, the curate of the parish (a poor man with a large family), who entertained a great hatred of Dissenters, entered the Independent chapel of that place whilst the minister was preaching, and, after blowing a horn, tried to put out the lights. A statement of this occurrence having been forwarded to Mr. Wilkes of London, the solicitor for the protection of religious liberty, that gentleman immediately indicted the curate, who, upon the evidence of Mr. Coombes's sons and other witnesses, was found guilty, at the Salisbury assizes, of the offence charged against him, and sentenced to an imprisonment of twelve months in the Queen's Bench Prison. After the curate's removal to the Bench, Mr. Jay, out of a feeling of compassion towards the large family he had left behind him at Tisbury, signed a petition for his release. Having received a letter from Mr. Jay requesting me to call without loss of time on Mr. Wilkes, to see whether I could not procure his influence to carry out the object of the prayer of the petition, I did so, accompanied by the curate's son. That gentleman, whom I well knew, said he would back the application by every means in his power. The petition was no sooner presented than the punishment was remitted, and, as I thought at the time, principally through Mr. Jay's signature.

The second domestic affliction which occurred in Mr. Jay's family was the decease of his daughter Statira, his youngest child, in the month of August 1820. It was the first time that death had entered his happy dwelling at Percy Place. Until then he knew not the full extent of a parent's feelings. In alluding to this bereavement in his Autobiography, he says: "I left her in perfect health to go and preach at the opening of a new chapel at Tavistock in Devonshire; but I had not proceeded further than Totness, before a messenger overtook me with foreboding intelligence. I hastened back, in anxious trembling suspense, only just in time to see her dying of typhus fever. She was incapable of knowing the father around whose neck she had so often hung. I turned away, and was led by her mother into the solitude of my study. We kneeled down, hand in hand, to pray; but not a word we uttered. At such a season how poor is speech! and how surprising it is that persons should employ it, and not yield to the devotion of silence and tears! . . . . . One thing I perfectly remember as arising from our affliction. Though I was not wanting in love to my wife before, yet now I felt her the more singularly endeared. No thought of her seemed so sacred and tender as that of the mother of my beloved and glorified daughter; and so I commonly addressed her in my letters."

The senior deacon of Argyle Chapel, a rough but good man, on hearing of Mr. Jay's bereavement, called at Percy Place to offer his condolence; but seeing his pastor in a state of deep despondency, he slapped him on the back, saying: "Why, my good sir, you have been all your life comforting others under affliction; but now that it has overtaken you, it appears that you are quite unable to perform the same office for yourself." Mr. Jay felt the rebuke.

I should here mention, that my late sister was named Statira after a lady of the name of Pool, who some years after her widowhood was united to an eminent barrister of the name of Smith, the father of the author of the *Rejected Addresses*. This second marriage took place at Bath, and Mr. Jay gave the lady away. At the time of my sister's death she had nearly completed the translation of a volume of sermons from the German, which Mr. Jay highly estimated, and intended to edit it and write a preface.

Some years afterwards, Mr. Jay received intelligence of the death of a little grandson of his at the Mauritius, of the name of William Jay, whose father (an architect) held a government appointment in that colony. His affectionate and amiable mother wrote a small but interesting tract on the occasion, entitled *Little Willy; a widowed Mother's Memorial of a beloved Child*. The tract having had a great sale, and a second edition being required, Mr. Jay, upon the solicitation of his daughter-in-law, wrote, in a style of great simplicity, a few lines by way of preface, wherein he says: "A small house should not have a large porch. I therefore only observe that no one will greatly wonder at my readily yielding, when it is known that the lovely infant was my own grandson; and that I am persuaded, though it was written with a maternal pen, there is nothing in the narrative but the words of truth and soberness. An infant more attractive, more engaging, more intelligent, and more pious, as far as piety could display itself in such childhood, I have never seen. Some of this estimate I might have suspected was owing to relative partiality, had not the same opinion been entertained and expressed by all who had opportunities to remark." The narrative went through several editions, the preface giving it currency.

It was about two years after the death of "Little Willy" that Mr. Jay received, whilst at Worthing, a letter from the Mauritius announcing the death of his eldest son William in that colony; a man who, besides possessing great talents as an architect, was of a most amiable disposition. Although much affected by the intelligence, he did not appear to exhibit the same intense feeling of grief as he did upon the death of his daughter Statira; but this might have been the effect of his son's absence from England (a period of more than three years), and of his own increasing age. His son was buried by the side of Mrs. Newall, the wife of the American missionary, in the same grave where repose the remains of his child "Little Willy." After the decease of her husband, Mrs. William Jay returned to England with a youthful son and daughter. The son (Ernest Jay), who lately left the Dissenting College at St. John's Wood, is now settled at Stockport over a large congregation there, with whom he is very popular.

The next death which occurred in Mr. Jay's family much affected him. It was that of a much-loved granddaughter, Abbey Bolton, a young lady of great piety and talent, who died of consumption at Pelham Priory, near New York, in 1849, at the early age of twenty-two, shortly after her return to America (where her father then resided) from a visit to this country, whither she had come as well for the benefit of her health as to meet many dear relatives. The closing scenes of her life have been presented to the public by a sister of hers in a little volume entitled *The Lighted Valley*. It is elegantly and touchingly written, and there is an excellent preface to it from the pen of Mr. Jay. It has found much favour from the public, and has passed through several editions

Abbey Bolton's chief delight, during her visit to England, was to listen to the discourses of her much-loved grandfather. "No one," said she, "can possibly imagine our feelings, when the venerable silvery head appeared in the pulpit, and then bent in silent prayer. The expression with which he reads is wonderful; his words distil as the dew,—so softly, yet so effectually do they fall. His manner of emphasising some passages merely, gives you an entirely new view of them."

The next death which occurred in Mr. Jay's family during his lifetime was that of his wife, who departed this life in the year 1845, at the advanced age of seventy-nine years. As I have at the conclusion of the second chapter of these Recollections set forth Mr. Jay's recorded opinion of my mother's character, it absolves me from the necessity of making any observation other than this,—that the husband had not over-painted the character of the wife to whom he had been united for the long period of fifty-four years. For the first thirty years of the marriage my mother was in the enjoyment of continual good health; but illness overtook her in 1830, the effects of which acting upon her nervous system paralysed her faculties, which, though slightly affected at first, became gradually stronger as age produced greater weakness. For the last few years of her life, although she had a proper apprehension of most things, yet she expressed herself in a manner very imperfect. Her speech was not incoherent as to ideas, but singular as to phraseology. Thus, she spoke of a *drop* of bread, and a *thin bit* of water. She often complained that, although she knew every thing, she could not command the right words. To relieve her embarrassment, she ingeniously had written for her, by her own desire, the names of a number of persons and things of which she was likely to speak; and often after a pause or effort she would refer to the little book, which she always carried about with her. Mr. Jay, speaking of her infirm and dependent condition, said, that she needed and occupied much of his attention, but that such attention endeared her the more to him.

Her death was an event which could take none of her family by surprise. When informed of the probability of her approaching dissolution, I lost no time in taking my departure for Percy Place, and arrived there a few hours after my mother's decease. Mr. Jay having requested me to go up-stairs to see her after death, I positively refused, saying that my recollections of her were so pleasing and happy, that nothing should induce me to have them erased from my memory. Upon which Mr. Jay, bursting into tears, said: "I think you are right, Cyrus; and I wish I had adopted and acted upon the same resolution as you have."

My mother was buried in a vault wherein reposed the remains of her daughter Statira; on whose decease Mr. Jay wrote a touching letter to the deacons of Argyle Chapel, in which he solicited them in the words of Abraham: "Give me a place where I may bury my dead." They gave him a vault under the burying-ground house; so that he stood upon his own tomb whenever he addressed the large audiences there.

CHAPTER XXV.

The female Servant and the Mechanic—Mary Rogers—Cleaving wood—Lodging-house servants—Cooper the novelist—The garden at Percy Place—Advice to Mistresses in their conduct towards Servants—Mary Upstal.

One day I was walking out in the Strand accompanied by Mr. Jay, when he directed my attention to what is so common in London that it is seldom noticed, viz. to a working mechanic, worn out by the toils of the day, carrying on his shoulders a box for a servant-girl, who was evidently going to a new place. "How I feel for that poor girl!" said he; "who knows what she has had to endure in her last situation, or whether she was not obliged to leave it from the vulgarity or harshness of some upstart mistress? Perhaps she is going to a fresh situation, where she will enter upon her duties a complete stranger to the whole household, little dreaming of what she may have to endure from the cruelty, temper, whims, and caprice of a new mistress. What a good-hearted man," continued he, "is that overworked mechanic, who undertakes, after his daily labour, to perform, without fee or reward, so kind an office for her! You observe that there is no conversation passing between them; the poor man is intent upon taking care of the box, which contains all she possesses; whilst she appears all anxiety and timidity, but not in respect of that box, which she knows is in safe keeping in the custody of her kind-hearted companion. How different it would have been had you observed her at a railway-station, where porters are paid for taking charge of the luggage! She never would have taken her eye off the box until she saw it safely deposited in the train."

His sympathy for female servants was not confined to mere expressions, he being in his own person a kind and considerate master. The consequence was, that his domestics performed their duties with cheerfulness, alacrity, and fidelity, and never sought a change of situation, thereby becoming as it were part and parcel of the household. I have often heard him declare, with much feeling, that the most interesting testimony which he had ever received during his pastorate at Argyle Chapel was the presentation to him of a silver sugar-basin, in the early part of the year 1846, by the female servants of his congregation, out of their united contributions through the hands of his long-attached, ancient, and venerable servant Mary Rogers, who is still living, and mourning the loss of her beloved master. In a letter which he sent to this faithful domestic, acknowledging the tribute of affection and regard towards him, he said that from no class could the offering have been so welcome, and desired each of the female donors to accept in return one of his publications, inscribed with their names and that of his own, as a memento of him when the lips upon which they then hung should be silent in the grave.

At the back of Mr. Jay's house in Percy Place there was a paved yard, which was separated from the garden by a low wall. It was here that, for many years of the earlier part of his life, he employed himself almost every fine morning, even after a walk, by cleaving into pieces, with a mallet and wedges, large roots of old trees, which were made a present to him by a gentleman of landed property; he considering that exercise of some sort before breakfast was conducive to health. During the latter years of his life, when cleaving the roots became somewhat too laborious an occupation for him, the same gentleman supplied him in lieu thereof with limbs of fir and other trees, which he, after sawing in lengths of about a foot each, split with a hatchet into thin pieces for lighting the fires. This being his almost daily occupation, there was always a large quantity of this wood (which he with his own hands deposited, in different piles, in one of the outhouses) ready for use.

I recollect one morning, when I was in the outhouse with him, that he called out to a new servant, —a young girl, who had only been in his house for a few days, and who during this brief period had been continually breaking china, crockery, and other articles, probably through a high flow of spirits,—that he wanted to speak to her. She no sooner made her appearance than, after telling her which pile of wood she was to use first, he pointed to an empty bin in the outhouse, and drily said, "Here you may throw your broken crockery," upon which both of them laughed. Strange to say, the reproof had its full effect; for the servant, who was highly esteemed by the family, and who was with them many years, never afterwards broke any thing.

After the servant left the outhouse, we went into the garden; and in walking up and down it, I gave

Mr. Jay a description of some London servants, particularly in lodging-houses, where reproof would be a waste of words. "I lodged," I told him, "during my articles, at a house in Beaufort Buildings, when one morning I heard a tremendous crash, and at the same time the landlady calling out at the top of her voice, 'Rebecca, what's that noise?' who instantly and coolly replied, 'It is only a row of plates broken.' This is merely a sample of the unconcern of many of these lodging-house servants, who become hardened by hard work; for seldom does a lodging-house keeper have more than one servant in her employ. All the lodgers generally want their boots cleaned and their meals ready at the same hour; and the servant, after performing this part of her duty, has to go through the drudgery of the general work of the house, for the most part unassisted."

I then told him the following anecdote: Cooper the novelist took lodgings in Warwick Court, where all the lodgers required the same thing at the same time. On the first day he rang for some hot water for his tea. When brought up to him, which was some time after it had been ordered, he said, "*Thank you,*" upon which the girl appeared quite affected. "What's the matter?" said the novelist. "I have not been used, sir, to any such kindness; and it is the first time that I have been thanked for any thing I have done here." He soon gave up the lodgings; and meeting the poor girl (who was evidently on the town) some time afterwards in the street, he inquired of her whether she had left her place. "O yes, sir. My mistress kicked me out of the house, because, she said, I had been so long bringing her a pint of gin,"—the favourite beverage of lodging-house keepers.

During the flower-season, it was Mr. Jay's habit every Sunday morning to go into his garden, and pluck for each of his servants a good handful of flowers, arranged by himself, which they were desired on no account to bring home, but to give them away to some of the poor members of the chapel. This garden, I should mention, was not only a source of great delight, but a place of much occupation to him. He would wheel down into it the dung from the yard, dig up the beds, graft the trees, and attend to the flowers. He had a great variety of fruit-trees of all sorts, which he had procured from the different places where he had preached in England. There was a noted pear-tree in the centre of the garden, on which he had grafted with his own hand twelve varieties of pears. I have often heard him, in his sermons, allude to this tree, and compare it to a head (*i. e.* Christ), having thereunder different denominations of Christians, who are all one in Him.

Having in this chapter spoken about female servants, it does not appear inappropriate to quote some passages from one of Mr. Jay's published sermons, entitled *The Charge*, the text of which is "A prudent wife is from the Lord," wherein he thus tersely inculcates the duties of mistresses towards this class of domestics: "Surely in the treatment of your servants it will not be necessary to remind you that you have a Master in heaven, and that there is no respect of persons with God; He that made you in the womb made them. No being is despicable as a creature of the Most High, so fearfully and wonderfully made;

and no one is to be contemned even on the ground of power and influence. Domestics can injure you; their very situation gives them peculiar means and opportunities; and they may employ their advantage in ways of which you have no apprehension, and which render counteraction difficult or impossible. It is never desirable to wage war with inferiors. You must descend to the same lowness of contention, and employ weapons in the use of which they are likely to be much more expert than yourself; while the sympathy of beholders will be most naturally drawn to the weaker side. Think not a hint of this kind beneath your notice. It will procure you more discredit than you are aware of to be always, or often, changing your servants; or to wear the character of a harsh, scolding, close, stingy mistress.

"Sink not your proper distinction by suffering your affability to degenerate into familiarities. Neither let your kindness disappear in your authority. Servitude being established against the natural equality of mankind, should be softened as much as the duties of it will allow. Consider your servants as humble friends. Little minds endeavour to support their consequence by distance and hauteur, but true dignity is always condescending and tender; and in a woman we admire not what is stately, but what is endearing; not what is dazzling, but what is mild and lovely; not what is great, but what is graceful. Forbear threatening; distinguish between mistakes and the want of principle; pass by little infirmities. Is it reasonable that the mistress should exact from a servant the perfection the servant can never expect from the mistress? Afford your domestics occasional indulgence, and especially moments for reasonable visits to their relations and friends. Let the readiness to commend you to others—the tear when you leave home, the beaming countenance when you return, the eager and uncomplaining attendance and watching by day and night in your sickness—show that you have gained the heart as well as hired the hand; and are served not by the sullenness of fear, but the cheerfulness of affection."

It was Mr. Jay's universal custom, whenever a servant or other humble member of his church died, to allude to the event on the following Sunday with the same pathos and fervour as he would display for a member of rank or wealth. So late as the 1st of December 1850 he thus alludes to the death of a poor woman of the name of Mary Upstal: "She was near fifty years a member of our church, during which time she walked worthy of her profession. She was a widow in humble life and dependent circumstances; but through a series of changes and many relative and personal trials she adorned the doctrine of God her Saviour. The church overlooks none of her members, whatever be their outward estate; they are all joined together by faith and love in Christ Jesus; and little are many aware of the degree of mutual attachment between all those who are of one heart and of one soul, who have given up themselves not only to the Lord, but to each other, by the will of God, and have long frequented the same sanctuary and engaged in the same exercises. But the world knows not those who have no riches or rank to recommend them. Their life is a hidden one, not only in the spirituality and mystery of its principles and experience, but in the obscurity of its stations and movements. But their day is coming, and they are now great in the sight of the Lord.

> 'Laurels may flourish round the conqueror's tomb;
> But happiest they that win a world to come.
> Believers have a silent field to fight,
> And their exploits are veiled from human sight.
> They in some nook, where little known they dwell,
> Kneel, pray in faith, and rout the hosts of hell.
> Eternal triumphs crown their toils divine,
> And all these triumphs, *Mary*, now are thine.'"

CHAPTER XXVI.

The Rev. Matthew Wilkes—Charity collections—Singularity of texts—A few words upon the opening of chapels—Mr. Jay's dislike of letter-writing—Pastoral visiting—Requisitions to him to visit condemned criminals—A character.

The Rev. Matthew Wilkes (the father of the gentleman whom I have lately mentioned in these Recollections) was the stated minister at Whitefield's Chapel Moorfields, and at the Tabernacle Tottenham Court Road; and was also a supply at the Bristol Tabernacle. He was a shrewd, ingenious, and popular preacher, and well acquainted with human character; but, like Rowland Hill, very eccentric. He was, on one occasion, engaged to preach for some charitable purpose in Wiltshire with Mr. Jay, an intimate friend of his, and officiated in the morning. His audience consisted chiefly of small farmers.

Before the service commenced, Mr. Wilkes observed to Mr. Jay, that from the class of people before whom he had to preach, he could only hope to collect a small sum of money; inasmuch as farmers seldom gave money for the erection of chapels or for any charitable or religious purpose, or became subscribers to county hospitals. Mr. Jay differed in opinion from his friend, declaring that they were a liberal and hospitable race of men, when things went well with them.

After the conclusion of the service, Mr. Wilkes observing several farmers pass by the plate without contributing, opened the pulpit-door, and ran downstairs with great agility. Upon reaching the chapel door, quite out of breath, he snatched a plate from the hands of one of the holders, presented it to every person who passed him, and, in order to prevent a too free egress from the chapel, put his foot across the door. The first person who attempted to pass by him without contributing was one of the farmers of the place, whom he thus addressed: "Why, my good friend, you surely are not going to leave us in this way. You never will be blessed if you do so. Come, give me your subscription. How do you know but that your cow will have two calves, and each of your ewes three lambs?" The appeal was not made in vain; and addressing each person who passed him with some appropriate sentence, he collected a larger sum of money than was expected.

The above anecdote of Mr. Wilkes as a plate-holder brings to my recollection a reproof which I once heard Mr. Jay give to some of his auditory, on the occasion of his preaching for some charitable object. Towards the conclusion of his discourse, observing some of the crowded congregation leaving their seats to avoid the sight of the plates, he stopped for a moment, and eyeing the retreating parties with a look of pity, said, raising his voice, and pointing at them: "You must be sharp, my good friends, or the plates will be at the door before you can get off."

Very singular in the selection of texts was Mr. Wilkes. They were frequently very striking, and their announcement struck the hearer so powerfully, that it was some minutes before he could recover from the singular impression which the reading of them produced. He, as I heard from Mr. Jay, preached three admirable sermons from the words, "Heady;" "I am black;" "Lord, by this time he stinketh, for he hath been dead four days." But Mr. Jay was often more singular in this respect than his friend Wilkes. What strange texts to preach from *at the opening of chapels* were the following: "Is there any taste in the white of an egg?" "We are fearfully and wonderfully made." "There are three things which go well, yea four are comely in going: a lion, which is strongest amongst beasts, and turneth not away; a greyhound; a he-goat; and a king, against whom there is no rising up." "Take it by the tail."

I have now before me a long list of chapels opened by Mr. Jay during the extended course of his ministry, the names of which would, without doubt, be uninteresting to the reader. It will, therefore, be sufficient to say, that although he opened most of the principal chapels (of various denominations) in the metropolis and provinces, yet he seemed to take more delight in performing this part of his ministerial office in the small places of worship in the thinly populated districts. I remember his calling on me one day at Manchester, where I was then at school, and his taking me with him to Liverpool, in which town I witnessed his opening a chapel, built by the then well-known preacher the late Rev. Mr. Spencer. This edifice having been burnt down some years afterwards, it was rebuilt for the well-known popular preacher Dr. Raffles.

The introduction of the penny postage released Mr. Jay from an onerous tax; for numerous were the letters daily addressed to him from all parts of the country, soliciting his services either to open chapels, or preach missionary or charity sermons. Many of the writers never thought of paying the postage, probably considering that the compliment of the invitation was an ample recompense. I have before mentioned his great disinclination to letter-writing, which was the more remarkable, as he excelled in epistolary correspondence. Many a time have I seen my mother go into the library with a number of letters in her hands, begging that he would give a reply to them, stating, by way of inducement, that it was not gentlemanly to neglect to do so. After some little entreaty on her part, he would throw aside the books or papers he had before him, and reluctantly comply with her request; but the answers were, for the most part, very brief. Innumerable were the letters he received after my mother's long illness, most of which remained unanswered; an act of inattention for which he incurred, and very justly so, much blame.

Mr. Jay, in his Autobiography, in alluding to *pastoral visitation*, and that complaints had been made against him on the score of his neglect of *pastoral visiting*, after declaring that no little of this censured neglect was *voluntary* with him, and therefore did not affect his mind, goes on to state the several reasons why he could not be a pastoral visitor in the fullest sense of the word. He had begun his career young; he had four services a week at home, besides calls abroad; his congregation extended over the whole of a large city; his place of residence exposed him to many interruptions; he was necessarily engaged to visit strangers who came to Bath for their health, away from their usual pious helps; and he was moreover an author of much acceptance, whereby he was able to disseminate the truths of the Gospel beyond the narrow precincts of his chapel. Knowing that he was well employed, he felt persuaded that he was better promoting the welfare of his people and the public in his study, than, to use his own language, "in gadding about without an aim, and wasting time in idle intercourse and nursery talk."

But one thing he did to remedy, in a degree, his deficiency, through the causes just enumerated, in visiting. For the sake more expressly of the busy, the poor, and the aged, he had a meeting in the vestry of his chapel on the Monday evening, in which he always sat for an hour, and spoke in a more free and familiar manner than it became him to use in the pulpit.

There was no part of his duty as pastor which he so readily and cheerfully performed as that of visiting the afflicted and dying at their own houses, whenever his ministerial services were expressly required and called into requisition.

But Mr. Jay always expressed a great disinclination to visiting criminals in prison, and never was solicited, except upon two occasions, during his ministry to do so; he was, however, through unavoidable causes, unable to comply with the second requisition.

The first of these requisitions was in the case of a young man carrying on some occupation in London. He had formerly resided at Bath, and formed part of the congregation at Argyle Chapel. He was courting a young girl, in humble circumstances, living on the first-floor of a small house in one of the narrow streets of the City. She, after many entreaties and much pressing on the part of the suitor, positively refused to marry him. After this refusal, he called upon her late on a winter's night, when he repeated his offer; but it meeting with no better success than before, he suddenly drew from out of his pocket a loaded pistol, and pulling the trigger, shot her through the head, and saw her fall a lifeless corpse at his feet. He then jumped out of the window of the poor girl's room; but fortunately for the ends of public justice, his hat was left behind. It was afterwards ascertained, through the hatter, what sort of a person it was who had purchased the hat of him; but still no intelligence of the whereabouts of the murderer could be obtained, until about a year afterwards, when he was discovered working as a ploughman on the downs of Wiltshire. He was immediately taken into custody, brought to London, and tried (on a Friday) at the Old Bailey. Mr. Jay, who was then supplying Surrey Chapel, was in court on the trial of the young man, and sat next to the late Duke of Sussex. After a most patient investigation, the prisoner was found guilty of wilful murder, chiefly upon the production of the hat, the evidence of the hatter, and his absence from his situation. Upon being asked what he had to say why sentence of death should not be passed upon him, he most solemnly protested his innocence, declaring that he was not the man who committed the deed. Sentence was then passed upon him, and execution ordered to be carried into effect on the Monday; for that was the sole time allotted in those days between sentence and execution, unless extended by a reprieve. After the trial, Mr. Jay received a pressing invitation from the sheriffs to dine with the judges; but he was too much affected at what he had witnessed in court to accept it. He, later in the day, at the earnest request of the prisoner, backed by the sheriffs, had an interview with him in the condemned cell, and implored him, with much earnestness, as a preliminary step towards seeking for forgiveness of the Almighty, to make a confession of his guilt, the evidence against him being too conclusive to admit of the least doubt; but the murderer still protesting his innocence, Mr. Jay took his departure, saying, that it was useless in such a state of things to talk with such a man on the subject of religion. On the Sunday night's service, after preaching at Surrey Chapel, the under-sheriff and another gentleman sought Mr. Jay out at the vestry, who, at their request, accompanied them to the convict's cell, where he had a lengthened interview with him. The next morning the murderer publicly confessed his guilt on the scaffold.

I will now speak of the second requisition made to Mr. Jay to visit in Newgate a young man of education condemned to death for forgery. He was acquainted with the convict's father (a member of the Wesleyan persuasion), who justly maintained in the city of Bristol a position of importance, both as a merchant and a member of its corporation. The bearers of the requisition were Dr. Bunting and another Wesleyan minister, who having heard on the day of the conviction that Mr. Jay was staying at a friend's house in Piccadilly, called upon him there late in the afternoon of that day. Their message was soon delivered. It was an earnest request from the convict that the friend of his father should visit him in his cell. Mr. Jay, after expressing to them his deep sorrow at not being able to comply with the request, not only on account of extreme indisposition, but also from the circumstance of having just booked his place by the Bath mail, which would leave town in a couple of hours, thus addressed himself to Dr. Bunting: "I do not know, doctor, who can afford so much religious consolation to the young man, in his pitiable condition, as yourself. You are far more able to perform that serious office than I am; for I confess that I am but a poor minister in the cell of a prison." The doctor replied: "You have underrated yourself; but as you have stated sufficient reasons why you cannot possibly attend, I will not press you to visit the prisoner, but will be your substitute."

A man of depraved character, who had been an occasional attendant at Argyle Chapel, having been convicted of murder upon the clearest evidence, at the Somersetshire assizes, was sentenced to death, and died on the scaffold protesting his innocence. There was a young gentleman of the county, of an eccentric character and of a disordered turn of mind, who was never so much in his element as when he visited condemned prisoners in their cells, and narrated either to friends or strangers the conversations which had passed between him and the criminals, giving, at the same time, an account of their birth, parentage, education (if they had any), and personal appearance, and how they fell into their evil courses. Late one Friday, about seven o'clock (the prisoner then awaiting his doom in prison), this gentleman rapped at the door of Percy Place, and upon the servant opening it, informed her that he wished to see her master. Although Mr. Jay was then busily employed in the preparation of his sermons for the Sabbath (always devoting to that purpose the whole of Friday in preference to Saturday), yet he desired the servant to show the gentleman into the library, thinking that he should not be detained by him more than a few minutes. But he reckoned without his host; for the stranger, for one full hour, narrated, to his (Mr. Jay's) annoyance, what he (the stranger) had said to the convicted murderer, and what he (the convicted murderer) had said to him, as if the details had the same interest to others as they had to himself. I was in the passage whilst Mr. Jay was showing the gentleman out at the door, and upon closing it, he turned round to me with a smile, saying, "Cyrus, I should think the murderer would like to be executed at once, to get out of that man's company."

CHAPTER XXVII.

Baptism of infants—Celebration of the Lord's Supper and Marriages at Argyle Chapel.

Mr. Jay, throughout the long course of his ministry, always avoided, except in cases of exigency, to baptise children at the houses of their parents, but used to contrive to set apart, every three months, an entire afternoon of a Sunday for the express purpose of performing that portion of his ministerial duty, in which he seemed to take an especial delight. On these occasions the attendance of the parents of the children and their friends was extremely numerous. It was a general remark, that he could handle an infant with more ease, and take up one after the other with greater rapidity, than most ministers. Let not the word "rapidity" startle some of my readers; for I must inform them that among Dissenters there are neither godfathers nor godmothers; a class of functionaries whom Robert Hall used to designate to Mr. Jay as "goosefathers and goosemothers."

The last time I was present at one of these afternoon services, I saw him take up a beautiful rosy-cheeked infant, and looking at it, he said: "I could give thee a thousand kisses;—Mary, I baptise thee in the name of the Father and of the Son and of the Holy Ghost." When he returned home in the evening, I asked him who had originated the ordinance of baptism. "I should be a clever man if I could tell," was his sole reply.

I remember his christening, in my youthful days, one of his grandchildren in his summer-house,—his favourite retreat in the garden, and where he would ofttimes sit either with a book before him, or preparing himself for his next discourse.

There were generally a great many spectators present in the galleries of Argyle Chapel at the celebration of the Lord's Supper, all of whom were anxious to hear the address of Mr. Jay to the communicants, which though, for the most part, brief, yet contained sentences of great pathos. I remember being a spectator on one of these occasions, when he was very argumentative and striking in his address on the subject of the Sacrament. On my return to Percy Place after the ordinance, I heard him complain to my mother that the deacons were always raising objections to prevent persons from joining the church and becoming communicants; in the course of which he said: "I was present at the last church-meeting; and a very good man wished to partake of the Lord's Supper; but one of the deacons objecting as usual, I flatly told him that he objected to every one." Then turning round to me, he said: "I regret the strictness of Dissenters towards those who wish to become members of our church, and have done every thing in my power to relax it; the consequence has been, that I hardly know a person expelled from my chapel." Perhaps some of my readers may not be aware that every Dissenter, before he can be permitted to be a communicant at the chapel wherein he worships, must be an *admitted* member thereof, approved by the church, the minister, and deacons, unless he has previously been a communicant at any other place of worship.

Some time afterwards Mr. Jay reproduced the same arguments, used by him in the address to which I have recently referred, in one of his Morning Exercises, taking for his text these words: "Except ye eat the flesh of the Son of Man, and drink his blood, ye have no life in you."

On the subject of these words, one of great interest at the present time, Mr. Jay says, in relation to the language employed by our Lord, that "it certainly requires some explanation, for it has given rise to several abuses or mistakes. We may remark two of these. The first takes it in a sense too gross. It is the doctrine of transubstantiation, which has rolled down from age to age in blood. According to this, it is believed that the words, 'This is my body, and this is my blood,' do not mean emblems of them, but the things themselves; and that as soon as the bread and the wine have been consecrated by the priest, they are changed into the very body and blood of Christ, and that He is thus eaten, and may be eaten by thousands at the same time. In the same way they may as easily prove that He consists of boards and nails; for He says, 'I am the door.' What a strong delusion to believe a lie is here! Be it observed, our Lord has here no reference at all to the Sacrament, for this was not instituted till long after. Besides, the participation of his flesh and blood, of which He speaks, is inseparable from salvation: 'Whoso eateth my flesh, and drinketh my blood, hath eternal life, and I will raise him up at the last day.' But are all saved who partake of the Lord's Supper? and do all perish who never received it?—The second takes it in a manner too refined, and is derived from the enemies of evangelical truth, who have always shown a peculiar aversion to the death of Christ under any other notion than that of an example or witness. They tell us the diction is very strong, and must be much qualified. Our Lord, say they, is here speaking of himself as a teacher, and refers to the design of his doctrine; for knowledge has always been considered as the food of the mind. This is readily allowed. Yet what teacher ever said to his pupils, You must eat, not my instructions, but myself; not my lessons, but my flesh and blood? The language is certainly very metaphorical; but it is founded in truth, and designed to convey an important reality. The thing is, we live not by the life of things, but their death. It is so with vegetables, and birds, and fishes, and beasts; they serve to nourish us by their deaths. We live spiritually by the dying of the Lord Jesus; and the allusion refers to his mediatorial offering for our sins, and teaches us that faith is necessary to our deriving benefit from his sacrifice: 'Except ye eat the flesh of the Son of Man, and drink his blood, ye have no life in you.' For this eating and drinking represent our believing on Christ. The resemblance between these and the exercise of faith appears in four things. There is in each of them *appetite.* Our Saviour speaks of hungering and thirsting after righteousness. Hunger and thirst are natural, powerful, returning appetites. Such are the desires which all believers feel towards the Lord Jesus. There is in each of them *application.* A man may hear of food, see it, hold it in his hand, present it to his lips; but this is not eating. In eating there is an actual reception of the food into the animal system. And in believing we receive Christ Jesus the Lord. His suitableness and all-sufficiency to our case are made known in the Gospel, and all the blessings of his salvation are brought nigh; but still we perish, unless we are made partakers of Christ. How often does the old and good divinity tell us that an unapplied Saviour is a nonentity to us! In each case there is *satisfaction.* Medicine may be necessary, but we are not said to eat medicine—we take physic; but we eat meat because there is pleasure in it. Food is essential to our subsistence; yet when we sit down to a well-spread table, we never perform it as a duty to save us from death. There is immediate gratification in the action, and this secures the performance. The reception of Christ is not only indispensable, but free and delightful. Like Zaccheus, we receive Him joyfully. We not only submit to the method of his grace; but we acquiesce, we glory in it. We love his salvation. We rejoice in his name. In each there is *nourishment.* This is the design and effect of food. It is thus the child grows; it is thus the man is sustained, and rendered equal to his labour. And 'the just shall live by faith.' 'The life that I live in the flesh,' says Paul, 'I live by the faith of the Son of God.'"

I never thought that Mr. Jay excelled in the performance of the marriage ceremony; but it should be remembered, that the act of parliament allowing Dissenting ministers to marry in their chapels had passed at a time when he had reached an advanced age. He looked upon the day as one of rejoicing; and always let off some piece of witticism, which was ever appropriate, and made the parties smile.

Some of the marriages celebrated by him in Argyle Chapel were important as to property. I was present at the House of Lords when, it becoming necessary to prove a marriage of this description which had been celebrated there, the late Earl of Shaftesbury, the chairman of committee, said: "Why, I had no idea that persons of property would think of marrying at a Dissenting place of worship." Well done, prejudice!

One of the most singular marriages solemnised in a Dissenting place of worship since the passing of the act was that between a bridegroom (a widower of the age of seventy-seven) and the bride (a spinster of the age of seventy-two), the parties being no less personages than Mr. Jay himself and a Miss Head.

Considering that at the time of this union Mr. Jay had been before the public as a popular preacher for nearly sixty years, and was then, as he is now, well known in the religious world as an author of much acceptance, I do not think it will be deemed irrelevant if I, in the following chapter, enter into some particulars, and make a few observations and remarks upon it.

CHAPTER XXVIII.

Mr. Jay's second Marriage.

At the latter end of the month of August 1846, having received a most pressing invitation from Mr. Jay to spend a few days with him at Worthing, prior to his return home to Bath on the following week, and wondering why I had not as usual paid him a visit without an express invitation, I left town in the afternoon of the same day, and arrived at that watering place late in the evening. I found him in the company of the late Mr. and Mrs. Ashton, and of Miss Head, the maiden lady referred to in the conclusion of the preceding chapter.

Early on the following morning Mr. Jay accompanied me on my way to the sands to bathe. After a few minutes conversation on trivial matters, he informed me that he was shortly going to be married. "To be married!" I exclaimed. "To whom?" To my utter astonishment he replied to my interrogatory, "To Miss Head, who, as you know, is a very pious lady; but," continued he, after a short pause, "you must view the union, at her time of life and my own, to a certain extent, as a matter of companionship on both sides. You and my other children are now removed at a distance from me, and my home is a place of desolation to me. Miss Head's state too is one of desolation; for she, to use the words of

Byron, is the 'sole heiress of her house and line.' I have known her and her parents from my youth, through the introduction of my good tutor Cornelius Winter. Then she has been an inmate at Percy Place for several months for some years past, and cheerfully performed the part of a Christian friend to your dear mother in her many years of affliction." At the conclusion of this statement, which I heard with patience, I simply said: "The marriage is your affair, and certainly as to your ages there is no disparity; but you may depend upon it that the religious world will not look upon it with a favourable eye. How it will astonish your hearers at Argyle Chapel and the citizens at Bath!" He calmly, but seriously, replied: "It is too late to alter our united decision, even if I wished it: every thing is fixed for the union, which will take place in the course of a few days. Having acted in the matter from conscientious motives, why should I fear the world's opinion?" The conversation upon the subject then dropped.

On my return from bathing, I could evidently discover from Miss Head's countenance, and her overstrained attention to me at the breakfast-table, that she knew that I had been informed of the intended marriage.

The breakfast finished, I took a stroll, and met a friend of mine, Mr. Edmonds, a solicitor at Worthing, a gentleman much respected, and who holds the principal professional situations in that town. I accompanied him to his office, on entering which, he said with a laugh: "Look there, Jay," pointing to a piece of paper stuck to the wall by four wafers, announcing that a marriage would take place between the Rev. William Jay and Miss Head. By the side of it there was stuck up a printed handbill announcing the sale of seventeen acres of potatoes. My friend, as well he might, expressed his astonishment at the contemplated marriage, and said that most of the persons who had heard of it shared in the same feeling.

I could only guess by the preparations which were going on, that the marriage would speedily take place; for I had no doubt spoken my mind too freely to Mr. Jay to be intrusted with his confidence in the matter. Be that as it may, he informed me one morning, after a few days' visit to him, that the marriage would take place on the following day; upon which announcement I said, "Then I shall start for London to-night." He requested me to remain and be present at the ceremony, and so did the bride elect; but I was firm in my purpose, and left Worthing the same evening.

The next morning the marriage was solemnised at Worthing Chapel by its then pastor Mr. Brewer, since ordained into the Church of England. Shortly after the ceremony they started off for Windsor; and after remaining there a day or two made their appearance at Bath as man and wife, and on the Sunday after the marriage Mr. Jay occupied the pulpit of Argyle Chapel as usual.

This strange marriage, I need not inform the reader, was the subject of the general conversation of the inhabitants of that city, and it greatly detracted from the high respect and veneration which had hitherto been paid to Mr. Jay. The London papers, by way of ridicule, contained the following paragraph, which went the round of all the country journals: "A *gay bird* has just married a *young girl* with a very large fortune; we understand that she is not one-and-twenty." The day I saw this announcement in the papers, I sent to him, advising him to write to the several editors who had inserted it to contradict the statement as to *age*, the money part being perfectly correct,—for she was possessed of 30,000*l.*, independently of a freehold house and grounds at Bradford. But he refused to do so, saying, "I never take notice of such misrepresentations. I made up my mind early in life, through the advice of Mr. Wilberforce, not to notice any attacks made upon me either publicly or privately, to which advice I have always since adhered."

In tendering this advice to Mr. Jay, Mr. Wilberforce related to him the following circumstances under which an unfounded charge had been made against himself: "I was walking," said this eminent individual, "in the Pump-room in conversation with General ——; a passage was quoted from Horace, the accuracy of which was questioned, and as I had a Horace in my pocket, I sought and found and read the words. This was the plain *bit of wire* which factious malignity sharpened into a *pin* to pierce my reputation. It was said of me in Benjamin Flower's *Cambridge Journal*, 'Behold an instance of the pharisaism of Wilberforce! He was lately seen walking up and down in the Bath pump-room reading his prayers, like his predecessors of old, who prayed in the corners of the streets to be seen of men.' I never thought it worth while to attempt to refute or rectify what I could so easily have done."

Although Mr. Jay, following the advice of Mr. Wilberforce, took no public notice of the newspaper paragraphs announcing the marriage, yet he felt their full sting; for he was of a very sensitive disposition.

A very old friend of his, carrying on his professional business at London, being on a visit to Bath, where he had formerly for many years resided, called on him shortly after the union. Mr. Jay, after introducing his friend in all due form to his wife, took him into his garden, and whilst walking up and down it said: "What do the public say of my marriage?" "I shall reply, sir," said his friend, "in the spirit of frankness. They say it is a very strange one; but of course you had a perfect right to act for yourself in so delicate a matter." The interrogator had heard enough from the lips of a very old friend to be convinced that the step he had taken was not generally approved; and the conversation at once took another direction.

Although the second marriage never met with general approbation, I feel it incumbent on me to vindicate Mr. Jay's character in the eyes of the religious world from the imputation that he had allied himself to an elderly lady through mercenary motives. From the influence he possessed over her, he could have had such a marriage-settlement executed as he wished, or none at all; but instead of exercising any such influence, the lady's property was, by his wish, settled on herself, with power of appointment reserved to herself; Mr. Jay only limiting to himself, in the event of his surviving her, a life-interest arising out of the annual income thereof. At the time of the settlement, she, unsolicited, made a will, leaving a legacy to each of his children; but after his death she revoked it by another will (two of those legacies having then become lapsed), wherein she bequeathed me a life-interest in 500*l.*, which I refused to accept. Thus, the only result which Mr. Jay gained for himself by the marriage was ridicule and a diminution of respect and regard, and for his family a few crumbs which fell from the rich woman's table.

I may err in opinion when I say that I never considered Mr. Jay the same man, in regard to matrimonial happiness, after his second marriage as he was before it. His former cheerfulness and fine flow of spirits seemed, unless some friends were around him, to have deserted him. I was the more struck with this alteration when on my first visit to him at Bath after the union, I saw him sitting in his arm-chair one evening in his library before the fire-place, whilst Mrs. Jay was reading aloud to him, which she was in the habit of doing every evening. He appeared to be extremely depressed. I heard him repeatedly sigh, and saw a tear or two roll down his cheek. I said to him, when Mrs. Jay left the room, more as a prelude to bringing him into conversation after his melancholy feelings than for any other purpose, "You will read Mrs. Jay blind if you continue to allow her to do so every evening." "What can I do?" said he. "You cannot expect that my present wife can ever be what your late dear mother was,—a *companion*." In this he spoke truly; for there was a decided contrast in intellectual endowments between them.

Mr. Jay never seemed so happy as when, after the marriage, he could entertain under his roof his children and grandchildren, or whenever he had society in his house. Whatever his inward feelings were respecting the union, he never allowed them to be manifested before his friends, nor even before his family; the scene in the library being the sole exception. One thing is quite manifest, that whilst in his Autobiography, written within a year of his death, he alluded in terms of tenderness and affection to the wife of his youth, he did not mention a single word respecting his second marriage. But I must add, in reference to the second Mrs. Jay, that her kind and Christian attentions to my venerable mother in her final and protracted illness were highly exemplary.

CHAPTER XXIX.

A fortnight's visit to Starcross—Mr. Jay preaches at Exmouth—Excursions from Starcross to Litscombe and Teignmouth—His visits to Bradford.

In the autumn following the marriage, I accompanied Mr. and Mrs. Jay into Devonshire for a fortnight; an excursion which I extremely enjoyed, as we were all alone, Mr. Jay having determined to keep himself quite private, and not to officiate at any chapel during this short trip. On passing through Exeter, we went on to Starcross, a lovely spot, and took up our abode at an inn in that village, the landlord of which I soon discovered knew Mr. Jay. The solitude of the spot was slightly relieved by a small railway station near it. At nine o'clock in the evening of the day of his arrival at the inn he rang the bell, and upon the waiter making his appearance, desired him to inform his master that he should feel pleased with his attendance, or that of his family or domestics, at his family worship. The landlord and many of his establishment gladly availed themselves of this invitation during the fortnight we were staying there.

The windows of the inn looked upon a fine creek of the sea, on the opposite sides of which were little green hills dotted about with woods. Many were the walks and rambles we took in the neighbourhood. Although a great lover of a country ramble, yet nothing would prevent his going to the small station to see the train come in from London on its way to Torquay, and he took great delight in timing its arrival. On one occasion, whilst standing on the platform, he discovered, in a first-class carriage, a young gentleman, of about eighteen years of age, in a deep decline. A mother and two sisters accompanied him. It being the prescribed time for him to take his medicine, a man-servant from another carriage brought it to him whilst the train was stopping. He looked as if he never would arrive at his destination. His mother was in tears, and two beautiful sisters were seated on either side of him, intently gazing, with deep anxiety, on a brother they so fondly loved. The whistle sounded, and off went the train. A savage-looking porter came up to Mr. Jay, who I observed was much affected, and said to him: "To-day they take mighty care of that young gentleman; but we shall have him back before a month in a horse-box." "How like," I observed, "is this man to his appearance!" "I do not know that," replied he; "for he must be accustomed to these sights in the train, since Torquay is the place where the consumptive repair under the advice of their medical attendants; and besides, it cannot be expected that these working men can have very fine feelings. The earning of their daily bread occupies their time, and prevents reflection." On his return to the inn he touchingly related this circumstance to Mrs. Jay.

One morning, near the close of a week, Mr. Jay espied from the window of the inn a boat coming up the creek to Starcross, containing, as he afterwards discovered, a deputation from Exmouth, requesting him to preach on the Sunday at that town; for it soon got wind that he was in the neighbourhood. After some little entreaty, he consented to preach at the two chapels there on alternate Sundays. On both occasions there were very crowded audiences. What interested him very much was, that he met with Captain Hunter of the Dragoon Guards, who, with his lady, had come from Exmouth, from their residence at Leamington in Warwickshire. He had a very great regard for this officer, who, whilst quartered at Bath for a very long time with his regiment, always, after marching his men into the Abbey, left them, and betook himself to Argyle Chapel, where he was a most attentive hearer.

During our stay at Starcross, Mr. Jay and myself crossed over to the beautiful village of Litscombe; and after sauntering about, we went into the churchyard, and near the porch of the church Mr. Jay discovered a tombstone erected to the memory of a very old friend of his (a Mr. William Moseley), who had been very many years in business at Westminster as the largest manufacturer of planes in England. It was at the residence of this gentleman's brother-in-law, Mr. Walker, who resided in Piccadilly, that Mr. Jay spent more of his time than at any other house in London.

Another day's excursion which he made from his retreat at Starcross, in which I was his companion, was to Teignmouth. The inducement which caused him to visit that delightful watering-place was once more to behold a large and commodious chapel which he had some fifty years prior thereto opened, and where he had again some twenty years afterwards officiated. Upon our getting out of the train, he remembered, notwithstanding the long lapse of years, the direction of the chapel. On finding out where the clerk lived, we directed our steps to his residence, in order to obtain from him the key of the chapel. He appeared disinclined to lend it, until Mr. Jay informed him what his name was, and that he it was who opened it. Upon hearing the name he appeared delighted, and voluntarily offered to accompany us. Mr. Jay, on inquiring of him after some early friends in the neighbourhood whom he had previously known and visited, found that they were all dead. "O," said he, "that is one of the disadvantages of a long life: we lose all our early friends. At my time of life I have no desire to make fresh ones." What arrested my attention whilst we were in the chapel was, that he remembered and repeated the texts of his sermons in the morning and evening of the day on which he opened it. The text in the morning, he said, was "Holiness becometh thy house, O Lord, for ever;" that in the evening, "Now Hannah, she spoke in the heart; only her lips moved, but her voice was not heard: therefore Eli thought she had been drunken."

Mr. Jay, in his Autobiography, alludes to the gentleman (Mr. Holmes) who built this chapel at his own expense; and thus quaintly relates a circumstance respecting the minister who had, on occasion of its opening, delivered the introductory prayer: "Being a hypochondriac, he had left his pastoral office; I never had the pleasure of seeing him again. But I afterwards heard of his misfortune, shall I call it, or happiness? He was a man of sober years, and was going to be conjugated to a dame of discretion; but happening to pass a fortnight with her at the house of a relation previously to union, they gained such a mutual increase of knowledge as induced them to remain *in statu quo*."

Mr. Jay, after his marriage, resided for short periods at Bradford (a town about eight miles from Bath), where Mrs. Jay had a house, the establishment of which she kept up until the day of her death. The house, rather a commodious one, presented the same appearance as when her parents resided there (the last of whom died about thirty years ago). In fact, every thing in and about it was old,—the furniture, fire-places, china, fruit-trees, and even servants, two of whom had lived in the family upwards of forty years each. Nor must I omit from this list a number of engraved likenesses of ministers, whose names are, and likely to continue to be, unknown to fame; some of whom had such queer-looking countenances, that Mr. Jay declared he could not refrain from laughing whenever he cast his eyes upon them. The library, a gloomy-looking place, contained a number of old books upon divinity, amongst which figured the heavy commentaries of Gill, an engraved likeness of whom met your eyes as you entered the room.

The house cried out loudly for improvement, but in vain. The flooring of the front bedrooms sloped so much towards the street, that Mr. Jay expressed to me with a smile, when I was staying in the house with him, a fear that it might cause him one day to slide into the street. In summer the house was hot to suffocation; in winter the cold was most piercing, the old-fashioned grates having the unfortunate propensity of sending all the heat up the chimney. But nothing could induce Mrs. Jay to have these defects remedied, or the house repaired; she expressing her determination that it should present the state, both internally and externally, it did in the lifetime of her parents and brother.

Mr. Jay, finding it useless to persuade Mrs. Jay to improve the house, betook himself to the garden, which, upon his first visit there as her husband, presented a neglected appearance. He purchased garden tools, even to a wheelbarrow, planted new trees and trimmed old ones, and devoted upon each visit the greater portion of his time to making improvements in it.

Close to the residence was a shut-up factory, where Mrs. Jay's father and brother acquired their property. Mr. Jay, on looking upon it, said: "Although that long-deserted building now looks so melancholy, yet it gives me much pleasure in reflecting, that the manual toil and labour formerly there expended, is now performed by machinery; by means of which the public have been the gainers, being enabled to obtain a better and cheaper article than under the old system." He was always in favour of improvement in machinery; and agreed with Sir Robert Peel, in that statesman's argument in the House of Commons, that if you once admit the utility of the spade, there is an end to raising any objection to the use of machinery.

Mrs. Jay, on coming into possession of her property, kept up the good old custom of her parents and brother, having a joint of meat cooked every day for the poor. With this exception, she had the reputation of being what is termed close-fisted, the result, no doubt, of early education. It should, however, be added that she was a contributor to many religious societies. But upon this point I have often heard Mr. Jay remark, into what a common error many religious persons fall by contributing only to Bible and religious societies, and the erection of chapels; and that if you asked them to subscribe to hospitals or any local improvement, they would refuse, and say: "O, worldly people can take care of these things, without our interference. We have enough to do for the cause of God." "This," said he, "is quite a mistake, because religious people ought not to be exclusive; it is unlovely, and does an injury to the cause of Christianity."

Mrs. Jay originally attended the Baptist Chapel at Bradford, but was driven away from it by the Antinomian minister, who, for a long time, preached *at* her (a most improper act certainly), through her having expressed dissent from his high doctrines. She then betook herself to the Independent Chapel of the town, where Mr. Jay, after the marriage, occasionally preached; but he could not fail to observe that it was less crowded than any other in which he had, during a long ministry, preached.

Mr. Jay's chief inducement to go from Bath to Bradford was to enjoy the trip by water by the boat plying between the two places, the canal passing by some of the most beautiful scenery in the West of England.

CHAPTER XXX.

Sermons for the British and Foreign Bible Society—Sermons for the Home Missionary Society on five different occasions—Mr. Jay's last appearance in the pulpit of Surrey Chapel.

Mr. Jay, during the whole course of his ministry, took a very great interest in the dissemination of the Holy Scriptures, not only in the British Isles, but amongst all the nations of the earth; and annually preached a sermon at Argyle Chapel in advocacy of the claims of the British and Foreign Bible Society. One of these sermons, delivered by him on the 11th of March 1832, was, at their special request, published, and had an extensive circulation, which was of much benefit to them. It now appears in the uniform edition of his works. The text of the discourse was, "Then took Jeremiah another roll, and gave it to Baruch the scribe, the son of Neriah; who wrote therein from the mouth of Jeremiah all the words of the book which Jehoiakim king of Judah had burned in the fire; and there were added besides unto them many like words."

A few days after the commemoration of the fiftieth year of Mr. Jay's pastorate, the Bath Auxiliary Bible Society unanimously passed, at a very full meeting, the following resolution: "That this committee, participating in the prevalent disposition of the Christian public to glorify God in the long course of consistent piety and extensive usefulness maintained for half a century in this city by the Rev. William Jay, and fully appreciating the value of his unwavering attachment to the British and Foreign Bible Society from its earliest formation, do appoint a deputation to wait upon him, and request his acceptance of the office of a Vice-President of the Bath Auxiliary."

The deputation who waited upon Mr. Jay to present him with the above resolution consisted of the Rev. John East, Rector of St. Michael's, Bath, its mover, W. T. Blair, R. Perfect, and W. Sutcliffe, Esqrs., all of whom had filled the office of mayor of that city. He accepted the honour, and his name was henceforth enrolled as one of the vice-presidents of the Bath Auxiliary.

Mr. Jay's annual visits to London drew him into connection, in early life, with some of the eminent and excellent men of that day who formed the plan of the London Missionary Society, which was founded in 1794. He preached, at different periods of his life, upon five several important occasions at the meetings of this society in the metropolis; an honour which has seldom fallen to the lot of any other individual.

At the first anniversary of this society, May 1796, he was unanimously selected, young as he was (being then only in the twenty-seventh year of his age), to preach before them. The sermon which he delivered on this occasion, the text of which was, "Let the whole earth be filled with His glory, amen. The prayers of David the son of Jesse are ended," was published at the time, and met with general acceptation. In this discourse he expressed himself thus on points which must command as much attention now as they did at the time he delivered it: "It has frequently been charged upon the Scripture as a defect, that it does not sufficiently inculcate patriotism, or a love to a particular country; a virtue celebrated among all nations of the globe; a virtue which so long secured Greece, and so highly extolled Rome; a virtue practised in former times, and professed in our own; a virtue of which, among many, nothing is left 'but loaves and fishes.' . . . But, after all, what is patriotism? Is it such a partial attachment to a particular country as leads us to disregard the liberty and happiness of every other nation? Is it such an exclusive attachment as would lead us to oppress every other country for the sake of our own, and destroy thousands who would not acquiesce in our opinion, avarice, and ambition? What was a Roman? A proud unfeeling tyrant, who placed right in power, who triumphed remorselessly over undefended weakness, who gloried in proportion to the number of cities and provinces he had taken or destroyed. What was the patriotism of a Roman? A false virtue, the destruction of all justice and beneficence; and this false virtue has always been admired, because it conceals self-interest under the mask of public spirit, and gives license to inflict injuries not only with impunity, but with applause. It is the glory of the Gospel to say nothing of such patriotism. It is the glory of the Gospel to set us above the prejudices which have so long and so unhappily kept men at variance; and to teach us that God has made of one blood all the nations of the earth, that men are not enemies because they live at the other side of a channel or mountain, and that they are not to be bought and sold as slaves because the sun has jetted their complexions. Christianity commands us to love all the human race, and to regard as our neighbours the inhabitants of the remotest regions. . . . . The more minutely we examine prophecy, the stronger is the confirmation of our hope that a day will come when 'wars shall cease to the ends of the earth;' when the animosities which have so long prevailed amongst Christians shall subside; when idolatry and superstition shall vanish; when truth and holiness and the pure worship of God shall abound. We are authorised to expect that a period shall come when not only individuals in different nations of the earth shall be devoted to Christ, but also potentates of every state, whose example is influential, and whose authority gives them a peculiar advantage, shall own their subordination to Him, and make their dominion subservient to his; considering themselves, in their different departments, as delegated to rule by Him, they will rule for Him. . . . . How little, alas, of the knowledge of the Gospel have the heathens for ages derived from their connection with evangelised nations! It has been justly observed that this is the crying sin of Christian lands; a sin too of which they have been quite insensible; a sin never lamented in our sermons for national humiliation. Without using the means to save men, are we not answerable for their blood? Is it not owing to our criminal indifference that millions are sitting in darkness and in the region of the shadow of death? Viewing ourselves in a national capacity, as Englishmen, the providence of God has furnished us with peculiar advantages for this service. Our arms and commerce have opened us a passage to the most distant parts of the globe; but our designs have not been formed with a view to benefit the heathen, while our conduct has commonly left a sad impression of the Christian name. We have all been culpable; too long have we stood idle: we have not sought occasions; we have neglected opportunities. . . . . We rejoice that there are those whose zeal for the Lord of Hosts disposes them to renounce the comforts of civilised life, to devote themselves to the service of savage tribes."

It was about four or five years after the delivery of this sermon that Mr. Jay, in the service of the society, visited Scotland. On his way to the north, he preached, on public occasions, at Birmingham, Manchester, Halifax, Hull, and York, where he drew very large audiences. The principal places he preached at in Scotland were Edinburgh, Falkirk, Stirling, Dumblaine, Glasgow, Paisley, Greenock, Largs, and the Isle of Bute. In four of these places he preached in the Established Kirk, as well as amongst the Seceders and Congregationalists.

In the year 1826 he preached his second sermon at the anniversary of that society to its juvenile friends; and in 1834 he preached a third time at their May meeting.

In 1844 he came up to London, at their express desire, to preach their jubilee sermon; and having after his arrival in town two clear days before the service, he employed his time in sight-seeing, being desirous during this interval of seeing the sights of London. The service took place at Surrey Chapel in the morning, and I found a very large congregation there. The text from which he preached was the single word "Ebenezer." The discourse commanded great attention, and was printed.

After the service he returned to Albemarle Street, where he was stopping, very exhausted and languid, not only from the exertion of preaching for an hour and a half, but having to shake hands with many of his friends after its termination. In the evening Dr. Raffles had to preach at Craven Chapel, and Mr. Jay requested me to accompany him to hear him, having a great regard for the doctor. He was soon recognised, and was glad to get into the vestry. He heard part of the sermon, which he admired both for its style and delivery. I now mention a little circumstance which much struck me. He beckoned to me, and said in a whisper that he must leave the chapel, not only on account of being very much fatigued, and unable to remain any longer on account of the heat being very oppressive, but wanted to purchase for each of his servants a dress, and was afraid the shops would be closed. I took him, on his way home, to a first-rate shop in Bond Street, where he was recognised by some of the young men of the shop. He quickly chose the dresses. I soon discovered that, at his time of life, the two or three days' sojourn in London was quite long enough for him, and that he was sighing for his house, library, and garden.

The fifth and last time he preached for the society in London was at Surrey Chapel in 1851, an interval of fifty-five years between his first and then present sermon for them. As he ascended the pulpit, and presented his venerable silvery head to the congregation, I could hardly contain my feelings. My mind rushed back to the long period of sixty-three years, when he, a ruddy-faced and interesting youth of nineteen years of age, there presented himself for the first time to a London audience, and gained a popularity which he maintained to the day of his death. But time had failed to diminish the lustre of his eye, the melody of his voice, the style of his delivery, and the able handling of the text. At the commencement, and during the delivery, of his discourse, he was at times very sensibly affected; he having determined that this should be, what it really was, his last address to a London audience. But he wanted nerve to announce such a resolve to the congregation. At the conclusion of the service, he was followed into the vestry by a number of his friends; and after receiving their congratulations, he left the doors of the chapel for ever.

On the afternoon of the same day he and Mrs. Jay, accompanied by myself, started for Cambridge, on a visit for a few days to his daughter and son-in-law, Mr. and Mrs. Ashton.

CHAPTER XXXI.

Mr. Jay's last visit to Cambridge and London.

On the Sunday after his arrival at Cambridge he delivered the same sermon at the Baptist Chapel of that town as he had preached at Surrey Chapel. The congregation was very numerous, and many gentlemen of the University were present, amongst whom was the late Mr. Gunning the Esquire-Beadle, who published in two volumes his recollections of Cambridge. I perceived that that gentleman was much pleased with the discourse; and at its conclusion he turned round to me, and said: "What a fool I have been for the last thirty or forty years of my life, in having let so many opportunities slip by of enjoying the gratification which I have this day experienced in listening to Mr. Jay. I have, during my long residence in Cambridge, heard all the popular preachers of the day; but I must say that, in my opinion, Mr. Jay is not excelled by any of them." This was the last appearance of Mr. Jay at Cambridge. On his return from thence, he stopped for the last time a few days in London.

On the day after his arrival in town, I accompanied him to the Crystal Palace in Hyde Park, and fortunately it was a most brilliant morning. I shall never forget the astonishment which was depicted on his countenance upon entering the exhibition. I was fearful that the sight would be too much for him. As it was, I observed that his eyes were suffused with tears; but quickly recovering his self-possession, he wished to see every part of it. He could not have had a better conductor than myself; for having repeatedly visited the palace with a season-ticket, I well knew what departments would most amuse him. He viewed with much pleasure all that I pointed out to his observation; but that which produced the greatest impression on his mind were the strains of the organ, the building, and the mass of persons of all ranks congregated under the crystal roof. I endeavoured, but in vain, to get him to view the steam-engine which kept all the other machinery there in motion. He said: "No; I could never understand the steam-engine, and I am certain I am not going to learn the mechanism of it in this magnificent structure at my time of life." I found him, as ever, the true son of nature; for he was perpetually endeavouring to get back to the fountain, trees, and flowers.

It so happened that the Duke of Wellington was in the Palace that morning, whom I pointed out to him. With what pleasure did he gaze upon that great man, and watch his movements! After the duke, who was born in the same year as Mr. Jay, had passed by, Mr. Jay said: "I think the duke will outlive me, after all;" but he was not a true prophet, for he survived his grace several months. It was remarkable how many persons recognised the venerable preacher, and how benignantly they smiled upon him, no doubt from either having heard his discourses or read his works. A fine gray-headed old mechanic came up to me whilst my father was gazing at the duke, and abruptly said: "Sir, I would rather be William Jay than the Duke of Wellington."

I will just mention one other circumstance which took place at the Exhibition. A lady (the widow of a Baptist minister who had lately died), dressed in deep mourning, accompanied by her son, a fine boy of about eight years of age, suddenly came up to Mr. Jay, and lifting her black veil, accosted him thus: "Sir, you do not perhaps recollect me?" to which he replied, "Yes, I do; and have often thought of and prayed for you;" and then putting his hand in his pocket, and drawing out from thence a sovereign, presented it to her child. On her taking leave of him, he said: "I always feel commiseration for the widows of clergymen and ministers; for when their husbands are dead, they are generally neglected by the public." He said nothing more on the subject of the lady; but I thought I could observe in his countenance that this incident added to the happiness of the day.

Just prior to leaving the Crystal Palace, a gentleman came up to Mr. Jay and informed him of the death of Ebenezer Foster, a rich banker of Cambridge, who had formerly served the office of high-sheriff of the county. The news affected him, not only from entertaining a high respect for that gentleman, but from having preached at Cambridge the previous week, at which time the deceased was in perfect health. He always spoke with great pleasure of the kindness of Mr. Foster towards the late celebrated Robert Hall.

Mr. Jay having expressed a great desire to visit the Zoological Gardens in Regent's Park, I accompanied him thither. The fine collection of animals and birds much astonished and highly gratified him. He was always fond of viewing collections of this nature, and would never allow a menagerie to leave Bath without taking my sisters, brothers, and self, when children, to see it, and explaining to us the natural history of the principal animals. Perhaps that which most arrested his attention were two otters, which were disporting in a pool of water; and whilst looking at them, he related to me with much humour many stories of his hunting those destructive animals when a boy. I could hardly draw him away from this spot; and although I observed on this occasion that his strength was breaking, and that he appeared fatigued, yet he nevertheless persisted, before leaving the gardens, in taking a view of the beautiful flowers.

The next day being Sunday, I paid an early visit to him, for the purpose of accompanying him to some place of worship. I was anxious to know whom he would hear, and in answer to the inquiry, he said that he and Mrs. Jay were going to Baptist Noel's chapel in John Street, Bedford Row. I accompanied them thither. Mr. Jay, after being seated, was soon recognised by most of the congregation, and removed by a gentleman to a seat nearer the pulpit. He admired the discourse delivered by Baptist Noel, to which he paid much attention. After the service, the preacher sent a message to Mr. Jay, to request him to come into the vestry. I accompanied him to the door of it, and heard him say on entering it, "Well, Mr. Noel, I am *half* a Baptist." Upon which Mr. Noel, after shaking hands with him, inquired how that could be. "Why," said he, in a laughing manner, "if you must know, my wife is a Baptist, and a bigoted one too."

I walked with him and Mrs. Jay from the chapel to a neighbouring coach-stand; and on the road he informed me that Mr. Noel had pressed him very urgently to preach in the evening, and that he refused the application very reluctantly, it having been made to him in so gentle and flattering a manner. He said he was much struck with the truth of an observation which the Earl of Ducie made to him respecting Mr. Noel. After praising that well-known preacher for his religious qualities, that nobleman said, "I have always been struck with Noel's manners as a gentleman. They are more polished than any I have witnessed at court or in society." Mr. Jay had known Baptist Noel from a child, being well acquainted with his mother, Lady Barham, and his grandfather. Just as we were getting into the carriage, Mr. Heald the M.P. for Stockport, and Dr. Bunting, introduced themselves to Mr. Jay, and requested him to preach at some chapel, the name of which I have forgotten; but of course he declined to do so. Not being far from Surrey Chapel, he thought of going there in the evening to hear Mr. Sherman preach; but he soon abandoned his intention, saying it would be too much for his feelings to enter again that place of worship.

The following day (being the day prior to Mr. Jay's leaving London for ever) I accompanied him to the City. On reaching St. Mary Woolnoth Church, he let go of my arm, and looking up at the building, heaved a sigh, and appeared deeply affected: "Ah, poor Newton," said he, "what a good man he was; and how often have I worshiped there, and heard him with profit and delight!" And then pointing to his residence, he said that many were the happy hours he had spent there. As we proceeded towards the Mansion House, he asked me whether Roger Cunliffe's banking-house was not close at hand, and on replying that it was, he said, "I will call upon him. I met his lady and family at Worthing this last season, and was much pleased with them. I recommended a school at Bath for one of his daughters. I observe that Mr. Cunliffe, like many others engaged in the City, leave town by the last train on Saturday, and return back by the first train on Monday, so that I could only see him when I was in the pulpit; besides, I have a great respect for gentlemen diligently engaged in commerce and trade." We accordingly called at the banking-house, and saw Mr. Cunliffe, who was pleased with Mr. Jay's visit, saying that he esteemed it a very great compliment. I mention this trifling circumstance because it was the last call that Mr. Jay ever made in the City of London, after visiting it annually for sixty-three years.

Mr. Jay, on this his last visit to London, was staying at the house of Mr. Rice Hopkins, whose lady was the granddaughter of a Mr. Nicholls, one of Mr. Jay's earliest friends at Bath. Her father, Mr. Long, lived at Kingswood, near Wootton-under-Edge.

CHAPTER XXXII.

The Rev. Mr. Vaughan—Reference to Mr. Jay's closing Sermons at Argyle Chapel in 1852—Extracts from them.

Mr. Jay having expressed, about the time of his second marriage, that he felt the want of *assistance* rather than an assistant, many of the ministers of the neighbourhood frequently preached at Argyle Chapel. In the month of April 1848, the Rev. R. A. Vaughan, the son of the eloquent and learned Dr. Vaughan, the late President of Manchester College, was unanimously chosen assistant-minister, he having previously officiated at the chapel occasionally for several months. If Mr. Jay could have been pleased with an assistant, no individual could have better met his views than this young minister, who not only possessed considerable talent, but was a gentleman. In 1850 Mr. Vaughan resigned, and removed to Birmingham, where he preached with much acceptance; but was cut off very early from his useful labours, much to the regret of his congregation and of the religious public, by a pulmonary complaint. The well-known disinclination of Mr. Jay to plurality of pastorate was the immediate cause of the young minister's resignation, his general observation being, that "No horse could carry double." Like most persons who for a long period of years have maintained an undiminished popularity, he had a jealousy of letting the reins go out of his own hands, he saying, "I always like to drive from the box, rather than be a postillion." Subsequently he regretted the separation of Mr. Vaughan, and I heard him express, after his own resignation, how gratified he should have been if that young minister, whose talents he highly appreciated, had been his own successor. Mr. Vaughan, during the time he was the assistant-minister, always preached in the evening, and was a favourite amongst the young members of the congregation, Mr. Jay preaching in the morning.

During my visits to Bath at the time that Mr. Vaughan was the assistant-minister at Argyle Chapel, I was frequently in his company. He expressed to me the pleasure he experienced in listening to Mr. Jay's discourse, saying, "If your father can preach thus energetically and eloquently at his advanced time of life, what must have been his powers formerly!" I replied, "I think he preaches as well now as ever he did: I see no change in him." I spoke truly; in fact, his venerable aspect made his discourses more impressive.

Indeed, at this time, and up to the termination of his pastorate, his hearers were particularly struck with the increasingly devotional character of his preaching.

I will now more particularly refer to Mr. Jay's discourses in the year 1852, delivered on the Sabbath morning at Argyle Chapel, the last of which closed his ministry there. I only heard one of these discourses; but I am enabled, through the kindness of a lady who took them down in shorthand, to quote a few passages from them, in this and the following chapter, which may perhaps interest the reader, as the sermons do not appear in Mr. Jay's published works. His Sabbath-morning discourses, notwithstanding his advanced age, extended to sixty minutes, often beyond, and were delivered (with the aid of notes, sometimes more or less copious, for reference) with all his accustomed distinctness and emphasis; and I should add that the fine melody of his voice had not departed from him. At the time of which I am treating he seldom offered up prayer before sermon himself, generally having that part of the service performed by the officiating supply; but when he did conduct the devotional exercises, it was quite a treat to his people. His texts, during the closing period of his ministry, were commonly short, and very striking; and one discourse, for the Bath City Mission, on the following words, "Bring him unto me," produced a deep impression on his numerous congregation. He often suffered much from his Sabbath-morning's exertion, especially from the excitement occasioned. Few would have supposed this when they observed his calmness and self-possession in the pulpit. Even up to the last hour of his ministry he drew crowded audiences.

The sermon which I heard was delivered in the early part of the year; the text of it was, "O taste and see that the Lord is good:" it was worthy of the preacher's best days, and the subject-matter of it was most ably handled. The following passages, in which liberality and singularity were blended together, attracted my attention. "'*Tasting*' has several things connected with it worthy of renewed and continual attention. It is very distinguishable from *party zeal.* There are some individuals who are never satisfied without bringing others over to their own peculiar views and feelings. It is not enough for them that persons should follow *Christ*; they must walk with *them*. It is not enough for them that a man should say '*Sibboleth*,' but he must say '*Shibboleth*,' or they will slay him as an Ephrathite. There is too much of this low base kind of spirit, that would increase proselytes to a party instead of increasing disciples to Christ; but

'Let names and sects and parties fall,
And Jesus Christ be Lord in all.'

I remember the words of Mr. Cecil to a female who addressed him, saying, 'Sir, I was once a Dissenter, but am now turned to the Church.' 'Madam,' said he, 'take care; you are turning from nothing to nothing.' And so it is with many. Would it bespeak loyalty to the queen, or love to your country, or add to the strength of the army, if you were to take soldiers out of one regiment to augment another,—for instance, if you transferred them from the Scots Greys to the Oxford Blues? But if you bring in fresh recruits,—ah, then there is real increase and strengthening. I recollect hearing the late Mr. Newton say, 'When I was taken into the ministry, I determined, if I was any thing in it, I would be a physician, and not a tailor. I would venture to restore my patient; but, having given him health and ease, I would not determine the cut of his coat; and I would leave all this to his own taste and fancy.' We may have our preferences, but let us take care; we may wish persons to be according to our respective views,—we may wish them to be Episcopalians or Independents, Baptists or Wesleyans; but let us remember there is a *name above all these,* and that the disciples were called Christians first at Antioch."

I have, in a former part of these Recollections, stated how singular and striking were the commencement of some of Mr. Jay's sermons. I am now going to bring before the eyes of the reader the commencement of three of his closing discourses at Argyle Chapel. Before I do so, I should state that he had to the last a most remarkable sight, and could observe almost every individual before whom he preached. In his sermons he was particularly careful in his introductory remarks, and nothing annoyed him so much as when, upon giving out the text, he saw his congregation hunting out for it in the Bible instead of listening to his first sentences, which he prepared with great industry and thought, terming them the key of his discourses. I have even known him give out and repeat the text without stating the chapter and verse, he remarking that it was strange that his hearers could not believe him without resorting to the Bible to prove that he had repeated the passage correctly.

But to return from this digression. Mr. Jay thus commences a sermon preached by him upon the Character of Christ as a Friend, the text of which was, "*Is this thy kindness to thy friend?*"—"Friendship is the state of minds united by mutual benevolence. It has often been deemed one of the essential articles of human life and comfort. Men have pursued it for their honour, as well as for their happiness; for it is considered as disgraceful as it is distressing to be without a friend. And who are those who, after a while, lose social intercourse and kind regards, but those who deserve it?—as whisperers, tale-bearers, backbiters, despisers of them that are good, and lovers of themselves. For he that will have friends, must show himself friendly; 'and there is a friend that sticketh closer than a brother.'

"General associations will not supply the place of a friend. Gossipers and visitors and acquaintances are not friends unless such as Cowper speaks of 'belonging to the lady who has her dear five hundred friends,' whom she always found sycophants in her house, and every one of whom, before they reach their homes, are running her down. For, while the friendship of the world is 'enmity with God,' it is hypocrisy with man; and no condition or rank places a man above the attractions of friendship. Kings have laid aside their royalties to indulge in it. Alexander would have found a conquered world a void without an Hephæstion.

"The dearest relations in life cannot supersede friendship. To the beloved name of a brother and sister, husband and wife, must be added that of a friend, in order to fill up the comforts of human life. O friendship, thou benefactor and comforter of the human race, how necessary art thou in a vale of tears, and in a world full of 'vanity and vexation of spirit'! Thou art the delight of sanguine youth, and the prop of trembling age; thou art the sweetener of prosperity, and the solace of adversity! The hardened heart at thy presence is relieved, and afflictions by thy hand are deprived of their tears!

"But, my hearers, while we hail the individual who has found a real friend, we are constrained to observe that it is not very easy to find one. And when you have laid down the infallible marks of a real friend, many who have worn the title will be found unworthy of the name, and, 'weighed in the balance,' will be found wanting. Besides, the present is a state of imperfection, and friends partake of this imperfection, as well as every thing else; therefore, if you would enjoy friendship in its highest and noblest degree, you must look above, and place yourself in connection with the Friend of sinners."

On the Sunday following the above discourse, he thus commenced a sermon from the text, "*Our liberty which we have in Christ Jesus.*"—"Liberty is our subject this morning. Liberty has always been highly prized, and can never be prized too highly. There is something animating and ennobling in the very sound of liberty. The word is sweet, but the thing itself much sweeter. Slavery is always disgraceful and hateful. By depriving a man of his freedom, you reduce him to a brute, or a mere machine. He is unworthy to bear the name of a man who can be reconciled to the absence of it; and, as Cowper finely says,

> 'Who lives, and is not weary of a life
> Exposed to manacles, deserves them well.
> 'Tis liberty alone that gives the flower
> Of fleeting life its lustre and perfume;
> And we are weeds without it.'

Well, we have liberty, we have *civil* liberty, we have *spiritual* liberty, we have liberty as Britons, and we have liberty as Christians.

"Yes, we have liberty as Britons. You would suppose from the language of some that we live in the regions of wretchedness and slavery, and that we have the notion of liberty rather than the reality. But

Britain is *free*. We acknowledge that every thing is imperfect under the sun; and whatever is human will always betray its origin by its defects. But while we have the four P's, even in the degree in which we have them, Britain can never be enslaved. We have a free Parliament, a free Pulpit, a free Press, and a free Platform.

"But what now is liberty? It is as remote from licentiousness as it is from despotism. It is not a permission for us to do as we *would*, but for us to do what we *ought*. Perfect beings may indeed be indulged with the former; depraved beings can only be intrusted with the latter. Burke finely said that 'Persons are enabled to enjoy civil liberty in proportion as they impose moral fetters on themselves.' And Newton has said,

> 'Men toil for freedom in a senseless mood;
> But he who loves it most, must first be wise and good.'

All persons prize liberty. The most tyrannical beings I have met during a long life have been in their own connections and dependencies the most zealous for liberty,—that is, *for their own*.

"But you must not suppose that I am going to speak this morning only or principally of civil liberty, —no, but of *spiritual;* not the liberty we have as Britons, but of the liberty we have as Christians; or, as the apostle finely phrases it in the text, 'the liberty we have in Christ Jesus.'"

Mr. Jay thus commenced a discourse which he preached from this text, "For I am in a strait between two, having a desire to depart and be with Christ; which is far better; nevertheless, to abide in the flesh is more needful for you:"

"Nothing is more unpleasant or distressing than a state of uncertainty and indecision, in which the mind is equally poised between two contrary directions. Now one side predominates, now the other. Shall I take such a journey or not? Shall I make such a purchase or refuse? Shall I form such a connection or forbear?

"Sometimes the case is very important and interesting, and requires much attention, deliberation, and reflection. Such, for instance, as marriage, where the connection is for life, and upon which so much of our happiness or misery depends.

"What a strait was poor Jacob in between starvation at home with his family, and letting his beloved Benjamin go down into Egypt! And what a condition must David have been in one morning when Gad gave him, from the Lord, three things to choose,—the famine, the pestilence, and the sword! No wonder he exclaimed, 'I am in a great strait.' Well, Paul was now in a strait, but it was an inviting and a blessed strait. He was not in a strait between two evil things, but between two good things, both having powerful claims upon him. It was the strait of a man in a garden between a peach and a nectarine,—between a rose and a lily. He was in a strait between living and dying; but as Christ was connected with both, the thing was whether he should die and enjoy His presence in heaven; or whether he should live and serve His people upon earth,—'Having a desire to depart and to be with Christ, which is far better. Nevertheless,' says the apostle, 'to abide in the flesh is more needful for you.'"

CHAPTER XXXIII.

Rev. Dr. John's visit to Mr. Jay—Present at Argyle Chapel at one of the closing Sermons—His opinion of Mr. Jay's preaching—Extracts from two of the Sermons.

WHEN these sermons were drawing near their conclusion, the Rev. Dr. Johns, rector of Christchurch, Baltimore, then on a visit to this country, obtained, through his friend Mr. Bolton, an introduction to Mr. Jay, whose guest he became for a few days. As the doctor, who was present at Argyle Chapel at the last of these discourses but three, is deservedly held in high estimation in America as a divine of much learning and piety, I do not think it will be deemed out of place if I quote the following passages from a letter which he wrote to Mr. Bolton from America on hearing of the death of Mr. Jay. "I arrived at Bath on Saturday, June 26, 1852, and was kindly received by your aged relative, then, I believe, in his eighty-third year. I can never forget the sentiments with which his form and face, his dignified and easy manner struck me. . . I asked him if he was in the habit of preaching from notes. 'From catch-words on a slip of paper,' he answered; 'but I wish I had never used even these; for the memory is like a true friend,—it loves to be trusted.' . . . He informed me that he endeavoured to select his text on Monday morning, stating that, by so doing, he could meditate upon it all the week; 'for,' said he, 'no clergyman ought to study on Saturday, but should allow his mind perfect rest at that time.' . . . On Sunday, June 27th, I heard Mr. Jay preach at Argyle Chapel. His text was, 'Hold thou me up, and I shall be safe.' The passage was sent to him by a friend, with a request that he would preach from it. . . . His manner was calm, and his voice clear and distinct. His object seemed to be to show the sinner's weakness on the one hand, and his safety on the other; and these points, sustained from Scripture, were also illustrated by one or two quaint but very forcible anecdotes. No one but a person of his age could have used them with advantage; but with his peculiar manner they told with great effect upon the audience, reminding me of Bishop Latimer's favourite style. I have never heard more of the Gospel in a single sermon; and in reply to the inquiries of American friends, as to whose preaching I liked best of all I heard in England and Scotland, my answer has uniformly been, 'The old preacher at Bath, whom you all know as the author of the *Morning and Evening Exercises.*' His sermon was full of Christ, discriminating and searching, while in point of style I did not notice a sentence 'out of joint' from the beginning to the end, and it was an hour in the delivery. . . . Conversing with Mr. Jay seemed like speaking with a past age. He had seen and known and heard nearly all the distinguished men in both church and state for more than sixty years; and, as his memory was fresh in reference to early incidents, he described Whitfield and his contemporaries, with the leaders in parliament, and in all the important movements of benevolence, with a minuteness and graphic power that no studied writer could well give to them. How few have lived so long, and lived through an age so abundant in events so deeply interesting to the Christian!"

The doctor having in his letter alluded to the *Morning and Evening Exercises,* I may just mention a circumstance he told me, and which I had read in the life of one of the American presidents,—that a gentleman having occasion to call upon the then president, was shown into his library, and there found him reading one of the Morning Exercises for the day.

It was on Sunday morning the 25th of July 1852 that Mr. Jay preached what proved to be his last sermon at Argyle Chapel. The text was, "O God, thou art my God; early will I seek thee: my soul thirstest for thee, my flesh longeth for thee, in a dry and thirsty land where no water is; to see thy power and glory so as I have seen it in the sanctuary." He delivered a most impressive discourse on these words; but it was observed that at times there was a peculiar sadness about his manner, as if he had a presentiment that this was to be the closing scene of his labours at Argyle Chapel, after a pastorate of sixty-three years.

In one of these closing sermons, Mr. Jay, in speaking of the utter degradation and moral helplessness in which the children of men had involved themselves, thus with graphic beauty addresses his congregation: "Yet, notwithstanding this, what a world has God made and furnished for their residence and enjoyment! He has varied the seasons, and made them softly melt into each other, so that 'the year is crowned with His goodness.' He hath clothed the earth with verdure, and has caused a sweet interchange of hill and dale, of wood and plain, of land and water. He also feeds you and clothes you all your long life.

"And this is not all. He not only supports you, but 'gives *you all things richly to enjoy.*' If He were only concerned for your being, and not for your comfort and pleasure, why does He furnish such colours to charm the eye, such sounds to delight the ear, such fragrance to gratify the smell, and such relishes to please the taste? Fruit was not necessary to our subsistence; and if it were necessary, it could have been made to grow without the previous process of the beautiful *blossom.* And why, then, those lovely tints,—why the sweet mixture of red and white,—but to please us before we gather the produce? We see how things that are necessary contribute more or less to our pleasure. Behold the helpless infant! But its helplessness is provided for in another, all without its care; its wants are all supplied by her who bore him. So that I never see an infant dandled upon the knee or sleeping in its mother's arms, reclining on the carpet or playing on the lawn, without being reminded of *Him,* who 'even out of the mouth of babes and sucklings ordaineth praise.'"

The following quotation from the same sermon is highly characteristic of the preacher's style:

"We live in a land of vision, and in a land of Bibles. There are many among us who know the grace of God in theory only, and not in spirit and in truth. They are strangers to an experimental acquaintance with all this. And these are characters the most unlikely for us to make useful and saving impressions upon of all with whom we ever have to deal. When we address those who have not heard the Word before, we entertain a hope that they will hear to profit. But as for you who have from your *infancy* known the Gospel, so as to be distinctly and familiarly acquainted with its contents,—as for you who know every thing we can advance, who admit every thing we affirm, and who are able to 'contend for the faith once delivered to the saints,' and here rest, without any concern to feel the influence of these things in your hearts and in your lives,—*you are the hearers that drive your preachers to despair.* And how strange is all this! You assent to all the doctrines we teach, and yet you show no more practical regard for them than if you believed them to be idle tales and 'cunningly-devised fables.' You acknowledge there is a hell, and that its miseries are inconceivable; but you never 'flee from the wrath to come.' You acknowledge there is a heaven, whose blessedness is beyond what the mind of man can conceive, and into which the righteous only shall enter; but you strive not to 'enter in at the strait gate.' You acknowledge the value of the Gospel, and may be concerned externally to endeavour to diffuse it, while you prefer every trifle to its glorious truths and 'the things that belong to your peace.' *O the misery of preaching to such persons,—to such characters as these,*—these, who need no information, who are sensible to no motive, —these, who feel no emotion,—these, who are *sermon-proof,*—these, whom we have preached *blind,* so that they cannot *see,—deaf,* so that they cannot *hear,* and *dead,* so that they cannot *feel!* O what a perpetual contradiction is there between your creed and your conduct! You are not happy,—you *cannot* be happy,—and yet, somehow or other, you contrive not to be miserable. You are '*at ease in Zion.*'"

The following is a quotation from another of the sermons on the subject of the iniquity of covetousness, from a text taken from the seventeenth chapter of Isaiah, the seventeenth and eighteenth verses:

"Now, you who are prone to confine the love of money to misers. They, indeed, love it, and in order to hoard and to hide it. But then there are others who equally love it, for expenditure and extravagance, for the purposes of the pride of life, or excess in dress, or in ornaments, or in expensive amusements and travels. There are many who idolise money as much as ever old Elwes the miser did. Have you not heard even of families of rank and fashion, who have stolen ornaments of finery, and have been tried for the same, though, alas, they have seldom been convicted? 'Money is a defence,' and 'money procureth all things.'

"But, 'the iniquity of his covetousness.' Why, then, covetousness is iniquity. Well, so the apostle considered it, or he would not have called covetousness 'idolatry.'

"All idolatry is not gross, or corporeal. Much of it is refined and mental. We read of some 'who make gold their hope, and fine gold their confidence;' who 'love the praise of men more than the praise of God;' who are 'lovers of pleasure more than lovers of God;' who 'love and serve the creature more than the Creator,—God over all, blessed for evermore.' They transfer to some other being the love, the hope, the confidence, the dependence, the homage of the soul which is supremely due to God's holy name. This is idolatry. Idolatry is the alienation of the heart from God to something else.

"'The iniquity of his covetousness.' Why then there is iniquity in covetousness. And what else is there not in it? The apostle tells us that 'they that will be rich fall into temptation and a snare, and into many foolish and hurtful lusts, which drown men in destruction and perdition; for *the love* of money is the root of all evil.' What crime has it not led to the perpetration of! See the influence and effect of it in Balaam, in Gehazi; see it in Judas, who, for thirty pieces of silver, could even betray the Lord of life and glory."

CHAPTER XXXIV.

Mr. Jay's last visit to Worthing; his illness there—His return home, and tender of his resignation as Pastor of Argyle Chapel.

On the day succeeding Mr. Jay's closing sermon at Argyle Chapel, he took his departure from Bath to Worthing, to enjoy his usual relaxation.

Two or three days after his arrival at this watering-place there was a very heavy gale of wind blowing directly on the town, and bringing up with the waves and depositing on the beach large masses of seaweed. The storm was succeeded by very hot weather, and the rays of a summer's sun striking upon the weed, which was covered with innumerable insects, drew up an exhalation, from the effects of which he was attacked with diarrhœa, in an aggravated form, accompanied with violent sickness. Previous to this attack his appearance was healthy, and his spirits for the most part good.

Upon receiving an account of Mr. Jay's illness, I hastened down to Worthing without loss of time, and found him suffering much from the pain. He was soon joined by Mr. and Mrs. Ashton, and we all remained with him until his return homewards.

He was fortunate enough to have the professional assistance of the late Mr. Martyr, an eminent surgeon of Worthing, who generally attended him twice a-day, and by his skill relieved him for a time. I often walked with the doctor after his visits to his patient. On one of these occasions, he informed me that he had seldom seen a man at the advanced age of my father whose flesh was so firm, appearance so healthy, and intellects so clear as his; "And this," said he, "is the more remarkable, for, notwithstanding the cheerfulness your father exhibits under his affliction, he must at times be suffering very acute pain; for the attack of the diarrhœa cannot fail to aggravate the complaint under which he has been previously labouring. If we can subdue the diarrhœa, and bring the tone of his stomach to a healthy state, he may be spared to you some years longer. I have never had a patient in whom I have taken so great an interest as I have in your father."

I accompanied the doctor one day to the apartments of Mr. Jay, whom he found sitting on a sofa with a book in his hand. The doctor, on entering, said, "Why, we are better to-day!" to which his patient, with a smile, replied, "Why, you have said that every day since I have been under your care; so that I ought to be well by this time."

Mr. Jay, notwithstanding his illness, took an airing almost every day either by the seaside or along some of the lanes. He frequently called upon the Rev. John Clayton, who resided at the Crescent, Worthing, and whose chapel in the Poultry he had opened, the pastorate of which, after many years' services, that gentleman resigned.

On my return homewards with Mr. Jay after the last of these calls on his friend, he said, "Do you know, Cyrus, I think I shall do the same as Mr. Clayton has done, and resign my pastorate at

Argyle Chapel." Strange enough, when we arrived home, Mrs. Ashton showed me a letter addressed to her father, which the ladies had opened in his absence. I think it was from the deacons of the chapel, intimating that Mr. Jay ought to resign; but I cannot any further recollect its contents. We all felt very distressed at this unexpected communication, and resolved that it would be the height of imprudence to show it to him in his present critical state of health. Mr. Martyr, whom we also consulted on the matter, was of the same opinion.

A day or two after this communication, his physician and friend, Dr. Bowie of Bath, paid him a visit at Worthing, and remained one or two days with him,—I forget which. Upon my informing the doctor that a letter had arrived from Bath urging Mr. Jay's resignation, but that his family would not allow it to be shown to him, he stated that we had acted with great judgment in withholding it from his knowledge. Whether the doctor was aware that such a letter had been written or not, I do not know, nor did I ask him. He was an especial favourite of Mr. Jay's, and felt much regret on leaving him.

During this his last visit to Worthing, Mr. Jay delivered one address at the chapel there, from a chair placed under the pulpit, to a very crowded audience. The text was, "A broken and a contrite heart, O God, thou wilt not despise." I recollect the first sentence. It was, "We have heard a great deal of people dying of a broken heart. I will tell you to-night how you may live with one." It was a beautiful address, and delivered with animation.

A few days after the delivery of this sermon, Mr.

Jay bade adieu for ever to Worthing, a place connected in his mind with so many reminiscences. To his family and attendants he said, "I am going home —to go home." Being in very great pain, he took the whole of the carriage to Reigate, and from thence to Reading, where Dr. Bowie came expressly from Bath to conduct his friend and patient home.

After a few weeks, his sufferings, to the astonishment of almost every one, were greatly alleviated; and it then became a question with him whether he should resign or not; for said he, "the members of my church will never allow me, after my many years' services, and at my time of life, to want a supply." But his hesitation was of short duration. He resigned not exactly voluntarily, as the following statement will show. On his arrival home from Worthing, he sent for his daughter, Mrs. Bolton, to pay him a visit, who was too happy, in her father's state of health, to comply with his request. One morning Mrs. Jay asked her, as she was going into the city, to call at a tradesman's house (an influential member of the chapel, and, I believe, one of its deacons) to pay a bill and get a bank-note changed. On calling upon the tradesman, he invited her into his counting-house, and, after deducting the account out of the note and giving her the change, he abruptly said, "Really Mr. Jay ought to resign; it has been notified to him by letter; we have had several supplies, and the congregation are talking of the expense; and as to myself, I am tired of entertaining ministers at my house." Mrs. Bolton, on her return home, finding her father in the library alone, innocently told him of what had occurred, upon which he instantly burst into tears.

"This is no time for me," said he, "to deliberate; after such an announcement, I will send in my resignation at once. I should have wished it to have proceeded more spontaneously from myself, so that I might have taken a farewell of my congregation as their pastor." He then, full of pensive thought, took up a pen, and addressed the following letter to the deacons of the chapel:

Bath, October 4, 1852.

To the Church of Christ assembling in Argyle Chapel: To the Deacons and all the Members assembling in Argyle Chapel.

My most dearly beloved,

I had fully intended to send from Worthing an official intimation of the resignation of my pastorate January next; a measure to which my mind has been brought by various considerations and proprieties of things; but a dreadful and painful assault of disorder prevented my doing any thing. As soon as possible I now thus announce officially what I had intended, and had mentioned to my deacons before. Had I my usual ability, I should do this in a very different manner; but you must now excuse a want of enlargement dictated by extreme depression and weakness.

The Lord bless and direct you, and enable you to preserve the union and harmony and prosperity and reputation of a church which has been exemplary in the world, endeared by the affectionate and happy connection of more than sixty-three years to your now resigning minister,

William Jay.

After reading the letter to Mrs. Jay and his daughter, he directed it, saying, "There, let it go. I have asked for nothing for myself; but I presume the deacons will consult their old minister upon the choice of a successor. Such has been the unity of the church in my time, that every attempt to form a separate congregation has failed. God grant that that unity may continue! I trust I have written to the deacons in a spirit of Christian charity." He was then made acquainted, for the first time, with the communication which had been sent to him at Worthing, suggesting resignation; upon the hearing of which he again wept, saying it was very considerate of his family to have concealed the fact from him.

CHAPTER XXXV.

The acceptance of Mr. Jay's resignation as Pastor of Argyle Chapel; and reflections.

SHORTLY after Mr. Jay's letter to the deacons of Argyle Chapel, I paid him a short visit at Percy Place; and upon being informed by him of the circumstances which had induced him so suddenly to tender his resignation, I said, "They surely will never accept your resignation, but will allow you to die their pastor. It will be a reproach to the members of the church if any contrary decision be adopted." He shook his head sorrowfully, but made no reply.

I had not been at Bath for more than two days before I could plainly discover that there was a variance of opinion about accepting Mr. Jay's resignation, and as to the most eligible person, in that event, to be his successor; and that a few of the influential younger members of the church were desirous of introducing a new minister, to the exclusion of their venerable pastor, without any sufficient reason except a love of change; whilst there were others who were looking forward to a successor who would devote more of his time to *pastoral visitation* than ever Mr. Jay had done.

The deacons were not long in calling a meeting of the members of Argyle Chapel to deliberate upon the subject of Mr. Jay's letter of resignation; and on the 30th of October 1852 they passed a resolution accepting it as from the 30th of January then next, that day completing the sixty-third year of his pastorate.

When this resolution was communicated to him he was deeply affected; the more so, as, although it professed to express *sympathy* towards him on account of his affliction through illness, yet the word *regret* at the dissolution of his long connection with the chapel did not once occur in it. As soon as he recovered his composure, I said to him, "How different would have been the feeling expressed towards you had you been a political character instead of a preacher! I remember being at Drury Lane Theatre at a dinner given to the late Mr. Byng, the then member for Middlesex. When the Marquis of Tavistock, the chairman, proposed his health as the father of the House of Commons, that gentleman rose, saying, 'I have served you and your fathers faithfully for fifty years;' upon which the whole audience instantly rose, and cheered him most enthusiastically for several minutes."

Mr. Jay, pausing for a few seconds after my relation to him of this affecting mark of respect to a long-tried public servant, exclaimed with a sigh, "Ah, Cyrus, Mr. Byng died the member for Middlesex; but they will not permit me to die the pastor of Argyle Chapel." "You have lived so long," I remarked, "that you have lost all your old friends." "Yes, they are nearly all gone; and I now love my burying-ground better than the chapel. Only think of Mr. ——" (alluding to the tradesman upon whom Mrs. Bolton had called, as stated in the last chapter) "having expressed a wish to my own daughter that I should resign! and also that the young man's father, grandfather, and uncle were all deacons of my church, and most esteemed friends of mine! and that it is less than two years ago that I preached the young man's father's funeral-sermon!" He gave a sigh, and the subject dropped.

To show the high estimation in which the father and family of Mr. —— were held by Mr. Jay, I quote the following passages of the sermon, as it does not appear amongst his published works. "He" (meaning the young man's father) "doubtless had his infirmities; but I know not what they were, and if I did I would not mention them, assured that none are free, and that he had none but were compatible with an Israelite indeed, in whom is no guile, and with a conscience void of offence towards God and towards man.

"He had sufferings relative and personal, but they are all over; and all tears are now wiped from his eyes.

"I believe he was the first I baptised when I came to Bath. I have now seen his family in three generations, and this desk has been in mourning three times for its bereavements; for the father of the deceased was one of our first deacons, and a great blessing in his day and generation. His elder brother also was a deacon, and one of the best men I was ever acquainted with.

"He has left a widow to finish her journey alone; and yet not alone, because the Father will be with her, and she is coming up out of the wilderness leaning upon her Beloved.

"He has left three children. They are all members of this church, and they all rise up around his memory this morning, and call him blessed.

"He has left other more near or remote relations, some of whom are walking in the way everlasting, and others of whom will, we hope, be affected by this providence; for we have often observed that the death of one has proved the life of another.

"He has left a pastor who, in the course of nature, will soon follow him,—a pastor whom, I believe, it was impossible for him to have loved more,—a pastor who always found him his credit and his comfort. This has been also the case with many more; and I hope they will prove the same to my successor, when those lips which have fed you so long are sealed in silence for ever.

"He has left a church bewailing the loss of one of its most active and useful members and deacons.

"He has left a choir, which he generally led, and amongst whom he sung, if ever a man did in this world, with melody in his heart, as unto the Lord. O may you, singers, sing with him for ever! and may none of you be wanting in the day when the Saviour shall make up his jewels!

"He has left a Sunday-school which he loved, and which he delighted to serve, and where he often caused, out of the mouth of babes and sucklings, the praises of God to be perfected.

"He has left the poor, whose distresses he so often relieved.

"He has left neighbours, who held him in high respect.

"He has left a large circle of affectionate friends.

"What a number of immortals has he left behind

in this large congregation, whom he is now, by my mouth, addressing, calling upon you from the very grave, 'Seek ye the Lord while He may be found; call ye upon Him while He is near!' 'Be ye also ready; for in such an hour as you think not the Son of man cometh.'

"'Arise! let us go hence, and sit down with Abraham, Isaac, and Jacob, in the kingdom of God.'"

Let me notice, in passing, that I believe that the Christian names of the three deacons of the young man's family were respectively Abraham, Isaac, and Jacob.

Having concluded the quotation, I have only this remark to make, viz. that Mr. —— had a perfect right to express a wish for the resignation of the friend of his family; but I claim an equal right, as the son of that friend, to let the public know how a good man may be treated after a faithful and devoted service of sixty-three years.

To the above remark let me add, that all through life Mr. Jay disregarded the offers made to him from time to time, many of which were extremely lucrative in comparison to the income he was receiving as the pastor of Argyle Chapel, to change his situation. This was the more self-denying, because his salary was limited, and quite disproportionate to his talents, popularity, and services; and had it not been for the sale of his works, and the munificence of noblemen and gentlemen who visited Bath, it would have been quite insufficient to enable him to bring up his large and expensive family. I remember being one day in what they call a commercial-room at Taunton, when a burly-faced traveller, who knew that my name was

Jay, and that I was the son of the preacher at Bath, walked up to me, and abruptly asked me what salary they gave my father. I without any hesitation informed him; when he said, "Why, I make double that money by selling Emden grits."

I trust that I have not spoken my mind too freely in this and the preceding chapter, in setting forth the circumstances which led to Mr. Jay's resignation as pastor of Argyle Chapel; the editors of his Autobiography having passed over this most painful event of his life—no doubt from praiseworthy motives—in almost perfect silence.

CHAPTER XXXVI.

Mr. Jay's final addresses to the members of his congregation—The choice of his successor—His visit to Gloucestershire—Opens a chapel for Earl Ducie.

DURING Mr. Jay's illness, and after he had tendered his resignation, there were many supplies of ministers at Argyle Chapel, some of whom were anxious to become his successor. Amongst the most prominent of these supplies was the Rev. William Dyer, of West Bromwich, Staffordshire, a gentleman of talent and high respectability. This minister soon gained supporters amongst the congregation, not by his mere preaching alone, but by his great attention to pastoral visiting; which was a point, as I have before observed, much neglected by Mr. Jay, who, when some gentleman remarked to him in my presence that he ought to have visited his congregation more frequently than he had done, replied quaintly, "Granted; this has been my vice."

In the early part of 1853, Mr. Jay upon a few occasions addressed the members of Argyle Chapel on a Monday. These services, except upon the last occasion, were performed in the vestry. On Monday evening, March 28, his auditors were so numerous that he adjourned from the vestry to the chapel, and addressed to them from a chair a solemn and edifying discourse from this text: "This is the heritage of the servants of the Lord, and their righteousness is of me, saith the Lord." At the conclusion of his address, he observed, "I shall never enter this place again;" adding some remarks of great tenderness and solemnity to his friends, who stood around him. Prior to leaving home for this service, he said on entering his carriage, "This will be my last journey to Argyle Chapel."

Whilst Mr. Jay was thus delivering his final addresses to the congregation of Argyle Chapel, not as their pastor, but as a long-tried friend, a great amount of canvassing was going on amongst its members, without his knowledge, for the election of a new minister. No sooner was he made acquainted with this fact, than he expressed his fears that the acceptance of his resignation had led to much disunion, and that his old congregation would not be sufficiently united either in the person of Mr. Dyer, or in that of any other of the candidates for the filling up of his vacant seat, and that therefore it became his duty to enunciate boldly his opinion in the broad face of day. "I am resolved," said he to me, "not to lend a hand to leave the church over which I have so long presided a disunited one, and therefore it is my firm determination to vote against Mr. Dyer at the forthcoming election." Upon hearing this intention, I said, "I advise you most earnestly not to interfere. You will be sure to have your conduct criticised, if you do so. Let the members of the church choose whom they like. There must be a division amongst the congregation in their choice, which will assuredly lead to a separation, and the establishment of another chapel." To my remark he curtly replied, "I have given out that I shall vote against Mr. Dyer being my successor. In adopting this course I shall act according to my conscience, and leave the consequences to God."

I was astonished at his proposed interference, because throughout his long life he had been remarkable for the exercise of common sense. And here I will mention, in illustration, what frequently took place during his extended ministry. A lady or gentleman would call upon him to consult him about marriage; and the first question he would put to either of them was, "Are you married?" and on hearing the monosyllable "No," he would quickly put an end to the interview by saying, "I never have given advice upon this matter, nor will I depart from my rule on any consideration." His reason was this, that if he had given it against him or her, they would have married notwithstanding, and one party would have told the other that Mr. Jay's advice was against the union, and thus he would have made himself an enemy for life; and if he had, on the other hand, given his opinion in favour of the union, and the marriage should turn out an unhappy one, the whole blame would have been cast on his shoulders. In reference to this point I have heard him say: "When a patient called upon the famous Abernethy for a prescription, he would refer them to his book on Indigestion, saying, 'Go and read it; you will find all necessary advice in it.' I have often acted in a similar manner with some of the persons seeking my advice upon the subject of matrimony, by saying, 'Go and read my Essay on Marriage.'"

This essay was written and published in the year

1806, at the especial request of the members belonging to an association in the West of England. It had an immense sale, and was spoken very highly of by the reviewers. It is the only work that I am aware of that he wrote in the form of an essay, and is divided into these seven sections, viz.: "1. The peculiarity and importance of the marriage relation,—the possibility of knowing the will of God in this affair. The law laid down. 2. This law argued and established. 3. The evils of transgressing it variously viewed. 4. The mischief historically considered. 5. Excuses to justify deviation from it examined. 6. In what cases this law is not broken, though both the parties be not religious. 7. Disregard of this principle lamented. But piety, though essential to choice, not sufficient alone to justify it. Ministers under peculiar obligation to marry discreetly. Prudence needed and recommended."

Mr. Jay was considered an authority upon the subject of marriage. So far back as the year 1801, he published a sermon on marriage, entitled "The mutual Duties of Husband and Wife." Again, he published a sermon in the year 1829, entitled "The Wife's Advocate," preached on a marriage occasion; and subsequently he published a sermon entitled "The Charge," addressed to the wife of a minister, the text of which is, "A prudent wife is from the Lord."

We will now turn back, after this digression, to the most distressing circumstance of Mr. Jay's sunny life. At the day of election, for the choice of his successor, he attended at the vestry of Argyle Chapel to exercise his right of voting. It was pretty well understood that if the Rev. Mr. Dyer was elected, it would be only by a small majority, so nearly were the congregation divided in opinion. Upon presenting himself in his turn to tender his vote, I was informed by him, and afterwards by two ladies, that he was rudely pushed aside in the aisle of the chapel by a thin, pale, and uneducated deacon, who said, "Your vote is now of no more importance than mine," and voted before him. Mr. Jay then came up to the table, saying, "I vote, not against Mr. Dyer, but against his coming here." I saw that he was much distressed in relating the unfeeling and insulting conduct of the deacon; and I said, if I had been present, I would have knocked him down, regardless of the place. He made no reply.

The Rev. M. Wallis, a member of Argyle Chapel, says: "Few will, perhaps, feel much astonishment that Mr. Jay's people found it impossible to agree in the choice of a successor;—for, 'what shall the man do who cometh after the king?' and our late brother might be styled, in some respects, the King of Preachers."

A secession followed, as a matter of course, and that portion of the congregation who did not approve of the choice of the majority retired from the chapel in Argyle Street, and repaired to the Assembly Rooms, where they worshiped until a commodious place of worship was built. The Rev. Mr. Brindley, for whom Mr. Jay had a very high respect both on account of ability and character, was ultimately chosen its pastor. It is an elegant building and very well attended. The retiring party, constituting the most respectable portion of Mr. Jay's congregation and his stanch friends, wished to call the chapel "Jay's Chapel;" but Mr.

Henry Godwin, who was the most active member of the new interest, thought it would be better to name it after his venerable friend's house, "Percy Chapel." Mr. Jay, the day before his death, asked me if I had seen Mr. Godwin, saying, that he had always been treated by him as a gentleman;—and inquired very particularly after the health of his highly estimable lady. It was at this gentleman's house that Miss Prothero, a lady alluded to in Mr. Jay's reminiscences, died. Her uncle was member of Parliament for Bristol, and her cousin member for Halifax. She had been a resident for some time in Mr. Jay's family, after his children had been dispersed.

The election of his successor having severed him for ever from Argyle Chapel, and finished his ministerial labours at Bath, he was enabled, through the improved state of his health, to take, during the spring and summer of the year 1853, short journeys, and enjoy the society of his friends. He visited Bradford, and preached there, and at Bratton between April and the end of August.

Early in September he visited his daughter and son-in-law, Mr. and Mrs. Bolton, and preached at the opening of Lord Ducie's new chapel at Tortworth, from this text, "Jesus saith unto her, Mary. She turned herself, and saith unto him, Rabboni, which is to say, Master." On the following Sunday he again preached there, from the text, "How shall we sing the Lord's song in a strange land?"

He was entertained by the new earl and his lady with every mark of kindness and attention, and as an old and esteemed friend of the family. In his Autobiography there is a very affecting letter which he wrote, in the month of June 1853, to Dowager Lady Ducie, on the occasion of the late earl's death. He had, not very long before this event, been in his lordship's company and prayed with him.

It was quite refreshing to observe the interest he took in amusing and playing with his great-grandchildren, while on this his last visit to Mr. and Mrs. Bolton.

In the next week after his last sermon at Tortworth, he paid a visit for a few days to his old friend Mr. Long, at Kingswood, near Wotton-under-Edge, the son-in-law of the late Mr. Nichols, one of the first deacons of Argyle Chapel. He was remarkably cheerful during the time he was this gentleman's guest, and every day walked out and visited several friends in the neighbourhood.

Speaking of his visit to Mr. Bolton, after his return home, he says: "How I valued and enjoyed it! Nor could it be otherwise, when every attention was exquisitely paid me, as though I had been a prince-royal; and besides, I was in the midst of such a family as I never witnessed elsewhere."

On Sunday, the 18th of September, he delivered a discourse at Kingswood meeting-house from this text: "Behold, I am vile." This was the last sermon he ever preached, and it occupied fifty minutes in the delivery.

It was whilst staying at Mr. Long's house, some time in the preceding year, that Mr. Jay went over to Wotton-under-Edge, and opened the chapel of his late old friend, Rowland Hill, upon its being rebuilt; he preaching in the morning, and the Rev. Mr. James in the evening. Mr. Jay's old friend

Dr. Raffles came from Liverpool purposely to see him and hear him preach. The doctor delivered on the following day an eloquent sermon in the same place of worship.

CHAPTER XXXVII.

Mr. Jay's return to Bath—Female Biography of the Old and New Testament Scriptures—Extracts from the Lecture entitled "Hannah"—Dr. Hunter.

Shortly after the delivery of Mr. Jay's final discourse as a minister of the Gospel, he with a sorrowful heart took leave of his daughter and son-in-law, Mr. and Mrs. Bolton, and all his friends in Gloucestershire,—a county to which he was greatly attached, having preached in it oftener than in any other county of England, with the exception of that in which Bath is situated. He then went on to Bradford, where he intended to have made an extended stay; but, after having been there for a short time, his complaint returned upon him in an aggravated form, and his spirits became daily more depressed. This compelled him to hasten his return homewards (some time about the latter end of September 1853), in order to be near his medical advisers.

He was deeply affected on returning to Bath as a simple individual, and not as William Jay, the pastor of Argyle Chapel. This reflection would often cause a tear to start from his eye. "I will," said he to me, "throw aside all melancholy feelings; and although I am no longer a minister at Bath, I will, in order not to be wholly useless to the public, endeavour yet to serve them in my old age. Amongst my manuscripts, which I lately looked over, I found a number of lectures, delivered by me nearly fifty years ago, on the subject of the female biography of the Old and New Testament Scriptures. It is my intention, please God, to publish and dedicate them to the Dowager Countess of Ducie, whose son's new chapel at Tortworth I have so recently opened, and which I look upon as the last important act of my ministry. This will be a work of some little labour; for I shall have to revise and introduce much to present the lectures in a fit state to meet the public eye."

I approved of his resolution, saying, "What do you think now of the *voluntary system*, which could so suddenly snap the tie which connected you with Argyle Chapel?" "Why," said he, "I must confess that the system is not over-prolific in liberality. I remember, when once preaching a sermon in aid of some institution, I finished it by saying, 'I shall presently see by the contents of the plates what the voluntary system will do this morning.' But this exclamation did not prevent many people passing them by unnoticed."

"You know," I said to him, "that it was my most earnest wish that you should die the pastor of Argyle Chapel; but since it was not permitted that it should be so, what a benefit it would have been to the religious world at large if you had resigned upon the death of my dear mother, and devoted the remainder of your life to authorship!" "That was the only consideration," replied he, "that could have induced me to have resigned; but I looked upon myself as wedded for life to my late congregation. Could I have devoted a few years solely to my pen, I think I should have written essays on various religious subjects; but it is a style which in my opinion is ill adapted to the pulpit. But, do you know, I think I can preach now as well as ever I did, and certainly with greater ease." And here let me remark, that after ceasing to be the minister of Argyle Chapel, he was unwilling to retire from the pulpit; and those who heard the sermons which he delivered in Gloucester, Bradford, and Bratton, describe them as being worthy of his well-established reputation.

Although Mr. Jay was labouring under acute pain and extreme languor from his complaint, yet such was his strength of mind and anxiety to send forth his lectures on female biography to the world, that in every intermission of pain he laboured diligently in his library to carry his intention into effect; and it was gratified, the dedication to the Dowager Countess of Ducie and the preface to the biography being written in his bed four days prior to his death, and the last sheet of the work passing through the press when the venerable author was summoned to his rest.

In his dedication to the dowager countess he truly says that, "In the lamented death of Earl Ducie has been removed the singularly-attached husband, the tender father of a large and noble family, the delight of his friends and acquaintances, the praise of his neighbourhood, and the subject of a widened fame in the county of which he was the ornament and benefactor;" and that "it would not, perhaps, be easy to find another in the same elevated sphere so free from prejudice and bigotry; so firm in the essentials, and so tolerant in the circumstantials, of religion; so open and fearless in the profession of the truth as it is in

Jesus; so abhorrent of hypocrisy, formalism, and cant; so attached to the sacred volume; so concerned for its diffusion; so regardful of the poor, and so anxious for their instruction."

In the preface, the very last effort of his pen, he says, "I delivered these lectures on Sabbath evenings, from short notes; but afterwards, as soon as possible, while the subjects were fresh in my recollection, I wrote them at full length, or nearly so.

"This was the case with all of them, except the lecture on the Poor Widow, on the Elect Lady, and on the Mother of our Lord. The two former of them were indeed so far written out that I have recently been able with tolerable ease to complete them; but those (for I have five) on the Virgin Mary had been left in so imperfect a state, that I found it was too much for me to think of filling them up at the time.

"Though indisposition and various other interruptions prevented me for a while, I hoped for some few leisure moments when I might recover and transcribe what I had delivered on this extraordinary personage; but, alas, the moments never came, or came in vain.

"I lament this, as I had thought much on the subject, and had wished to steer between the idolatries of the Church of Rome and the excessive fears of some Protestants, which have betrayed them into a degree of the opposite extreme."

I perfectly well recollect being present in Mr. Jay's library upon his perusing the manuscript of one of the lectures entitled "Hannah." After its perusal, he appeared deeply affected, and laying it down on the table, said, "How well I remember delivering this lecture, even after the lapse of nearly fifty years!

What a crowded congregation listened to it! But there is one circumstance which most distinctly impresses itself on my mind; it was the deep interest with which your dear mother listened to the discourse, and the admiration she expressed at two of the passages, which I will read to you." After doing so, he threw down the manuscript, looked pensive for a few minutes, as if thinking of past times, and then recovering from his reverie, which I forbore to disturb, he began to discourse upon a few of the leading subjects of the day.

The first passages of the lecture he read to me were its commencement, and were in these words: "The birth of a child is one of the most important events that ever takes place in the world. But for the frequency of the occurrence, it would be deemed little less than a miracle of nature and Providence. The structure of the body, the powers of the soul, the union of flesh and spirit, the provision made to nourish and preserve life,—all proclaim that we are fearfully and wonderfully made.

"The birth of any infant is a far greater event than the production of the sun. The sun sees not his own light, feels not his own heat, and, with all his grandeur, will cease to be; but that infant which began to breathe only yesterday will hear the heavens pass away with a great noise, and see the elements melt with fervent heat. That infant is possessed of reason, conscience, and immortality. It is true these principles are not yet developed; but they are in embryo, and the oak is contained in the acorn, and the day in the dawn."

The other passages from this lecture which Mr. Jay

read to me were in relation to a common and, as he feared, an increasing evil,—the abandonment of maternal nursing, upon which subject he thus expresses himself:

"Surely nothing can be a more ungrateful return than to treat with neglect and disdain the provision which the goodness and kindness of God have obviously made for the performance of this duty.

"And is it not a violence offered to nature, and such a violence as is unknown to all the inferior animals, and to the most barbarous nations, and to the polished Greeks and Romans in their purer ages?

"Were I to speak of its physical injuriousness, I might seem to get off my own ministerial and moral ground; but here I can appeal for my censure to proper and qualified authorities. Have not the most eminent physicians told us that the sudden check of the nutritious fluid may be of the worst consequences to the mother, by gendering disease, and even risking life itself? Have they not told us that there are many disorders incident to women of which their nursing is the most effectual cure; that delicate constitutions are strengthened by it; that when a mother suckles her children, her complexion becomes clearer, her spirits more uniformly cheerful, her appetite more regular, and her general habits stronger? Have they not affirmed, even, that fewer women die while they are nursing than at any equal period of their lives? Have they not told us what injury the babe may sustain by being deprived of its own natural nourishment; yea, and that a far greater number of those children die that are nursed by aliens than of such as are nursed maternally? And is it not strange that a mother should deprive herself of the most exquisite pleasure of tender and endeared sympathy and kindness; or that a woman of sensibility can see the darling of her soul hanging on the breast of another, and stroking the cheek of a stranger, engrossing her maternal rights, and sure to be more loved than herself?"

At the time Mr. Jay delivered these lectures it was his intention to have published them; but he delayed doing so for these two reasons, viz. that Dr. Hunter, for whom he entertained a great friendship, and whose talent he highly appreciated, had written on several female scriptural characters; and that Dr. Cox of Hackney had also anticipated him on the same subject.

The mention of Dr. Hunter brings to my recollection an anecdote which I have often heard Mr. Jay relate, respecting the intrusion of a queer stranger into that minister's chapel in London. In a letter which he wrote to his wife, he thus describes the incident: "My dearest love,—Last night I preached for a Sunday-morning lecture, in commemoration of the accession of this family to the throne. Dr. Hunter prayed. The congregation was large; and just as I was concluding the sermon, there was a general consternation and outcry. All was confusion, the people treading on one another, &c. It was rather dark, and the pulpit-candles only were lighted. I saw something moving up the aisle towards the vestry. It was a bull! we presume driven in by pickpockets, or persons who wished to disturb us. We were talking on the affairs of the nation, and *John Bull* very seasonably came in. But imagine what followed: the bull could not be made to go backwards, nor could he be turned round;

five or six persons, therefore, held him by the horns; while the clerk, as if bewitched, gave out, in order to appease the noise,

> "Praise God, from whom all blessings flow,
> Praise Him, *all creatures* here below," &c.

O that the bull could but have *roared* here in compliance with the exhortation! I looked down from the pulpit, and seeing the gentlemen who held him singing with their faces lifted up, as if returning thanks for this unexpected blessing, I was obliged to put my hand before my face while I dismissed the congregation. This, I think, is enough for once. I long to receive a line from you, to tell me all your plans. Love to the dear children."

Mr. Jay, in relating to me the above anecdote, stated two other circumstances, which, he said, annoyed him quite as much as the intrusion of the bull. The first of them was, that during the greater portion of the sermon he observed Dr. Hunter was fast asleep; and the second was, that whilst standing by the side of the gentleman holding the plate, the bull began cantering up the aisle towards the door in so furious a manner, that, in his eagerness to escape out of the chapel, he knocked against the plate and upset the money on the ground. Mr. Jay, who was a great admirer of the doctor's writings, attended him on his deathbed.

CHAPTER XXXVIII.

The rapid decline of Mr. Jay's health, and daily prostration of strength—His cheerfulness and resignation.

AFTER remaining at Percy Place for a few days, I was compelled by professional avocations, much to my regret, to return to London. On my departure, I promised Mr. Jay that I would pay him a prolonged visit at Christmas. "Ah," said he, "who knows whether the Almighty will spare my life so long? If He does, it is my wish that I should then see all my family in England around me."

Having received, in the month of November, a letter from my sister stating that her father's strength was daily declining, and the paroxysms of pain arising from his disorder more frequent and intense, I hastened without loss of time to Percy Place. I found him not much changed in appearance, but greatly prostrated in strength. He was, however, at times very cheerful, and would, after the devotions of the morning had been concluded, request me either to read to him the leading articles of the *Times*, or any book which would amuse him and divert his attention for a while: the greater part of the day was, however, occupied by him in completing the female biography alluded to in the preceding chapter. And this was not a very easy task; for he had great difficulty, after the lapse of so many years, in reading his own writing: for it should be stated that he was a rapid writer, his thoughts flowing very quickly from his pen; and that he had, moreover, in early life, invented a shorthand of his own, which he had nearly forgotten. In fact, reading, being read to, and attending to the completion of the biography, seemed to be now his sole delight. Numerous were the calls at Percy Place to inquire after his health; but he seldom saw any person, being anxious for retirement. Dr. Bowie and Mr. Brown (a celebrated surgeon at Bath, and an old friend of Mr. Jay's) were constantly in attendance on him, and endeavoured by every means in their power to ease his pain and cheer his mind. Beyond the professional and friendly calls of these gentlemen, he received the visits of no one; the society of his own household and that of his relations being all he cared for. He had now given up walking in his garden, but was constantly looking into and giving directions to the gardener about it.

During this visit, I observed that he would frequently throw himself back in his arm-chair, and appear as if half asleep, on which occasions his family would keep perfect silence, fearful of disturbing him. He would generally, after the lapse of half an hour, start up, and addressing himself to me, say, "Cyrus, why don't you talk; I know you can always amuse." My talking would generally be the precursor and prompter of his own. One evening, he was very animated in conversation, and narrated to his family circle various anecdotes connected with his native place, Tisbury, and Fonthill Abbey, and expressed a great desire to visit once more, ere he died, the place of his birth.

I particularly remember the following statement he made to us respecting the tower of Fonthill Abbey: "On a very clear day," said he, "my two nephews were riding on horseback; and whilst looking at the elegant structure at the distance of two miles, and expressing their mutual admiration of it, they saw its very high tower fall instantaneously, and vanish like a dream. They thought they had lost their senses, the shock being so sudden. I always thought that such would be its fate; for my father, who worked at it, told me that the masons who were employed in erecting it predicted its sudden downfall. The head-mason, who had the superintendence of laying the foundation of the tower, when dying, sent for Mr. Beckford, and confessed to him that the base was defective, and that the building would one day tumble down. Mr. Beckford inquired of him whether it could not be remedied; and the reply was, 'Certainly not. The only thing is, to take the tower down and rebuild it.' What a providence it was that the tower did not fall when the building was crowded with nobility and visitors at the several weeks' sale of its furniture and articles of virtù!"

Another anecdote which Mr. Jay related to us was respecting an act of nervousness exhibited by Lord Nelson when on a visit to Fonthill, after one of his great naval victories, little to be expected from one whose acts of bravery were the admiration of the world, and who had then lost an arm and eye in battle. Mr. Beckford being desirous to drive his distinguished guest round the grounds of Fonthill, both of them took their seats in an open phaeton, drawn by four horses. Mr. Beckford, in order to show his lordship the improvements on his large estate, and point out the most interesting pieces of scenery to him, drove the phaeton at a very moderate rate. They had not proceeded very far before Nelson began to exhibit much restlessness, and after a few minutes said to Beckford, "Really this is more than I can stand. You must set me down. I cannot ride any longer behind the horses." It was in vain that Mr. Beckford assured him that the animals were perfectly tractable and entirely under his command. His lordship descended, and Mr. Beckford had to take the phaeton back again at a walking pace.

Having mentioned the name of Mr. Beckford in connection with Fonthill Abbey, in the erection of which Mr. Jay, when a youth of fourteen, had been employed under his father, I may observe that it could not fail to be a source of great satisfaction to him to find that a gentleman of such high literary attainments and exquisite taste had purchased his works. *The Christian Contemplated* was much admired by Mr. Beckford, as appears from numerous notes written on its leaves in his own handwriting, and from one of which the following is an extract: "This man's mind is no petty reservoir supplied him by laborious pumpings. It is a clear transparent spring flowing so freely as to impress the idea of its being inexhaustible. In many of these pages the stream of eloquence is so full, so rapid, that we are fairly borne down and laid prostrate at the feet of the preacher, whose arguments in these moments appear as if they could not be controverted, and we must yield to them. The voice which calls us to look into ourselves, and prepare for judgment, is too piercing, too powerful, to be resisted; and we attempt, for worldly and sensual considerations, to shut our ears in vain."

Mr. Goodridge, an eminent architect of Bath, and who had been professionally employed by Mr. Beckford, and that gentleman's son-in-law, the late Duke of Hamilton, says, "I was on one occasion at the Horticultural Exhibition, Sydney Gardens, with Mr. Beckford: Mr. Jay being there also, I pointed him out; and as Mr. Beckford was desirous of seeing him, we walked towards the place where he was standing, and I exchanged salutations, but there was no introduction. On the publication of his *Recollections of Alcobaca* he sent a copy to Mr. Jay, inscribing (in his own handwriting) *From the Author* on its pages. 'Take this,' said he, 'to the good and holy man, say all that is kind from me to him, and beg his acceptance of it.'"

The Rev. Mr. Neale, in relation to the closing scenes of Mr. Beckford's life, states that that gentleman, in a conversation with him, said, "Jay of Bath was one of the finest preachers he had ever heard;" and, that "he had had a correspondence with him (Jay) about the bad poetry, both in the Church and among Dissenters, as exhibited in the hymns and psalm-versions which they used."

One evening, after Mr. Jay had been narrating to us many reminiscences of his early life, to which he was now very fond of recurring, he requested me to read to him some of the letters of his dear and early friend Newton, of whom he says, in his Autobiography, "I deem him the most perfect instance of the spirit and temper of Christianity I ever knew—shall I say with the *exception?* no, but with the addition, of

Cornelius Winter." After I ceased reading, he retired to bed; but I fear had little rest.

The next morning being very fine he took a short drive upon the road; but, on his return home, said that it had so shaken and given him such pain that he should be obliged to forego his much-cherished wish to take a last farewell of Tisbury. "I shall never leave my home again," he exclaimed, "except to my place of burial." He spoke these words with the firmness of one who had made up his mind to die.

In the afternoon of that day I was with him in his library, when he was looking over some of the manuscripts of his life. I observed that he perused one of them very particularly. After a few minutes he read it to me, but in doing so was at times much affected. It contained an account of his parentage, the dwelling of his parents at Tisbury, and the early effects of scenery upon him. The following passages of the manuscript, having reference to the home of his parents and the scenery surrounding it, may perhaps interest the reader: "Our dwelling, which was my father's own property, consisting of a double tenement, too large for a cottage, had attached to it a proportionate garden and orchard. It was situated about an equal distance from Wardour Castle, the seat of Lord Arundel; Pithouse, the seat of Mr. Bennet; and Fonthill, then the splendid mansion of Mr. Beckford. The village in which it stood was wide and varied, and abounded with lovely and interesting aspects,

'And the sweet interchange of hill and dale and wood and lawn.'

It was impossible to express the intense pleasure I

felt from a child in the survey of rural scenery, while standing on the brow of an eminence, or seated upon the upraised root of a branching tree, or walking through a waving field of corn, or gazing upon a clear brook with fish and reeds and rushes. How vividly some of those spots are impressed upon my memory still; and how recoverable, at this distance of time, are some of the rude reflections so early associated with them!"

After finishing the reading of this manuscript, he said to me, "Cyrus, my children must not consider me unjust in having left my freehold cottage, garden, and orchard at Tisbury to the Independent chapel there, which I opened. I feel such an interest in the place, that I think it is the best appropriation I can make of the property."

On the following morning, I left Bath for London; but my next visit to Percy Place was to witness the death of a dear and venerable father.

Although Mr. Jay was suffering during the whole of this visit under frequent and acute pain, yet he nevertheless bore it as a Christian, and felt grateful for the slightest act of attention. His complaint affected neither his memory nor recollection, and in the intervals of cessation from pain he exhibited a cheerfulness of spirit which made one forget that his race was nearly run.

CHAPTER XXXIX.

The closing scenes of Mr. Jay's life—Christmas-day.

On the Wednesday before Christmas-day 1853, I was summoned to Bath by a telegraphic letter from my sister, Mrs. Ashton, stating that her father had just taken to his bed, and could not possibly survive many days.

I was not long before I arrived at Percy Place, and found that Mr. Jay had not much altered in personal appearance since my recent visit to him. Although he was at times suffering the most excruciating pain, he was, in the intervals of its cessation, cheerful, a smile oftentimes beaming on his face. His voice was firm and intellect unclouded.

He was most assiduously attended by Mrs. Jay, my sisters Mrs. Bolton and Mrs. Ashton, and his sons-in-law, all of whom were almost constantly with him.

The day after my arrival (Thursday), when left alone with him in his chamber, I expressed my satisfaction to him in having about him such excellent and sympathising nurses as his wife, his daughters, and his servant Ellen. "They are," said he, "too good and too attentive; but I should feel happier if I were left more alone to my own reflections; besides, their sorrowful faces disquiet me in these last moments of my life. As to my wife, she seems always in distress,—in fact, so much of her life has been spent in a sick room, that she ever appears to anticipate the worst results. I wish I could see her more cheerful." "A physician," I said to him, "once remarked to me, that he would rather have *paid nurses* than any other; for they are stronger and healthier, do their work without sympathising, and are free from that melancholy countenance which tends to disquiet and disturb a patient." "I think the physician was right in his observation, Cyrus," said Mr. Jay; "and one thing is quite certain, and a great blessing it is to reflect upon it, that the poor who go to hospitals receive the best advice, and the best-regulated attention."

On the following day (Friday), after prayers had been read to him, and he had passed some time in devotion, he fell back in his bed and composed himself for a while, Mrs. Jay and myself remaining in the room with him. It was a brilliant but frosty morning, and the sun shone directly upon his bed. After reposing for about half an hour, he raised himself up in his bed, saying he felt much easier. The sunbeams seemed to exhilarate his spirits. To my surprise, he began asking me about the Russian war. After I had given him all the information I could about it, he said he should feel much obliged to me if I could read any thing very short, which would divert his mind for a while. I said, "If you recollect, I read to you, at your last visit to Worthing, Dickens's Notes on America, which much amused you, although you were then suffering great pain, and which you informed me had also amused your friend Foster the Essayist, when read to him just before his death. I remember you laughed very much at the humorous description by Dickens of the New York pig in the Broadway. Shall I read it to you?" "O, I should like to hear it very much again; for I recollect it much diverted me when you last read the Notes to me."

Having procured the book from the library, I read to him the following account of the pig:

"Here is a solitary swine lounging homeward by himself. He has only one ear; having parted with the other to vagrant dogs in the course of his city rambles. But he gets on very well without it; and leads a roving, gentlemanly, vagabond kind of life, somewhat answering to that of our club-men at home. He leaves his lodgings every morning at a certain hour, throws himself upon the town, gets through his day in some manner quite satisfactory to himself, and regularly appears at the door of his own house again at night, like the mysterious master of Gil Blas. He is a free-and-easy, careless, indifferent kind of pig, having a very large acquaintance among other pigs of the same character, whom he rather knows by sight than conversation, as he seldom troubles himself to stop and exchange civilities, but goes grunting down the kennel, turning up the news and small talk of the city, in the shape of cabbage-stalks and offal, and bearing no tails but his own; which is a very short one, for his old enemies the dogs have been at that too, and have left him hardly enough to swear by. He is in every respect a republican pig, going where-ever he pleases, and mingling with the best society; on an equal, if not superior footing, for every one makes way when he appears, and the haughtiest give him the wall if he prefer it. He is a great philosopher, and seldom moved, unless by the dogs before mentioned. Sometimes, indeed, you may see his small eye twinkling on a slaughtered friend, whose carcass garnishes a butcher's door-post; but he grunts, buries his nose in the mire again, and waddles down the gutter,—comforting himself with the reflection that there is one snout the less to anticipate stray cabbage-stalks, at any rate. They are the city-scavengers, these pigs;—ugly brutes they are, having, for the most part, scanty brown backs, like the lids of horsehair trunks, spotted with unwholesome black botches. They have long gaunt legs too, and such peaked snouts, that if one of them could be persuaded to sit for his profile, nobody would recognise it for a pig's likeness."

I asked Mr. Jay if I should read any more of the book. He said, "No, I thank you, Cyrus; it has relieved me a little." Mrs. Jay, who, I observed, was very restless whilst I was reading, then began talking to him, upon which I left the room.

The next morning (Saturday), he, after devotion, sat up in bed correcting the last of the proof-sheets of the Female Biography, and getting Mr. Ashton to read them to him, he still having as clear an intellect as ever, notwithstanding the violent paroxysm of pain which oftentimes rendered his frame a machine of agony. After the proof had been finally perfected, I induced him to allow me to send to the hair-dresser to shave him, thinking it would refresh him. He acquiesced; and on the hair-dresser's arrival, we lifted him into an easy-chair. He appeared much refreshed after being shaved, saying to the operator, whom he knew very well, "This will be the last time I shall ever require your services." The hair-dresser asked him whether he would like to have his hair cut. He replied quickly, "No;" and it struck me by the look of his eye that he had an idea, which proved to be correct, that his hair was required for distribution amongst his admirers: for after his dissolution numerous were the applications even by the post to obtain a lock of it. After we lifted him into his bed, I asked him whether I should read any more out of Dickens's book to him. He said, "Yes, you may, Cyrus. I feel myself much easier than I lately did, and this sunny day cheers me. I remember that there is another story about a pig, which you can read to me." And here I should remark that he always had a great partiality, as Dickens professed he had, for pigs, and when in a farm-yard found a source of amusement, when every other failed, in watching the proceedings of these odd animals.

I then read to him the story which Dickens, with his usual humour, thus narrates:

"As we were riding along this morning, I observed a little incident between two youthful pigs, which was so very human as to be inexpressibly comical and grotesque at the time, though I dare say in telling it is tame enough.

"One young gentleman (a very delicate porker with several straws sticking about his nose, betokening recent investigations in a dunghill) was walking deliberately on, profoundly thinking, when suddenly his brother, who was lying in a miry hole unseen by him, rose up immediately before his startled eyes, ghastly with damp mud. Never was pig's whole mass of blood so turned. He started back at least three feet, gazed for a moment, and then shot off as hard as he could go: his excessive little tail vibrating with speed and terror like a distracted pendulum. But before he had gone very far he began to reason with himself as to the nature of this frightful appearance; and as he reasoned he relaxed his speed by gradual degrees, until at last he stopped, and faced about. There was his brother, with the mud upon him glazing in the sun, yet staring out of the very same hole, perfectly amazed at his proceedings! He was no sooner assured of this, and he assured himself so carefully that one may almost say he shaded his eyes with his hand to see the better, than he came back at a round trot, pounced upon him, and summarily took off a piece of his tail, as a caution to him to be careful what he was about for the future, and never to play tricks with his family any more."

Mr. Jay seemed to enjoy the story of the delicate and youthful porker even more than he did that which I had read to him the day before. This was the last time I ever read to him; and I observed that, on this occasion, Mrs. Jay seemed pleased, because the story had pleased my father. It appeared to me as if, after the mental exertion which the completing of the Female Biography entailed upon him, he liked to hear something sprightly; for he was ever of a happy disposition. After the completion of this work, his spirits gradually sunk, and conversation disquieted him.

The next day was Christmas-day, which fell upon a Sunday, and it was ushered in by the paroxysms of pain being more intense and frequent. He occasionally groaned much. We tried to soothe him, and to divert his mind from the agony of pain. He said, "I do not murmur; allow me to groan, it seems to ease my pain. Objects most dear and attractive now fail to interest. I have made some little stir in life, but now I am nothing; God seems to be saying, 'I can do without you.' An official character is not to be judged of by his ministerial work; he is compelled often to administer comfort to others, when perhaps he is not enjoying it himself."

Dr. Bowie's appearance during the day seemed to work like magic upon him, making him momentarily forget his pain. "O," said he to him, in a firm voice, "what a Christmas-day we shall spend! But I can say, 'Thanks be unto God for His unspeakable gift,'" and then quoted the text, "Blessed be the God and Father of our Lord Jesus Christ, which according to His abundant mercy hath begotten us again unto a lively hope by the resurrection of Jesus Christ from the dead, to an inheritance incorruptible, and undefiled, and that fadeth not away, reserved in heaven for you, who are kept by the power of God through faith unto salvation ready to be revealed in the last time."

Almost immediately after Dr. Bowie's departure, the paroxysms of pain returned upon him with such intensity as to cause him to exclaim, "I fear God has forsaken me," and, after a slight pause, he added, "let me not be impatient, let me repose in His love. I fear I am impatient." Mrs. Jay replied, "Think of the feelings of your precious Saviour: like you, He said, 'My God, my God, why hast Thou forsaken me?' He has promised never to forsake you. His grace is sufficient for you." He then replied, "I mourn, I do not murmur; 'It is the Lord, let Him do unto me what seemeth Him good.' I desire to lie passive, and know no will but His. 'In patience possess ye your souls.' Lay no more upon me than Thou wilt enable me to bear, and I will glorify Thee in my sore affliction. The language of the publican did, does, and ever will befit me, and even down to death must be my cry, 'God be merciful to me a sinner.'"

Even in the very height of agony, his recollection was as unclouded, and his quotations from Scripture as appropriate as if he had been in a pulpit, and not on a dying bed. And so appropriate, too, to his sad state! Sometimes, when Mrs. Jay wished to draw his attention to particular passages of Scripture, he would say, "Pray do not speak to me upon the subject, for it will distract me. I know the Scriptures better than you do, and I deeply meditate upon them." And how often did we see his lips moving as if in devotion, and a transient smile playing across his face, reminding his family of what he was in the days of health! Such was his last Christmas-day on earth: the evening saw his agonies somewhat abated, but that was only the precursor of the near approach of death.

I shall describe the last two days of his life in the next chapter.

Sketched by Walter Mosley.

CHAPTER XL.

The Death of Mr. Jay.

Monday morning saw him more composed, in fact he seemed to have made up his mind to bear pain without repining. He spoke little, but apparently was thinking much. After the morning's devotion I left the room, but returned again in the early part of the afternoon. The day was very frosty and cold, and the sky unclouded. He said to Mrs. Jay and his family, that he should like to have one more look at his favourite garden, and the beautiful prospect surrounding it, before he died. His family, with the exception of myself, dissuaded him from getting out of his bed, fearful that the exertion would be too much for him; but I urged that his wish ought to be indulged. Having carefully and warmly wrapped him up, Mr. Ashton and myself got him out of bed, and placed him in an easy-chair, which we wheeled to the window, where he remained for upwards of an hour. I was standing close by his side and watching him: he was quite silent, but I observed that his eye first alighted on his garden, wherein he had spent so many happy hours, and that he was looking at the various beds, plants, and trees in it. He then cast his eye upon the meadows by the river-side, and said, "There is the milkman feeding his cows with hay;" then towards the hill beyond the river, on the side of which runs a canal, then crowded with skaters, but their heads alone were discernible from the window; and then his eye alighted on the castle at the top of the hill, but he made no remark. After viewing the beautiful surrounding prospect for some time, he cast his eye again on the garden. It was remarkable that although it was so sunny when he was wheeled to the window, after the lapse of half an hour, the clouds began to gather, and at length a heavy snow-storm set in, and large flakes beat against the window. He appeared affected and fatigued, and said, "The prospect of my garden is now hid from my sight; I have nothing to do but retire to my bed and die." Whilst Mr. Ashton and myself were lifting his heavy frame into his bed, he said, "Here is the end of the popular preacher." He spoke but little when he got into bed, and seemed anxious not to be spoken to. He occasionally dozed; but nothing that could be called sleep came to his aid.

The morning of Tuesday the 27th December, the day of his death, at length came, and as soon as the light dawned upon the earth a cheerless scene presented itself—a clouded sky above, and the snow-covered earth below. But it accorded well with the gloomy scene of death. Occasional paroxysms of pain had racked his enfeebled body during the night, but they now became less frequent and painful. He spoke but little, only his lips were occasionally in motion; and whilst I was close to his bed during one part of the day, I heard him softly whispering forth a prayer; his eyes were closed, and he did not observe me. He afterwards fell into a slumber for a short time, and upon opening his eyes, a smile illuminated his countenance, as he beheld his family, like a dying patriarch of old, around him. He then closed his eyes, but it was not to sleep; it was merely the languor of a dying man, who thought that darkness best suited his exit from this world. After a little while, he opened his eyes for a moment, as if endeavouring to arouse himself, and said to us in a firm and pathetic tone, "O, none of you know what it is to die." From that time he spoke little, but sank gradually into the arms of death, becoming so still and calm, that the precise moment of his death could not be ascertained.

I am not superstitious; but there was such an indescribable smile playing on his countenance during his dying moments, that it strongly impressed my mind with the idea, that he had caught a glimpse of the glory of heaven, and that his soul was passing to uncreated light; and then, under such impression, these passages, which I had often heard my dear parent repeat, came to my remembrance: "Thus he came up to the gate. Then the King commanded to open the gate, that the righteous which keepeth the truth may enter in. Now just as the gates were opened, I looked in, and, behold, the city shone like the sun; the streets were paved with gold, and in them walked many with crowns on their heads, palms in their hands, and golden harps to sing praises withal. There were also of them that had wings;—and they answered one another without intermission, saying, 'Holy, holy, holy is the Lord.' And after that they shut up the gates; which, when I had seen, I wished myself amongst them."

I cannot conclude this chapter more appropriately than by availing myself of the following able observations, made on the occasion of the death of my revered parent, by the editors of his Autobiography:

"Thus closed the lengthened earthly career of this eminent servant of Christ, who, through the period of *sixty-three* years, faithfully discharged his ministerial commission, and diligently served his generation, in a city distinguished indeed by its fashion and gaiety, but yet not wholly insensible to the attractions of his eloquent and evangelic labours.

". . . . . . The truths he has embalmed in his writings, or by his eloquent tongue upon living hearts, will retain their interest and influence undiminished amidst all material ruin and desolation; and the writings of William Jay will continue to shed light upon the pathway of many a traveller Zionward, and to train many of the heirs of immortality for their mansion in the skies.

"When William Jay died, the city in which he had so long laboured lost one of its most honourable patriarchs, one of its richest ornaments and holiest attractions. *There*, under his ministry, senators, wearied with the cares of state, had listened gratefully to the Saviour's invitation, 'Come unto me, all ye that labour and are heavy laden, and I will give you rest;' and found that repose which only faith and hope can impart. *There* many of the slaves of dissipation and vice were emancipated, by the gracious words which proceeded out of his mouth, from the fetters of their fatal enchantment, and were brought into the glorious liberty of the children of God. *There* the eager votaries of fashion, thirsting for the pleasures of sense, and proving the emptiness of the wells from which they had hoped to draw them, were allured by his mellifluous tones to taste the fountain of living water, and found the bliss which they had in vain sought from worldly sources. *There,* too, the victims of fell diseases, who had tried many remedies and were nothing bettered, were directed by him to the Divine Physician of their souls, and received that healing which made their bodily afflictions light, by teaching them to triumph over death."

CHAPTER XLI.

Funeral of Mr. Jay—And passing notices of the deaths of his daughter, Mrs. Ashton, and her husband, and of his son-in-law, the Rev. Mr. Bolton.

A FEW minutes after the decease of my venerable parent, my sisters and brothers-in-law retired to the library, there to deliberate upon the steps necessary to be taken consequent on the melancholy event. Unwilling to interfere with their wishes in the matter, I left them, and betook myself to the green-house, and from thence walked about the garden, covered as it was with snow. I thought of the deep interest he took in this earthly paradise of his, and the tasteful and elegant disposition, by his own hand, of his little beds of flowers.

On returning to the library, full of mournful reflections, I espied, in the passage of the house, hanging on a peg, and in the same position as my father had last left it, his garden-hat. I observed that there were several green spots upon it, occasioned by its having rubbed against apple or other trees, when he was pruning or grafting them. While I was looking at it, one of the servants came out of the kitchen and said: "Only think, sir, of a mistake which occurred to my dear master a year or two ago. One Sunday morning, he had rather over-stayed in the garden. After leaving the house, I discovered that his garden-hat was missing, and going into his library, I found that he had gone out of doors with the wrong hat. I ran after him with his best hat in my hand, and soon overtook him. The hats were exchanged, much to the amusement of several persons who were near him. I and my late master laughed heartily at the occurrence."

Upon my return into the library, I was informed by my sisters that they and their husbands had been discussing by whom the funeral service should be performed, and where the funeral sermon should be preached, and that they were unanimously of opinion that the burial should be conducted by the minister of the Vineyard Chapel, and that Mr. Jay's friend, the Rev. John Angell James, should be requested to preach the funeral sermon at the same chapel. This resolution, in the propriety of which I perfectly acquiesced, was taken in consequence of the *virtual dismissal* of the deceased (for his family, like himself, could not look upon it in any other light) from the pastorate of Argyle Chapel, after his long and faithful services there. I suggested, however, that the Rev. Mr. James should be consulted on the subject. An electric message was immediately sent to him, who, without loss of time, returned an answer to it, stating that, under all circumstances, the resolution of the family was the best course which could be adopted; and that he would readily perform the promise which he had made to his much-esteemed friend (some short time before his death) by preaching the funeral sermon.

The news of Mr. Jay's death soon spread through the city of Bath, and produced a universal feeling of sorrow amongst its citizens and visitors; and I may say throughout the nation, for he had occupied the public attention, both as a preacher and writer, for a longer period than what is generally allowed to man. The Bath papers published, on the day of his death, a supplemental sheet, containing a history (of many columns) of his life, and a critique on his preaching and works, from the able pen of his old and esteemed friend Mr. Wood.

Numerous were the calls made at Percy Place to view the corpse of my late father; but, with the exception of a few particular friends, the wish was not gratified.

There were also many applications made to the members of Mr. Jay's family to open his body, in order to ascertain of what disorder he died; but I interfered effectually to gratify such an act of curiosity. I said, "The complaint was ascertained by an eminent surgeon, when he was last at Worthing; but the *real cause* which *hastened* his death was that of *a broken heart;* and I am sure that in mangling his body you will find your science will avail you but little." The family agreed with me in opinion, and on the manner I had expressed myself on the subject; consequently there was no dissection; and so was he buried with the same placid smile on his face as he exhibited when his spirit took its flight.

It was the anxious and understood wish of his family that the funeral should be conducted as privately as possible, such being the desire of the deceased, often expressed by him during his illness.

The day of the funeral (the 3d of January 1854) was one of the most inclement in a winter of extraordinary severity; and so had it continued ever since the decease of Mr. Jay, destroying the greater portion of the shrubs and laurels in the garden of Percy Place.

The mournful procession left the house in a snowstorm; but nevertheless it did not deter a multitude of persons, some of them worn down by age and infirmity, from following to the grave the remains of one whom they so much revered in life, regardless of the drifting snow and piercing wind. I observed that on the line of procession all the shops were closed. On arriving at Snow Hill, the burial-ground of Argyle Chapel, we found that numbers had also there collected, who, mixing with those that had accompanied the procession, formed a great body of spectators. In this ground there was the same ceremony about to be performed over the remains of Mr. Jay as he had performed over his flock more than a thousand times.

The Rev. John Owen, of the Vineyard Chapel, officiated on this occasion, and in the course of the funeral oration paid the following tribute of affection and respect to the memory of Mr. Jay:

"In referring to our departed friend, whether we regard him as a believer in Christ, as a minister of the everlasting Gospel, as a pastor of a Christian church for so long a period, as a philanthropist, as an author, as a citizen, or as a friend, we cannot but sorrow, but most of all that we shall see his face no more on earth. There are circumstances, we admit, my dear friends, which greatly soothe our pain under the loss we have sustained, and which tend to moderate our regret, and to chasten our grief on this occasion. When we call to mind the early commencement and lengthened period of his religious course, the remarkable and increasing acceptableness and usefulness of his ministrations, the variety and unique excellence of his published works; when we look at the unsullied purity of his moral character; when we reflect on his peaceful end, and think of his present blessedness in the presence of Jehovah,—there is much, my brethren, to soothe our griefs. We mourn, but not on his account. No! He has fought the good fight, he has finished his course, he has kept the faith, and has now joined the general assembly and church of the first-born which are written in heaven; he is with the spirits of just men made perfect; he is with the Saviour he loved, the Saviour he proclaimed, and will be with Him for ever.

"And yet we cannot but mourn on our own account. We suffer a loss—a great loss—by his removal from our midst. We lose his wise counsels, his instructive example, his ready coöperation, his tender sympathy, and his fervent intercessions; and therefore we mourn. Jesus wept at the grave of Lazarus, and we may weep at the grave of the venerated Jay. His name will for ever be imprinted on my memory. For fifty years I have known it—for forty in connection with religion, for thirty-five as a fellow-minister of the Gospel; and especially during the last twenty-five have I regarded him as a son would regard connection with his father. From my first taking up my residence in this city, to the last day of his life, there was never a mis-thought or a mis-word between us, and therefore I cannot but mourn his loss on my own account."

After the delivery of the address, during the course of which many a tear was shed, Mr. Owen offered an impressive prayer; and having pronounced the apostolic benediction, the funeral procession was again formed, and the coffin having been deposited in the vault, we left the ground. Prior to the mortal remains of William Jay being consigned to their last resting-place, the numerous persons who had congregated together to pay their last respects towards one whom they so much venerated, looked with intense interest on the coffin whilst it was in the chapel; and upon it this inscription presented itself to their eyes:

REV. WILLIAM JAY,

DIED

27TH DECEMBER 1853,

AGED 84 YEARS.

On looking into the vault, I observed the coffins of my dear mother, my sister Statira, my brother Edward's wife, and Miss Prothero; and now there rested upon its brink another coffin, containing the remains of a dear parent, to add to the number. When the family beheld the heavy coffin lowered into the vault, it was some consolation to them to reflect that he was now free from all pain and anxiety.

On returning from the funeral, I could not help thinking of his old friend Mr. Titley, for many years his deacon, whom Mr. Jay had some years previously buried at the Snow-Hill Cemetery. They were sitting together one morning in a carriage, on their way to the burial-ground; and no conversation passing between them, the deacon suddenly patted his pastor on the thigh, and said, "Thank God, my dear sir, it will soon be my turn to be carried here;" and so it proved. I merely mention this circumstance, as it was alluded to in the oration which Mr. Jay made over the tomb of his friend, of whom he said, "He had more faith than any man I ever knew."

The funeral sermon was delivered two days afterwards by Mr. Jay's old attached friend, the Rev. John Angell James, at the Vineyard Chapel. It was a most impressive and excellent discourse, the text being, "Where is the Lord God of Elijah?" This sermon was printed, and had an extensive sale.

Funeral sermons were also preached on this occasion in Argyle Chapel, on the following Lord's Day, by the Rev. James Sherman of London, and by the Rev. Mr. Dyer; but for certain reasons, which the public can pretty well understand, the family of the deceased did not attend there. There was also a funeral sermon preached by the Rev. Richard Brindley, to the separate congregation worshiping *pro tempore* in the Assembly Room.

Some time after the decease of one so long known as *William Jay of Bath*, a tablet was erected to his memory in Argyle Chapel; but how or by whom the funds were collected, or who was the author of the ably written inscription, I know not; for I never visited Bath after my return to London, except for one day, and that was to attend the funeral (some four years afterwards) of his second wife. The tablet, which bears the following inscription, may be taken as an expression of sorrow on the part of the congregation that they did not allow the "faithful and beloved pastor" of Argyle Chapel to finish his career in their service:

SACRED TO THE MEMORY OF
THE REV. WILLIAM JAY,
FOR MORE THAN 62 YEARS
THE FAITHFUL AND BELOVED PASTOR
OF THE CHURCH AND CONGREGATION
ASSEMBLING IN THIS PLACE OF WORSHIP.
HIS DISTINGUISHED GIFTS, HIS HOLY LIFE,
AND HIS UNWEARIED LABOURS WERE CROWNED,
BY THE DIVINE BLESSING, WITH EXTENSIVE USEFULNESS,
AND HE LEFT A CONVICTION OF HIS INESTIMABLE WORTH,
WHICH THIS TABLET,
ERECTED AS A TRIBUTE OF AFFECTION,
IS DESIGNED TO COMMEMORATE.
HE WAS BORN MAY 8, 1769; ORDAINED JANUARY 30, 1791;
DIED DECEMBER 27, 1853, IN THE 85TH YEAR OF HIS AGE.

He was a good man, and full of the Holy Ghost and of faith.
Acts xi. 24.

Yes! this is the tablet erected in Argyle Chapel to the memory of a man who, thirty-four years previously thereto, when in the intensity of sorrow at the death of a beloved daughter, wrote an affecting letter to the deacons of Argyle Chapel (to which I have before alluded), soliciting a place where he might bury his dead, in which he says, "*Having passed the best part of my life amongst you, it is my wish to die in your service.*" This was not an aspiration uttered in the fervour of youth, for he was then of the matured age of fifty.

The Rev. John Angell James, in speaking of the

close of the earthly career of his friend, says, "The city that possessed his pulpit, around which such distinguished assemblies crowded, now exhibits his sepulchre. From the one they heard his living voice, from the other they will learn the silent but eloquent lesson of his death. No saintly shrine will be erected to court and stimulate the incense of superstitious and idolatrous worship, though he was a saint in the church below, and is now a glorified one in the church above; yet to his tomb a pathway will be worn by the foot of many pilgrims of affection from various parts of the earth, who will inquire for the spot—not where rest the ashes of the great dramatist, poet, philosopher, or statesman, but where, till the morning of the resurrection, repose the mortal remains of the wise and good and holy *William Jay*, the great and useful preacher of the Gospel of our salvation."

I will conclude this chapter with a few lines respecting his family. And here I must bestow unqualified praise on the deep and unremitting attention they paid to their deceased relative. Their first act, prior to taking their departure from Percy Place homewards, was a unanimous resolution on their part to allow his second wife to have the benefit of the house, and the use of the furniture and valuable library, during her lifetime, notwithstanding his will authorised the sale thereof, for distribution amongst his children in equal proportions. And here let me observe, that he left but little property behind him.

Death soon closed the career of two of the faithful attendants of the dying patriarch. The day after Mr. Ashton's arrival at Cambridge, from the house of mourning, he was smitten with an alarming stroke of paralysis, under which he became a nearly helpless man. But almost at the very commencement of this prostrate condition he had to endure a bitter trial. One Sunday afternoon (five weeks after the death of Mr. Jay), Mrs. Ashton, whose attentions to her husband were most unremitting, was, whilst walking in the beautiful grounds attached to the villa, taken suddenly ill. She hastened into the house, was seized with a fit, and expired in the room, and before the eyes of her suffering husband. Death, after an illness of about sixteen months, came to release him from pain and sorrow. Mr. Jay's other son-in-law, the Rev. Mr. Bolton, a gentleman of unblemished integrity, and of whom I have previously in these Recollections made mention more than once, has recently taken his departure, at a good age, leaving behind him a very interesting and talented family.

CHAPTER XLII.

Remarks on Mr. Jay's private character.

Mr. Jay's life was essentially one of sunshine, almost up to the termination of his lengthened career. Even whilst the victim of a painful disorder, he was, as each paroxysm passed away, still the same cheerful man in disposition as when he first started into public life.

But there were many circumstances tending, even in the early days of his boyhood, to render his disposition a happy and contented one. His parents, besides being religious, kind, and tender, were of cheerful dispositions, and much beloved and esteemed by all the neighbourhood of Tisbury. It was in this village that he acquired that love of nature which never departed from him; and the last wish which he expressed upon his death-bed, as previously stated, was to cast his eyes once more, before they were closed for ever, upon hill, dale, and running stream. Then, again, he found in the days of his youth a kind and cheerful friend in his tutor Cornelius Winter, acquired an early popularity which never spoiled him, and contracted in early life a happy marriage.

Indeed, so cheerful was Mr. Jay during the whole course of a long life, except in those moments when he was weighed down by domestic affliction, that it was almost at its very close that he takes this retrospect of it. "But you may ask, should I be willing, such as I have found it, to go over life again. I should not shrink from the proposal of repetition. Goodness and mercy have followed me all the days of my life. My duties have not been burdening and irksome. My trials have been few compared with my comforts. My pleasures have been cheap and simple, and therefore very numerous. I have relished the bounties of Providence, using them with moderation and thankfulness. Preaching has been the element of my heart and head. The seat of my residence was of all others the place of my preference. My condition has been the happy medium neither of poverty nor riches. I had a most convenient habitation, with a large and lovely garden,—a constant source of attraction, exercise, and improvement. I had a sufficient collection of books of all kinds. My wife was a gentlewoman, a saint, and a domestic goddess; my children were fair and healthy and dutiful; my friends were many, and cordial and steady. Where shall I end?

> 'Call not earth a barren spot,
>   Pass it not unheeded by;
> 'Tis to man a lovely spot,
>   Though a lovelier waits on high.'

I do not believe that in this earth misery predominates over good. I have a better opinion of mankind than I had when I began public life."

The primitive manner in which he lived tended greatly to make him a happy man; and so did the distribution of his time; the early part of the day being devoted to his pulpit and press studies, and the after part being usually spent in exercise or reading.

But there was another reason which tended to render him a cheerful man. It was in his extreme temperance both as regarded eating and drinking. He seldom partook of more than one joint; and as to drinking, he had been all through life extremely temperate, and for many years of his life constantly and entirely a teetotaler. On one occasion, when dining with him at a gentleman's house, he, upon observing that I had been taking several glasses of wine, said, "Cyrus, I could make an affidavit that I never in any one day during the course of my life took more than two glasses of wine;" upon which I remarked, that I never observed him take more than one, and that very seldom. "You are correct," said he. His love of temperance did not go to the extent of denying the proper use of wine to others. He was always happy to see his friends enjoy it in moderation. Upon this subject, he, in a spirit of liberality, remarks, that, "Even temperance, so useful and commendable, may become a snare: there have been instances of persons, under a religious motive, injuring themselves by self-denial and abstinence. Timothy was in danger of it. Up to this time," that is, the time when Paul wrote these words, *Drink no longer water, but use a little wine, for thy stomach's sake and thy often infirmities,* "Timothy used water only; but he was following this abstemiousness too exclusively and too long. His system now required something more generous and restorative and strengthening." But nothing could overcome Mr. Jay's aversion to the use of ardent spirits. Speaking in reprobation of the crime of drunkenness he says: "It takes away the man, and leaves the brute. It dethrones reason from its seat. It covers the wretch with rags. It reduces his wife and children to beggary. It impairs appetite; produces trembling of the limbs; and such sinking of the spirits as compels the repetition of the offence: so that, physically as well as morally, it is almost impossible to cure it." He had the greatest detestation of what he designated the wretched habits of snuff-taking and smoking. In speaking of the several kinds of visitants whom he did not think he was called upon to follow, he enumerates, "the smokers furnished with a pretty pipe and its usual concomitant at every house of call."—"We have," I have often heard him remark, "plenty of necessary wants, without adding to them any artificial ones."

Mr. Jay was not only cheerful himself, but delighted to see others so. Whenever any one remarked to him that a person who had been known to have led an irreligious or dissipated life had reformed his conduct and become *serious*, he would reply, "I do not approve of the term 'serious;' for religion never was designed to make our pleasures less. I always say that such a man has become *happy*."

Indeed, he had all the requisites to make his society much coveted. He was extremely lively, vivacious, and witty. He abounded in genuine and dry humour, and in his conversation there was a considerable play of imagination and range of thought. The great extent of his reading (the public journals and the serials forming part of it), and the retentiveness of his memory, gave him in society many advantages;

added to all this, his residence at Bath, and his ministrations in Ireland, Scotland, and various parts of England, afforded him opportunities during the course of a long life, not only of multiplying friends, acquaintances, and connections, but also of studying the human mind.

Not long after his settlement at Bath, he found there a coterie of celebrated as well as singular characters, many of whom occasionally attended at Argyle Chapel, and became his friends.

Mr. Jay was seen to the best advantage in a small party; he disliked a large set company, but delighted to have around him a little quiet circle, the select few, persons of intelligent, accomplished, kindred minds.

His annual supplies at Surrey Chapel, for nearly fifty years, drew him away from Percy Place more than he could desire; for when absent from home, where his sweetest pleasures and highest gratifications were realised, he always sighed for his return back to it. In affording these services, he yielded to the importunity of his friend Rowland Hill, and the express wish of the admiring congregation there.

During many years of these annual visits, he was for the most part the guest of Mr. Walker, a gentleman of large property and of a liberal disposition, living in a spacious house in Piccadilly. Mr. Jay could not fail to find himself at home here; for his kind host did every thing in his power to make him happy, and would often invite a select few to meet him. On these occasions, and whilst the wine was circulating round the table, he would, much to my regret, beckon me out of the room, saying, "You have had quite wine enough; you observe that I have not taken more than one glass. I like to see the mail-coaches come up to the Gloucester Coffee-House, and start for the different parts of the west of England; so come along with me." He would stay till the last of the coaches left; and what astonished me much was, that the coachmen and guards appeared to know him as well as he knew them. If on our return back he found his kind host and the company still over their wine, he would retreat into the drawing-room and join the ladies; for he was always partial to their society. The death of Mr. Walker deeply affected him.

It was at the house of a relative of this gentleman, Mr. Hawker of Piccadilly, that Mr. Jay became acquainted with Dr. Hawker, the rector of Plymouth, and the author of the *Daily Bread*; and I have heard him say that the reading of it gave him the first idea of writing the *Morning and Evening Exercises*. He did not entertain a very favourable opinion of the religious creed of the doctor, on account of his being so high in his Calvinistic notions.

The last journey but one that Mr. Jay took to London, I received a note from him dated from the Golden Cross. On my entering his private apartment at that hotel, he said, "Cyrus, it is come to this,—all my friends are dead; and I have just been thinking that in passing through London I really do not know any body that I could take the liberty of asking for a bed." I observed, that I should prefer an inn. He replied, "Why, I have never been accustomed, like you, to an inn, having always been so kindly treated wherever I went. I never could agree with Tillotson, who said that he should like to die at an inn, as it represented the termination of the journey of life."

Mr. Jay disliked above all things a censorious man and a tale-bearer, being ever desirous to view the actions of others in as favourable a light as possible. This state of mind enabled him to overcome many an annoyance and disappointment; but this was ofttimes no slight effort, for his character was marked by great sensibility. He was a man with whom no one felt he could take a liberty; but this deference towards him was not without its occasional defects, as it tended at times to make him rather too positive. To a great manliness of character there was united much simplicity of manners; he was quite devoid of affectation, the same man from year to year, and one upon whose judgment those seeking advice could rely. In fact, he was ever consistent with his avowed opinions, and disliked a fickle-minded man.

He took the greatest pleasure in noticing little children; and whenever I have gone with him to a collection of paintings, he would always admire those which represented them in their innocent sports. He used to say that there was poetry in their every movement, and called them "little honest men and little honest women," which I think is a quotation from Pope. Frequently have I seen him, when approaching in his walks a group of boys and girls, put his hand in his pocket and throw amongst them a handful of halfpence; but he always gave his throw in favour of the girls. "How easily and cheaply," said he, "children may be amused!"

I will conclude this chapter by the following quotation from one of Mr. Jay's works, as illustrative of his great and patriotic love for his native country; and here again was a cause of cheerfulness to him:

"People are naturally attached to a land in which they were born and brought up, and with which all their earliest recollections and feelings are associated. It has pleasures and charms for them that others know not of. And who would be cruel enough to deprive them of their preference, and make them miserable by comparison? Rather, who would not rejoice that there is no region so absolutely dreary and barren as to have no flowers and attractions scattered over it by the kindness of Providence, to bind them to their native soil, and to make it painful to leave their own country and their father's house?

"And how much is there, whatever view I take, to induce the acknowledgment, 'The lines are fallen to me in pleasant places; yea, I have a goodly heritage!' Let me think of our insular situation, in consequence of which we are open to commerce, guarded from invasion, and even in war itself know so little of its ravages, never hearing the confused noise of warriors, or seeing garments dipped in blood. Let me think of the temperature of our atmosphere, in which we are not frozen to statues or dissolved in heat. Let me think of our freedom from tornadoes, hurricanes, earthquakes, pestilences. Let me think of a country where the seasons regularly return and melt into each other,—where are the sweet interchanges of hill and vale and wood and lawn,—where the pastures are clothed with flocks and herds,—where the fields and valleys stand thick with corn,—where we are fed with the finest of the wheat. Let me think of a country whose merchants are princes, and whose traffickers are the honourable of the earth,—a country ennobled by the zeal of patriots, enriched by the blood of martyrs, endeared and sacred by the dust of a pious multitude without number,—a country illustrious by every kind of genius, and by every improvement in science and in art,—a country in whose well-balanced constitution are blended the advantages of monarchy, aristocracy, and democracy, without their defects,—a country whose government is equally averse to tyranny and anarchy; where none are above law, and none below it; where liberty has so long fixed her abode; where religious opinions produce no civil disabilities; where all persecution is excluded; and where every man sits under his own vine and vineyard, and none can make him afraid. Let me think of a country where charity and compassion reign, not only in numberless personal acts, but in a thousand institutions to meet every kind of distress, and lessen the sum of human woe. Let me think of a country possessing, not only so many natural, intellectual, civil, and social advantages, but so many moral and religious privileges; where not only the darkness of paganism, but of superstition, is past, and the true light shineth; where the Scriptures are found in our own language, and all are allowed to read them and able to procure them; where the word of life is preached, and we can hear the joyful sound of the truth as it is in Jesus; where the gospel of Christ is not only spreading widely among ourselves, but zealous and persevering efforts are making by individuals and communities to convey it to others. And can I glance at all this, and not say, 'It is a good land which the Lord our God hath given us'? Ought I not to be thankful to

Him who determines the bounds of my habitation, and performeth all things for me? Ought I not to bear with patience and cheerfulness a few difficulties and trials inseparable from a condition so favoured and indulged?"

CHAPTER XLIII.

Mr. Jay as a Preacher.

Before I enter upon the subject of this chapter, and that of the succeeding one, wherein I shall say a few words of Mr. Jay as an author, it seems necessary that I should, in the first instance, take a slight glance at those studies, upon the superstructure of which he raised his fame.

No sooner had Mr. Jay been admitted into the academy of his kind friend and tutor, Cornelius Winter, than his thirst for knowledge led him to appreciate those advantages which would ensue from the studies requisite to form the preacher.

That he must have made much proficiency in Latin at the age of seventeen is manifest, for, in a letter which his worthy tutor wrote to him from Bristol, in September 1788, he says, "I have not much time to write to you in Latin, nor indeed much in English." And in another, written by Winter to him in the same year, he says, "Be sure to preserve some time for attending to Latin and Greek, and, by carrying your wits about you, get a knowledge of men and things." Mr. Jay attended to this advice; but, I believe, never acquired any other than a slight knowledge of Greek, but was well versed in Latin, although he never paraded himself before the public as such. He read with deep attention all the classical authors, and the works of the ancient fathers, as rendered into English by our best translators. I remember his informing me, in allusion to his Latin studies, that Mr. Winter would frequently say to him, "Billy" (for he always addressed him as such), "I am going to preach at a place a few miles off, and I wish you to accompany me; so ride behind me on my horse. Whilst on the road, he examined me upon Latin syntax, and made me scan some of the verses in Virgil. This was his invariable practice." After he left Marlborough College he studied the French language, in order to be able to understand more perfectly the French divines, and made himself so completely a master of it that he could read and translate it with great facility, but I believe he seldom spoke it.

Whilst he was at Marlborough College he had begun preaching with so much success, that the question was mooted by some of those who took an especial interest in the future welfare of the youth, and who were themselves moderate Episcopalians, whether he should be sent to the University and enter the Church; but Sir John Thornton, the philanthropist, and Sir Richard Hill, objected against the proposition, saying that "God has opened the young man's mouth, and we dare not shut it." Probably this was a right decision. A university education might have cramped his genius; for it was in the union of this gift of nature with diligent application, and an earnest thirst for knowledge, that he acquired his fame as a preacher and writer.

I have related, in the first chapter of these Recollections, that, whilst Mr. Jay was a student under Winter, he preached in the open air at Calne, and that, whilst addressing the rural audience from a wall bounding the Marquis of Lansdowne's estate, he observed the Marquis and Dr. Priestley on the other side of the wall, attentively listening to his discourse. I have often heard him say that the attention of these two eminent men was of the greatest advantage to him, and that from that time he had made up his mind that he would, by diligence, under God's blessing, make his name known as an acceptable preacher.

It was his determination, when he first settled at Bath, to become one of the most useful and efficient preachers of the city; and the history of more than sixty years showed that he did not labour in vain in this laudable ambition.

Indeed, he was compelled at the very outset of his ministry at Bath,—then the resort of statesmen, of the wits of the age, of learning, and of fashion,—to set about this task in earnest; for many of these distinguished visitors at this *metropolis of the west of England*, as Canning styled it, occasionally formed part of his audience. Hence it was that he deeply studied the subject of every discourse before he entered the pulpit; for what he was obliged to do at the commencement of his pastorate at Argyle Chapel became afterwards a matter of habit. All through life he was anxious to advance, having an abhorrence of any thing like indolence or remaining stationary. I could fill pages with a list of the distinguished individuals who had attended Argyle Chapel. Poor Sheridan had often heard Mr. Jay preach, and said that he was the most natural orator he had ever heard. Thelwall, so long known to the public from having been tried with Horne Tooke and Hardy for high treason, came to Bath to lecture. He occasionally frequented Argyle Chapel. He much admired Mr. Jay's preaching. He was a master of elocution, and took pupils for the purpose of qualifying them for the senate. He came to Bath to lecture, and was found one morning dead in his bed. He was consequential, but had the merit of being politically consistent.

I remember, after one of the Sunday morning services at Argyle Chapel, observing near its door the late Sir William Owen (who afterwards changed his name to Barlow), one of the oldest baronets in the kingdom, in close conversation with Lord Wynford (then Chief Justice of the Common Pleas). Just as I came up to them, his Lordship took his leave, upon which I accosted him, and, after shaking hands with me, he said, "Do you know, Lord Wynford and myself have been talking about your father. His Lordship has just remarked to me that the Church would be sure to be upset. I asked his Lordship how. He answered, 'If there be many such fellows as that d—— Jay, it will soon be accomplished. Look at the carriages that have just left the chapel. I suppose you have been fool enough to go there?' 'Precisely so,' I answered; 'and I think, in spite of your prejudice, that you would, if you were to go there once, repeat the visit.'" The baronet, although a high churchman, subscribed liberally to the fund presented to Mr. Jay on the occasion of the jubilee.

Mr. Jay was always the advocate of arrangement and division in his discourses, it being his opinion that it relieved and quickened the attention, apprehension, understanding, and memory of the congregation, particularly those of the uneducated portion of it. "But it is much to be wished," said he, in allusion to this subject, "that the divisions should be short, simple, and easy, the language every where plain, and the exemplifications natural and familiar. Few can imagine how much I have always made this my aim and effort; nor have I less wished and endeavoured to be, in some measure, not only intelligible but impressive. This is no easy thing."

Although Mr. Jay was thus the advocate of arrangement and division, yet he considered it essential, in order to fix the attention of his hearers, to introduce variety into his discourses. Speaking upon this subject, he says, "May not the want of unity be more than compensated by variety? In the drama much has been written of the unities by the French, who have always boasted of their maintaining them. But has any one of their authors any thing equal to the mixed productions of Shakespeare, who often violates all the unities? But, in preaching, it should be remembered what diversities of persons and cases there are before us at every service, and how unlikely those diversities are to be reached by the very same thing."

Mr. Jay, with great frequency, illustrated his discourses by apt historical allusions, and quotations from the poets, which, uttered by his fine voice, were very effective. He also, when occasion required, would make quotations from our best prose writers, and divines of eminence of all persuasions. He greatly excelled in quoting passages from the Scriptures, which were not only pertinent, but glided harmoniously into his own language. He once commenced a sermon where, after the interrogatory, the whole of the sentence consists of quotations, thus: "And what is life? 'A vapour, that appeareth for a little time, and then vanisheth away,'—'a flower of the field,'—'a flood,'—'a sleep,'—'a dream,'—'a tale,'—'nothing,'—'surely every man at his best estate is altogether vanity.'"

I have mentioned that Mr. Jay would select rather strange texts for charity sermons. He states his reasons for so doing thus: "Though I have not been much at sea, I have observed that a kind of side-wind is the best for filling all the sails, and for securing speed. I have therefore, for some years past, been led to preach very few *direct charity* sermons. Many of the subjects of the appeals are well known, and the common enlargements upon them are become trite and satiating, when a peculiar frame of soul in the audience is necessary, and I regard it as a kind of desecration of the place, and debasement of the glorious gospel, to deal much in pounds, shillings, and pence. I, therefore, more generally have chosen a very evangelical or experimental subject, the warm discussion of which was more likely to produce in my hearers a favourable state of mind and feeling for every good work, so that at the close of the service their inquiry would be, 'Lord, what wilt thou have me to do?' and I have only to present the case, with its nature and claims, all tricks and teasings being unnecessary."

Mr. Jay, whenever occasion permitted, uttered extremely patriotic sentiments from the pulpit, particularly during the threatened invasion of England by the first Napoleon; but during the whole course of his career as minister never introduced what might be termed politics, except upon one occasion. This act of indiscretion is thus alluded to by Cyrus Redding, in his work entitled *Fifty Years' Recollections, Literary and Personal, with Observations of Men and Things.* He says, "There was a Dissenting clergyman whose conduct I cannot forget, being truly Christian, and worthy of himself. The Rev. Mr. Jay, a well-known name, had, for the first time in his life, introduced politics into a sermon. I did not hesitate to notice and reprove it—I hope not too violently. On the following Sunday, he apologised to his congregation for the remarks he had made, and cast blame upon himself in a manner so honest and truly Christian, that I almost felt sorry I had not let his comments pass; but then I should not have had his virtuous recantation. His discourses were marked by earnestness, simplicity, and perspicuity of style. He had nothing lofty, none of the scholastic finish of Robert Hall; but he was perhaps, on that account, more extensively useful in his day."

Mr. Jay had preached more sermons upon jubilee occasions, and upon the deaths of kings, queens, princes, princesses, poets, and statesmen, and upon occasions of victory, than perhaps ever fell to the lot of any one minister of the gospel.

As a preacher, Mr. Jay was neither highly doctrinal nor drily practical. His discourses were distinguished by what should be called experimentality, or a constant blending of the practice and doctrine of the gospel. His sermons were full of Christ, and his whole ministry was emphatically a gospel one. He discarded the introduction, as much as possible, of metaphysical theology or allusions into his discourses.

We have already spoken, in some of the preceding chapters, of many of the excellencies of Mr. Jay as a preacher, both as to voice, emphasis, pathos, and style.

But he had other qualifications than those already described to form the preacher. He possessed an extraordinary fascination of power over his audience at once. The rivet was instantly through you. Consciously or unconsciously, it was impossible to withhold the profoundest attention and sympathy. Your heart, your mind, your tears, your smiles, were the speaker's—at least for the hour. No other preacher but one possessing his tact could dare to introduce into his discourses occasional sallies of wit, humour, quaint expressions, and anecdotes; but he had the faculty of turning them to advantage, and if they raised a smile, it was only momentarily.

Mr. Jay, in speaking of his own style of preaching in comparison with that of Robert Hall, says, "It is very different from that able preacher. My object has been *impression*, and I have adopted a plain, manly, and, what I wanted to make, a direct, straightforward, penetrating style—one which every person would feel. I know I am very defective in this respect, when compared with Mr. Hall. His chasteness, his elegance, his classicality, I cannot too much admire; still, every man in his own order."

In his religious views, Mr. Jay was a moderate Calvinist, but his Calvinism was diffused, not concentrated, implied rather than expressed. It was, in truth, the grand object of his life to understand the Scriptures, the result of which was a maturity and ripeness of theological knowledge such as has seldom been attained. Addressing, one Sunday morning, his congregation at Argyle Chapel upon the subject of the betrayal of our Saviour by Judas, he said, "He was *foreordained* of God to betray the Saviour, and yet he betrayed Him *willingly,* and is damned for the deed. Now, do not look at me for an explanation of this subject: both statements are true—the foreknowledge of God, and the free agency of man; and when we reach heaven, and not till then, shall we be able to understand all which in our imperfect condition is quite beyond the grasp of our finite minds."

In describing Mr. Jay, throughout the whole of these Recollections, I have made no distinction between what he was when I could first appreciate what preaching was, and what he was in the last year of his pastorate. He appeared to me always the same, except that in his latter years his gray hairs and venerable aspect seemed to command reverence as well as attention. The same observation applies to his writings. His earliest writings and his latter productions exhibit the same style, beauties, and defects.

In the *Pen-Pictures of Popular Preachers,* sketched by a very able writer, the following faithful portraiture is given of Mr. Jay in the latter days of his ministry:

"While you are singing the first line of the first hymn, the vestry-door opens, and a gentleman clad in the vestments of his sacred office appears. He ascends the stairs with a slow and solemn step, holding firmly, yet not feebly, the railing of the staircase. Beneath his left arm is a large Bible. He is of the middle height, stoutly built, and his broad shoulders are bowed by age. Gracefully fall the folds of his gown about his form; yet withal, there is a carelessness apparent in its disposition. He enters the pulpit, sits down, and for a time we see nothing of him but the upper part of his white head. But now he rises, and, after taking a careful survey of the multitude below, he opens the Bible, and presently commences reading.

"His voice strikes you at once; it is rich, deep, and musical. He reads slowly, and with remarkable dignity, occasionally lifting his eyes from the sacred page, and fixing them earnestly on his hearers. The solemnity of his manner is in harmony with the majesty of his subject; every word *tells;* and, as Mr. Jay proceeds, every faculty of every listener is absorbed in a deep attention to the subject he is introducing, whatever that may be.

"And now we have a better opportunity of observing his head and face, which, as yet, no artist has succeeded in transferring to canvas. I ought to say rather, that no painter has succeeded in depicting the peculiar expression which belongs to, and is so characteristic of it.

"There is something in the massive head of Mr. Jay which reminds one, at times, of the grand old head of some ancient statue of Jupiter. It is large, and abundantly covered with silvery hair, which, sweeping from one of the temples, discloses a splendid forehead. The eyes are peculiar, being dark, extremely bright and lively, and of a most searching expression. Eyebrows large, of a darkish gray, overshadow these 'windows of the soul,' as some old writer has called them.

"Taken as a whole, the face is an extremely fine one; and, stamped as it now is with the radiance of a good old age, few can behold it without a reverential feeling. It is capable of a great variety of expression; and so does it change with the changes of the preacher's subject, that an intelligent *deaf* person once told me he could almost understand Mr. Jay's sermon by the mere looking at him. Deep pathos, genuine humour, sly sarcasm, biting irony, and boundless benevolence, are by turns indicated. As we sometimes behold on a hill-side, now the shifting shadows made by the clouds sailing above, and anon behold bright patches of sunlight where gloom had been but a moment before; so, on the countenance of the subject of our sketch, the mind's varied emotions are alternately depicted; and each so imperceptibly blends with the other, that, though fully conscious of the changes, we do not discern the precise moment when those fine transitions of thought and expression occur."

CHAPTER XLIV.

Mr. Jay as an Author.

UPON this subject I can say but little in the way of criticism, as I confess my incompetency to analyse the beauties or defects of Mr. Jay's works in so perfect a manner as I could wish.

From the number, well-known character, and wide circulation of these works, one would be led to suppose that he appeared as an author very early in life. Such was not exactly the case. He did not present himself in that capacity before the public until he had reached, as I believe, the age of thirty.

His popularity as an author commenced almost as soon as he devoted his talents in that direction. His really first publication, by which he established his fame, was a discourse sent forth to the world in 1801, entitled *The Mutual Duties of Husbands and Wives.* (I use the word 'really' because, prior to that time, he had published a few sermons, at the especial request of his congregation, and for their perusal only, respecting which he says that, as they did not deserve much notice, he on that account omitted them from the list of his works.) This discourse was received with marked public favour, was much commended by the periodicals of the day, and passed rapidly through five editions. Thus encouraged, he advanced in the path of authorship far beyond what he originally intended. Distinguished as a preacher, he became equally distinguished as a writer, in connection with experimental practical theology. And here let me remark, that his language in the pulpit was for the most part the same as it appears in print. But this was not much to be wondered at; for he never delivered a discourse, as I have stated in the preceding chapter, without deeply studying and meditating upon the subject of it. To illustrate this remark: I was present one Sunday morning, in the vestry of Argyle Chapel, when Dr. C—— had been invited, a week prior thereto, to preach on that particular day. Mr. Jay was conducting the Doctor from the vestry to the pulpit-stairs, as was his usual custom, when the Doctor suddenly turned round, and said, "What text shall I preach from?" The reply was, "I am not going to tell you; but this I know, you should not have preached at all, if you had asked me the same question a few minutes ago;" and then, pointing to the pulpit, added, "I never enter that desk without many hours of deep and anxious study on the subject of the text."

Mr. Jay's first success as an author led him to believe, and rightly too, that he might effect even more good to the public in that capacity than as a preacher, and hence it is that they are indebted for the numerous works which from time to time he presented to them.

Whenever he sat down to write for the press, he had always a great design in his "mind's eye"—it was usefulness. He aimed at doing good in the most extensive sense of the word.

His works, notwithstanding their high price, have always commanded an extensive circulation; have ever been good property, sell steadily, and a demand from all parts of the empire is continually made for them. They have been perused by royalty, and all the intermediate classes of society. They are to be found in the library of almost every dignitary and clergyman of the Church of England, and on the shelves of many a humble dwelling. In America, the circulation of these works has not only been wide but universal, being held there in as high repute as they are in England. They have found their way, for the benefit of thousands, not only to our Australian colonies, but to other parts of the world.

As evidence of the value put upon the works of Mr. Jay, I have only once, during a residence in London of forty years, observed any of his works on a book-stall, and they were marked at almost the selling price. I mentioned this circumstance to an eminent bookseller, who assured me that he had never seen any of them either on a book-stall or in a second-hand shop. This is a clear proof that there never was, nor is there now, any occasion for an alteration of price, as has been suggested.

In the writings of Mr. Jay you find nothing sectarian. He wrote, not as a nonconformist minister, but as a true and large-hearted Christian. Avoiding every thing controversial, he opened the New Testament, and inculcated its principles, as a man and disciple of catholic views and catholic spirit. In fact, he did not address himself to one class of the public, but to the whole body.

His writings, independently of these qualifications,

recommend themselves to the reader by their vigour, manly simplicity, sagacity, freshness, and originality; by their soundness and theological accuracy; by their clear and beautiful exhibition of evangelical sentiment; by their just and striking delineation of character; by their illustration and enforcement of great practical principles; by their devotional richness and elevation; and lastly, by their application to Christian experience in its numerous and diversified forms.

Mr. Jay's style of writing, so far as it refers to his sermons, like that of his preaching, was essentially *sui generis*. He was fond of antithesis, as being a mode whereby he could secure attention, and had a partiality to alliteration, wherever it could be used with effect. His sentences are short, pithy; frequently epigrammatic; and many of them amount to aphorisms and maxims. But his peculiar style of writing led occasionally to a want of consecutiveness. A sudden idea, or impression foreign to the subject, ofttimes flows from the pen of an author dealing in short sentences, who does not, in the midst of them, readily detect the incongruity.

Having made these preliminary observations, I will now proceed to give a list of the principal works ushered by Mr. Jay into the world after the publication of the discourse entitled *The Mutual Duties of Husbands and Wives*.

The first of them, in order of date, is a collection of twenty-four sermons (called his longer discourses), written in the year 1804, and published in two volumes octavo (now contained in one volume), and dedicated to the church and congregation of Argyle Chapel. The religious public bought them with great avidity, and the several reviews spoke of them in the highest terms, especially *The Monthly Review,* then a work of much authority. They are very striking and admirable, and permanently established his reputation as an author.

I believe his next publication was the work entitled *Short Discourses for the Use of Families,* which, in succession, was sent forth to the world in four volumes. These discourses, in the opinion of the religious world, are amongst his best and happiest efforts. They are numerous, varied, appropriate in their subjects, not too extended; and have commanded, from year to year, since the date of their publication, a large and steady sale. In the midst of thousands of families they are read, and at the time they were ushered into the world were particularly acceptable, as there were then very few churches, and not many chapels, wherein evening services were performed. Indeed, had he written nothing else, he would have conferred an inestimable benefit on multitudes of Christian households.

Many were the discourses of Mr. Jay, upon stated and other subjects, published by him, from time to time, shortly after their delivery. A selected portion of them was afterwards published in two volumes, and is known to the world as his *Occasional Discourses* (the third series of his collection of sermons). They are full of excellencies, and there is something in them which you cannot find in connection with other sermons.

The discourse already alluded to, entitled *The Duties of Husbands and Wives,* and which heads the first of these volumes, is an extremely fine specimen of composition and sentiment, and abounds in the most admirable counsels, tendered in an affectionate and faithful manner. It is a discourse which, as a friend of the author suggests, should be published separately, in a neat and elegant form, as an appropriate wedding present.

Another of Mr. Jay's happiest efforts, which we find in those discourses, is his *Charge to a Minister's Wife*. It is very sage and comprehensive.

His funeral sermons are particularly touching and effective, and abound in strokes of the tenderest and most beautiful pathos.

The discourses delivered by him at the ordination of ministers are amongst his best. I shall name three of them here as being highly worthy of perusal: one at the ordination of the Rev. James Stretton of Paddington; one at the ordination of Dr. Burder of Hackney; and one at the ordination of Dr. Tidman of Salisbury. And here, speaking of ordination, I have heard Mr. Jay state that, when he was once performing this duty at a market-town, many of his congregation, amongst whom were several Presbyterians, wished him *to lay hands on*, it being, as they alleged, a scriptural mode. "I will do so," he said, "if you will adhere to the whole verse by *fasting*." He cunningly knew that they would object, there being an ordinary at two o'clock at the Red Lion. "They thought more of the ordinary," I have heard him say, "than the ordination."

Indeed, all the discourses contained in these two volumes have their excellencies, and were called forth upon a variety of occasions, so that there is no sameness of language to be found in them.

The Morning and Evening Exercises for the Closet, by Mr. Jay, have, ever since their publication, procured an extensive circulation; and it is a work which will ever perpetuate his fame as a scriptural author, being written, as it were, for all time. It cannot fail, therefore, to be the daily companion and the instructor of generations yet to come. Each of these Exercises is, in point of fact, a study; and, as it was once appropriately remarked, they are seventy-four-gun ships cut down to little frigates.

He first published the *Morning Exercises* in two volumes, which soon reached a tenth edition. The work was dedicated to Lord and Lady Barham. About three years afterwards he produced (in two volumes) *The Evening Exercises,* and dedicated them to William Wilberforce. When we take into consideration that there are two subjects for every day in the year in these works, we may pretty well estimate the amount of labour which must have been bestowed upon them. The author, speaking of these Exercises in his Reminiscences, says: "I cannot but hope from their wide circulation, and the testimonies I have received from so many quarters, that they have been owned of God, and will continue to be useful after my death." It gave him much satisfaction to receive from the American publishers presentation copies of this work, with letters highly commendatory of it.

It was between the publication of the *Morning and Evening Exercises* that Mr. Jay delivered a course of twelve lectures at Argyle Chapel, which he shortly afterwards published, in one volume, under the title of *The Christian contemplated.* These lectures are entitled, in succession, "The Christian in Christ,"

"The Christian in the Closet," "The Christian in the Family," "The Christian in the Church," "The Christian in the World," "The Christian in Prosperity," "The Christian in Adversity," "The Christian in his Spiritual Sorrows," "The Christian in his Spiritual Joys," "The Christian in Death," "The Christian in the Grave," and "The Christian in Heaven." To these twelve lectures he, in the published work, added another lecture, entitled "The Result," the words of the text being, "Almost thou persuadest me to be a Christian." This work, which went through many rapid editions, is in constant request, has a character of much originality about it, and is admirably carried out. *The Church-of-England Quarterly Review* very truly described this volume as one of the most poetical of his practical works; and the public generally estimate it as his very best. The introductory essay to the volume, on effective preaching, is full of the most valuable remarks and suggestions. So pleased was one of the Church-of-England bishops with *The Christian contemplated,* that he recommended all his candidates for holy orders to purchase it.

Mr. Jay's *Biographical Memoirs* have been so deservedly esteemed, that it makes us regret he did not send forth to the world a greater number of them.

The first of these productions was the life of his much-revered friend and tutor Cornelius Winter, a work which claimed the especial admiration of Southey, who, in his *Life of Wesley,* said that "the best account of Whitefield was to be found in the memoirs of Winter by Mr. Jay."

In the preface to this work, Mr. Jay, speaking in

the third person, says that "he has laboured with pleasure and rejoiced in the entertainment, from the persuasion that what he has written from the warmest affection and the highest regard will at the same time be ratified by a large proportion of the public voice: and that he is doing good to others while he has an opportunity to indulge his own feelings, and to acknowledge the obligations to his dear and honoured friend and benefactor, which he will never be able to discharge. To him he owes all his respectability in life, and all his opportunities of public usefulness. Though not a child by birth, he has been one by adoption; and he closes this preface by a line borrowed from Homer, which our admired Cowper, with some little deviation, inscribed on a bust of his Grecian favourite:

'Loved as his son, in him I early found
A father such as I will ne'er forget.'"

The death of the good Cornelius Winter was an event which caused the deepest anguish to Mr. Jay. Although solicited to deliver the funeral oration over his remains, and preach the funeral sermon, he found that he would be totally unable to perform the task; for his feelings would have choked his utterance, and left nothing but a few incoherent sentences, mixed with sighs and tears. This was the cause which determined him to publish these Memoirs as a lasting tribute to his memory. Speaking of his revered friend, he says: "It is goodness that makes one man a god to another: we are only to be won by kindness: they are the cords of love by which hearts are irresistibly drawn, and indissolubly bound together. Who, therefore, that knew Mr. Winter, can wonder at the sensibility his loss produced? The intercourse of the friends that assembled in his own house previously to the funeral was carried on by looks and tears rather than words. When the procession came out of his dwelling, the spectators that lined the street all melted into emotions of grief. When the corpse entered the chapel, and when it was laid low in the dust, the audience could hardly be restrained within the bounds of decency,—all seemed to feel and to verify the words of our great moralist: 'The blameless life, the artless tenderness, the pious simplicity, the modest resignation, the patient sickness, the quiet death, are remembered only to add value to the loss, and to deepen sorrow for what cannot be recalled.' Many who never heard him came to bedew his grave. Persons of religious sentiments widely different from his own opened their houses to accommodate those who came from a distance. The rector, with a liberality of mind and tenderness of heart that did him honour, apologised for his inability to attend, as he expressed it, 'the funeral of the ever-to-be-lamented Mr. Winter.' Attendants who had waited upon him, the driver at the inn who had carried him to his house when he fractured his bone, the coachman who had driven him when he was seized for death at the house of his friend,—all seemed glad to remember, and to divulge any little kindness they had shown him."

The accident alluded to was upon his return homewards on foot, on a rainy November night in 1800, after visiting a venerable dying woman, his foot slipping at the bottom of a declivity, breaking the master bone of his leg in two places. His death occurred in January 1808, and was hastened by the effects of an inflammation which broke out in this leg. It was in April 1808, that Mr. Jay sent forth to the world the memoirs of his much-loved friend and benefactor, consisting of more than 500 pages, so eager was he to fulfil what he considered to be equally an act of duty and affection. It was always his wish that the names of Winter and Jay should be associated together. The tutor lived to see the fame of his pupil both as a preacher and author.

The second of these biographical works was the *Memoirs of the Rev. John Clark,* which Mr. Jay states occasioned him more pains than any other of his works; but it did not sell so extensively as any other of his publications.

The Female Biography of the Old and New Testament Scriptures (the last proof-sheet of which was, as I have stated in the thirty-seventh chapter of these Recollections, passing through the press when its author was summoned to his rest,) is a work of exquisite beauty. Throughout the whole of these biographical lectures he seems to have departed somewhat from his usual style of scriptural writing. The language appears to me to be less sententious, and more in the essay style.

The last biographical work of his to which I shall allude is that of his own *Autobiography,* sent into the world some months after his death, containing charming slight biographical sketches of a variety of celebrated characters who were his friends and contemporaries. It is much to be regretted that he did not devote more of his time to it, so as to have made it a complete history of his life; but the fact of it was, that he commenced it at an age when the performance of two things at a time became too arduous a task for him. He therefore sacrificed his authorship in order to fulfil his duties as minister of Argyle Chapel. In the preface preceding that part of the autobiography containing the reminiscences of his departed friends, he says, that "almost every memento of celebrated personages is desired and welcomed, and readers are anxious to catch any trifling anecdote that helps to form a conception of their individuality, or to connect their private history with their public fame."

The only comment which I need make upon this work is that, like the *Female Biography*, it is written in an easy, flowing, and simple style, and has, like his other works, met the acceptance of the public, has passed through several editions, and is still in much request.

The Domestic Minister's Assistant, or Prayers for the Use of Families, alluded to in a former part of these Recollections, is still in great request, and has commanded the largest sale next to that of *The Morning and Evening Exercises*.

It was always Mr. Jay's custom, whenever he published a work, to send a presentation copy of it to his friend Mrs. Hannah More, a mark of attention which was highly appreciated by her. In presenting this lady with a copy of a second edition of the above-mentioned work, she, in a letter to him, thus acknowledges this act of attention towards her, not only on this but on other occasions: "I know not how to express the gratitude I feel for the very excellent works you have had the goodness to bestow upon me. To feel deeply their inestimable value, and to offer my fervent prayers to the Almighty Giver of every good gift, is all I *can* give. May He enlighten and strengthen me more and more by the constant perusal! Your last bounty, the new edition of your prayers, with the valuable additions, is a great additional treasure. We fell upon it with a keen appetite this morning, and I hope I shall be the better for it so long as I live. My truly pious friend Mr. Elven, who is my chief spiritual visitor, said, when I showed him your volumes, 'Mr. Jay has more ideas than any man I ever knew.' I could not prevail on myself to keep this remark from you."

Independently of Mr. Jay being a very voluminous writer himself, he was often dragged into print much against his will. The *Pulpit*, a weekly religious publication, reported, from its first starting, many of his sermons (taken down verbatim by a short-hand writer), and they constitute several volumes.

The various prefaces penned by Mr. Jay to many of his works are perfect specimens of that style of writing.

When he commenced his career of authorship, he was very anxious to have his works printed at Bath, and his paper manufactured in one of the mills near that city, the owner of which, though a good man, was a bad paper-maker. I had often, when a youth, gone out with him when trout-fishing upon his friend's mill-stream, and heard him give directions for the making of the paper. This laudable rule of his did not improve the appearance of his work entitled *Short Discourses* when in print. I have a copy of the first edition before me, and never did I see a book so wretchedly got up, both with respect to paper and printing, and can truly say that the paper was not good enough to have had printed on it the last dying speech and confession of a murderer at an assize town. Editions were subsequently printed in London, and a beautiful edition was published by Mr. Wood, of Bath, a short time prior to Mr. Jay's death.

But nevertheless he was very fortunate in having had for his sole publishers Messrs. Hamilton, Adams, and Co., of Paternoster Row, for a period of forty years, between the first of whom and himself a friendship sprang up, which lasted uninterruptedly during the whole of the life of the deceased. Whilst these gentlemen were Mr. Jay's publishers, the sale of the works, as well as the profit, was great.

In an unfortunate moment, and just a few years prior to his decease, he was influenced by my brother, a resident at Bath, through very laudable motives, to employ another house in Paternoster Row to publish, in ten volumes, a cheap and stereotyped edition of the greater portion of his works, at 7*s*. 6*d*. each volume; and it was to be so published that each volume should be complete in itself. The expense of the stereotyping came to more than a thousand pounds, as I understand; but the same satisfactory pecuniary result did not follow from the sale of the works as formerly. Whenever Mr. Jay, who could never understand accounts, complained to my brother (who was the medium of communication between him and the publisher) on the subject, he was informed that the money arising from the more quick sale of some of the volumes was required to purchase paper, &c. for the others of them, for each volume came out every three months. This explanation was but of little avail to him, he saying, good-humouredly, "My works have got into such a muddle, that it is confusion confounded. I wish I had not taken them out of Mr. Hamilton's hands."

And here let me bring under the notice of the reader observations which I have often heard Mr. Jay make, as to the necessity that there should ever exist between author and publisher confidence and friendship, such as always existed between himself and Mr. Hamilton, and that of late years such a desirable state of things had disappeared. These observations are exactly in accordance with those expressed by Mr. Cyrus Redding, in his late interesting work, who says, "The project of a really good work, that forty years ago would have been grasped at by the leading houses in London, would now have no chance, the object being to make the public awake to a name, sell off an edition, and have done with the work for ever. The way of doing business among the old bookselling firms was rational and considerate. There was a friendship between the author and publisher, which has disappeared, literary bargains being as much of a huckstering as a purchase in Clare Market. The old houses, on my first coming to town, surprised me by their urbanity, and the opportunities given at set seasons for the facility of intercourse and business. On such occasions, the authors of that time were certain to meet with friendliness, and the conversation was useful and improving."

Nothing can be more fortunate for an author than to have as his publisher a well-known and respectable gentleman. This observation brings to my recollection an anecdote of Dr. M'Guin. He was walking one day, in Fleet Street, with a literary gentleman, who, in the course of conversation, stated that he was going to remove the publication of a work of his to a court opposite; whereupon the Doctor said to him, "You had better not do so: for whenever an author takes a work to any of the publishers there, the sale instantly drops. They are the knackers of the press." I can in truth say that the Doctor's advice to his friend is not applicable in my case; and therefore, if this volume fail to meet with public approbation, it will be entirely through the demerits of one who presents himself before them for the first time as a writer.

In portraying the character of Mr. Jay as a man, preacher, and author, I trust the reader will not deem that I have been too eulogistic. At all events, it has been my aim throughout these Recollections to take as fair a view as I could of the mind and character of a revered parent; and it will be seen that I have frankly declared my opinion in relation to one or two acts of his life which I considered laid him open to remark. I may have written, as his son, with a certain bias, but of this there can be no difference of opinion—that the world has unanimously proclaimed *William Jay of Bath* a good man, a good preacher, a good author.

THE END.

CPSIA information can be obtained
at www.ICGtesting.com
Printed in the USA
LVHW040633310123
738243LV00003B/169

9 783375 142018